Fortuné Du Boisgobey

The Cry of Blood

Le cri du sang: A story of crime and its penalty

Fortuné Du Boisgobey

The Cry of Blood
Le cri du sang: A story of crime and its penalty

ISBN/EAN: 9783337393984

Printed in Europe, USA, Canada, Australia, Japan

Cover: Foto ©Andreas Hilbeck / pixelio.de

More available books at **www.hansebooks.com**

THE
CRY OF BLOOD

(LE CRI DU SANG)

A Story of Crime and its Penalty

BY

FORTUNÉ DU BOISGOBEY

AUTHOR OF "THE BLUE VEIL" "THE CONDEMNED DOOR"
ETC., ETC.

Sole Authorised Unabridged Copyright Translation

LONDON:

JOHN AND ROBERT MAXWELL

MILTON HOUSE, ST. BRIDE STREET, LUDGATE CIRCUS,
AND
SHOE LANE, FLEET STREET.

THE CRY OF BLOOD.

CHAPTER I.

PARISIANS adore the country. This is a well-known fact, and as soon as the new leaves appear upon the trees in spring, they swarm there like bees.

Two months later the environs of the capital are almost as crowded as the city itself. The wealthy have castles there, and the middle classes, cottages; while plebeians flock to the public-house, where they regale themselves upon fresh fish and claret. These last, however, visit the country only on Sunday, and they enjoy themselves with all their hearts; but the others, who have taken up their abode there for the summer, only pretend to enjoy themselves, and are in reality bored to death.

No better proof of the truth of this assertion is needed than the fact that they never neglect an opportunity to visit the city. Monsieur is called there by business; madame must go there to try on a gown at her dress-maker's, 'or do a little shopping, and the much-coveted villa is left in charge of footmen who do not deprive themselves of the pleasure of visiting the wine-shops, while the maids go to the woods to flirt with the dashing soldiers of the nearest garrison.

Still, there are days when the family remains at home; days when it receives its guests; there are even times when it does penance for a whole week by remaining at home to entertain friends.

At such times the host and hostess rack their brains to

devise ways of amusing their guests. In the evening they have whist for the elderly people, and dancing, to the music of the piano, for the youthful members of the party. In the morning come the letters and papers, which are always awaited with impatience. In the afternoon everybody takes a walk, and goes to see the train pass, as the inmates of provincial châteaus went out on the highway to watch for the passing of the diligence in former times.

It is not so very amusing, this mode of diversion, but it whiles away an hour or two, and in the country amusements are rare.

Chatou is a coquettish village, surrounded by lovely villas, whose inmates spend their leisure time in the usual way.

So it happened that one day last June, a goodly company that had emerged from a castle that stands on the edge of the rather insignificant forest of Vésinet, slowly wended its way along the dusty road toward the line of railroad that connects Saint-Germain with the capital.

This party gradually divided itself into several little groups. At the head of the procession walked a number of young girls, protected from the sun by umbrellas of all colors. In the middle marched a corps of middle-aged men. A well-matched couple formed the rear-guard; a gentleman about sixty years of age, but of distinguished presence, and still hale and vigorous; and a lady considerably younger, who must once have been very handsome, and who could still hope for admirers.

No connoisseur could have failed to notice her, and her imposing carriage would have exerted an irresistible fascination over a collegian.

This couple had purchased the pretty château known as the Oaks, about six months before, but they had been residing there only about six weeks.

The husband enjoyed his new existence very much; the wife was nearly bored to death. The husband, Count Jacques de Muire, was a nobleman of the old school: his wife, *née* Louise Plantier, had brought him a large fortune in exchange for an ancient title, and from this union of two very different races, had resulted a charming daughter, Marcelle de Muire, who was already old enough to marry, as she was nineteen years of age.

Her parents had just celebrated their silver wedding, and the wedding of their only daughter would have closely followed it, had the parents been able to agree in their choice of a husband for Marcelle. But the count favored a suitor whom his wife refused to regard in that light, though he was a welcome visitor at the house.

He had even been invited to pay them a visit on that very day, and they expected him to arrive on the train that reached Chatou at 5:56.

Upon this very occasion the diversity of opinion that existed between the husband and wife, revived a discussion which had begun that morning, shortly after breakfast; but which had been interrupted by the arrival of some friends of M. de Muire, gentlemen belonging to his club, and moving in the best circles of Parisian society.

"My dear Louise," began the count, "I have never been able to discover the cause of your prejudice against Médéric. His father, Colonel Baron de Mestras, was my chum at Saint-Cyr, and we remained intimate friends after I resigned my commission as captain, to marry you. When he met with a glorious death at the head of his cuirassiers, on the battle-field of Gravelotte, he had been a widower for many years, and it became both a duty and a pleasure for me to exercise a guardian's care over his son. I wanted to make him a soldier, but he failed in his examinations both at the Polytechnic and Military Schools. The magistracy in these days is not a very enviable vocation, and Médéric has no talent whatever for what is known as business. He has a taste only for the fine arts, and for horses —tastes which certainly are not likely to enrich one, but he has plenty to live upon as he inherited a fortune of three hundred thousand francs, and perhaps a little more, from his father. He leads a very creditable life, and I have never heard any one accuse him of aught dishonorable. He is a very worthy young man in every sense of the word, and a very handsome one—which certainly is no objection. He is ten years older than Marcelle, and consequently just the right age for her, as she still needs some one to look after her a little."

"Even more than you think," interrupted the countess.

"Yes; I know that advice seems to be rather thrown away upon her, and that she generally manages to have her own way; but love is a powerful master, and she loves Médéric, who is positively daft about her."

"She thinks she loves him. At her age a young girl hardly knows her own mind."

"Take care, my dear," said M. de Muire, laughing; "you were only eighteen when I married you, and I have always believed that ours was a love-match, and I think so still. Do not try to destroy the illusion."

"You never will be serious, my poor Jacques. You turn everything into a jest, and this time your pleasantry is in very poor taste."

"But, my dear, I was thoroughly in earnest in what I have said about our daughter. I repeat that you would do her a grievous injury by preventing her from marrying Médéric; and if you persist in your opposition, you will certainly cause her to do something desperate. The children love each other devotedly, as you know perfectly well. Médéric is coming to dine with us this evening, and I have a presentiment that he will make a formal demand for Marcelle's hand before he returns to Paris."

"Very well; you can reply that the marriage will not take place while I live."

This was said in such a tone that the count paused and looked his wife full in the face. Her countenance wore an expression of inflexible determination, and her husband saw that this was no time to continue a discussion which could hardly fail to become acrimonious; besides, M. de Muire held domestic quarrels in holy horror.

"We will talk the matter over at some future time," he remarked. "I think we had better rejoin our friends now."

"You can rejoin them without me," replied the countess, dryly.

The count hastily availed himself of the permission. He understood his wife's temperament thoroughly, and knew that she was subject to fits of ill-humor, that soon abated, however; but he was none the less hurt by the haughty refusal she had just uttered, and his resolve to have his own way in the matter became still more firm.

"In case of a difference of opinion between the husband and wife, the father's consent suffices—at least, so says the Code," he said to himself, as he quickened his pace.

His friends waited for him. There were three of them: two well-preserved old beaus, who had been shining members of the *jeunesse dorée* that adorned the reign of Louis Philippe, and another, much younger, but equally polished gentleman of distinguished appearance and unmistakable military bearing.

This last was the intimate friend of the Count de Muire, in spite of the difference in their ages; but he was not as great a favorite with the countess as the other gentlemen, for Major George Roland, who had resigned his commission only a year before, was not nearly as well informed in regard to the sayings and doings of the fashionable world as the Marquis de Brangue and the Viscount de Liscoat, who were able to regale their hostess with the choicest bits of society gossip.

When the count overtook them, he found them both busily engaged in slandering one of their fellow-men.

"Young Mestras is going it pretty strong," remarked

M. de Liscoat. "Only night before last, he was fleeced out of a thousand louis in some low gambling-den."

"How do you know?" inquired M. de Muire, hastily.

"I heard so, through one of my friends who was inveigled into the same den, and who shared the young man's fate."

"You surprise me very much, for Médéric rarely plays."

"You surprise me, too," remarked the major. "I served under his father, who was a brave soldier, and one of the most exemplary men I ever knew, and good blood will tell."

"Nonsense, major! Do you really think that virtues and vices are transmitted from generation to generation, like real estate?"

"Generally, sir."

"According to that, I, who am the son of a pious nobleman, who was a devoted servant of God and the king, ought to be a saint, and I assure you that I am not leading a life that will result in my canonization after death."

"By no means!" exclaimed the Marquis de Brangue, who knew his old friend well.

"We had better change the subject, I think," said Marcelle's father.

"Bah! what if the countess does hear us."

"But my daughter is approaching with her friends and her governess," replied M. de Muire, severely.

In fact, the flying squadron that formed the advance-guard were retracing their steps, and the young ladies were already within hearing.

"A morsel for a king, that governess!" muttered the incorrigible viscount.

Mlle. de Muire was the first to rejoin the group of gentlemen. She was a tall, beautiful blonde, with large, clear, blue eyes, a transparent skin, and delicately chiseled features.

Hélène Lanoue, the governess, was a beauty of an entirely different type. A decided brunette, with much less regular, but more expressive features; her mouth was adorable, and her teeth something wonderful; and she was tall and *svelte*, with a waist one could span with two hands.

The criticism of Liscoat, who was a connoisseur in such matters, was eminently just.

Hélène was twenty-five years of age, though she did not look so, for age had not impaired her matrimonial value, and to be a fit bride for a prince or a millionaire, she lacked only one thing—a dowry.

That day she had with her, in addition to her pupil, three young girls, nieces of Mme. Muire, just out of a convent, well-dowered, and anxious to marry, so that they would have a right to waltz at balls and wear diamonds.

"Father," began Marcelle, "we have just decided unanimously to go to the station. In the first place, Monsieur de Mestras is coming, and he will be disappointed if he does not find us there; besides, we are not at all anxious to see the train pass. That is all very well on days when we are expecting no one, but when we are, it is much more pleasant to meet them at the station."

"But your mother wishes it, my dear," replied M. de Muire; "besides, your decision is made too late. I hear the train now. It has just left the station, and will pass here in less than three minutes."

"That is true. We should be sure to miss Médéric, and now we are here, we may as well enjoy the diversion— if diversion it can be called."

"Why, I think it is really quite amusing, mademoiselle," said the viscount, laughing. "When one is standing on the bank close to the track, one commands a view of the whole train, and one occasionally sees some really ludicrous sights in the first-class carriages."

In another moment, the entire party had ranged itself in line on the low embankment that borders the track at this point. The countess, who had overtaken them, placed herself at the end of the line nearest Vésinet, the next station, and furthest from the station from which the train was coming. M. de Brangue stationed himself at Mme. de Muire's right, between her and M. de Liscoat; then came M. de Muire, and then the four young girls, at the other end of the line.

The locomotive approached, snorting and wheezing like some asthmatic monster, and the noise of its wheels drowned even the voices of the young girls who were jabbering with all their might. It soon passed them, and the cars it was dragging moved by them with steadily increasing swiftness.

While his friends were watching the passing train, the Marquis de Brangue allowed his eyes to linger admiringly on the graceful shoulders and Juno-like form of his fair neighbor; but suddenly he heard her utter a quick cry, and saw her stagger, as if about to fall, and though he hastily caught her in his arms, she swooned in his grasp; and not until then did he perceive that her breast had been pierced by a bullet, and that from the narrow opening was gushing a torrent of blood that inundated the light robe of Marcelle's mother.

The train that had brought Médéric de Mestras was already out of sight.

"Help!" cried M. de Brangue, scarcely able to support the weight of the body he was holding in his arms, for the old beau was not a Hercules, by any means, and Mme. de Muire was very heavy.

M. de Liscoat sprung to his friend's assistance, and by their combined efforts they succeeded in preventing the unfortunate woman from sinking to the ground.

She still breathed, but her life was fast ebbing away with her blood, and her wide-open eyes already wore a vacant stare. She managed to falter the words: "It is he!—it is—" but she was unable to finish the sentence, and this effort was her last. She was already dead when her frantic husband reached her side.

Marcelle was entirely ignorant of what had happened. She was too far off, and too much engaged in jesting with her friends, who were laughing at her because she pretended to have seen Médéric de Mestras on the train; but on turning she perceived her mother, supported in the arms of the gentlemen, and heard her father's despairing cry.

She was rushing toward her, when the major hastily interposed.

Taking very little interest in the commonplace sight that had drawn the others close to the track, he had remained a little in the rear of the party, and from the spot where he stood he was better able to explain what had just occurred than his companions: A shot fired from the moving train: the countess struck full in the breast by a bullet.

He was now anxious to spare Marcelle the horrible sight of her mother's bleeding form.

"No, no, mademoiselle!" he cried, stretching out his arms to prevent her from passing.

"Let me pass!" cried the young girl, wildly.

"I swear that you shall not go a step further, mademoiselle," replied Roland, firmly. "Your mother has just met with an accident. Your presence would only prevent us from giving her the attention necessary. Return to the château with your friends."

Then, turning to the governess, who had just joined her pupil, he added:

"I must ask you to take Mademoiselle de Muire home immediately. This is no place for her."

Hélène Lanoue cast an inquiring glance at the major, saw there was no hope, and led away Marcelle, who was also beginning to understand, and who offered no further resistance.

"Send us the barouche," George Roland called after them.

The other young girls had already fled, like larks who had just seen one of their number fall under the fire of the fowler.

It was very fortunate that the governess had not lost her wits, and that the major succeeded in preserving his presence of mind on this terrible occasion. But for Hélène, there would have been a frightful scene, and M. de Muire had quite enough to bear as it was.

His daughter was forgotten for the moment, and kneeling beside his wife, whom his friends had laid gently on the turf, he labored in vain to revive her, calling her frantically by name, and trying to warm her cold hands by covering them with kisses.

As yet it did not seem to have occurred to him to ask how the catastrophe had happened.

Brangue and Liscoat, stunned by the shock, exchanged frightened glances. These gentlemen not being accustomed to such scenes, were utterly at a loss what to do. The affair had occurred upon a piece of ground dotted with stunted trees, about fifteen hundred yards from the railway station at Chatou, and beyond the reach of any immediate aid.

No individual nor habitation of any kind was in sight, and the Oaks was a good twenty minutes' walk from there.

It was time, indeed, for the major to interfere. He had already, however, done the only thing that would be of the slightest use. On days when the owners of the Oaks entertained guests the barouche stood harnessed in the courtyard ready for their use at any moment. Thanks to the order given to Mlle. Lanoue, in half an hour the vehicle would therefore reach the scene of the tragedy to transport the body to the château, for no human power would be able to restore Marcelle's unfortunate mother to life.

"Come, Jacques," Roland said to his friend, taking him by the arm and assisting him upon his feet.

M. de Muire obeyed; then standing there with set teeth,

distorted features, and tearless eyes, asked in evident be-
wilderment:

"How did it happen?"

"A shot was fired from the train—by accident, undoubtedly."

"No, not by accident," muttered the marquis, wiping
his blood-stained hands with his handkerchief.

"Why, in that case it was a murder!" exclaimed M. de
Muire. "And who could have had the heart to kill her?
She hadn't an enemy in the world."

"And nothing will ever make me believe that a person
on a moving train could have aimed so correctly," added
Roland.

"Some people make wonderful shots," remarked Liscoat.

The major did not feel inclined to discuss the question at
such a moment, so turning his back on the skeptical viscount, and taking his grief-stricken friend by the arm he
led him far enough away to attempt to console him without
being overheard by the others.

"Courage, my dear Jacques," he said, with an emotion
he could not repress in spite of all his efforts. "Recollect
that your daughter is still spared to you, and that she has
no one but you to look to now—that is, until the day of her
marriage to the young man she loves—"

"Ah, I wish that might take place to-morrow; but that
is not to be thought of now we are plunged into mourning."

"The children love each other. They will wait."

"I know it; but it is by no means certain that they will
ever be happy. What would you think if I should tell you
that my poor wife was bitterly opposed to their union?"

"You are telling me no news. I had guessed as
much."

"But what if I should tell you that just now, only a few
moments before she met with this terrible death, she de-

clared to me that the marriage should never take place while she lived.''

"What reason did she give for this refusal?"

"None whatever.''

"That is strange. She has known Médérie from his childhood, and Médérie's father was an intimate friend of hers and of yours.''

"Where is Marcelle?''

"She has returned to the château. She could not remain here, and I insisted upon her immediate departure.''

"You did right. I too will go.''

"I see a carriage coming,'' cried M. de Brangue.

"It is yours,'' said the major, turning to the count. "I requested Mademoiselle Lanoue to send it, but she must have met it on the way. I had forgotten that the coachman was to meet us for fear the ladies might become fatigued. I see him on the box, and the footman is with him.''

"Listen,'' said the count in a voice hoarse with emotion, "we shall have to send the body home in the carriage. I will accompany it; but I must go alone. I will have no one with me.''

"I will take it upon myself to dismiss these gentlemen. They would only be in our way; besides, I think they are anxious to get away as soon as they can.''

"Let them go. They are mere acquaintances; and I need the assistance and sympathy of a true friend. You will remain with me, will you not, my dear George?''

"As long as you wish. You can return home in the carriage, and I will rejoin you in a few moments at the château, where I think we shall find Médéric, who must have left the train at Chatou.''

The marquis and the viscount had become tired of standing guard over the lifeless body of the poor countess. A train from Saint-Germain was nearly due, and they did not care to be seen watching over a dead body, so they left it and approached M. de Muire, ostensibly to condole with him, but really with the firm intention of hastening back to Paris as soon as they could do so with decency.

The major felt that he would confer a favor upon his unfortunate friend by shortening their leave-taking as much as possible, so advancing to meet them, he said to them in subdued tone:

" Shake hands with him and then let him depart in the same carriage that takes away his wife's body. "

" Certainly, certainly," replied both gentlemen in the same breath.

" I will remain a moment longer, for I wish to have a talk with you. Afterward, I shall return to the Oaks on foot.''

" While we make our way back to Chatou," replied Liscoat promptly.

In the meantime the barouche had come up, and George Roland, who seemed to think of everything, gave the necessary orders to the servants—for M. de Muire seemed equally incapable of thought and of action—and he also held the horses while the coachman and footman, two stalwart men, lifted the body and placed it carefully in the carriage.

The blood had ceased to flow. It must have returned to the heart.

The major assisted his friend into the carriage, and then made a signal to the coachman, who started his horses on a walk in the direction of the château.

" Poor Jacques!" sighed Liscoat, " this will make a great change in his life; but fortunately he is a philosopher, and he will become consoled in time.''

" One becomes consoled for everything, even for the loss of one's wife," added the Marquis de Brangue.

" Especially for the loss of one's wife," corrected Liscoat, who had very little faith in lasting regrets, and still less in conjugal love. "But to lose her in such a strange and tragical way. It is a very uncommon case, and quite enough to shock the most indifferent husband. What do you think of this sudden death, my dear major?"

"I was about to address the same question to you," the major responded coldly; "and I beg that you will not noise the unfortunate affair abroad, but be silent in regard to it, at least until we have discovered the cause of it."

"Be silent in regard to it!" exclaimed Liscoat. "What good would that do? By to-morrow everybody in the neighborhood will know what occurred here. I defy Jacques to conceal it. His servants will spread the news if no one else does. Besides, it will be necessary to report the death to the authorities; and the physician who will come to verify the report will see that the poor countess was shot, and shot by a pistol, probably, for one can not handle a gun very conveniently in the compartment of a railway carriage."

"Be silent!" repeated M. de Brangue. "You certainly do not advise that, my dear major. Such a course would compromise us all very seriously; and I really think it my duty to inform the station-master of the affair on passing through Chatou. We ought to inform the commissioner of police, but it is necessary for me to get back to Paris as soon as possible."

"And for me as well," chimed in Liscoat. "After such an ordeal I need a bottle of Château-Margaux to revive my spirits. Catch me coming into the country again to dine!"

"I pity you most sincerely, sir," interrupted the major, deeply incensed by this display of heartlessness; "but I pity my friend Jacques de Muire far more; and I once more entreat you not to hawk this sad story about the streets."

"I decidedly object to the word hawk in this connection," retorted the viscount, straightening himself up.

"No quarrel here, I beg of you. If your sensitive nature is wounded I shall be entirely at your disposal to-morrow; but in the meantime I particularly request that you will not meddle with this affair."

"You certainly are taking a prominent part in it, however."

"It is different with me. I am the count's most intimate friend. I have been intimate with him for years. We were under fire together at Buzenval, where he did his duty bravely as a member of the national guard, by my side."

"Very well, sir, we are by no means anxious to figure in a criminal case," retorted M. de Brangue, who had taken refuge in England during the siege of Paris. "I made the suggestion merely to quiet my own conscience. I thought it of the utmost importance to insure the immediate arrest of Madame de Muire's assassin; and the surest means of accomplishing this would certainly be to telegraph on to Saint-Germain, where he will probably leave the train; but I would much rather say nothing whatever about the affair to the station-master at Chatou, for he might take it into his head to detain us until the arrival of the commissioner of police."

"Who might decide to keep us in custody until he was able to secure further information," added Liscoat. "Your shirt-bosom is all stained with blood; and my clothing being in a similar condition, he might conclude to send both of us to jail, and to be confined in the Chatou Jail of all others, would certainly be a bitter pill to swallow. Let us take the first train, marquis. It will be time enough to tell what we know when we are examined in Paris."

"And what do you know?" inquired the major, "and what did you see that I did not see? Merely a passing train and Madame de Muire falling, shot through the heart."

"I saw the smoke, and I know what car it came from. It was fired from the last car on the train."

"And I heard the last words Madame de Muire uttered," added the marquis.

"What! did she speak after she was shot?" asked George Roland.

"She said very distinctly 'It is he!' So she must have recognized the man that fired the shot."

"Impossible! The train was moving too rapidly."

"She at least suspected some one of the deed. The 'It is he' signified 'It is the man I feared,' and she was about to mention the name when her breath failed her. She added, 'It is—' and that was all."

"Are you positive of this?"

"I will testify to it under oath if any judge should take it into his head to summon me before him for examination; but that is all I shall say. I intend to keep my opinion to myself, and allow the authorities to solve the mystery as best they can."

"What is your theory on the subject?"

"I might reply that this is no business of yours; but I will merely remind you that only one man had an interest in putting Madame de Muire out of the way."

"I can't imagine who you are referring to. Be more explicit, if you please."

"I am referring, of course, to the young man about whom Jacques de Muir is so daft as to be willing to accept him as a son-in-law."

"Médéric de Mestras! You dare to accuse him?"

"I don't accuse him. I merely say that Madame de Muire was bitterly opposed to the match. Her husband has told me so a hundred times, and I think the poor woman was perfectly right."

"She would certainly have withdrawn her opposition eventually; and no one but yourself would ever think of suspecting the son of my old colonel of murder."

"I hope not, indeed, sir. You defended him before the crime was committed, and I am not surprised that you still defend him; but you are very much mistaken if you think that he will not be called upon to give an account of the way his time was spent."

"He will have no difficulty in proving his innocence, I am sure. He left the train at Chatou, where he probably expected to find Monsieur and Madame de Muire, with their daughter and guests. That was the arrangement; and it was not until after we had begun our walk that Madame de Muire changed her mind. Médéric could not have foreseen this, and by this time he must be at the Oaks, where a frightful surprise is awaiting him."

"If he was not on the train he will have no difficulty in establishing an *alibi*," remarked Liscoat; "but unfortunately Mademoiselle de Muire declared to her friends just now that she saw him in one of the compartments."

"She was mistaken," replied the major quickly. "How could she possibly have recognized him in a moving train?"

"She loves him, and lovers are endowed with extraordinary keenness of vision, as I have had occasion to observe more than once in my life; and so, I presume, have you."

George Roland did not smile at this display of vanity on the part of this antiquated beau who pretended to have been the idol of every woman he had met in years gone by. He was beginning to be seriously troubled by these open accusations against a young man he loved and esteemed. He thought them absurd; but he could not blind himself to the fact that they might be believed by some magistrate, and even in the circles in which these gentlemen moved.

Médéric did not figure in what is generally styled high life in fashionable journals. The mediocrity of his fortune forbade that, and so did his tastes; but he was known in those circles, the news of his intended marriage with Mlle. de Muire having been pretty generally circulated, so there were not a few persons who envied him his good fortune; and those who are envied always have enemies in plenty.

The major also said to himself that Marcelle's father would be sure to remember the words of his wife, who, only a few moments before her death, swore that her daughter should never marry Médéric de Mestras with her consent; and now would Jacques de Muire, after the tragical event that had made him a widower, have the strength of will not to be influenced by the strongly expressed wishes of a mother who certainly loved her daughter devotedly? And what would he say if the shameful rumors his club acquaintances seemed more than likely to circulate should reach his ears? What would be the consequences if outraged justice should open an investigation in which Marcelle's betrothed was involved, if only for a day?

George Roland had not a moment to lose if he desired to avert these misfortunes.

"This much is certain," continued M. de Liscoat, carelessly, "the poor countess was fatally wounded in the left breast; and unless you think the bullet was intended for one of us, or that some senseless practical joker was amusing himself by discharging his revolver at random, you must admit that a crime has been committed, and that the affair will not be allowed to end here."

"I quite agree with you, sir," interrupted the major; "and I have only one request to make, and that is that you will keep the matter a secret, if possible, until to-morrow."

"Oh, so far as that is concerned, we will say nothing about it until we are questioned."

"I shall rely upon your promise, and in return I give you my word of honor that justice shall be done, for I assure you that I am no more anxious to have the culprit go unpunished than you are. I am going to begin an investigation on my own account, and you shall know the result whatever it may be. Need I add that I shall begin by questioning Monsieur de Mestras?"

"Then I would suggest that you embrace the same

opportunity to advise him to frequent no more low gambling dens," said M. de Liscoat, with a malicious smile.

"I shall not advise him, I shall question him, and I assure you that I shall compel him to tell me the truth. He is probably at the château now, and I must see him without delay. Return to Paris, gentlemen, but rest assured that you will soon see me again, and as our paths diverge here, you must now allow me to take leave of you."

"Certainly, certainly, major," replied the marquis. "I think, however, that the viscount and myself had better walk down the railroad track, so we shall be in no danger of losing our way."

He was about to turn on his heel and walk away when his friend Liscoat exclaimed:

"Look, major, you will not be obliged to return to the château to question your protégé. Here he comes now, and strange to say he is coming from the direction of Vésinet."

He was right. Médéric was approaching at a rapid pace, in fact almost on a run, and he was coming from the direction of Vésinet.

The major could not believe his eyes.

"We will leave you, so as not to intrude upon your interview with him, my dear sir," cried Liscoat, hastening off with his friend in the direction of Chatou.

With folded arms and frowning brow, the major awaited the approach of his young protégé, who had recognized him at a distance, and was already making signs of recognition.

CHAPTER II.

Mederic de Mestras, whom the two old fops accused
so rashly, had neither the expression nor the bearing of a
man who had just committed a great crime, for he was
laughing heartily, and amusing himself by leaping lightly
over the clumps of furze that bordered the railroad track.

He was a tall, well-built youth, very dark-complexioned,
and as straight and slender as a reed. He had eyes of
extraordinary vivacity and clearness, a soft silky mustache,
lips of a vivid scarlet, white teeth, and best of all, an
expressive, mobile face that reflected every thought and
emotion.

"A man with a face like that could not possibly tell a
falsehood," thought George Roland.

"How do you do, major?" cried Médéric. "I see that
I am a little too late. I made the best time I could, but
when one has only one's legs to depend upon—"

"Where did you come from?" asked the major, sternly.

"From Vésinet, of course. It is quite a long story.
Would you believe it, I fell asleep on the train. It was
unpardonable in me, I know, but I did not go to bed until
very late last night, and my eyes would close in spite of all
my efforts to keep them open. Suddenly, I heard the
guard call out 'Chatou! Chatou!' I rubbed my eyes, and
tried to rouse myself, but was still half asleep when I
jumped out of the car. I expected to find the ladies at
the gate where the man takes the tickets, for Marcelle told
me yesterday that she would be at the station with her
mother and her young friends, but though I looked, I could
see no one. So I imagined that I must have misunderstood
her, and that they were to meet me at Vésinet, which is
quite as near the Oaks as Chatou is, so without pausing to

reflect, I leaped aboard the train, which was just moving out of the station, and had barely time to jump into a compartment which was so crowded that I landed straight in the lap of a gentleman who uttered a cry of pain. Up to the time of my arrival at Chatou, however, I had been the sole occupant of another compartment that I was unable to find again—"

" And after that?"

" Why, I of course reached Vésinet, where a fresh disappointment awaited me, for there was not a soul at the station to meet me. I decided to leave the train for good this time, however, though the gate-keeper at first refused to let me pass, because my ticket was for Chatou, but he finally consented on the payment of the fare between the two stations. Then I started off on the run, but though I am quite out of breath, I have missed the ladies. It serves me right, however. It will teach me not to go to sleep on the cars again."

The major listened to this explanation with close attention, but his contracted brow did not relax. He had formed a plan from which he did not intend to deviate in the slightest particular. This was to allow Médéric to go on with his explanation, wait until he had finished, and then abruptly inform him of Mme. de Muire's tragical death.

No judge of instruction could have done better,

" That is all very well," he remarked, quietly. " But on leaving the station, why didn't you take the road leading directly to the Oaks?"

" I don't wonder at your astonishment, but I forgot to tell you that from the window of the car, I caught sight of Monsieur de Muire, his wife, his daughter and their friends, standing in line near the track. I even took off my hat to them, but they did not see me."

" You are mistaken; some one did see you."

" Who?"

"Marcelle."

"She must have laughed heartily. How much fun she will make of me when I relate my adventures! How provoked I was with myself when I saw her! I had half a mind to shout: 'Stop the train, conductor! stop the train!' or to jump off, while the car was in motion; but I was afraid you would all laugh at me, and also that I might break my neck. The ladies got tired of waiting and have returned to the château, I suppose?"

The major replied only with a nod, and remained standing in such a position as to conceal from the sight of Marcelle's betrothed the pool of blood in which the body of the unfortunate countess had lain.

"So those antediluvians I see going down the track have given up the idea of dining with us, I suppose. So much the better! I can't endure them, with their dyed whiskers and their pompous airs—above all, that Viscount de Liscoat, who reminds me of an old battered butterfly. I am almost sure that he wears corsets."

"Have you any particular cause to dislike him?" inquired George Roland, who had not forgotten the spitefulness which had characterized the viscount's remarks about Médéric de Mestras.

"No; but I feel sure that he dislikes me, and he is just the kind of a man I heartily despise. I don't meet him very often, and it's a good thing that I don't, for at the very first innuendo he cast upon me, I am sure I should not be able to resist my desire to slap him in the face."

"I advise you to do nothing of the kind," remarked the major, coldly. "Monsieur de Muire will certainly close his doors against you if you insult one of his friends."

"One of his friends! Nonsense! He invites Liscoat to his house merely because he is a good whist-player, and he likes to have him for a partner, but he understands the old fossil's real character perfectly. You will say, perhaps, that Madame de Muire finds him very entertaining; but I can reply that Marcelle hates him, and I always agree with Marcelle. But, by the way, speaking of the ladies, how does it happen that you did not return with them? I don't suppose you preferred the society of those two old peacocks to theirs."

"If you had not come, I should have accompanied them to Chatou. They were just speaking of you."

"They said no good of me, I am sure."

"One of them told me that you had quite recently lost twenty thousand francs in a low gambling den."

"It was Liscoat who told you that. I am sure. The scoundrel! I'll pay him for meddling with my affairs."

"It is true then. You have been gambling, and you have lost in a single night, a sum of money that represents, if I am not very much mistaken, a fifteenth of your fortune—even admitting that you had not impaired it very considerably before you committed this act of folly."

Médéric blushed to the very tips of his ears; but he did not shrink from a full confession of his wrong-doing.

"I never told a falsehood in my life, major," he said, bravely, "and I certainly am not going to begin now. It is true that I did allow myself to be decoyed into a pretended club-house which turned out to be a mere gambling den. I had an irresistible longing for a two hundred louis horse I saw at Tattersall's the other day, and I knew that my circumstances would not justify me in purchasing it—you see how sensible I am. Ah, well, it was my prudence that ruined me, for I said to myself that by risking a few louis, I might win enough to gratify this whim, without making any inroads on my capital, and—you can guess the rest. But I assure you that the lesson has been a good one, and that I shall never be guilty of a like imprudence. I am such a poor hand at card-playing that I should be sure to ruin myself in six months."

The major could not help smiling at this naïve confession, and his confidence revived. A young man who confessed his faults so frankly, could not have been guilty of any very atrocious crime.

"I really hope that you will not say anything to Marcelle about it," continued Médéric. "I should die of shame."

"You deserve to be reported both to her and to her father," replied the major, "but though I have no intention of doing it, others may. Besides, you have no suspicion of the danger that surrounds you at this very moment. This, however, is no place to explain your situation to you. I am going back to the Oaks. Will you accompany me?"

"Most assuredly. If you only knew how anxious I am to see Marcelle, you would not ask such a question. I have so many things to tell her that I scarcely know where to begin. I hope I shall be seated next to her at the table, though the last time I dined there I was placed between her governess and an elderly relative of Madame de Muire."

The major took Médéric's arm, and together they wended their way in the direction of the château.

"I don't know what has turned Madame de Muire against me," continued Médéric. "She used to make a great deal of me in former years, but since there has been any possibility of my marriage to her daughter, she has treated me coldly, and almost rudely."

"I have noticed that fact, and being unable to account for it, I thought I would ask you the reason."

"I assure you that I haven't the slightest idea, major. I am really very fond of her, and I have tried to convince her of the fact by redoubling my respectful attentions, but without avail."

"It is certainly very strange."

"It is incomprehensible, for you must recollect that if Marcelle and I have grown to love each other, Madame de Muire might, with justice, be held accountable for it. While my father lived, I was always at her house, and yet I never seemed to go there often enough. After my father's death, Monsieur de Muire became my guardian, but it was the countess who came to school to see me, and I spent my holidays in playing with her daughter. Marcelle grew up; I attained my majority, and I remained on the same intimate footing with the family. What followed was only natural. I fell violently in love with Marcelle, and had the good fortune to win her love in return. Her father encouraged us; I finally declared my love to him, and he did not repulse me. He only imposed a year's probation upon me before he gave his full consent. It was not until then that the manner of the countess underwent an entire change. I pleased her as a protégé; but I begin to think that she does not want me for a son-in-law."

"She told her husband this very day that while she lived, you should never marry Marcelle."

"Ah, well, we can wait," replied Médéric, stoutly.

"What do you mean?" exclaimed the major, startled by this unexpected declaration. "You can wait! That probably means that you are wishing for Madame de Muire's death."

"I!" exclaimed Médéric, no less vehemently. "I, who have always regarded her as a second mother! My feelings toward her have not changed, nor will they ever change any more than my love for her daughter. In answering you as I did, I only meant to give you to understand that time can make no change in hearts that truly love. We shall marry, Marcelle and I, ten years, or even twenty years hence, if they will not allow us to marry before."

"You talk like a child," said the major, partially reassured. "Mademoiselle de Muire will not consent to become an old maid for your sake, and you, yourself, would soon weary of loving without hope. Instead of indulging in vain protestations, examine your own conscience, and try to discover how you can have displeased a lady who once loved you fondly, for she reared you, so to speak. She was the much-esteemed friend of your father, who commended you to her care before he departed to engage in that disastrous war of 1870. She treated you like her son, then, and for years afterward; how then does it happen that she casts you off now?"

"I again assure you that I have no idea."

"Can it be she has heard that you gamble?"

"I am not fond of cards. It so happened that I yielded to temptation once, but it was only a passing weakness. I am afraid of the gaming-table. I always shun it; and I think you will need no further proof of the truth of my statements than the fact that I belong to no club."

"Are you entangled in any *liaison?*"

"Why, major, I certainly hoped that you had a better opinion of me. If you had asked me the same question three years ago, your inquiry would not have wounded me, and I should not have hesitated to answer you frankly in the affirmative; but if I had bestowed a thought on another woman since I declared my love to Marcelle I should be the basest of men."

This reply pleased Roland, but threw no light upon the cause of the dislike that the countess seemed to have suddenly conceived for the son of Colonel de Mestras.

"Some one must have slandered you," he muttered, "and now the evil is irreparable."

"Why? If she will but tell me of what I am accused I can vindicate myself, I am sure."

The major was almost on the point of replying, "Because Madame de Muire has just been murdered," but this announcement would have been premature, so he said, instead:

"Do you think it probable that the governess has influenced the countess against you?"

"Hélène Lanoue? That noble girl is incapable of such perfidy. She loves Marcelle as she would love a sister, and she is Marcelle's only confidante. Hélène knows that the breaking off of this marriage would ruin our happiness, and I can trust her as unreservedly as I can trust you, major. Besides, she is no longer in Madame de Muire's good graces, for that lady sees very plainly that her daughter's governess is on our side. But enough of these surmises. There is a much easier and surer way to learn the cause of Madame de Muire's ill-will. That is to question her, and that I have resolved to do. I did think of doing so this very evening, but abandoned the idea because I supposed those gentlemen would be present. Now they have gone, my mind is made up, and after dinner I shall have an interview with Marcelle's mother. I shall request Monsieur de Muire to be present, for I count upon his assistance as confidently as I count upon yours."

The major made no reply, and Médéric, astonished at this silence, turned and looked at him; but had hardly done so, when he vaguely comprehended that his old friend was concealing something from him.

"Why did those gentlemen hurry back to Paris?" he inquired, suddenly. "They were invited to dine at the Oaks, were they not?"

"I will tell you, sir, in a moment," said the major; "but, before I tell you, there are some questions I would like to put to you."

They had been walking on quite briskly while they talked, and the *façade* of the château, which was really only a large and beautiful villa, built of brick and stone, in the style of Louis XIII.'s time, was already visible through the trees.

They would soon reach the gate, and Médéric could hardly enter the court-yard without hearing the terrible news, for the wildest confusion must reign at the château, and the servants would, of course, be talking of nothing else; so George Roland decided, and with reason, that the time for casting aside all disguise had come.

"Tell me, Médéric, what occurred while you were going from Chatou to Vésinet?" he began, in a much graver tone.

"Nothing—absolutely nothing. The trip, you know, occupies only about four minutes."

"Where did you sit?"

"I sat on this side of the car, with my back to the engine. I could find no other seat. All the others were occupied. Besides, I had just as lief ride backward as not."

"Then your seat was next to the window, I suppose?"

"No; between me and the window there was a stout gentleman, who grumbled all the time because he was too much crowded. It was my fault, I admit, for on leaving the train at Vésinet, I noticed that there was only one solitary passenger in the compartment of which I had been the sole occupant until I reached Chatou. But I was in such a hurry that I did not have time to choose when I got aboard the train a second time."

"You told me so before. Still, in spite of the close proximity of the gentleman, you were able to see the land on this side of the track, were you not?"

"Yes, for a few seconds, though if I had not excellent eyes I should not have seen you at all, for the train moves quite rapidly, even through the outskirts of the village."

"And you saw or heard nothing?"

"Yes; I heard the whistle of the locomotive, which is the most disagreeable of sounds, whatever the enemies of music may say to the contrary," replied Médéric, laughing.

"So you did not hear any shot fired?"

"Any shot? Certainly not. The hunting-season has not begun. It is true that a duel is occasionally fought in this neighborhood, but—"

"No, no; I mean a shot fired from the train."

"Certainly not. Such a thing would not be allowed. I might have amused myself by shooting from the car-window, as I always carry a revolver in my pocket; but I should have been fined for it, even if my traveling-companions had allowed me to do it."

"You had a revolver in your pocket?" exclaimed tho major.

"Yes. I got into the habit of carrying one soon after I took up my abode on the Place Pigalle, for as I often return home late at night, some means of self-defense was not amiss. You know the weapon well, for it was you who gave it to me for a New-year's gift last winter."

"That is true. I recollect it now."

"Would you like to see it?" asked Médéric, putting his hand into his trousers pocket.

Then, almost instantly, he exclaimed:

"Why, it isn't here, though I am sure that I slipped it into my pocket before leaving home. How could I have lost it?"

The major turned very pale. All his former suspicions had returned.

"Oh, I have it! It must have fallen out of my pocket while I was asleep in the cars. I was alone, so I stretched myself out at full length on the seat, and the revolver must have dropped out without my noticing the fact. This is certainly a piece of bad luck, for, you see, I prized the pistol very highly, because you gave it to me. But I shall find it again. I will telegraph to Saint-Germain for it this evening, and some of the employés must have found it on going through the cars on the arrival of the train."

"Was the revolver loaded?" asked Roland, in a voice husky with emotion.

"Of course. I don't carry it for a plaything."

"Then I advise you not to make any effort to recover it."

"Why?"

"Because Madame de Muire was just killed by a shot fired from the same train."

"Marcelle's mother—dead?"

"If you doubt my word, look in the court-yard."

The servants of the château were rushing wildly to and fro, making frantic gestures. The barouche, from which the horses had been removed, was standing in front of the open door. A gentleman dressed in black, doubtless a physician, was just leaping from a tilbury, and through the open windows of the main dining-room Médéric could see Marcelle and her father kneeling beside a sofa upon which the lifeless form of their loved one had been laid.

"I will avenge her!" cried Médéric, making a sudden movement as if to rush into the court-yard.

But the major prevented him from doing so, and said to him, in a tone that was almost curt:

"Don't you understand that you will be accused of having killed her? You are suspected already."

Then, seeing that Médéric was about to burst forth into vehement protestations:

"Not a word here!" continued Roland. "If you are not guilty, I will plead your cause, and I shall gain it. But you shall not enter this house to-day. Depart instantly. Return to Paris. Early to-morrow morning I will be at your rooms, and I hope that you will be able to prove your innocence. If you can not, blow your brains out this very night."

Médéric stared wildly at the major, and then fled like a madman.

CHAPTER III.

For several years, Médéric de Mestras had been living in a rather strange part of the town, but in one that suited not only his tastes, but the state of his finances.

He loved painting; he even painted tolerably well; so nothing would do but he must have a studio, and he had found one on the Place Pigalle, in a house built expressly for artists.

He lived there very comfortably in a tolerably spacious and well-lighted suite of apartments, not too far from the

Muire family, who occupied a large and handsome house on the Boulevard Malesherbes, close by the Park Monceau.

There, he led the comfortable and independent existence possible to any young man of moderate fortune, breakfasting at home on a cutlet and eggs prepared by his one servant, dining at a restaurant, and spending his evenings at the theater or in society.

This quiet life had been disturbed by a few short-lived love-affairs, but they were only fleeting fancies, very unlike his profound love for Marcelle. This last love, born of a friendship between a youth and a mere child, had been of slow and gradual growth, and it was a wonder it had sprung into existence at all, for a young man rarely falls in love with a child he has seen playing with her hoop and doll.

But what is the use of trying to discover the cause of this psychological phenomenon?

Love comes because it is obliged to come, and its victims find it difficult to say when and how it first began.

Nevertheless, this was a very unusual case.

Médéric, on leaving the lyceum, spent two years in the preparatory schools, which had only prepared him to dabble a little in painting, and he entered society the very winter Marcelle entered a convent to complete her education. Consequently, he lost sight of her entirely for a time, and while he was sowing his wild oats, he scarcely bestowed a thought on this school-girl, who was still wearing short dresses. But when he met her again, five years afterward, Marcelle had already become a charming young lady. All childishness had disappeared, but it had not been replaced by the coquetry so common in young girls of that age. The two seemed to have been created for each other, and they appeared to become conscious of the fact immediately.

They resembled each other greatly in temperament, being impulsive, generous to a fault, and exceedingly kind-hearted, though extremely quick-tempered. If they had not adored, they would certainly have detested each other; but they adored each other in the most complete acceptation of the word, and this enforced delay was beginning to make them both impatient.

Marcelle saw that her mother was strongly opposed to the marriage, but she knew that she had her father's approval; and after consulting with Médéric, she, too, had decided that the matter should be settled on the very day the countess fell a victim to an assassin's bullet.

The poor child little thought that at the very time she was praying beside her mother's body, open accusations were being made against the man she loved, and that Médéric, instead of joining her, as he had at first intended, was rushing back to Paris in a state of mind closely verging on frenzy.

He had fled in obedience to the advice of the major, who was the only person that had much influence over him—fled without knowing where he was going or what he was going to do. He had rushed blindly on through the forest, turning neither to the right nor to the left, pursued by a recollection of George Roland's terrible words:

"If you can not prove your innocence, blow your brains out this very night."

If the revolver he lost on the train had still been in his possession, it is more than likely that he would have put it to that use at the very first turn in the road, for he did not see how he could vindicate himself.

One can defend one's self against a clearly formulated accusation; one can answer the question of the judge of instruction who questions one, and try to convince him of one's innocence; but one can not refute vague presumptions.

"I was on the train when the shot was fired," poor Médéric said to himself; "how shall I prove that I was not the person who fired it? How can I find the persons who traveled in the same compartment with me? And as several people know that Madame de Muire refused to consent to my marriage with her daughter, they will suppose that I killed her to remove the only obstacle that separated me from Marcelle. They are saying this already. The major gave me to understand that those old knaves suspected me. They will spread the news everywhere, and hint that I am the only person who could have committed the crime. I shall be summoned before a magistrate who will compel me to give an account of my every act; and even if I should succeed in convincing him that I have a clear conscience, Monsieur de Muire will know that I have been accused, and that will be enough to make him close his doors against me. Marcelle, too, will know it, and she will never marry a man who has been accused of murdering her mother; so I am lost, whatever happens, and I had better follow my old friend Roland's advice. "

The poor fellow had lost his wits completely, and instead of going to Chatou, he hastened toward Bougival, which place he reached almost as soon as if he had traversed the distance in a carriage. On the bridge he paused, seized with a frantic desire to retrace his steps, force an entrance into the château, and throw himself at M. de Muire's feet, entreating to be heard.

But, in a moment, he muttered between his set teeth:

"No, no; I should seem to be asking his forgiveness. There is nothing left for me but to die; and I will die at my own home."

Seeing a passing street-car, he jumped into it without noticing where its route terminated, but subsequently found that this extended through Courbevoie and Neuilly to the Arc de Triomphe. He left the car at the Place l'Étoile, however, and, without knowing why, began to walk down the main avenue of the Champs Elysées.

It was one of the longest days of the year; but night was approaching, and a long line of carriages was proceeding toward the Bois, laden with persons anxious to take advantage of the superb summer evening.

This gay throng of equipages had no attractions for Médéric; but the appetite never fails to assert itself in one of his years, and he suddenly discovered that he was almost fainting with hunger and fatigue. The intense excitement which had sustained him during his mad flight had subsided in a measure, and his limbs now refused to support him.

To rest himself and appease his hunger he only had to choose between a dozen or more restaurants on either side of the avenue. There was one that he had often patronized, especially in the summer-time, and this happened to be the first one he reached after leaving the car.

It was located on the left side of the avenue between the Circus and the Avenue Gabriel. The establishment was crowded that evening, and the waiters were hurrying to and fro, scarcely knowing which way to turn, and listening to no one. All the tables were occupied; but it was growing late, and some of the guests were preparing to leave, so by waiting a little, Médéric was able to secure a seat in a corner, next to a table occupied by two other gentlemen, at whom he did not even glance so profound was his preoccupation. He ordered the first dish he happened to see on the bill of fare, and a bottle of champagne on ice. This is certainly a rather festive beverage, and had Médéric been in his normal condition he would have reproached himself for drinking it on the evening of Mme. de Muire's tragical death; but he was completely enervated and overcome, and he knew by experience that this wine would prove a powerful stimulant.

Besides, there was no one present who would be likely to criticise, at least he thought so, and he congratulated himself upon the comparative isolation he was able to secure among this crowd of strangers. Moreover, he had no intention of remaining long in this public place; on the contrary, he intended to regain his apartments on the Place

Pigalle as soon after dinner as possible. He had little expectation of finding there the healthful slumbers of which he stood so greatly in need; but remembering the old proverb, he began indeed to hope that the night would bring counsel, and that he should discover some means of speedily establishing his innocence.

Gradually his thoughts assumed a less gloomy character, and his situation seemed less desperate in its aspect. He said to himself that though he had enemies, he also had warm friends who would defend him: George Roland, the stern but just major; Hélène Lanoue, the devoted governess; and last, but by no means least, Mlle. de Muire herself, who, after her first paroxysm of grief had subsided, would certainly take his part in a very energetic fashion if any one should venture to attack him in her presence.

Besides, there was nothing to prove that the authorities would see a crime in what might have been only an accident, nor impute the crime to him merely because he had been on the train at the time; and Mme. de Muire had been unwilling to grant him her daughter's hand in marriage.

The revolver he had lost during his trip from Paris to Chatou would be no conclusive proof against him, even if it should be taken to a commissioner of police or a judge of instruction; on the contrary, the finding of it would be a positive advantage to him, as it would establish the fact that neither of the six cartridges with which it was loaded had been fired.

Somewhat consoled by these reflections, Médéric was finishing his dinner, with his hat drawn down over his eyes, when his attention was attracted by the conversation of two gentlemen seated on the veranda just outside the window by which his table stood. The gentlemen had evidently stepped out upon this veranda, which overlooked a small garden, to smoke their cigars and continue a conversation which had been begun at the table.

There was nothing surprising about this, and Médéric would have paid no attention to the incident, much less would he have listened to a conversation between strangers, had he not recognized one of the two voices as that of the Viscount de Liscoat.

The two gentlemen were talking quite loudly, and they were so close to Médéric that not a word escaped him, for he, feeling sure that the tragedy at Chatou was the subject under discussion, it is needless to say that he listened with all his ears, for he was too deeply interested in knowing what they thought of the affair to reveal himself, as he would not have failed to do under other circumstances.

"No one will ever convince me that it was not the young man in question that committed the crime," said the Viscount de Liscoat.

"I differ with you," replied his companion, who was no other than the Marquis de Brangue. "I do not believe that the fellow possesses sufficient spirit, nor sufficient skill in the use of fire-arms to kill poor Louise in that way. It would require even more skill than the feat of shooting partridges while one's horse was going at a full gallop, as they say General Margueritte—the one who was killed at Sedan—used to do in Africa."

"If it was not young Mestras, who fired the shot? It must have been some one else; and the person who did it can truly boast of being as dexterous as the hero you just mentioned: that is, unless the bullet that struck Madame de Muire was intended for you."

"For me! Really that supposition is absurd. No one has any interest in sending me into the other world, and I have never injured any one."

"Hum! you have given several husbands just cause of offense in your life-time; besides, you have a nephew who would not be sorry to step into your shoes."

"Husbands do not avenge their wrongs thus late in the day; and as to my nephew, I disinherited him, by will, long ago. He must suspect as much, for he is now sojourning in some unknown country. I haven't seen him for twenty years."

This beginning was not unpromising, and Médéric, who had not lost a word of it, listened with redoubled attention.

" By the way, speaking of injured husbands," continued Liscoat, " you probably are aware that poor Jacques de Muire has been one of the most notable examples of his time."

" I have heard so; I have even heard several names mentioned; but I, for my own part, have seen nothing—"

" Then you haven't very sharp eyes. Jacques had an intimate friend whom you knew well, and who held an exalted place in madame's good graces. Jacques, too, could not bear him out of his sight."

" At what date did this happy trio exist? I have no recollection of it."

" Oh, a long time ago! It was formed only three or four years after our friend's marriage."

" And how did it end?"

" With the death of the lover. You can imagine how Jacques mourned his loss. His death occurred fourteen years ago; and I don't believe that he is yet consoled for the cruel loss he sustained. His wife recovered from her grief more quickly, for she had an admirable consoler in the person of Dubrac, who was a captain in the Guards before the war."

" I do recollect that Dubrac was always at Muire's house. But who was the other man? I assure you I can't imagine."

" Think again. Muire introduced him at the club, and you must have seen him there, though he was not a regular visitor."

" An army officer, wasn't it?"

" You are burning, as the children say."

"A handsome man, and rather distinguished-looking, though his bearing was a little too much like that of a drum-major."

"Yes, and he was killed at Gravelotte on the sixteenth of August, 1870."

Médéric started violently; his father, too, had fallen upon that famous battle-field, hewing down the Prussian dragoons at the head of his regiment.

"I have it!" exclaimed M. de Brangue. "You mean Colonel de Mestras, do you not?"

"You have guessed at last," replied the viscount.

"But this Mestras was the father of the young man in question."

"Yes; and before he left for the war he commended his son to the care of our friend Jacques, and so effectual did the recommendation prove that the Muires looked after the child as carefully as if he had been their own."

"That is true; but why the deuce did Madame de Muire take such a dislike to him of late?"

"I don't know, nor am I particularly anxious to know; no more anxious, indeed, than I am to become involved in the affair of the shooting. I love my ease above every-thing, as you know; and if you will be guided by me, you will allow Jacques and his friend Major Roland to man-age the affair as they think best. The news of the event has not yet reached Paris, as no one at Chatou knew any-thing about it when we purchased our tickets at the station, and I certainly feel no desire to spread the news."

"It will become known soon enough without the aid of any one. But I shall do as you suggest; keep quiet at least until I have had another interview with that formida-ble major who promised to see us again very soon, you recollect?"

"Was he also an admirer of the poor countess?"

"No, indeed. She could not bear him. He is a very unsociable fellow; and I have always wondered how Jacques could take any pleasure in the society of a man who is as stiff as a crowbar and about as uncompromising. Nevertheless. Jacques insists upon inviting him to the house on all occasions, and it seems to be no fault of his that the man hasn't become a member of the family. The governess is the only member of the household in whom I feel any particular interest, however. She's a beauty, and if she should ever feel a desire to own a pretty little establishment on the Avenue de Villiers, and a handsome victoria to take her to the Bois, I know some one who would be delighted to offer them to her.''

'' You are not the only one, for I haven't seen a handsomer creature for many a day. But it would be a waste of breath. She is too conscientious for such a life to have any charms for her. She will live and die a governess.''

'' Don't be so sure. Mademoiselle de Muire will marry sooner or later, and the handsome Hélène will then lose her situation.''

'' She will find another; that is, unless she marries some worthy clerk. But it seems to me that it is getting rather too cool here. Suppose we step into the Circus to finish our cigars.''

'' I have no objections. That arrangement suits me; and after the performance is over I'll go to the club. It isn't ten o'clock yet, and I am anxious to have my revenge upon that rascal, Golymine, who won three thousand francs from me yesterday.''

'' And I can have my usual game of whist. Decidedly everything is for the best in this best of worlds. We should have spent a frightfully dull evening at the Oaks.''

With this cynical remark M. de Brangue left the balustrade against which he had been leaning, and his worthy companion did the same.

It was time, for Médéric would not have been able to restrain his indignation much longer. He had found considerable difficulty in doing so already, and his patience was now exhausted. These men excited both contempt and loathing, for though he himself had led that gay Parisian life which vitiates and depraves, he had not sunk to the level of such degrading selfishness and skepticism as this; and the climax was reached when this licentious sexagenarian congratulated himself on the death of Mme. de Muire because her death spared him a few hours of *ennui*.

Rising from the table, Médéric settled his bill, entered one of the carriages that were standing in front of the restaurant, and ordered the driver to take him to the Place Pigalle.

A great surprise awaited him there.

It was not late; and this square, which is the center of the artists' quarter—of the New Athens, as it is called—is crowded nearly all night, especially in the summer, when the air is mild, and its inhabitants can sit and chat comfortably upon the benches and even upon the curbing that surrounds the basin of the fountain.

Consequently Médéric was not at all surprised to see two men talking upon the pavement in front of the house in which he lived, and he paid no attention to them.

On alighting from the carriage he paused to pay the coachman, and this took some time, as he had no small coin about him, and the driver, faithful to the habits of his class, drew out the change, piece by piece, from the depths of a leather bag.

When this operation was concluded, Médéric turned to ring the door-bell, and as he did so noticed that the talkers had vanished, but a man, who was probably one of the pair, was standing a few yards off on the corner of the Rue Duperré, and before Médéric could place his hand on the bell-knob, he started toward him. Wondering what this stranger could want with him, Médéric went half-way to meet him, and they came face to face directly under a street lamp only a few steps from Médéric's door.

Médéric had at first supposed the individual to be some

artist of his acquaintance, but on approaching the gentleman he perceived that he was mistaken.

He was a remarkably good-looking man, however, very
handsomely dressed, and still young, though he had a
rather haggard face. It was evident that he belonged to
the upper classes, but that he had spent much of his life in
bad company.

He bowed to Médéric with perfect ease of manner, and
asked politely:

" Is it to Monsieur de Mestras that I have the honor of
speaking?"

" Yes, sir," replied Médéric, greatly astonished. " But
you must excuse me for not recollecting when and where I
met you before."

" I do not wonder that you have forgotten. We spent
only one evening together, and that was in Rome two years
ago, at the house of a *pensionnaire* of the Academy of
Design."

" I know one, it is true, and I used to go and see him
quite often during the winter of '83, which I spent in Italy."

" But you do not remember my face, and you have forgotten my name. That is only natural, for I am not sure
that I was even introduced to you. I will now introduce
myself, however. I am Count Serge Golymine."

Médéric made a gesture which said as plainly as any
words: " Pardon me, but that name is wholly unknown to
me."

It seemed to him, however, that this was not the first
time he had heard it, but he could not recollect where or
under what circumstances.

So he contented himself with replying:

" Very well, sir. You have taken the trouble to come
to my apartments at an hour when one usually receives
only one's intimate friends, and from this fact I conclude
that you must have some communication of an important
nature to make to me."

" Both important and delicate, sir."

" I am ready to hear it, though the place is not very well chosen for a conversation which must be of a private nature, I judge."

" Strictly private, sir; and it is no fault of mine that it is not held elsewhere than on the sidewalk. I reached here about nine o'clock, but your *concierge* told me that you were not at home, and that you often did not return until very late. It was of the utmost importance that I should see you this evening, so I decided to wait for you, and my decision was a wise one, as here you are."

" Will you go up to my rooms?" inquired Médéric, who, having regained confidence, now felt sure that he was dealing with a gentleman.

The visitor hesitated a moment, but finally replied:

" That is not necessary. I hope you will do me the honor to receive me on some future day; but we are now comparative strangers, and this time I feel justified in trespassing upon your attention only for a moment. The evening is superb, and there is nothing to prevent us from walking about while we talk. If we continue to stand here on the pavement people will mistake us for conspirators."

Médéric began to feel a little surprised at these precautions, but being anxious to bring the interview to a close as soon as possible, he said rather curtly:

" As you please, sir."

CHAPTER IV

So Médéric allowed himself to be led toward the double row of trees that extend down the middle of the Boulevard de Clichy. This dimly lighted promenade is a favorite resort of lovers, but lovers are not in the habit of troubling themselves much about other passers-by, and no one paid any apparent attention to the two gentlemen as they walked slowly down the path side by side.

After they had walked about thirty yards in silence, Médéric becoming impatient, paused abruptly, and turning to his companion, said:

" And now, sir, what do you want with me?''

" I want to proffer you my assistance. "

" Will you be kind enough to explain what you mean by that?"

" I will. You were invited to dine at the Count de Muire's villa this evening, I believe?''

" Yes, sir. What of it?''

" And you took the 5:30 P. M. train from the Saint-Lazare Station, but instead of stopping at Chatou you went on to Vésinet. "

" Was it merely to tell me this that you brought me here?'' asked Médéric, angrily.

" Yes, this, and something more. Madame de Muire was killed by a pistol shot fired from the train. "

" How do you know?"

" I was on the same train. I saw the lady fall, and I saw you leave the train a few moments afterward. I recognized you instantly, for I have a remarkably good memory for faces. I knew that you were expected at Monsieur de Muire's house, for one of my friends who was also to dine there told me so, just before he left Paris on the 4:25

train. I was invited to dine with a party at Saint-Germain, but on arriving there I excused myself to my host, whom I found waiting for me at the station, and immediately returned to Chatou, for I was anxious to know the condition of affairs at the Oaks.''

"Why should that have interested you so deeply? You are not acquainted with the Muire family so far as I know.''

"It was in you that I felt an interest chiefly, and I intended to apply to you to learn whether or not Madame de Muire had been dangerously wounded. At the station I inquired the way to the villa, and hastened there afoot. On my arrival I asked for you, and learned that nothing had been seen of you. At the same time I learned that the countess was dead, and that the authorities were to be apprised of this strange event. The footman who told me this gave me your address, and I returned to Paris immediately, for I was anxious to see you without delay.''

"Why were you in such haste to see me?'' inquired Médéric, unable to understand the cause of this solicitude.

"Ah! this is the very point,'' replied the stranger, with an air of real or pretended embarrassment, "and I trust you will not take offense at what I have to say to you. Since I first came to Paris, several months ago, I have often heard you spoken of at the club to which I belong. Several of the members are acquaintances of yours—the Marquis de Brangue and the Viscount de Liscoat among them. They have often met you at the house of Monsieur de Muire, and it was one of these gentlemen—Monsieur de Liscoat—who told me that he was going to dine with you at the Oaks to-day. Having previously met you in Rome, and having been very favorably impressed with you, I have taken advantage of the opportunities thus afforded to make some inquiries in regard to you, and was much pleased to learn that you were about to make a very brilliant match by wedding Mademoiselle de Muire——''

"You are really too kind,'' interrupted Médéric ironically, "but I should like to know what right Monsieur de Liscoat had to circulate this report about me."

"Oh, he had no evil intentions, I assure you; quite the contrary. He even expressed a fear that Madame de Muire might refuse to grant you her daughter's hand, but you can dispense with her consent now she is dead."

Médéric started violently and looked straight in the eyes of his new acquaintance, who continued tranquilly:

"After the tragedy which I witnessed from a distance, the idea suddenly occurred to me that this lady's untimely demise might cause you no little annoyance."

"I fail to understand you. Explain more clearly, if you please."

"That is the very thing that puzzles me. I am afraid of offending you, and on the other hand, I should blame myself very much if I kept anything back. So I shall venture to run the risk, and I beg that you will listen to me without losing your temper. I am your sincere well-wisher, and any misunderstanding between us might be very disastrous in its consequences."

"No further introduction is necessary. The facts, if you please."

"The facts are these: A crime has been committed— the authorities have been apprised of it, and it is of such a very peculiar nature that it will not only cause a great sensation, but the investigation will be conducted with the greatest care. They will move heaven and earth to discover the assassin, and they will perhaps look for him in the wrong place. There is an old and generally received axiom: *Is fecit cui prodest,* that is to say: 'The crime is always committed by a person who will profit by it.' When a wealthy man is murdered, suspicion immediately falls upon his heir. This is not the case in the present instance, however, as Madame de Muire's fortune goes to her daughter; still, the lady's death has been a decided advantage to one person."

"To whom, if you please?"

"Advantage is not exactly the word, perhaps; still, this unexpected and untimely death has removed a very serious obstacle from—"

"My path, I presume you mean."

"That is it precisely."

"Then why can you not muster up courage to say openly that you suspect me of the crime?"

"I do not, but others will not fail to do so."

"Then I will find an effectual way to silence them, and I defy them to produce a shadow of a proof against me."

"Are you very sure that you left nothing of a compromising nature behind you on the Saint-Germain Railway?"

"I have no intention of concealing the fact that I took the 5:30 train."

"But I presume you are not particularly anxious for people to know that you had a six-shooter in your pocket when you left Paris."

This blunt retort, for which Médéric was utterly unprepared, disconcerted him completely.

How could this man have heard of the loss of the revolver? Major Roland was the only person who knew the story, and it certainly was not the major who had related it to the so-called Count Golymine.

It suddenly occurred to Médéric that this strange person must be a detective who had been sent to make him commit himself before he was formally examined by a magistrate, and he resolved to waste no ceremony upon him.

"Who doesn't carry a revolver in his pocket, nowadays?" he retorted, shrugging his shoulders. "Besides, I expected to dine in the country, and the suburbs of Paris are more unsafe than the city itself."

"I admit all that," replied the stranger, coldly; "but even when one is provided with fire-arms one isn't in the habit of amusing one's self by firing in the air, so if the authorities should discover that one of the cartridges of your pistol has been fired, and that there are fresh traces of powder in the barrel—"

" I fired at no one."

" That is something you would have to prove; and if you had this pistol about you, it would probably be best for you to take it immediately to the commissioner of police of this precinct."

Then, as Médéric evinced no intention of replying, Golymine added, coldly:

" But it is not in your possession?"

" How do you know?"

" Because I have it."

" Did you find it?" exclaimed Médéric, thoughtlessly.

" Yes, and it is fortunate for you that it did not fall into other hands, for it would have been in a magistrate's possession before this time."

" Where did you find it?"

" In a compartment I entered at Saint-Germain. I was the sole occupant of it, and the weapon had fallen under the seat. I stepped on it, and so very naturally picked it up."

" How did you discover that it belonged to me?"

" You forget that your name is engraved upon it. Judge of my surprise on seeing it! You can no longer wonder at my anxiety to see you. The finding of this revolver furnishes abundant grounds for a formal charge against you, for I examined it, and found that a shot had just been fired from it."

" But not by me. I must have dropped it, and so left it in the car when I got off the train at Chatou; and some other person must have found it and used it."

" I should advise you not to offer that explanation if you are questioned by a magistrate. I, for my own part, can only wonder at your carelessness. To leave a pistol that had your name upon it, in the car, was certainly the height of imprudence."

"And proof positive, it seems to me, that I was not the person that fired the fatal shot. Had I done so, the very first thing I should have done afterward would have been to conceal the weapon."

"Yes; but I can *very* readily understand why you should not have felt inclined to replace it in your pocket, for you were liable to be arrested on leaving the train. But as for getting rid of it, you would probably have found that no easy matter. Had you thrown it out of the window, the track-walker would have been sure to find it. Had there been any river where the train passed over a bridge, you could have disposed of it there, but the railroad does not cross the Seine between Chatou and Vésinet."

"But of course it is all right, sir, as you found it; that is, unless you intend to denounce me and surrender this weapon to the government procureur."

"For what do you take me? I never informed on any one in my life, and I certainly shall not begin with you, for whom I have felt a strong liking ever since we first met at the house of a mutual friend, in a foreign land. Had I entertained any such unfriendly idea, I should have made no effort to find you, but should have gone straight to the authorities."

"Then you will give the revolver back to me, I presume."

"No; but I have it, and you have nothing to fear. It is in good hands."

"I don't doubt it; but what do you intend to do with it?"

"I should like to keep it as a souvenir of you."

"And you have no intention of ever returning it to me?"

"That is saying too much. I shall keep it—for awhile."

"I understand. You intend to blackmail me."

"Really, sir, you use very harsh language, and when you come to know me better I am sure that you will regret having suspected me of such infamous intentions. The fact is, I have a favor to ask of you—"

" And in exchange for this service, if I should consent to render it, you will return my revolver?"

" That is about it. Permit me to explain, however, and in the first place please to recollect that this weapon is much safer in my hands than in yours. No one will think of coming to my rooms to look for it, while your apartments are liable to be searched at any moment; and if the weapon should be found in your possession you would be seriously compromised. Do not fancy that you could devise a way to get rid of it with safety. You would not dare to intrust it to the keeping of any one; and as to throwing it into the street, or into the river—that would be still more dangerous. Nothing is lost in Paris. Some fine morning the Seine would be dragged, and the pistol found. "

" What of that? I shall not deny that it belongs to me. "

" Such a confession might cost you dear. For your own sake, I should strongly advise you to leave this very damaging article in my possession. "

" I can not take it from you by force; but if you should decide to show it, I shall not hesitate to tell the truth about it. So you had better do as you like without counting upon any assistance from me. "

" I only ask you to remain neutral. The question is just this: The Viscount de Liscoat was to introduce me to Monsieur de Muire, whom I have not the honor of knowing, but who may, perhaps, be of great service to me in an important business enterprise I think of undertaking. All the arrangements had been made, and the presentation would have taken place in a few days if this misfortune had not occurred. When we were talking about it, Monsieur Liscoat and I, he happened to speak of you. I instantly recollected our meeting in Rome, and I hoped, by reason of our former acquaintance, that you would not be unfriendly when we met again at the Oaks. The catastrophe which I witnessed has necessitated the postponement of the introduction, but it has only been deferred, I trust, and we are likely to meet, sooner or later, at the count's house."

"Pardon me, sir," interrupted Médéric, suddenly struck by a serious discrepancy in this singular person's statements; "you tell me that you do not know Monsieur de Muire, and yet you said, just now, that you saw Madame de Muire fall a victim to an assassin's bullet."

"I know Monsieur de Muire only by sight, but my acquaintance with the countess is one of much longer standing. Some time ago she was in the habit of going to the springs of Aix, in Savoy, every year. She went there without her husband, and I was one of her favorite partners in the dances at the Casino."

Médéric started violently. The conversation he had overheard in the restaurant recurred to his mind, and he wondered if this Count Golymine had also been one of the lady's admirers.

"Whether our future relations are to be friendly or unfriendly depends entirely upon you," continued the stranger; "but for your own sake, as well as mine, I earnestly hope that they may be truly amicable. I must add that you would make a great mistake if you impute to me motives that I do not possess, for I shall not only carefully refrain from doing anything to injure you in the estimation of any member of Monsieur de Muire's household, but if I should ever see an opportunity to say a word in favor of your marriage, I shall certainly avail myself of it."

"I do not need your assistance," retorted Médéric, dryly, "and if this proposal of yours is to be regarded in the light of a bargain—"

"By no means. You are at perfect liberty to make use of me or not, as you please. I retain possession of the revolver only because the authorities will not think of looking for it in my house; and I will restore it to you as soon as all danger of a search for it has passed. If you should become alarmed, or if you should need my testimony to establish your innocence, I will not even shrink from falsehood to assist you. I can say, for instance, that I traveled in the same compartment with you, and that you did not fire your pistol during the journey. My very best efforts are at your disposal, and I seek nothing from you in return except that you will not try to injure me in the count's estimation."

Médéric was really too much bewildered to reply; so Golymine continued:

"Take notice, I beg, that you are not to vouch for me in any way whatever. I am to be introduced by Monsieur de Liscoat; besides, I am a member of the same club to which Monsieur de Muire belongs—a club which admits to membership only persons of the highest respectability. I am very well known there; and every one is aware of the fact that I am one of the prominent members of a firm of wealthy capitalists whose principal office is in Vienna. I am not the only nobleman who is engaged in business, and I think that even Monsieur de Muire will not consider that he is degrading himself by associating himself with us in our enterprises, as I am anxious to persuade him to do. Now I have said all I have to say, sir. I was anxious to inform you that I have your revolver, and that, consequently, you need feel no fears that it will fall into your enemies' hands. I have done this, and you know the only favor I ask in return. There is nothing for me to do now but take leave of you, which I will proceed to do by saying '_Au revoir._'"

And Golymine bowed politely and walked away before Médéric could decide what to say in reply. He saw the stranger disappear down a side-path, and it seemed to him that a man who was sitting upon a bench rose to join him.

That mattered very little to him, however. He knew enough about the projects of this friend of the Viscount de

Liscoat, and he did not try to blind himself to the fact that the overtures to which he had just listened concealed a covert threat. After all, he had promised nothing; and as the conversation had had no witness, he could keep it a secret and profit by it. But he was no longer capable of reasoning calmly. So many exciting incidents closely following such a frightful catastrophe had bewildered him, and he felt like a man who, having lost his way, finds himself surrounded by precipices on every side, and dares not advance a single step.

Besides, he was overcome with fatigue, and he could do nothing until after he had seen Major Roland.

So he went up to his rooms, threw himself on the bed, and, as not unfrequently happens after great crises, fell into a leaden slumber that lasted until the next day.

It was the brawny hand of the major that awakened him. George Roland was a frequent visitor at the apartments of his old colonel's son, and when he presented himself there every door flew open. The *concierge* and Médéric's servant had both received orders to always allow him to enter unannounced, so the major made his way straight into the chamber, and up to the bed upon which Médéric was soundly sleeping.

This profound slumber appeared a good omen to M. Roland. A person who has a crime upon his conscience does not usually sleep so soundly. They are troubled, generally, by bad dreams.

The major laid his hand heavily upon the shoulder of the sleeper, and shook him, calling him by name. It is in a similar manner that the superintendent of the Roquette prison arouses a man on the morning of his execution. The circumstances were not identical, but the major was anxious to see what Médéric would do and say in the first moment of surprise.

Médéric opened his eyes, closed them again, and then turned over, and his old friend was obliged to repeat the operation three times before he succeeded in thoroughly arousing the sleeper.

At last the young man raised himself up on one elbow, and, gazing around him with an air of astonishment, exclaimed:

" What! is it you? What time is it?"

" Upon my word! one would suppose you were not expecting me!" exclaimed the major. " You have a very short memory. Still, I am happy to find that you did not blow your brains out last night. "

Médéric suddenly recollected all that had occurred.

" I have made a mistake in not doing it, perhaps," he exclaimed. " But tell me, I beseech you, what occurred at the Oaks after my departure?"

" Nothing that you have not guessed already, probably. Two physicians who had been summoned from Saint-Germain arrived. The one from Chatou was there already. They could only certify to the death. The bullet penetrated the breast below the left collar-bone, and severed the aorta. Madame de Muire was killed almost instantly. "

" I know that; but—"

" But you would like to know what the authorities are doing? I am not able to say. Chatou is in the department of the Seine and Oise, so the officials of Versailles were the proper persons to be consulted. The government attorney did not arrive until after midnight. He ordered a *post-mortem* examination, and it will be made to-day. They wish to extract the bullet, which, judging from the size of the wound, must be a pistol-ball. "

" The magistrate probably questioned—"

" Everybody, including Marcelle, who was hardly able to reply, however. The poor child had a frightful attack of hysterics, and is so ill that her father will be obliged to bring her back to Paris this morning with her governess. Of course, she could tell the magistrate nothing of any importance, and the servants were equally ignorant, as they were not present when Madame de Muire was shot. The count has lost his wits completely, and suspects no one. In fact, he seems to feel sure that it was an accident."

"That is very fortunate," replied Médéric. "But you, too, must have been examined, major?"

For an hour or more. I was asked what I thought of this strange affair, and I endeavored to prove that the catastrophe was the result of an accident—that some careless traveler must have involuntarily pulled the trigger while playing with his revolver. But the magistrate who questioned me did not seem to share this opinion."

"The magistrate must have learned that guests were expected yesterday?"

"Probably; and he may learn their names, but yours was not mentioned in his presence."

"What, did Marcelle evince no astonishment at my absence? She must have been surprised not to see me at such a time."

"Marcelle was so overcome with grief that she scarcely spoke to me. Besides, as you can very readily understand, I was much less anxious to know what the poor girl thought, than the action the authorities were likely to take in the matter. The case was put in the hands of a judge of instruction this morning, and an investigation must have been begun before this time. This investigation will probably bear more upon the attendant facts than upon the causes; and it is very difficult to determine where it will end. All the railroad employés who were on duty yesterday will be summoned to give their testimony—the conductor among them. It will be very strange if he did not hear the shot."

"He may be able to tell which car it was fired from; and the station-master at Chatou can testify that I entered a compartment occupied by several other persons. He knows me by sight."

"Still, he may not have noticed you, and I would advise you not to have recourse to his testimony. It would be very foolish to anticipate a possible charge against you, for very few persons are aware of the fact that Madame de Muire was opposed to your intended marriage."

"The Viscount de Liseoat and his friend, Monsieur de Brangue, know it," murmured Médéric, sadly.

"They are not particularly friendly to you, but they probably will not dare to denounce you openly. The greatest danger to be feared is that some one may find the revolver and discover that it belongs to you."

"Especially as my name is engraved upon it."

"You didn't tell me that."

"Because I thought you knew it. It was engraved upon it by your order, you remember?"

"I recollect the fact now, and a most unfortunate idea it was on my part. You are in much greater danger than I supposed. But, after all, there has been no trouble thus far, and there is not likely to be," added the major, encouragingly.

"Unless—"

Médéric did not finish the sentence. He had been on the point of telling the whole story of his interview with Count Golymine, but he feared that the major would blame him for having tacitly accepted the compromise offered by this person, whose real character was unknown to him; so he paused a moment, and then asked, earnestly:

"So you no longer suspect me of the crime?"

"No," replied George Roland. "I have reflected a good deal during the night, and am now convinced that you are guilty only of thoughtlessness and folly. The son of Colonel Mestras can not be a cowardly assassin. If I suspected you yesterday, it was your own fault. Your story of a journey in another compartment seemed so strange to me; besides, the insinuations of those old simpletons were not without their effect."

"What if I should tell you I had seen them since?"

"When? Where?"

"Last evening, before returning home, I stopped in a restaurant on the Champs Elysées to get my dinner."

"You could think of dinner at such a time?"

"Yes. I was nearly famished. The gentlemen in question were there, and I happened to seat myself in a place where they could not see me, but where I was able to overhear every word of their conversation. If you only knew what they said!"

"Did they say they were going to denounce you as the assassin?"

"No, though they believe, or pretend to believe, that I am guilty, but they set too much store upon their ease and their peace of mind to desire to become involved in a criminal suit."

"Then what could they have said to move you so deeply?"

"I can repeat what they said to no one but you. You served under my father. You know that he was a man of honor."

"In the fullest sense of the word, and if these scoundrels dare to assert the contrary I will cut their ears off."

"If you had heard them, major, you would have stayed and heard them through, until the end, as I did. They seem to have an entirely different conception of honor from what we have, and the crime they imputed to my father seemed to be scarcely worthy of censure to them. They only laughed about it, and seemed to consider it an excellent joke."

"Explain, if you please. I am becoming very impatient."

"They declared that my father was Madame de Muire's lover."

"It is an abominable lie!" exclaimed the major. "Your father was killed in 1870; I served in his regiment for a long time before the war, and I never saw anything that furnished the slightest grounds for such a supposition.

Your father was on very intimate terms with the Muires, it
is true, but—”

“ They spoke of the *liaison* as if it had been common
talk at the time. According to their story, Monsieur de
Muire was the only person who did not know of it. They
even added that my father had a successor in Madame de
Muire’s good graces in the person of a Monsieur Dubrac,
an officer in the Guards.”

“ Dubrac! I knew him. It is true that he was a frequent visitor at the house of the Muires for several years,
but that is no reason why people should believe that he
was ever the lady’s lover. As for your father I can swear
that he never betrayed the confidence his most intimate
friend reposed in him, and were it not for the scandal it
would create, I would publicly give the lie to these calumnies, sustaining my word by my sword if necessary. I
hope, however, to find some pretext for treating them as
they deserve to be treated, by and by. Just at present,
however, you and I have other work on hand, so forget
their foolish talk, and do me the favor to get up and dress.
You must breakfast with me, and after breakfast accompany me to the Oaks. I advised you not to enter the house
last evening; but it will occasion remark if you are not
seen there to-day.”

“ Who knows how I shall be received?” murmured
Médéric.

“ Like a son by the poor count; like a betrothed lover
by Marcelle, and like a friend by Hélène Lanoue, who is
a noble girl, and who has always embraced every opportunity to speak a good word in your behalf. These slanders
will soon die out, and in six months you will be Mademoiselle de Muire’s husband.”

“ Then you have no fears that this investigation which
has just been opened—”

“ Will implicate you? I think not; but if it should,
there will be four on hand to defend you. And to

strengthen your position I shall persuade Jacques to have you serve with him as one of the chief mourners at Madame de Muire's funeral. It will be well for every one to know that you were to have been her son-in-law."

"Heaven grant that you are right!" sighed Médéric, less sanguine than the major, who was ignorant of the existence of a certain Count Golymine, however.

CHAPTER V

FOUR days have elapsed. The magistrates summoned to investigate the murder committed at Chatou have concluded the preliminary investigation, and the body of the Countess de Muire has been taken back to Paris, and is about to be interred with fitting pomp and solemnity.

The front of the church Saint-Augustin is hung with black, and above the heavy folds that drape the portico is the coat of arms of the Muire family, surmounted by a coronet.

The nave, which is also heavily draped with black, is filled to overflowing, and more than thirty carriages are standing in line in front of the church.

At the foot of the altar stands the catafalque, surrounded with candles, and almost concealed by flowers. The solemn notes of the organ peal through the church; the simple chants of the burial service resound through the arches; and more than one poor wretch is thinking that with the cost of this handsome funeral he and his, who are perishing of hunger, might be made comfortable for life.

Upon the church steps is a crowd of fashionable people who arrived too late to gain an entrance into the edifice, and of reporters sent there to take the names of the prominent persons present.

All Paris is talking of the Countess de Muire's tragical death; and every one is looking forward with intense interest to a *cause célèbre,* though there have been no new developments, and no one has yet been arrested.

Marcelle is not present. She had insisted upon coming, but her father objected, though he expressed a desire that Médéric de Mestras should accompany him to the church and to the cemetery.

So Médéric occupies a seat at the count's left. Behind them sits Major Roland, with two or three personal friends of the count, who, being the last of his race, has no relatives except on his wife's side. These are only distant cousins of Mme. de Muire, *née* Plantier; and as they reside in the country they have not thought it necessary to attend the funeral.

The rest of the assemblage is composed of people belonging to the circles in which the countess moved, and as the deceased was very widely known, and exceedingly popular, there is a large but very elegant crowd, made up of men in Prince Albert coats, black cravats and black gloves, and ladies attired in mourning of the very latest style.

Every one is talking in whispers, but no one is weeping, at least no one except a young lady who is kneeling upon a *prie-Dieu,* near the coffin. This is Hélène Lanoue, the governess whose beauty had been so highly extolled by the Viscount de Liscoat. She would greatly have preferred remaining with her pupil, but Marcelle had insisted that she should attend the funeral, for she was anxious to know all that occurred there, and she had little hope of seeing Médéric or even her father again that day, for her parent's grief was so profound that he shunned the society of every one.

The major watched Hélène closely, secretly resolving to join her when they left the church, advise her not to follow the body to the cemetery, and escort her back to the house.

This would afford him an opportunity to see Mlle. de Muire, with whom he had been able to exchange only a few words since the catastrophe that had made her an orphan, and enable him to talk with her about the future. He already knew that neither she nor her father had suspected Médérie of the crime for an instant, and that they had no idea of breaking off the marriage, though it would necessarily be postponed on account of Mme. de Muire's death; but he was anxious that a day should be appointed for it, and that in the meantime Médéric should be admitted to the house on the same footing as in former times.

The doors of the church had been left open, and on the portico M. de Brangue stood talking with his inseparable friend, M. de Liscoat, both gentlemen being equally averse to entering the edifice which was already crowded to suffocation.

"A fine house," remarked the marquis, as if speaking of a first night at the theater.

"Yes," replied the viscount, "crowds of people have been turned away. Still, we must show ourselves."

"Oh, we have plenty of time. The friends and acquaintances have not begun to offer their expressions of condolence yet, and that will take at least twenty minutes. We shall be among the last, that is all. It will be enough if Jacques sees us."

"He will see many other acquaintances. All the members of the club are here, even Golymine, who doesn't know Muire, or who scarcely knows him."

"Who is Golymine? Oh, yes, that Pole who was recently admitted to the club, and who plays piquet every evening from five o'clock to seven. Who is the man, anyway?"

"A nobleman, and a great capitalist who is at the head of several gigantic enterprises. I don't know why I haven't introduced him to you."

"What would be the use. My property is all in real estate, and I have no idea of selling any of it in order to engage in speculation."

"Oh, he is not hunting for investors, though I think he

has his eye on our friend Jacques, for he asked me to introduce him to the count the other day. I understand now why he came to the funeral. It is a mark of deference which he wishes to show to his future associate in business."

"Your Pole is certainly reckoning without his host. Muire married under the dotal *régime*, and all the property belonged to his wife. The daughter will inherit it unless the countess made a will in her husband's favor, which is not at all likely."

"Golymine is going into the church now. Suppose we do the same," said Liscoat, elbowing his way through the crowd. "Follow me."

The Count de Muire and Médéric de Mestras, preceded by the undertaker, were advancing to take their places near the main door-way, there to receive expressions of sympathy and respect from personal friends as they passed out.

The major might have stationed himself beside them, but he was anxious by his voluntary absence to call attention to the fact that if Médéric stood beside M. de Muire, it was because he would soon become a member of the Muire family by a marriage with Marcelle.

So instead of following them George Roland stepped forward, offered his hand to Mlle. Lanoue, and led her gently toward one of the side aisles. She was too much overcome with emotion to speak, but she lifted her large, tearful eyes to his, and thanked him with an eloquent glance. Of course she and the major were not expected to salute M. de Muire formally, so instead of walking down the main aisle, they passed down one of the side aisles, but finally found themselves wedged in the crowd opposite the count, and only a short distance from him.

M. de Muire was very pale, but he mastered his emotion and acquitted himself very creditably of the trying task of returning bows and responding to formal expressions of condolence when one's heart is breaking.

A true nobleman of the old school, he even suited his acknowledgments to the rank of each person who saluted him, but he was suffering terribly, and it was evident that he longed for the ordeal to be over.

Médéric acquitted himself less creditably, and the majo fancied that several persons pretended not to see him as they passed. From this he very naturally concluded that the viscount and his friend must have been circulating evil reports about his protégé, and the natural animosity he felt toward them increased accordingly.

Very soon he saw the pair approach the count, closely followed by a gentleman who seemed to be in company with them, for only a moment before Liscoat had turned to beckon to him. The viscount and the marquis honored Médéric with only the semblance of a bow as they passed, but the stranger offered his hand, and George Roland was not a little surprised to see that Médéric ignored it. He was even more surprised to hear Mlle. Lanoue inquire in a low tone who that gentleman was, but he did not know what to say in reply, for Médéric had said nothing about Count Golymine's nocturnal visit.

What was there about this man that had attracted the attention of Marcelle's governess at a time like this? The major looked at him attentively, but did not recollect to have ever seen him before. He was a rather fine-looking man, at least forty years of age, the possessor of an energetic face, illumined by a pair of dark blue eyes of extraordinary brilliancy, and adorned by a long silky mustache of a bright chestnut hue.

And this gentleman evidently knew the Count de Muire, for the latter returned his bow with marked deference.

"Come, mademoiselle," said the major, who was in a great hurry to leave the church and get his companion back to the Muire mansion. "I can not answer your question, but Médéric can probably tell you what you wish to know."

Mlle. Lanoue had ceased weeping, but she seemed greatly agitated, and she paused on the portico and looked back, as if she were trying to catch another glimpse of some one in the crowd. The major led his companion to the coupé which had brought her to the church, and which was in waiting on the Boulevard Malesherbes, and after he had entered it with her he inquired in what way the gentleman she had pointed out could have interested her.

" I thought I recognized him," she replied, " but I presume I was mistaken."

" So far as I know, he is a stranger," replied George, " but he is probably a member of the club to which these gentlemen belong. I will make inquiries, however, and let you know."

" One sees extraordinary resemblances sometimes."

" To whom does this gentleman bear such a striking resemblance?"

The girl hesitated, but finally replied with evident embarrassment:

" A person I have not seen since my infancy, and whom I supposed to be dead."

The major abstained from questioning her any further, even while he mentally resolved to solve this mystery, though it interested him much less than the Chatou murder.

" Will you permit me to go in a moment?" he asked as the coupé drew up before the door of the Muire mansion.

" Marcelle will be very glad to see you," replied Mlle. Lanoue; " and it will do her good to talk with a true friend like you, sir. Her father is not in a condition to reason with her, and she has only had an opportunity to exchange a few words with Monsieur de Mestras since this misfortune befell her."

" Very fortunately for her she has had you with her," remarked George, as he assisted the young lady out of the carriage.

"I have tried my best to console her, but in vain." She worshiped her mother; and Madame de Muire's tragical death has unnerved her completely. The physicians and magistrates who questioned her have shown her no mercy. She will not believe that the catastrophe was the result of a crime; and they seemed to take a cruel pleasure in proving that the countess was foully murdered. They even asked her if she suspected any one. She has not yet recovered from the state of intense excitement into which she was thrown by these examinations, and the sight of her despair almost breaks my heart."

"Time is the only cure for sorrow like hers. But you, mademoiselle, what do you think of this terrible affair?"

"I can not yet bring myself to believe it, though I witnessed it. I saw Madame de Muire fall unconscious into the arms of the Marquis de Brangue, and the bullet that struck her must have come from one of the cars of the passing train; but for all that, it seems to me that I must be dreaming."

"Médéric was on the train, but he did not even hear the report of the pistol."

"What! Monsieur de Mestras?"

"Didn't you know that he went on to Vésinet instead of stopping at Chatou?"

"No; he has not mentioned the fact to me. Still, I have scarcely seen him since the catastrophe. I am surprised that he did not mention the circumstance to Marcelle, however."

"He was probably afraid of alarming her. No one has thought of suspecting him, thank Heaven; but it is not impossible that this absurd idea might occur to the minds of the magistrates. Madame de Muire has not been very favorably disposed toward him for some time past, and that is quite enough to give rise to the most absurd suspicion under circumstances like these."

"They would certainly be cruelly unjust. Madame de

Muire really liked him very much. I do not know why she objected to his marriage with Marcelle, but she would have yielded eventually, I am sure; and Monsieur de Mestras knew that she would sooner or later."

"What if I should tell you that there are persons who are already trying to prove that Médéric was the only person really interested in the lady's death?"

"Such persons must be either fools or scoundrels. I dare them to accuse Monsieur de Mestras openly."

"I hope that they will not dare to do it. Besides, Jacques de Muire has just given public proof that his intentions are unchanged, and that Médéric is to be his son-in-law. Still, I shall not be really tranquil in mind until after the real culprit has been discovered. Will you permit me to add that I am depending upon you to assist me in accomplishing this?"

"Upon me! How can I possibly assist you?"

"Yes, mademoiselle, upon you," replied the major, gently. "If my memory serves me, it is seven years since you entered the Muire family, and little that has happened in the household can have escaped your observant eyes. A day will perhaps come when a providential chance may recall to your memory some now forgotten fact that may set us on the right track. But I am detaining you, and Marcelle needs you. Tell her that I am here, and ask her if she will see me."

Major Roland and the governess had held this conversation in a small room on the second floor, a room in which Marcelle loved to sit because the windows opened upon a garden full of flowers and verdure. This favorite nook belonged to the suite of apartments set aside for the young girl's use, and upon the same floor with the apartments of the countess. M. de Muire occupied the story above; and the first floor of the spacious mansion was opened only for the large winter receptions.

That day the house seemed deserted. The servants, all

attired in deep mourning, had gone to attend the funeral, and there remained in the house only a footman to guard the door, and a maid who had been in attendance upon Mlle. de Muire from her infancy, and who never left her.

Marcelle received Hélène Lanoue with open arms, though she seemed inclined to reproach her for not having gone to the cemetery; but when she learned that Médéric's best friend was in the house she hastened to the room in which Hélène had left him, and held up her forehead to Major George, who imprinted a paternal kiss upon it.

"How kind in you to have come!" she exclaimed. "I have cried and cried until I can cry no longer."

Major Roland took both her hands in his, and seating himself beside her began to gently remind her of the duty of resignation to God's will, though he had no intention of confining his conversation with Médéric's betrothed to well meant attempts at consolation.

"He promised to bring my poor father back to me after the sad ceremony," was her only reply to the exhortations of her old friend.

He was evidently Médéric de Mestras; and this showed plainly enough that her betrothed was ever in the young girl's thoughts.

"Yes," replied George Roland, "and I assure you that it is no fault of his that you have not seen him often during the past three days. He has talked only of you and of the terrible bereavement that has overtaken us all. We both loved your mother, and the thought of her dying such a death is truly horrible."

"Then you, too, think that she was murdered?"

The major made a gesture that signified, "I can not deny the evidence of my own eyes." Then he said, in a less assured tone:

"But unintentionally. The pistol may have been fired by accident."

"Oh, yes; tell me that it was an accident, or that the

bullet that struck her was not intended for her. Tell me that there could not be found in the whole world a person wicked and cruel enough to injure her—one who was all kindness to every one, and who had not an enemy on earth."

Hélène and the major exchanged glances. The former knew now that several persons suspected Médéric of the crime; and she ardently desired that Marcelle should never know that any one had so wronged her betrothed. The major did not doubt Hélène's discretion, but his eyes said to her, "What would happen if our dear Marcelle should ever learn that the man she loves with all her soul is accused of the murder of her mother?"

"Do not excite yourself, my dear child, I beg," he replied after a short silence. "What good would it do to ferret out the cause of this terrible calamity? We are all born to suffer. Resign yourself to your lot, and think of the future. Your father is still left to you, and you will soon marry the son of my noble friend Colonel de Mestras. Why did he fall at Gravelotte? He would have been so rejoiced at this marriage! But you probably do not remember him, you were so young when he died."

"I was five years old, and I can see him still in his handsome uniform as plainly as on the day he left for that disastrous war. It was a superb summer evening, like that one on which my mother died fourteen years afterward. I was with her at the Oaks, and we were to join my father at Dieppe the next day, where we were to spend the rest of the season. The colonel was to start for the seat of war that very night. He came to bid us good-bye, and we met him at the station and brought him to the château in our carriage. He spent two hours at the Oaks. Just before his departure he took me up in his arms. He was so tall that I was afraid of falling, and clutched his coat-collar with all my might. He gave me such a long and close embrace that I cried. He, too, wept like a child, and that made me cry still harder. Ah! he was very fond of me! I remember, too, the day on which we received news of his death as if it were but yesterday. There was a children's ball at the Casino, and my mother had taken me there. I was dancing when my father entered the room. His face was distorted with grief, and he had a paper in his hand. He gave it to my mother, who fainted almost as soon as she glanced at it. I am paining you; but I take a sad pleasure in recalling all this. We did not know you then. You were in the army."

"Yes, in the very regiment that Mestras commanded. I saw him fall."

"Médéric was at school at the time; and my father immediately started for Paris and brought the poor boy back with him. After this he spent all his vacations with us. I was only a little tomboy, and he paid no attention to me. No one would ever have supposed then that we would fall in love with each other some day, and that a fresh bereavement would overtake us just as we were about to be united forever."

"Your father told me that your mother had seemed to be very much opposed to the marriage of late."

"I feel sure that she would have changed her mind. She had the deepest affection for Médéric, and had always treated him as if he had been her own son; but of late, when I said anything to her about our marriage, she always replied, 'There is no hurry. You don't know your own minds yet.' I thought this was only because she wished to keep me with her as long as possible. But she would not have turned a deaf ear to my entreaties when Médéric made a formal request for my hand, as he was about to do, it having all been arranged by my father. Joy and happiness were about to enter the household, but instead came death; and in the sleepless hours I have spent since the catastrophe I have more than once asked myself which of us God wished to punish."

"Do you know whether or not your father intends to remain in Paris?" inquired the major, rather irrelevantly.

"He has said something about our traveling for awhile," replied Marcelle; "but I don't think he has fully decided upon any plan for the future yet, and I hope that he will consent to do as I wish."

"What do you desire?"

"I would like to return to the Oaks, spend the summer there, and not return to Paris until after my marriage."

"Then you think that your father will consent for you to marry before the period of mourning expires?"

"I hope so. If he refuses, I shall beg him to allow me to enter a convent. I will not go on living as I am living now. Nor is Médérie any more willing to remain in such a false position. We shall be married in three months or we shall never be married at all."

George was surprised to hear this very clearly expressed resolve on the part of the young girl; but looking at her he saw an indomitable determination shining in her eyes.

"I have suffered too much," continued Marcelle. "Our marriage was decided upon more than a year ago; and I felt sure I should be able to persuade my mother to give her consent eventually. She is no longer alive, and I shall not have the happiness of seeing her near me at the altar; but she will bless us from on high, I am sure, and my father will not be so cruel as to delay our happiness. I am going to ask him this very day to appoint the time."

"What, to-day?"

"Why not? I am anxious for Médérie to be present when I make my request; and he has promised to bring my father back to me after the funeral. You spoke of the period of mourning: do you think that I shall ever cease to mourn? and that my mother's frightful death will not be ever before my eyes? There will be two of us to mourn her loss, for Médéric loved her dearly, and he never could be made to attach any importance to the ill-will she seemed to feel toward him of late."

"It troubled him sometimes, though," remarked the major.

"Then he was very foolish, as my father told him. You, my friend, know perfectly well that I would not act in direct opposition to my mother's wishes in marrying Médéric; but both my father and myself feel perfectly sure that she would have given her free consent eventually; and to prove that you agree with me in this, promise me that you will accompany us to Italy, where we propose to spend the winter."

"I should like to," replied George Roland, more and more surprised. "I should certainly enjoy the trip immensely, but—"

"Médéric will persuade you; and we will all start together on the day of my marriage—you, my father—"

"And Mademoiselle Hélène also, I presume?" added the major, who had just noticed a shade of sadness steal over the lovely face of the governess.

"I have begged her to do so, but she refuses. I shall persevere, however, until she yields."

"You know that it would be impossible, my dear Marcelle," said Mlle. Lanoue, gently. "Your education is finished, and you have no further need of my services. While you remained single, I could stay with you; your mother desired it, but when you marry —"

"You will still be my friend, and you shall never leave me."

"That is saying rather too much," remarked Major George, smiling. "Mademoiselle Lanoue will marry, too, undoubtedly."

Hélène blushed, but replied quietly, though decidedly:

"No, sir. I shall never marry."

"Oh, yes, you will," exclaimed Marcelle. "We will

find you a good husband, Médéric and I. One who is as good and kind as our dear major here."

"And much younger," added George Roland. "I am too old to enter the lists, and I am sorry for it."

As he said these words he cast a furtive glance at the governess, and noticed that her face suddenly assumed a stern expression that furnished him with abundant food for reflection. Had the compliment displeased Mlle. Lanoue, or did her apparent coldness conceal an entirely different sentiment? He was strongly inclined to find out, but the sound of carriage-wheels interrupted a conversation that had already lasted more than an hour.

"It is my father!" exclaimed Marcelle, running to the window. "Médéric is with him. He has kept his promise. They will both be very glad to find you here."

George had not expected them so soon, but he suddenly recollected that the interment was to be made at Montmartre, where the Muire family owned a lot, and the drive from the church to the cemetery, and from the cemetery to the upper part of the Boulevard Malesherbes was not a long one.

A moment afterward the count entered, leaning upon Médéric's arm, and his daughter ran to him, and threw her arms around his neck. For several minutes they wept together in silence. Médéric shook hands with the major, but Mlle. Lanoue held herself a little aloof. In fact, she was about to leave the room, when the count, hastily drying his eyes, requested her to remain.

He was very pale, and seemed greatly fatigued, but his face wore a determined expression that was not habitual to him, and the major felt satisfied that his old friend had just arrived at some important decision.

He even guessed, by Médéric's manner, that this decision must be in conformity with the wishes of the lovers.

He was not mistaken, for, seating himself in an arm-chair, M. de Muire motioned the others to gather around him.

"My dear George," he began, "I have just had with Médéric, who has so kindly assisted me in this trying ordeal, a conversation, the result of which I should like to submit to you. You are my tried and trusted friend; you have been such since my child's infancy, and I wish to consult you in a matter which involves the happiness of these young people, as well as the peace of my old age."

The major made a gesture, which said as plainly as any words: "Speak, and rely upon my devotion;" but the introduction frightened him a little, and the thought that he would be obliged to give his advice made him feel ill at ease.

Marcelle's marriage to Médéric would have delighted him beyond expression a week before; now, he could not entirely overcome a vague uneasiness.

"My own life is blighted, as you well know," continued the count. "My married life, thanks to the dear wife who is no more, was one of unclouded happiness. God has taken her from me. It was not right. I should have been the first to go; but I have no right to follow her. I am the guardian of others, since I have a daughter and a son," added the count, glancing at Médéric. "I hope that they will never leave me, and I want them to be happy. They already love each other, so there only remains for me to unite them."

The major bowed without replying, and the count, a little surprised at this silence, resumed with some hesitation:

"My mind is fully made up, and I think the sooner it is done the better. It makes very little difference to me what people say about this marriage, which will, of course, appear very hasty. I intend to lead a very retired life, sever my connection with the club, and perhaps even retire to the country—"

"With us?" exclaimed Marcelle.

"My children will be at liberty to follow me or to remain in Paris; and your approval will suffice, my dear

George. But I want that, and you can understand why I ask it."

"The only really serious difference of opinion that ever arose between Louise and myself was on this subject, as you know. She opposed this marriage, and though I begged her again and again to give me her reasons for this opposition, I could never obtain the slightest satisfaction. I now apply to you. To what cause do you attribute her persistence in this inexplicable refusal?"

"I could never understand it," murmured the major.

"Louise sometimes had strange fancies," remarked M. de Muire, evidently satisfied with this evasive reply; "but her heart was all right, and she never refused to listen to the voice of reason. This would certainly have been the case if she had lived, so I do not think that I am really acting in opposition to her wishes in giving Marcelle to Médéric. Were they not betrothed with her knowledge and consent? And if there had been any serious reasons for objecting to the marriage, would she have allowed Médérie to almost live at our house, as he has done ever since the death of the father we loved so much? No, certainly not; and I should do wrong to lay too much stress upon the transient opposition of a mother who certainly desired her daughter's happiness above all else. Still, I think it only right to mention these scruples to you. It will be an easy matter for you to allay them. Tell me that you think them unworthy of serious consideration, and the marriage shall take place in three months."

Never had Major Roland been placed in a more trying position, not even on the night following the battle of Sedan, when, as the only survivor of the commanding officers of his regiment, he found himself obliged to choose between two routes to save his men and his standard from falling into the hands of the enemy.

He decided wisely then, as he succeeded in getting his regiment back to Paris, where they did good service during the siege; but great as had been the difficulties and dangers of the successfully managed retreat, George Roland had been less perplexed than he was now when he found himself obliged to give M. de Muire a reply. He could not muster up courage to advise him to abandon this proposed marriage, which the major himself had so ardently desired a few days before; but, on the other hand, he hesitated to assume the responsibility of approving it; not that he really felt any doubts of Médéric's innocence, but he feared that the viscount and the marquis were industriously circulating reports which would result in a formal accusation against the young man and create frightful scandal.

In his perplexity, the major said to himself that, after all, the marriage was not to be solemnized immediately, and that during the three months' delay announced by M. de Muire, all these difficulties and doubts would undoubtedly be dispelled; so, forcing a smile to conceal the evasive nature of his response, he replied:

"Médéric would never forgive me for opposing this marriage, but I advise him to submit uncomplainingly to the delay you impose upon him. It would not look well to hasten the marriage, especially while the authorities are still engaged in endeavoring to discover the perpetrator of a possible terrible crime."

"They will never succeed," said M. de Muire, sadly; "and I am even inclined to think that they will soon abandon the search. The judge of instruction told me yesterday that he was beginning to think that it might really have been the result of an accident."

'I thought so, too, at first; but, on reflection, I came to the conclusion that if the shot had been fired by accident, the involuntary murderer would have denounced himself."

"The strangest thing about it all is that the conductor of the train declares that he heard no shot fired."

"Nor did I," murmured Médéric.

"True; you were on the train," remarked M. de Muire.

"I heard so a couple of days ago, but I had forgottten all about it, and I am under the impression that the judge is not aware of the fact. Would it not be well for you to mention it to him? He would probably examine you, and your testimony would serve to confirm that of the conductor."

"It would not set him on the culprit's track," interrupted Major George; "so I advise Médéric to wait until he is summoned before presenting himself. The authorities are naturally suspicious, and a voluntary admission of this character might be misunderstood. Why have they not issued a notice, inviting all persons who were on the train to come forward and testify? They would perhaps find some one able to throw some light upon the matter. I am not a magistrate, but I swear that if I should ever take it into my head to begin an investigation, I should arrive at some result. Still, what good would it do after all? All the discoveries one could make would not repair the misfortune that has befallen you. Let the magistrates continue their search. It will be time enough to think of this marriage after the investigation is concluded. Marcelle tells me that you are going to remain at the Oaks."

"Yes, until winter."

"Very well; I invite myself to become your guest. I have no idea of allowing you to remain by yourself in your present state of mind."

"Your room is ready for you," rejoined Marcelle, quickly. "It is next to Médéric's."

"Médéric will come to see us every day, but it would be better for him to retain possession of his rooms on the Place Pigalle until his departure for Italy," remarked the major.

"I submit," replied the young girl, "on condition that my father will appoint the day for our marriage."

And, as M. de Muire, who seemed to be greatly preoccupied, made no reply, she continued:

"I propose the 15th of October. You say nothing, and

Médéric seems afraid to speak. Can't you say a word in support of my suggestion, my dear Hélène?"

The governess raised the eyes that she had kept persistently fixed upon the floor ever since the beginning of the conversation.

"I think Monsieur Roland is always right, my dear Marcelle," she said, gently.

"And I thank him most sincerely for consenting to become our guest at the Oaks," added M. de Muire. "His society and advice will be an inestimable boon to us. We will leave it to him to appoint the day of your marriage; but I can now say to you, Marcelle, place your hand in the hand of Médéric de Mestras, in the hand of an honorable youth whose father was my dearest friend; and to you, Médéric, I can say, from this time forth, you are my son, and to you, I intrust the happiness of my only daughter. Her mother, who is no more, sends down a blessing upon you from on high!"

The two young people threw themselves with one accord into the count's arms, while the less enthusiastic major glanced at Hélène Lanoue, who seemed to be repressing some deep emotion; and thinking, from the expression of her face, that she shared his fears, he stepped toward her and silently pressed her hand.

In the midst of this outburst of feeling, the door suddenly opened, and the count's valet, an old family servant, who had accompanied his master to the cemetery, cautiously entered, and it instantly occurred to one and all present that something very unusual must have occurred to make him appear unsummoned, for he was a remarkably well-trained domestic.

M. de Muire freed himself from his daughter's embrace, and, turning, glanced inquiringly at the intruder.

"A person has called to see Monsieur le Comte with a message from the government attorney at Versailles," said the valet.

"What, to-day?" exclaimed M. de Muire. "He must be aware that I have but just followed my wife to the grave."

"He knows that, and begs that you will excuse the intrusion; but says he must speak to monsieur without delay upon a very important matter."

M. de Muire glanced inquiringly at Major George, who unhesitatingly replied:

"You must see him."

"Show the gentleman into my study, and ask him to wait for me," said the count.

"There must have been some new developments at Versailles," remarked the major.

"Perhaps they have discovered the culprit," exclaimed Médéric. "I hope so, indeed."

"We shall soon know," replied M. de Muire. "Wait for me here, all of you. The interview is not likely to be a long one, and I will return as soon as it is concluded."

The count went up to the floor above, where, at the further end of his suite of apartments, there was a room which was really a library, though he styled it his office.

It was very rarely used for the transaction of business, however, for it was Mme. de Muire that attended to all matters of that kind, as she understood them much better than her husband.

The fortune of the family consisted principally of stocks and bonds; and she managed it with remarkable financial ability, without any interference from the count, and even without consulting him in regard to her investments.

The burden of care and responsibility which his wife's untimely death would cast upon him was not the least of M. de Muire's troubles; and it was his intention to ask Major George's assistance in watching over the interests of Marcelle, her mother's sole heiress.

M. de Muire had felt almost certain that his visitor was a magistrate, so he was not a little surprised upon entering the room to find himself in the presence of a man who looked very like an army officer dressed in citizen's clothing, with closely cropped hair, heavy mustache, and a frock coat, buttoned to the throat, in true military style.

"To whom have I the honor of speaking?" he inquired of this person, whose vocation he was utterly unable to determine. "I was told that you came from Versailles—"

"Yes; from Versailles," replied the stranger, without seeming in the least disconcerted by the coolness of this reception, "and my intrusion here is in obedience to the orders of the superintendent of police."

"It was he who sent you to me?"

"Yes, sir, and I must add that in so doing that official was actuated by a desire to show you that he is fully cognizant of your unimpeachable integrity and high social rank."

"I do not understand you; but I certainly think if it is your intention to subject me to another examination that you might have chosen some other day."

"I know that the funeral of Madame la Comtesse took place this morning, but I am intrusted with a mission that can not be deferred, however painful it may be. I have in my possession a warrant—"

"For the arrest of the assassin? What! has he been discovered?"

"I am intrusted with the unpleasant duty of arresting a person against whom there are grave charges; and I have orders to arrest him as soon as possible without publicity or scandal. I could not have avoided either if I had arrested him in the street, and I knew that I should not find him at his home."

"What are you driving at?" demanded M. de Muire, sternly.

"I have to inform you that this suspected person is now in your house, and to request your assistance in executing the warrant that has been intrusted to me."

"You say that this man is in my house!" exclaimed the count, thinking he must have misunderstood the stranger.

"Yes, sir," was the calm reply.

"Some one has evidently deceived you, or you have deceived yourself. At the present time the only person in the house except the servants, are my daughter, my daughter's governess, Major George Roland, a retired army officer, and Monsieur Médéric de Mestras, who will soon be my son-in-law."

"I know it."

"And you dare to accuse one of these gentlemen?"

"I accuse no one. As I had the honor to tell you, I am the bearer of a warrant of arrest, and my duty is confined entirely to conducting the person into the presence of the government attorney at Versailles, who will decide whether or not the warrant of arrest is to be converted into a consignment to prison. This is a duty that is generally intrusted to a subordinate, but he might have shown a lack of deference in the discharge of his duty, so the prefect of police sent me. I am the chief of the detective service."

The Count de Muire was amazed beyond expression when the stranger thus revealed his identity, and the dread official himself seemed rather embarrassed, for he was not often obliged to act in such a capacity.

"Why, monsieur, to whom can you possibly refer?" exclaimed Marcelle's father, vehemently. "A man's life and honor are at stake, and you keep me in suspense. I demand an explanation."

"Excuse me, sir," replied the official, coldly. "I thought you understood that I came here for Monsieur de Mestras. I was at the cemetery, and I saw him enter the carriage with you, so he is here, and I trust that he will consent to follow me without any disturbance. It is now merely a question of a trip to Versailles, as it is quite possible that the young man will be released as soon as he has been questioned; consequently, it would be greatly to his advantage to promptly respond to the summons of the magistrate whose representative I am."

"Of what is he accused?"

"You can scarcely be ignorant. A crime was committed under your very eyes; the officers of the law were summoned to your country residence, your servants have given their testimony, other witnesses have been heard—"

"But no one has thought for an instant of suspecting Monsieur de Mestras, whom I brought up, and whom I have always treated as if he had been my own son. And now, after a three days' investigation, this absurd and disgraceful accusation is made against him. I protest against it, and I shall advise him to take no notice of this warrant."

"Then you will make a very great mistake, sir. I am provided with the means of insuring its prompt execution, but I certainly hope that you will not compel me to resort to force."

"No. That being the case I shall accompany Monsieur de Mestras to Versailles."

"The instructions I have received positively forbid that. I have even transgressed them by first mentioning the matter to you. I can do no more, and if I might venture to give you a word of advice I should say to you, sir, that it would be much better if you would refrain from being present at this unfortunate young man's examination."

This was said in an earnest tone that made a deep impression upon M. de Muire. Evidently, this official was a man of heart, and felt a sincere compassion for the trying position of an honorable man who, while lamenting the death of his wife, suddenly finds that his prospective son-in-law is accused of having murdered her.

"So you believe him guilty?" murmured the count, deeply agitated.

"I have no opinion to express on the subject. I am not allowed to even have one, much less to express it. But there is nothing to hinder me from telling you that from the very beginning of the investigation there has been circumstantial evidence which amounted almost to proofs against Monsieur de Mestras.''

'' What?'' inquired M. de Muire, eagerly.

'' I would like to be excused from replying.''

'' And I entreat you to answer me.''

'' Remember, Monsieur le Comte, that among these presumptions there are some of a purely personal character, and that if I should venture to mention them, you might, with justice, accuse me with meddling with family matters to which I should remain a stranger. The judge alone has this right.''

'' I understand, sir. You allude, I presume, to a diversity of opinion that existed between Madame de Muire and myself on the subject of my daughter's marriage. How this diversity of opinion came to the knowledge of the magistrates who are investigating the case I do not know. This opposition would have been withdrawn eventually, I am sure; and for any one to conclude merely from the fact of its existence that Médéric de Mestras is the perpetrator of a terrible crime is too absurd beyond measure. I am ready to explain all the facts of the case to the judge. He can not refuse me a hearing, and he will be compelled to acknowledge the injustice of his suspicions. Is it likely that he will succeed in making any one believe that a well-born young man, whose past is irreproachable, would suddenly enter upon a career of crime by killing the mother of a young girl whom he loved, and whom he was sure to marry sooner or later? And that merely to overcome an obstacle which it was in my power to remove by an exercise of paternal authority?''

'' I agree with you, sir, that the whole thing seems in the highest degree improbable; and if there was no other evidence against the young man—''

'' Can it be that he is accused merely because he was on the train when the shot was fired?''

"That was certainly an unfortunate coincidence, but—"

"But at least fifty other persons were on the train with him, and I am surprised that the suspicions of the authorities should fall upon the only person whose innocence is evident—upon a friend whom I regard as my own child, and who was to dine with us at the Oaks that very day. Instead of accusing him so rashly, it would certainly be well for them to question the employés of the railroad company, many of whom know him by sight."

"That is exactly what should have been done in the first place; at least such is my humble opinion, though I can confide it only to you, Monsieur le Comte. But since the murder a discovery has been made which throws an unexpected light upon the affair, and it was one of these employés that made the discovery."

"A discovery!" repeated M. de Muire, both alarmed and astonished.

"Yes. A six-shooter which had been recently fired was found in a compartment of a first-class carriage on the Saint-Germain railroad. This revolver was placed in the hands of the Saint-Germain station-master yesterday, and that official immediately carried it to the government attorney at Versailles. The employé claimed that he had just found it under one of the cushions, though it seems strange that it could have remained there so long without being seen, the cars being generally examined on the arrival of the trains; one must conclude either that this inspection was omitted, or that the weapon was concealed under the cushion three or four days after the crime. Up to the present time the employé has given only a rather confused explanation of the finding of the revolver, though he can not be suspected of connivance with the murderer, who would, of course, realize the necessity of concealing the weapon he used."

"Certainly, but I fail to see wherein this discovery compromises Monsieur de Mestras."

"The revolver belongs to him. His name is engraved upon it."

M. de Muire turned pale on hearing this startling announcement, but he quickly recovered himself.

"I have an indistinct recollection of having seen this weapon in Médéric's hands," he said, quietly. "I even recollect that it was given him by Major Roland, a mutual friend. But what does that prove? It might have been stolen from him, or he may have lost it."

"That is exactly what we shall give him an opportunity to prove; but until he succeeds in doing that the authorities must believe the contrary. I know, too, that there is other evidence against him. This, I am not at liberty to divulge, at present, however."

"You can at least question Monsieur de Mestras in my presence. He is here, and I will—"

"Summon him? I was about to request you to do so. But I can not question him before you. I have positive orders to bring him to Versailles without allowing him to communicate with any person whatever, and even without telling him why he is wanted. I have assumed the responsibility of informing you, however, in order to spare you a painful scene, and I trust that you will not cause me to regret the step, for I know that you are an honorable man. I was anxious, too, for you to view the situation as it really is, because illusions are always useless, and often dangerous. Now I must ask you to send for this young man, and I will tell him who I am, and the object of my mission, which is simply to conduct him immediately to Versailles— nothing more. He will probably suppose that he is summoned there as a witness, and I trust that you will do me the favor not to undeceive him. If he should succeed in proving his innocence, as I sincerely hope he will, there will be nothing to prevent him from bringing you the good news himself this evening."

M. de Muire, without uttering a word, rang the bell,

ordered his valet to go for M. de Mestras, and then waited without giving any sign of the inward torture he was enduring.

A moment afterward Médéric entered, with head erect. The visitor did not give him time to speak.

"I am the chief of the detective service, sir," he said very politely.

The young man changed countenance, and the count instantly perceived the fact.

"I have called to request you to accompany me to Versailles, where the government attorney desires an interview with you," continued the official.

"What does he want with me?" stammered Médéric.

"You will soon learn. I have a carriage at the door, and I beg that you will follow me."

The colonel's son turned pale, and between his set teeth, he muttered:

"I understand. Some scoundrel has denounced me because he found—"

"Wretched boy!" exclaimed M. de Muire.

"Come, sir," whispered the officer. "Take my advice, and avoid a scene here in this house."

Médéric glanced at the count, and read both anger and suspicion in his eyes.

"Ah, well! so be it!" he cried. "Let us go. It is time, indeed, for me to put an end to this most atrocious slander."

Marcelle's father allowed him to depart without even offering him a friendly hand.

"Of all whom I loved I have only my daughter left!" he murmured, burying his face in his hands.

CHAPTER VI.

Parisians have very short memories. Even a thrilling event like the tragical death of Mme. de Muire occupies the circles in which the victim moved only for a few days; in a week, their attention is engrossed by other topics, and before a fortnight has elapsed they have entirely ceased talking about it. Mere acquaintances have forgotten it entirely. Only relatives and intimate friends remember it. They suffer deeply, and time, instead of assuaging their grief, increases it, when to their regret is added a poignant anxiety in regard to the fate of one who is near and dear to them.

The Count de Muire, his daughter, and Major George, who had all taken refuge at the Oaks, had spent a fortnight of misery which had been fully shared by Hélène Lanoue, who certainly had a right to be regarded as one of the family.

Poor Médéric, who had been taken to Versailles by the chief of the detective service, had not returned, and what was worse, they had heard nothing in regard to what had passed between him and the judge of instruction. He was not only a prisoner, but he was kept in solitary confinement, and as these unusually severe measures had been adopted, his case must certainly be one of those which are almost certain to end in conviction.

M. de Muire had made no effort to secure any alleviation of the hardships imposed upon the poor youth who had once been Marcelle's betrothed.

M. de Muire was one of the most inconsistent of men, and one of the most impulsive. After siding with Médéric against the countess, after loving him like a son, he had abruptly banished him from his heart on hearing the terrible accusation made against him by the prefect of police. He did not even stop to ask if he was guilty. The fact that the young man was in custody was quite enough to make the count resolve never to see him again. Médéric no longer existed so far as M. de Muire was concerned.

It was in vain that his old friend, George Roland, assured him that Médéric had apprised him of the loss of the revolver on the very day of the crime. The obstinate nobleman silenced him by saying firmly:

"My daughter shall never marry a man who has been suspected of killing her mother, even if the man should be set at liberty to-morrow."

In vain, too, had Marcelle thrown herself at her father's feet, entreating him not to curse Médéric, and not to desert him in his hour of need.

The count had remained inflexible. When his daughter threatened to enter a convent he replied that she was not of age, and that he should exert his paternal authority, if necessary, to prevent her from abandoning his roof.

With his pride thus deeply wounded, and his dearest hopes blighted, the count led a secluded and gloomy life at the Oaks, which had once been so gay, but which was now so gloomy. He saw his daughter only at the table, and he left the house only for an occasional visit to Paris when business called him there on matters connected with the estate of the countess.

As a natural consequence, Marcelle led the dreariest life imaginable; and if she bore her burden of sorrow with comparative resignation it was because she still had a hopeful and devoted friend--that greatest consolation of the afflicted. She could not be brought to believe that Médéric was guilty, and felt firmly convinced that the day was near at hand when his innocence would be established beyond any possible doubt.

The major encouraged her in this belief, for he too felt sure that Médéric was the victim of a mistake which would become apparent sooner or later; and though the government did not feel justified in interfering between the father and daughter, she did her best to console Marcelle; and the better George Roland learned to know her the more he was compelled to admire her lovely and unselfish character. In fact he was already thinking of securing for her a situation which would assure her a comfortable future in case she should soon be obliged to leave her present home, as now seemed only too probable, for the count was talking of selling the Oaks, around which so many harrowing associations clung.

Hélène and the major, without acknowledging the fact to each other, were both trying to discover the perpetrator of the mysterious crime of which Médéric had been accused upon evidence that was purely circumstantial in its character.

At the risk of getting himself into serious trouble with the Versailles authorities the major had inserted in several papers an advertisement requesting any persons who took the 5.30 train for Saint-Germain on the 19th of June, to make known their names and whereabouts to George Roland, No. 37 Rue de Miromesnil, who was in possession of an article of value which had been found on this train and which he was anxious to restore to its owner.

There are persons who always present themselves as claimants for advertised articles, even when they have lost nothing, and he had some hope that this might be the case in the present instance; but though this notice had appeared in the Paris journals for more than a week, no claimant had yet come forward.

Hélène, though no one suspected the fact, was really more likely to secure trustworthy information than the major. As both M. de Muire and his wife had implicit confidence in her, she enjoyed perfect freedom of action, coming and going as she pleased about the Oaks, Vésinet, Chatou, and sometimes even further, for the countess, who was very charitable, constituted Hélène her almoner, and Hélène performed the rôle with great zeal and discretion.

There were very few poor families in the neighborhood, but those that were poor were very poor, being principally small market-gardeners, who led a precarious existence, and who were not unfrequently reduced to positive want in a single day by an early frost or a destructive hailstorm; and railway employés, burdened with large families, and poorly paid.

Mlle. Lanoue knew them all; and while the Muire family were domiciled at the Oaks a week seldom passed in which she did not visit these humble homes and inquire into the needs of their inmates.

She usually went alone, and she had nothing to fear, as all the people of the neighborhood knew and loved her. For a time after Mme. de Muire's tragical death she was unable to leave her grief-stricken friend; but she was now contemplating a speedy return to her former habits, and thought it not improbable that she might obtain some useful information on her round of visits. She had even confided her plans to the major, who cordially approved them; and she set diligently to work though without much success at first.

All the poor people she visited sincerely regretted the death of the countess, pitied the count, and cursed the assassin; but they did not know Médéric, nor were they acquainted with the particulars of the catastrophe.

But her usual round was not concluded; and one morning, when M. de Muire had gone to Paris, Marcelle was feeling too languid to venture out, and the major had some letters to write, Mlle. Lanoue—who had visited her poor at Chatou the day before—started out to visit the needy of Vésinet.

In that village there was one household that interested her particularly: a young woman with three small children, and a husband who earned barely enough to keep them alive, and who did not seem to care much about them. This husband was in the employ of the Western Railway Company, and was consequently rarely seen in the squalid rooms occupied by his family.

Mlle. Lanoue did not know him, nor did she know the precise nature of his duties; the fact that the woman was in want being quite enough to induce her to come to the poor creature's aid; but that day it occurred to her for the first time that her protegée might have learned through her husband what the other employés thought about the murder, and she resolved to ask her a few questions on the subject.

The cottage, or rather hut, in which the mother and children lived, stood on the outskirts of the village, and had formerly been used as a store-house for sashes and tools by a market-gardener. It was much more suitable for a sheep or cattle pen than for the abode of human beings; and Hélène could not help feeling surprised that any man, no matter how meager his salary, should allow his family to dwell in such a hovel.

This, too, seemed the more strange from the fact that the wife appeared to have seen better days. Once she must even have been·pretty; she was still young, and her features were not devoid of a certain air of distinction—nor, indeed, were her manners and language. She had a slight foreign accent, but she expressed herself in French with perfect ease and in well-chosen terms.

She was sitting in front of the door when Mlle. Lanoue approached, and she greeted her benefactress with these words:

"Ah! mademoiselle, how glad I am to see you! But for your coming my children would be without bread to-morrow, for their father has none to give them. He lost half his pay this month on account of that unfortunate pistol affair."

"Pistol affair!" repeated Mlle. Lanoue, who did not

quite understand, but who was beginning to foresee a possibility of securing some valuable information.

"Yes, mademoiselle," was the reply. "He was fined and threatened with dismissal, only because he did his duty. You know that he is a conductor on the road—not a regular conductor, of course, but he takes the place of any conductor who may be sick or absent. Ah, well, one day about a fortnight ago, while on duty, he found a pistol lying under a seat in a first-class carriage, and on reaching Saint-Germain he gave it to the station-master. To look up the owners of missing articles is not a part of his duty, so he certainly did nothing wrong; but bad luck seems to pursue us. It seems that this revolver belongs to the person who is suspected of killing the poor lady who has been so kind to me; but it certainly was no fault of my husband's that she was murdered, was it, mademoiselle?"

"No, certainly not," replied Hélène, maintaining her self-control in spite of the emotion she experienced. "It seems to me that your husband has no reason to reproach himself. Of what is he accused?"

"Oh, they do not really accuse him. It is not as bad as that. But they suspect him—"

"Of having been the murderer's accomplice?" inquired Hélène.

"No, but of having kept the revolver for awhile. They will not believe that he gave it up immediately, though that is really the truth. They pretend that he found it the day the lady was killed, and that he tried to profit by the discovery."

"But how?"

"It seems that the owner's name was on the pistol; and the officers of the road say that my husband intended to return it to this gentleman, and that he finally decided to turn it over to the station-master only because he found out that the owner was about to be arrested. As if Julien were capable of concocting such a scheme. He has his faults, but he is not tricky. Besides, he has suffered too much from poverty to run any risk of losing his place. He has no other way of earning a living.''

"Is your husband's name Julien?''

'' Yes, mademoiselle: Julien Maurevers; and he might, if he chose, write a *de* before his name, for he is of noble origin. But when one is poor one must renounce all such pretensions. No one knows that he still has influential relatives in France. But he is proud, and, forgive me, mademoiselle—and if he should learn that I had accepted aid from you he would be angry with me. I may have done wrong, but it was for my children's sakes; besides, I hope to be able to repay the obligation some time, for our situation may change at any moment, as Julien often tells me.''

'' I hope so, for your sake, madame; but you are under no obligations to me. I have only been the dispenser of Madame de Muire's bounty. It is to her that you must feel grateful.''

'' I was so grieved when I heard that she was dead! And to think that she died such a death! Ah, they certainly ought to hang the wretch who murdered her if they ever find him. My husband thinks they will not fail to do so; and yet, on the day of the crime—he happened to be acting as conductor on the train at the time—he neither saw nor heard anything unusual. The magistrate at Versailles examined and cross-examined him, but all in vain. My poor Julien could not tell what he did not know—and they had ceased to persecute him when he was so unfortunate as to find the revolver—and sometimes I ask myself if it would not have been better if he had kept it and said nothing about it.''

Hélène Lanoue, who had entirely recovered her self-possession, was fully aware of the advantage she might derive from a conversation which she intended to convert into a covert examination without delay. She felt satisfied that this woman was perfectly honest and sincere; but the husband's conduct seemed highly suspicious; and this opportunity to learn something about the man who had, perhaps, been the unconscious cause of Médéric's arrest was certainly an excellent one.

"Does Monsieur Maurevers know the young man who is accused?" she inquired, without appearing to attach any importance to the question.

"Yes, by sight. They say that he is a friend of the Count de Muire, and that he was a frequent visitor at the Oaks. Julien saw him one day at the Chatou Station; but he knows nothing more about him, though he seems inclined to believe that the gentleman is not guilty. Julien is always ready to take the part of genteel people—he has been a very genteel person himself, and he will be again when fate becomes tired of persecuting us."

"I do not doubt it; and you yourself, madame, must have been born in a very different sphere."

"I am the youngest daughter of Prince Orbitello, of Naples," replied the conductor's wife, straightening herself up, "and my father disinherited me because I married, against his will, Julien de Maurevers, whom I met at Ischia. That was ten years ago; Julien had some money then, and led a brilliant life; but that was not the inducement. I loved him madly, and I love him yet, though I have suffered much through him. Five years afterward, when every penny of his patrimony was gone, squandered in dissipation of every kind, and more especially in gambling, Julien decided to return to France. Not that he had anything to expect from his family. The only relative he had left had cast him off in his youth, and did not even know that he was living. Julien is his legal heir, however; but he would rather die than ask him for assistance, or even make himself known to the heartless man."

"Then it was not a relative that secured your husband his present position?"

"No; it was a foreigner who had known him well in better days. He pitied him; and as he has many influential friends in France, he managed to secure a situation in the employ of the Western Railway Company for Julien, though he had scarcely arrived at an age that made him eligible for appointment, being only thirty-four, while the required age is thirty-five. He is forty now, and you see where he is. It is not because he has not worked, however; he began as a brakeman."

"But how about the friend who secured him this place?"

"He spends most of his time in Germany and Russia, and so has rather lost sight of Julien. But he has just returned to France, and I hope he will save my husband from dismissal, but I do not know that he can do anything more for him."

The longer Hélène listened to this strange story, the more convinced she became that this woman's husband knew more about Mme. de Muire's murder than he was willing to admit. She did not believe that he was the murderer of the countess, for what could have been his object in committing such a deed; but she had a suspicion that he knew the murderer, and that he was paid to be silent.

In spite of the reticence of the unfortunate woman who had linked her lot to his, Hélène felt satisfied that Julien Maurevers had been nothing more nor less than a rascal all his life; and with such antecedents it was only natural to suppose him capable of accepting a bribe from a scoundrel whose secret he had detected.

He had been on the same train with the murderer, and might have seen him fire at the countess, so, on the arrival of the train, or even during the journey, as his position gave him a right to pass at will through the carriages, he had probably threatened to denounce him, and then proposed a bargain which had been instantly accepted.

It is true that in this case he ought to have considerable

money in his possession. This objection instantly presented itself to Hélène's mind, but she said to herself that there
was nothing to prove that he had not received it, and
afterward lost it at the gaming-table, without troubling
himself about the wants of his wife and children.

Still this reasoning did not explain how this very disreputable person had come into possession of Médéric's
revolver, and why he had placed it in the hands of a superior, at the risk of incurring either a fine or a dismissal, and
of exposing himself to the suspicions of the authorities.

Hélène, being unable to solve the mystery to her satisfaction, decided to submit the whole case to the judgment
of Major George, and resolved not to allow the daughter
of Prince Orbitello to suppose for an instant that she had
any special object in asking these questions, for it was of
the utmost importance that the young woman should not
take her for an auxiliary of the magistrates. The pretended princess seemed to have no such suspicion, however, for
she had given all this information with a readiness that
showed the utmost confidence in her visitor, and now she
added:

"If my husband knew I had told you all this he would
never forgive me: and if you should ever meet him, I beg
that you will make no allusion to our unfortunate history."

"I can promise you that, madame," replied the governess. "Besides, I have never seen Monsieur Maurevers,
and it is hardly probable that I shall ever meet him. I
come here so rarely—much more rarely, indeed, than I
would like. But now I am here, permit me to offer you
this slight assistance in the name of one we both mourn."

The princess accepted the proffered gold coin without
ceremony, and even kissed Hélène's hand. This is cus-
tomary in Naples in such cases, and she accompanied this
rather servile mark of her sincere gratitude with the warmest thanks.

The children had emerged from the cottage in which

they had been taking an afternoon nap, and stood looking at Mlle. Lanoue with wondering eyes.

"They will have some supper to-night, and I shall not have to endure the misery of seeing them cry for food even if Julien brings home no money," remarked the mother.

"Do you expect him home to-day?" inquired Hélène.

"Yes, but not until late. He will be on duty again to-morrow—that is, if he has not received his dismissal. He has been to Paris to see Count Golymine, and to beg him to intercede for him."

"Count Golymine?" repeated Mlle. Lanoue, who had never heard the name before.

"Yes, the foreign nobleman who interested himself in Julien's behalf and secured him this position."

"Is he a Pole?"

"I think he is a Russian."

"Will you think me too inquisitive if I ask how your husband made his acquaintance?"

"I don't know exactly. He knew him before he married me. I suppose he must have met him at Aix or at Monaco. They were both frequenters of watering-places, and especially of gambling-houses. But Count Golymine is very well known in Paris, and I should not be surprised if the people at the Oaks had heard of him."

Mlle. Lanoue secretly resolved to ascertain, and then proceeded to take leave of Mme. Maurevers. She was anxious to consult the major; besides, she did not want to leave Marcelle alone too long, for the poor child relapsed into a state of the deepest melancholy when left to herself.

But Hélène had no intention of saying a word about what she had just heard to her friend. What good would it do to trouble her already overexcited brain with such a recital? It would be time enough to tell her by and by, after Major George had investigated the matter.

To reach the Oaks she was obliged to take a wooden foot-bridge that formed a high arch, from the center of which one could secure an extended view of the railroad between Chatou and Vésinet. As Mlle. Lanoue reached the middle of the bridge, she paused not only to take breath, but also to glance at the spot where Mme. de Muire was killed. This was about two hundred yards below the bridge. Hélène took a melancholy pleasure in recalling the thrilling scene, and as a train that had just left Chatou approached, leaving a long trail of white smoke behind it, it occurred to her, for the first time, that a spectator standing on the bridge, as she was then standing, might have seen the arm of the assassin extended beyond the window, revolver in hand.

This was certainly a mere conjecture, for the distance was considerable; but giving a free rein to her imagination, she said to herself that the cowardly assassin of Marcelle's mother was perhaps in one of the cars that was about to pass under her feet, and she caught herself wishing that the train would run off the track.

The locomotive passed, bearing to the cheerful château of Saint-Germain a crowd of worthy people who were going to enjoy the cool air of the forest, quite unmindful of the tragedy of the 19th of June.

At the same time, but much more slowly, an employé of the company advanced up the track, clad in the uniform of the corporation. He advanced with swinging arms, bowed head and the heavy unelastic tread of a drudge who performs his daily task mechanically, knowing that the duties of the morrow will be no less irksome. He seemed to be on his way to Vésinet, and Mlle. Lanoue, without knowing exactly why, somehow fancied that this man was the husband of the strange woman who had so gratefully accepted her aid.

She had a tolerably good view of him from her lofty perch, and perceived that his appearance harmonized tolerably well with her idea of an impoverished gentleman. He was tall, slender, and slightly round-shouldered, but he still carried himself well, and his rather haggard features were not devoid of a certain air of distinction. His hair was light, but it was beginning to turn gray, though he was not old.

After he had passed under the bridge he turned to the right into a narrow footpath that led up to the village, and finally disappeared around the corner of a house that stood at a curve in the same road that Hélène had taken to reach the miserable dwelling inhabited by the pretended Neapolitan princess.

"Now, I am sure it is he," murmured the governess.

It would only be necessary for her to retrace her steps to satisfy herself of the fact; but it would have been a great mistake on her part to attract the attention of a man who perhaps knew Mme. de Muire's murderer, and whom she intended to have closely watched.

Besides, on glancing toward the other end of the bridge, she saw the major, who had sallied out for a stroll without anticipating a meeting, which could hardly fail to be agreeable to both parties, however, as they always had many things to say to each other.

CHAPTER VII.

"You have been to visit some of your poor people," remarked Major George, "and I suppose you are now on your way back to the Oaks, where Marcelle must be deploring your absence. I am anxious to be there myself when Monsieur de Muires returns, which will be very soon. Shall we return to the château together?"

"I was just going to ask you to walk back with me," replied the young governess, eagerly, "for I want to talk with you. I have just heard a very important piece of news which I can confide to no one but you."

"It concerns Médérie, does it not?"

"Yes, indirectly. I will tell you about it, and you can then decide what it is best to do."

And Mlle. Lanoue proceeded to give a full account of her visit to the Maurevers family, without omitting any of the strange revelations made by the unfortunate woman, but without adding any comments.

The account was as clear and yet as concise as a military report, and the major perceived with no little gratification, that in addition to all the other good qualities of which his companion had proved herself the possessor, she was endowed with one that is rare in young ladies—remarkable soundness of judgment.

"This man may know the assassin," he remarked, as soon as Hélène had concluded; "but his conduct is incomprehensible. Médéric told me of the loss of his revolver on the day of the murder, and this man must have found the weapon immediately afterward. Who knows but he may have been the very person that fired it?"

"He had no acquaintance with either Madame de Muire or Monsieur de Mestras," remarked Hélène.

"But he may have been hired to murder the countess and then cast the blame upon Médéric."

"In that case, he would have kept the revolver."

"It is possible, then, that he may have surrendered it in obedience to the orders of an accomplice. This conductor's past authorizes all sorts of suppositions; and the first thing for us to do is to satisfy ourselves beyond a doubt that his wife told you the truth. I have a friend who is one of the directors of the Western Railway Company, and he will not refuse to give me all the information in his power."

"But will you not try to see the judge of instruction?" inquired Hélène, timidly.

"Not now. He would not grant me an interview; besides, I have nothing of a positive nature to reveal as yet. I will present myself at his office by and by, after I have learned the real facts in relation to this man's origin. It is also necessary to ascertain whether or not there has ever been in Naples such a person as Prince Orbitello; nor shall I neglect to make inquiries about this Count Golymine, who is so well and favorably known in Parisian circles, according to the pretended princess, that Jacques de Muire must have met him there."

Médéric could have told the major all that he wished to know, but Médéric was in solitary confinement, and had said nothing to any one, except, perhaps, the judge of instruction, about his strange interview with the man who styled himself Count Golymine.

Prudence is a virtue, but it is also a fault when it is carried to excess.

"But I must say that I do not believe that reverses of fortune transform a gentleman into a scoundrel," continued the major. "One can become poor or rich without leaving the plane in which one was born. The contrary happens only in romances."

"You are mistaken," replied Hélène, quickly. "It also happens in real life, as I have reason to know."

The major glanced wonderingly at the young girl, who was already blushing deeply, as if she regretted having said so much.

"True," he said, after a pause, "you certainly could not have been reared to become a governess. I have never dared to question you on the subject, but I have often asked myself what events could have wrought such a change in your life. I am sure that your parents must have met with reverses. But nature has endowed you with gifts which are of much greater value than money, and there is nothing to prevent you, I am sure, from making what the world regards as an excellent match."

"I have never thought of such a thing, and if my history interests you, here it is. It is sad, but it is brief. My mother died in bringing me into the world. My father was in very comfortable circumstances; he even seemed likely to become very wealthy. I was only five years old when a financial disaster swept away half he possessed. He might have retrieved his fortunes, however, had not a brother, fifteen years older than myself, completed his ruin.''

'' And your father died of grief,'' concluded the major.

The girl hesitated a moment. Her eyes had filled with tears, but she kept them back, and in a firm tone, continued:

'' I have sufficient confidence in you to tell you the whole truth. My father committed suicide. He would have had courage to endure poverty, but he had not strength to face dishonor.''

'' Dishonor! Why! what do you mean?''

'' My brother committed a forgery. He was about to be arrested. His conviction was certain. Our name was about to be covered with disgrace. It was, and I obeyed [my father's last request in ceasing to bear it.''

'' What! the name of Lanoue—''

'' Is not mine. Madame de Muire knew it, and always guarded the secret I now fearlessly confide to you. Monsieur de Muire and Marcelle are ignorant of it. Madame de Muire learned the facts from the mistress of a boarding-school, who kindly took me under her protection, after my father's death, and gave me the education that enables me to earn my living honorably. I had just received my diploma when I had the good fortune to be selected by Madame de Muire to complete her daughter's education. I have found a home in the truest sense of the word, in the Muire family, and the thought that I shall soon be obliged to leave it fills me with dismay.''

'' If that day should ever come, mademoiselle, you will still have, and you will always have, one devoted friend,'' said Major George, warmly. '' But will you pardon me for asking what became of this erring brother?''

'' He was convicted, and sent to prison; but he succeeded

in making his escape, and I have never seen nor heard of him since. "All this happened twenty years ago. I was still very young when these misfortunes overtook me, and I did not hear of my brother's crime until long afterward. No one in France knows what became of him, and I suppose that he is dead."

"You should hope so; but even if he is not, it is not likely that he will ever dare to show himself again in this country. He might, however, do so with impunity now; for even in criminal offenses the law limits the period during which one is liable to prosecution to twenty years. But if he should ever have the audacity to return to France, it will be under an assumed name; and he will never think of trying to find the sister whom he impoverished and to whom he has never, apparently, given a thought since his flight."

"When he saw me last, I was a mere child, so he would not recognize me even if I should be so unfortunate as to meet him."

"And you, mademoiselle, would you recognize him?"

"I think not; and yet I can still see him as he looked then, when he dandled me upon his knee, for he often used to play with me, and I loved him dearly. But he is over forty years old if he is living now."

"And he must have changed greatly in appearance. Nothing ages a man like exile."

"Exile and disgrace," corrected Mlle. Lanoue. "When I think of him, I often say to myself that he must have sunk still lower. Heaven only knows the depths of infamy into which he may have fallen! And yet, he was born with traits of character that might have made him a remarkable man. I was too young to judge, of course; I speak only from hearsay. The lady who kept the boarding-school where I was educated, and who had known my brother well, often spoke of his remarkable intelligence, energy, and tact. More than once, too, she has assured me that he was one of the most fascinating of men. His vices ruined him."

"Do you ever see the lady now?" inquired George Roland, more and more deeply interested in this charming girl's mournful history.

"She died six years ago," replied Hélène, sadly. "But you asked me a moment ago if I would recognize Gaston. His name was Gaston. Yes; I should know him by his hands. He fought a duel when he was only nineteen years old, and on one thumb he had a deep scar."

"Which time has probably effaced."

"Ah, well, let us talk of something else. I don't know why I should have bored you with my past sorrows when we have so many of a more recent date to discuss. I yielded to a sudden impulse that I should have repressed; but it seems to me that we have known each other for twenty years."

"Let us continue the subject a moment longer. May I ask if you have any plans for the future, mademoiselle?"

"The future? Oh, that is all marked out for me. A governess I am, and a governess I shall remain."

"That is very much like my saying that I shall remain an old bachelor," replied the major, smiling. "It is quite possible that I may, but I assure you that I shall fight hard against it. I have never taken any vow of celibacy; nor have you, I fancy. The day will come when you will understand, as I am beginning to understand, that married life is much more desirable. You are happy now. Marcelle's friendship and the affection and esteem of those around you content you. I myself need no pity; nor have I any right to complain of my lot. I enjoy perfect health; I left the army with an excellent record, and just before I resigned I inherited a very handsome fortune from an aunt I knew very little about. Still, mademoiselle, you and I are both missing one blessing, in comparison with which all others are as nothing—the happiness of loving and being loved—that is to say, I lack only the happiness of being loved, for I love; and you, who, to my certain knowledge, are loved, lack the happiness of loving. So, you see, each of us has that which the other lacks. You frown? Have I offended you? I hope not; but I am very much afraid that all this sentimental talk seems supremely ridiculous to you. It would be much better for me to say to you simply and plainly: ' If I am not too unpleasing to you, and if my forty years do not frighten you, become my wife.' You might do much better than marry an old soldier like me; but I have a warm heart, and a sturdy arm, and if you can be content to be tenderly cared for and loved I am ready to devote my life to making you happy.''

Mlle. Lanoue, who had been slightly embarrassed ever since the beginning of this conversation, suddenly changed countenance when she heard the major make this offer of his heart and hand. Not that the proposal offended her—for she liked and admired the major exceedingly—but she thought it too abrupt, and she could scarcely believe that he was in earnest.

'' Come, come,'' continued the major, '' I see that I have shocked you. The old soldier can not get over his habit of going straight to the point; but I entreat you to believe that I am not a coarse old trooper at heart. I see that I have been too abrupt. Forget what I just said to you; but permit me to hope that we may resume this conversation at some future day after the situation has undergone a change. Both you and I have a difficult task to accomplish. We must prove that Médéric is innocent; and we shall succeed in doing that only by discovering Madame de Muire's real assassin. It seems to me that we are now on the track, thanks to you, and all I ask, at this present time, is that you will consent to accept me as an ally.''

'' With the greatest pleasure,'' replied Hélène.

'' Thank you. Now our treaty of alliance is concluded, allow me to say to you that it must remain a secret. We will pursue our investigation independently of each other, but though we will immediately apprise each other of any information we may succeed in collecting, it seems to me that it would not be advisable to keep Marcelle informed in regard to our movements. Above all, we must beware of giving her any false hopes."

"That is my opinion exactly. But how about Monsieur de Muire?"

"Oh, not a word to him on the subject. He has taken it into his head that poor Médéric is guilty, and if he should find out that we are trying to save him he would forbid our meddling with the affair. I should not obey him, nor would you; so we should become involved in a quarrel with him, and that is useless."

"I do not know whether or not you will succeed in saving Monsieur de Mestras; but whatever may be the result of your efforts I am very much afraid that Monsieur de Muire can never be induced to grant him Marcelle's hand in marriage."

"I shall attempt no interference on that point," said the major; "I shall do all I can to secure Médéric's release; but my efforts will stop there."

"But Marcelle counts upon your assistance, and if the marriage should not take place I really do not know what will become of her."

"The time has not yet come for me to take any part in this very delicate matter. In the meantime, we will give no further attention to it, if you please. We have more important work on hand. As I told you before I intend to at once make inquiries about the conductor who has played such a strange part in the affair, and also about his protector—the stranger with a Russian name."

"Golymine. He is really a Russian, I believe. At least, Maurever's wife told me so. She is under the impression that her husband made her acquaintance at Aix."

"A place which Madame de Muire visited every summer for several years. Jacques never remained there long, but he always took her there, and then went to escort her home. He may have met Count Golymine there, and, in that case, he will tell me all he knows about him."

" Madame de Muire must certainly have met him, and it seems very strange that this count should be the protector of the man who has just played such a rôle in the affair."

" It is a mere chance, of course. I shall be able to learn all I wish to know this evening, however. Jacques has gone to Paris to consult his notary, but he will return before dinner, and I will question him. And, by the way, speaking of this notary, you are probably ignorant that a very strange and inexplicable thing has happened?"

" What? No new disaster, I hope!"

" Yes; a financial misfortune this time. Monsieur de Muire's private fortune is very small; that of his wife very large. In addition to the house on the Boulevard Malesherbes, and the Oaks, which bring in nothing, and which it costs a good deal to keep up, Madame de Muire owned property which yielded her an income of from two hundred and fifty to three hundred thousand francs, and which consisted chiefly of stocks and bonds. These were deposited in the Bank of France for safe keeping some time ago, but Jacques learned yesterday for the first time that his wife had withdrawn them about three months ago. He supposed she had intrusted them temporarily to the keeping of her notary; but such was not the case. What the countess could have done with this large amount of personal property, no one has yet been able to ascertain."

" She certainly could not have lost it."

" Nor could it have been stolen from her; but up to the present time Jacques has discovered no trace of it. Perhaps she has concealed it in some piece of furniture. This is even quite probable; but if he should be so unfortunate as not to find it, Jacques will be cruelly punished for his carelessness about business matters. He never would pay any attention to his own financial affairs, much less to those of his wife, and, thanks to his culpable negligence in this respect, his daughter may find herself reduced to comparative poverty; for if the securities are not found her income will not amount to more than thirty thousand francs.''

"She will be much more easily consoled for this loss of fortune than for the loss of her lover.''

" Perhaps so; still it will be pretty hard for her. Jacques, who always looks at the dark side of things, considers himself ruined, and talks of selling all his real estate immediately. It seems that he has found a purchaser for the Oaks already, and that— But, look, here comes his valet, apparently on his way to Chatou!'' exclaimed the major, suddenly, for they had reached a turn in the road, and only a short distance from them was François approaching from the opposite direction.

"Has the count returned?'' inquired the major.

" Yes, sir.''

"Did he bring any one with him?''

And the valet replying in the affirmative, the major inquired:

"Is it Monsieur de Brangue or Monsieur de Liseoat?''

"No, major; it is a gentleman who has never been here before. It is the first time I ever saw him.''

" And you are going to Chatou?'' inquired the major, rather surprised to see this old servant going on an errand, for he did not usually condescend to perform a footman's duties.

"I am going to post a letter, which must be very important, as the count was not willing to intrust it to any one but me,'' replied François, proudly.

George Roland was too honorable to express a wish to see the superscription on this important missive; but he felt sure that something new must have transpired.

"Is mademoiselle still in her room?'' inquired the governess.

" No, mademoiselle; she is sitting under the trees at the foot of the garden,'' replied François, respectfully.

"Where are the gentlemen?" asked the major.

"The gentlemen are going through the château."

The major, understanding the situation tolerably well, now walked on, remarking to Hélène:

"I feel almost certain that Jacques has brought this stranger back with him, in the hope of disposing of the château; and this haste on his part makes me fear that his notary must have told him some bad news. That gentleman was to make inquiries at the different banking-houses and brokers' officers, in which Madame de Muire might have deposited her stocks and bonds, and I fear the notary has not succeeded in finding any trace of them."

"All this is certainly very strange," remarked Mlle. Lanoue.

"I shall soon know, however, for I am going to join Jacques, while you have a talk with your dear pupil. I feel some curiosity to see this possible purchaser."

The two entered the court-yard together. The open carriage that had brought the count was standing at the foot of the steps, and the coachman was sitting bolt upright on the box, with his whip held perpendicularly in the air, and the reins in his hands. From this fact, George concluded that he was waiting to take the visitor back to the station as soon as the tour of inspection was ended, and that his stay consequently would not be long, so the major had no time to lose if he wished to see the stranger.

Hélène was obliged to walk around to the other side of the house to reach the garden; but the major ascended the steps and entered the spacious hall which extended from one end of the house to the other, and which was lavishly adorned with flowering plants and exotics.

In the center of this broad and airy hall, which was open at both ends, was the broad stairway, leading to the floors above; but before ascending it the major paused a moment to glance out into the garden to satisfy himself that the two young ladies had found each other.

" The garden was large, and adorned with lofty trees that spread a welcome shade over the well-kept turf; and on reaching the further end of the hall George saw Hélène, who was already quite a little distance from the house, and also caught a glimpse of Marcelle, who was advancing to meet her friend. But he also saw, almost at the foot of the broad steps leading down into the garden, his friend the count, who was pointing out the beauties of the establishment to his companion with all the complacent pride of an admiring owner.

Both gentlemen were so intently engaged in gazing at the brick and marble façade of the château and its turreted roof that they failed to notice the major, who was now standing in the door-way, so he had an excellent opportunity to look at the visitor his friend Jacques had brought back with him from Paris.

Great was his astonishment on becoming aware almost instantly that he had seen this stranger somewhere before; and after reflecting a little he recollected that it was at the Church of Saint-Augustin, on the day of Mme. de Muire's funeral.

The gentleman had a face which was not easily forgotten; besides, one fact which had assisted in engraving it upon the major's memory was that after the ceremony, while Médéric was standing beside M. de Muire receiving expressions of condolence from those present, he had refused the hand offered him by this very gentleman.

Another fact suddenly occurred to George Roland. Mlle. Lanoue had asked him the name of this very stranger who by a strange chance now reappeared at the Oaks, brought there by the count.

"What can all this mean?" muttered the major. "And where the deuce can Jacques have picked up this would-be purchaser?"

He was not kept long in doubt, however, for M. de Muire, having finished his eulogium of the beauties of the villa, perceived the major standing in the door-way, and beckoned him to come down.

George instantly responded to the silent invitation. The stranger awaited his approach with his hat in his hand and a smile upon his lips, and was the first to bow when the count introduced:

"Major Roland, my most intimate friend."

George bowed, shook hands with M. de Muire, and waited for what was to follow. But instead of completing the introduction, M. de Muire remarked:

"I am glad to see you. I was told that you had gone to the city."

"That was a mistake. I am fond of walking; and this morning I took a tramp in the direction of Vésinet, where I happened to meet Mademoiselle Lanoue, who was visiting some of her poor people, so I returned with her. But you went to the city this morning, did you not?"

"Yes; and at my notary's I met this gentleman, who wishes to purchase the Oaks, and who was kind enough to return with me to take a look at the property."

"I have already done so," remarked the stranger. "I am much pleased with the establishment, and I think we shall have no difficulty in agreeing upon the price."

"To whom have I the honor of speaking?" inquired the major. "My friend Jacques just introduced me to you, but he forgot to present you to me."

"Count Serge Golymine," replied M. de Muire.

On hearing this name George Roland gave a slight start, but he quickly repressed his surprise, and said a little coldly:

"It seems to me that we have met before, sir."

"Possibly, monsieur; but I do not recollect it."

"I think you were present at Madame de Muire's funeral."

"That is true. I accompanied my friends the Marquis de Brangue and the Viscount de Liscoat there."

"This gentleman belongs to the same club that I do," interrupted Marcelle's father, "and our acquaintance is one of quite long standing. Several years ago the count was a regular visitor at Aix—"

"Where you always spent a week at the close of every season. I understand."

The major's doubts were dispelled now. He was in the presence of the person that Mlle. Lanoue had designated as the protector of the man who had found Médéric's revolver; and this would be an excellent opportunity to become better acquainted with him, and to make a beginning in the investigation he intended to undertake.

"So you are likely to become the owner of the pleasant country home which my friend Jacques wishes to sell," he said, courteously. "I congratulate you most sincerely. There is not a more charming place in the environs of Paris. There are some very unpleasant associations connected with it for us, but for you—"

"And for me as well," interrupted Golymine, hastily. "I, too, sympathize deeply with Monsieur de Muire in the terrible misfortune that has overtaken him; and it would be very unpleasant for me to live in this villa, but it is not for myself that I am purchasing it."

"For whom, then, may I ask?"

"For a company of capitalists who have their head-quarters at Vienna, but who wish to extend their business operations into France. I am a member of the firm, and I represent it here in Paris, so I am on the lookout for profitable investments in real estate for a portion of our capital. It is an excellent means of inspiring confidence— a fact to which most of your prominent insurance companies seem to be fully alive by the way."

"Then if you make the purchase you intend to leave the Oaks, I suppose?"

"Yes; and I should be very glad if we could secure Monsieur de Muire for a tenant; but I see that there is no hope of that, and that he would not consent to remain on any terms. "

" No, not on any terms," exclaimed the count. " But if you have not seen the garden, I should like to show it to you. You will be amply repaid for your trouble."

" Good!" thought the major. " Jacques has no idea that his daughter is in the garden with her governess. I am curious to see what they will think of this foreign nobleman. Hélène will certainly be very much surprised when she hears his name."

M. de Muire led his visitors toward the trees, in the shade of which the young girls, whom the gentlemen had not yet perceived, were seated. George Roland followed them, eager to note the effect of the *coup de théâtre*.

But the result did not equal his expectations by any means. Marcelle remained cold and indifferent when her father mentioned the count's name; Hélène manifested some surprise but no agitation, and immediately began to carefully examine the features of this man who had previously attracted her attention at Mme. de Muire's funeral.

" She has more strength of character than I thought," the major said to himself. " Any other woman would have turned pale on finding herself in the presence of this Golymine whose suspicious connection with Maurevers is no secret to her. But she has made no sign. I shall have a valuable auxiliary in her; and between us we shall certainly succeed in rending the veil of mystery that envelopes these men."

The interview had lasted but a moment; and M. de Muire was already leading the count away to complete the tour of the garden with him. George heard Golymine compliment the count on his daughter's beauty. He also inquired the name of the governess, whose loveliness could hardly have failed to excite his admiration.

But George Roland, before rejoining the gentlemen,

found an opportunity to exchange a few low and hurried words with Mlle. Lanoue.

" "Well, you see it is the same man you noticed on the day of the funeral. Do you know him?"

" No," was the reply. " He resembles a person I knew years ago; but I am now sure that he is not the same person—and I am equally sure that this Russian hired Conductor Maurevers to murder Madame de Muire."

CHAPTER VIII.

AFTER Count Golymine's visit the major became convinced that he should not advance Médéric's interests by remaining constantly at the villa.

The campaign so cleverly opened by Mlle. Lanoue could be conducted to much better advantage in Paris; and he made arrangements to do this without depriving himself entirely of the society of his friends at the Oaks, upon which he set greater store than ever, since he had declared his love to Hélène.

She had given him no decided answer as yet. Their interview had remained a secret, and he understood that Marcelle's lover must be restored to her before he could again venture to broach the subject nearest to his heart. This was to be the price of Mlle. Lanoue's consent; therefore he must needs find the ways and means to accomplish this result.

Without leaving Mlle. de Muire the young governess could serve the common cause by continuing to collect information in regard to Maurevers, the railway conductor and husband of a princess.

The major must watch Golymine, and keep himself thoroughly posted in regard to all his movements; and to do this he must bring himself into more intimate relations with the friends of this foreigner—M. de Brangue and M. de Liscoat, for example.

He must even make up his mind to associate more or less with Golymine if this should seem necessary. He had a long conversation with M. de Muire after the departure of the count, who remained at the château only about an hour, but in the course of the conversation no allusion was made either to Médéric or Marcelle. M. de Muire explained his plans very clearly, and announced his firm intention of converting all his property into ready money and retiring into the country with his daughter. He believed himself irretrievably ruined; and had given up all hope of finding the stocks and bonds that constituted the greater part of his wife's estate.

He did not even seem to wonder what had become of them, so completely did he appear to be crushed by these repeated blows. He seemed to think only of disposing of his property and getting away.

· George Roland tried hard to convince him that he had no right to sacrifice Marcelle's interests in this way, and that if he was unwilling to do so, some friend ought to watch over them in his stead; and he himself offered to confer with the family notary upon the best means of discovering some clew to the whereabouts of the missing securities. M. de Muire gave him full permission to follow the dictates of his own judgment in the matter; he even authorized him to make a thorough search in the house on the Boulevard Malesherbes to ascertain if the countess had not left some writing or memorandum there, indicating the use she had made of her stocks and bonds, or at least the numbers of them, without which it would be useless to endeavor to prevent the sale of these missing securities, which had very possibly been stolen, as they certainly had neither been given away nor destroyed.

George took advantage of this opportunity to make some inquiries in regard to their late visitor; but M. de Muire replied with an indifferent air that as the terms of sale were to be cash, he had not troubled himself in the least about M. Golymine's antecedents. He had met him several years before at Aix, in Savoy; if his memory served him it was the countess who had introduced the gentleman to him. He had met him again a few months ago in Paris at the club, and they had recognized each other, but that was all.

"Apply to Liscoat," said M. de Muire in conclusion. "Golymine is his partner at the whist-table almost every evening; but, as I said before, I take no interest whatever in this gentleman's origin or social status. If he hasn't the ready money necessary, I shall look for another purchaser; that is all."

Being unable to obtain any further information from his old friend, the major decided to begin operations the very next day; so he informed Mlle. Lanoue that hereafter he should go to Paris every morning, spend the day there, and return to the Oaks in time for dinner. In the evening Hélène was to meet him in the garden, and each of them was to impart to the other any information collected during the day.

This was a very sensible plan; but the major's part of the task was much the most difficult, for Mlle. Lanoue had only to question Mme. Maurevers to make her talk, while George Roland had no idea what course to adopt with M. de Liscoat.

The antiquated fop had never been a favorite with him, and the dislike seemed to be mutual. Besides, they had not parted on very good terms on the day of Mme. de Muire's tragical death, and the viscount was most unfavorably disposed toward Médéric.

George would much rather have led a charge against a battery composed of Krupp's cannon than endeavor to ingratiate himself into the favor of such a man; but he saw no other way to gain any reliable information in regard to

Golymine's past and present, so there seemed to be no help for it.

He resolved, however, that the meeting should appear to be the result of chance; and being tolerably familiar with the viscount's habits, he knew that Liscoat took a horse-back ride almost every morning, and generally breakfasted at the Café Durand, on the Place de la Madeleine, on his return. There, he generally met his chosen friends, the Marquis de Brangue among them, and these relics of a former era usually whiled away a couple of hours in anath-ematizing the present age and blighting the reputations of their lady friends.

The major, who had often met them there, did not re-member to have ever seen Golymine in the restaurant, so he decided to make the venture; but he had no time to lose, as the summer was fast passing and Liscoat seldom failed to finish up the season at Trouville or Luchon. If he had not left the city already, he would very soon; and he was not very likely to warn M. de Muire of his intended departure, for he had not even come to pay his friend a call of condolence. He seemed to have considered that he had done all that could be expected of him when he attended the funeral.

So the very next morning George Roland took the 10:30 train for Paris, and on reaching the Rue Miromesnil, about eleven o'clock, his porter informed him that no letters for him had yet been received. This being the case, it seemed more than probable that the advertisement he had inserted in several city papers would be productive of no result whatever, and that Médéric's fellow passengers on the 19th of June would remain forever deaf to the appeal that had been addressed to them at three francs per line.

Still, this failure only made an interview with the hated viscount all the more necessary, so the major wended his way toward the Place de la Madeleine, which was only a short distance from his rooms on the Rue de Miromesnil.

On the corner of the Rue Royale he paused to reconnoiter. The weather was very warm: all the doors and windows of the restaurant were open, and the major was consequently able to secure a look at the interior of the establishment before he entered it.

As good luck would have it, he saw M. de Liscoat there, glancing over the columns of a sporting paper, and breakfasting alone, so the major could seat himself at a neighboring table without seeming to have any special designs upon the viscount. In fact, it was not until he had called the waiter that M. de Liscoat recognized him, and laid aside his paper to remark:

"Why! is that you, major? I was not expecting to meet you here, as you rarely honor the establishment with your patronage; but I am very glad to see you, nevertheless."

George Roland, little anticipating such a courteous greeting, had carefully prepared a few remarks intended to break the ice; but it was not necessary to make use of them; and as Liscoat assumed this friendly manner the major lost no time in responding in the same tone.

"And I am equally glad!" he exclaimed. "Since that terrible catastrophe at Chatou I have been leading the life of a hermit, and I shall congratulate myself upon my sudden resolve to breakfast in Paris this morning if I am to have the pleasure of your company. I should certainly enjoy a chat with you above all things."

"And I shall be charmed. So you are staying awhile with our friend Jacques. It is very kind in you, for life at the Oaks must be intolerably dull now. I confess that I have not been able to summon up courage to go there. My physician will not allow me to make visits of condolence. He thinks them too much of a strain upon my nerves; besides, I hear that our poor friend does not care to see any company. I can very readily understand that. To lose his wife, and his prospective son-in-law, both at once, is certainly a crushing blow!"

This allusion to Médéric's misfortunes brought the blood to the major's face; but this was no time to lose his temper, so he said never a word, and the viscount, encouraged by his silence, continued:

"You see I was right in suspecting the young man. He was arrested only four days afterward, and they say that the evidence against him is well-nigh conclusive. The revolver he used has been found."

"Who told you so?" inquired George, quickly.

"Why, that is the report; and I am surprised that it has not reached you before. Golymine was speaking of it yesterday at the club."

"I am not acquainted with Monsieur Golymine."

"I congratulate you. If you knew him he would ask you to play piquet with him, and win your money, as he wins mine every day."

"I should not accept his invitation. But I wonder how he happens to be so well informed. Médéric de Mestras is kept in solitary confinement, and up to the present time none of the particulars of the investigation now in progress at Versailles have been made public."

"Nonsense! everybody knows the facts. Magistrates are only men after all, and no more prudent than other people. They have wives too, and intimate friends, and Golymine is a man who always knows what is going on. And by the way, speaking of Golymine, tell me, my dear major, is it true that he intends to purchase all the real estate that belonged to the late countess?"

"I am not aware that he contemplates purchasing all of it. I only know that he came to look at the Oaks yesterday, and that he and Jacques agreed upon the price—which is to be two hundred thousand francs. I suppose the gentleman is good for that amount."

"Oh, yes, I am sure of that."

"So much the better! But, as you know him so well, tell me who this Count Golymine really is."

George Roland, who had begun his breakfast, made this request in a careless tone as he attacked the delicious shrimps which had just been placed before him, for the greater his desire to become fully informed in regard to this mysterious foreigner, the less importance he must appear to attach to his inquiries.

"Well, really, my dear fellow, I scarcely know what to say," exclaimed M. de Liscoat. "I know Golymine exactly as I know a hundred other members of my club. I can assure you that he is well born, that he is well bred, and that he has plenty of money. He must be spending at least one hundred thousand francs a year here, and one meets him everywhere; but if you ask me to give you his complete biography, I must beg to be excused."

"Still, as he has been admitted into your club, some one must know—"

"Every one knows that his name was proposed by two honorable gentleman, and that suffices, as these gentlemen are responsible for him. He took up his abode in Paris only last year; but one would suppose that he had resided here all his life. He has traveled a good deal, I believe, and gambled a good deal, and I should judge that he had been a great ladies' man. He seems to have been wonderfully successful in everything. I should call him a lucky man; but he is also very talented, exceedingly well read, and full of tact. He is a genuine count, of very ancient lineage. Brangue, who pays much more attention to these matters than I do, and who knows all about the European nobility, declares that these Golymines were sovereign princes of some province of Poland. This one became a Russian to save a part of his domains, and afterward went into business. This descendant of the Jagellons is extremely practical in his ideas. He is a man of the times, and it is well for him that he is, for he is very wealthy, while many of his noble compatriots have been compelled to mortgage their estates to buy bread."

This information which M. de Liscoat evidently gave in perfect good faith, completely disconcerted Major George, who could not imagine why such an exalted personage should have bribed a poor wretch to murder the countess; besides, what possible object could he have had in doing it? But he finally came to the conclusion that Liscoat, like many others, must be greatly mistaken in regard to this foreigner.

"But now I think of it, Jacques de Muire must know as much if not more about Golymine than I do," continued the viscount.

"No, I think not."

"Then the poor countess could not have told him."

"Told him what, pray?"

"Why that Golymine was her most devoted admirer at Aix. He was ever at her side, and he must have told her all about himself. I don't much wonder that she kept it from her husband though. Muire is not a jealous man, still, he would certainly have been greatly displeased at her compromising herself as she did."

The major suddenly recollected the conversation that Médéric had overheard between Liscoat and the Marquis de Brangue at the restaurant on the Champs Elysées, and this being an excellent opportunity to settle some of the vexed questions in regard to Mme. de Muire's past, he instantly resolved to improve it.

"What!" he exclaimed, assuming an air of astonishment, "do you really think that the countess—"

"Was in love with Golymine? He certainly never told me so. He is too well bred to boast of his conquests, but every one at Aix thought so. I suppose you are not ignorant of the fact that the lady had other lovers."

"This is the first time I ever heard such a thing hinted."

"Indeed! Really, you amaze me, my dear fellow. Everybody else has known it for the last fifteen years; and you yourself have been well acquainted with several of the favored ones.''

'' Mention them.''

'' Colonel de Mestras was one.''

'' Nothing will ever make me believe that.''

'' As you please, my dear major. It is by faith we are saved, and I certainly shall not try to shake yours. Still you may rest assured that I am telling you the truth. People even pretended at the time that the famous colonel was Mademoiselle de Muire's father.''

'' That is an atrocious lie! Mestras left for Africa two years before Marcelle de Muire was born.''

'' Ah! is that really so? By the way, now I think of it, why was the countess so bitterly opposed to her daughter's marriage with the unfortunate young man in whom you appear to take such an interest, and who seems likely to end so badly?''

'' I have always felt a deep interest in him, and I am more and more firmly convinced that he is not guilty.''

'' You have a perfect right to your own opinion, of course. Stick to it, my dear fellow, and let us change the subject. Is poor Muire ruined financially, that he is trying to sell all his real estate?''

'' He wishes to leave Paris and retire to the country.''

'' He must have some reason for that. Between ourselves I should not be surprised if the countess has lost the enormous fortune she inherited from her father in unfortunate speculations. They say she has been dabbling in stocks of late, to console herself for a lack of adorers. Some gossips even pretend that she has loaned large sums of money to several unscrupulous men—''

'' Such as Count Golymine, for example.''

'' You seem to dislike Golymine. Have you any just grounds of offense against him?''

'' I don't fancy his looks, that is all.''

'' That is a mere matter of taste. I certainly have no

reason to love him, for he has been winning money from me like wild-fire. Still, I assure you that he is a very good sort of a fellow. Why, only a day or two ago, he was moving heaven and earth to save a poor wretch who was in imminent danger of losing his place somewhere or other. He took an interest in the fellow merely because he had known him at Monaco, where the poor wretch lost all his money. But I have no idea why I am telling you all this. Let us speak instead of that charming young woman, Mademoiselle de Muire's governess. What is to become of her if our friend Jacques carries out his intention of retiring to the country? His daughter is old enough to discontinue her studies; besides, she will marry one of these days. Even if she has no dowry, many a young man will be glad to marry her for the sake of her beautiful eyes. Still I would greatly prefer to believe that poor Jacques is not yet reduced to penury. But in either case, the lovely Hélène will probably soon find herself without house or home.''

'' Mademoiselle Lanoue, too, will probably marry,'' said the major.

'' Then she would make a very great mistake. I am sure she would not commit such an act of folly. Marry a poor devil of a clerk, when she might live in luxury! Why, she would create a perfect *furor* among the *jeunesse dorée*, and become one of the leaders of the *demi-monde* I am sure. I would gladly do all in my power to secure her rapid advancement.''

George Roland looked the viscount straight in the eyes, and said in an eminently aggressive tone:

'' Mademoiselle Lanoue is not only the instructress, but the friend of Mademoiselle de Muire. It has come to my ears that you have ventured to speak of her disrespectfully before; I advise you not to be guilty of a like imprudence again.''

'' Ah, ha!'' sneered Liscoat, '' **you undertake her defense very warmly.**''

"There is no necessity of saying anything in her defense, as her conduct has always been irreproachable; but I shall allow no one to attack her. You would do well to bear that in mind."

The old fop decided not to take offense.

"Take care, major," he said, smiling. "If you constitute yourself this young lady's champion, I shall begin to believe that you are in love with her yourself."

"Believe what you please, provided you change the subject."

"Certainly, certainly, my dear fellow," replied the viscount, who did not seem to be at all anxious to pick a quarrel with this irascible protector of innocence; but, really, I scarcely know what to talk about without giving offense. This is the only time I have ever had the pleasure of breakfasting with you, and it really grieves me to find that we do not seem to agree upon any subject. I begin by making an allusion to the former love-affairs of the poor countess, and you reply that I am slandering her. I venture to express a doubt of young Mestras's innocence; you declare that you will vouch for it. Let us then return to Golymine, though we are not of the same mind even in regard to him."

The major was already beginning to regret that he had spoken so curtly. This was not the way to extort further information from the viscount; besides, he felt that he had made a mistake in espousing Mlle. Lanoue's cause so warmly. A man, that is, unless he is a very old man, can scarcely defend a young lady without compromising her a little; and the major, who thoroughly understood all this, would have been glad to continue his conversation with the viscount in a calmer strain.

Liscoat seemed resolved to afford him an opportunity, for he remarked:

"I just met Golymine. He resides near here, on the Rue Boissy d'Anglais, you know."

"I was not aware of the fact."

"I live on the Rue d'Anjou; so we met in the Faubourg Saint-Honoré this morning, and had quite a little chat. I invited him to breakfast with me, but he had another engagement. It is a pity, as you seem anxious to find out what kind of a man he is, and you might have studied him at your leisure. He is a capital guest, and the table is a very good place to judge of a man's character. However, if he purchases the Oaks, you will probably have plenty of opportunities to meet him."

"Oh, I am not particularly anxious about that. I am much more interested in his financial standing than in the man himself."

"I thought you had heard of his old flirtation with Madame de Muire or I should not have said what I did. You must admit that there are strange chances in this life of ours. Here is Golymine, who probably hasn't given the countess a thought for several years, about to purchase the real estate she left. Nor is this all. Just guess why he was unable to come and breakfast with me—to his great regret."

"How can you expect me to guess?"

"Well, would you believe it? he had been summoned to Versailles. He was obliged to rush off almost on a run in order to catch the train."

"To Versailles? What for?"

"He had been summoned there by the magistrate who is investigating the charge against young Mestras—summoned as a witness. Isn't it strange, especially as he doesn't know, and has never even seen Monsieur de Mestras?"

The major, much less surprised at this news than M. de Liscoat, gave no sign of the satisfaction aroused by this unexpected intelligence—a satisfaction mingled with uneasiness, however, for he could not decide what would be the result of Golymine's unexpected appearance upon the stage of action, nor even the capacity in which the foreigner was about to appear before the judge of instruction.

M. de Liscoat declared that it was as a witness, but M. de Liscoat was only repeating what Golymine had just told him; as he was evidently ignorant of the true history of the finding of the revolver by a railway conductor who was the very protégé to whom he had referred a moment before, so the major felt some hope that this conductor on being closely questioned by the magistrate had finally confessed his guilt, and denounced Count Golymine as his accomplice.

On the other hand he strongly suspected that Golymine and Médéric must have met before the death of the countess, and that they were now on hostile terms, in consequence of that, as yet, inexplicable meeting, for the major recollected that at Mme. de Muire's funeral, Médéric had refused the hand proffered by Golymine; and Médéric would not have acted in this manner in a church, only a few steps from the bier, and under the very eyes of Marcelle's father, if he had not had good reasons for his conduct.

Consequently, if Golymine should be called upon to testify before the magistrate who had placed Médéric in solitary confinement, his testimony would certainly be damaging to Médéric, and it was more than probable that he had been summoned only as a witness, as he had gone to Versailles alone, and of his own free will.

If he had been under arrest, or even under the surveillance of an officer of the law, M. de Liscoat would have been sure to notice the fact, and to mention it to the major, for he spared no one, not even his most intimate friends.

"This much is certain," continued the viscount, "poor Golymine is not very well pleased. He is heaping curses upon the Versailles authorities, and also upon the young man who was the cause of all this trouble. The fact is, it is not very pleasant to be obliged to neglect one's business and pleasure to spend the day in a stupid humdrum place like Versailles, to say nothing of the annoyance of being questioned in regard to matters one knows nothing about, and of perhaps being obliged to cool one's heels for hours in the office of a judge of instruction, for these gentlemen take their time in dealing with their victims."

" If Golymine knows nothing about the affair, they will not detain him long," George said, principally for the sake of saying something.

As the antiquated beau's conversation no longer interested him, he was anxious to get rid of him as soon as possible, in order that he might proceed to carry into execution a plan that M. de Liscoat had just suggested to him, without suspecting it, however.

Golymine was now at Versailles, and the major said to himself that this would be an excellent time for him to present himself before the judge of instruction, not to again solicit the permission to visit Médéric, which had been twice refused him already, but to tell the magistrate what he had learned about Maurevers's antecedents and his connection with the count.

This step might be rather premature, but he would have ample time for reflection during the journey from Paris to Versailles; besides, there was a chance of meeting Golymine, in or about the Palace of Justice, and in that case this real or pretended count would not refuse to tell him why he had been summoned, for Golymine would naturally desire to avoid a semblance of anything like mystery with one of M. de Mestras's friends.

This programme was based upon mere conjecture; but instinct impelled George to make the journey, and he had a presentiment that it would not prove futile.

The repast was fast drawing to a close. Coffee had been served, and M. de Liscoat was preparing to light a cigar.

" Do you think that Jacques would be pleased to see me if I should call on him before my departure for Trouville, my dear major?" he asked, carelessly.

" He has received no visitors up to the present time," replied George, evasively.

"No one but Golymine, and Golymine called on business. I think it would be better for me to deny myself the pleasure, perhaps. My visit might not be agreeable to him, and it might embarrass the young ladies, so I will abstain, and if I should not see you again before my departure, I assure you that I shall ever retain a very pleasant recollection of our breakfast together."

Having said this, the viscount, who had previously asked for his bill, and paid it, rose and offered his hand to George Roland, who did not refuse it, though the old fop's disrespectful remarks about Mlle. Lanoue still rankled in his breast.

"We part friends, do we not?" said 'Liscoat, smiling, and balancing himself alternately upon his heels and toes, like a marquis of the olden time.

George bowed his assent, and saw him depart with pleasure, for he was impatient to regain his freedom. He did not regret his interview with the viscount, though the information he had extorted from him in regard to Golymine's past was rather vague in its nature.

Still, it was something to have learned that this mysterious individual had just been summoned before the judge of instruction, and that he had recently been interesting himself in the welfare of a poor devil who had lost all his money at Monaco.

Though the viscount had not entered into particulars, this protégé was evidently the conductor who had played such a singular rôle in the affair of the shooting, and this fact, which George Roland had just verified, might be the beginning of a series of startling discoveries which would prove of the greatest service to Médéric.

CHAPTER IX.

IT was necessary to act immediately, however, and the major did not lose a moment. Hastily settling his bill, he started for the station, which he reached just in time to catch the 11:30 train for Versailles.

The train was not crowded, for Parisians rarely visit the museum and go to see the fountains play except on Sunday; and the major found himself alone in a compartment with a very respectable-looking but extremely portly man—a worthy *bourgeois*, who seemed likely to prove a rather tiresome traveling-companion.

All went well until they reached the junction at Asnières. George had been quietly smoking his cigar, and his companion had spent most of his time in looking out of the window, though he was evidently dying to enter into conversation.

The costume of this worthy citizen strikingly resembled that of the legendary Joseph Prudhomme, as created by the celebrated actor, Henry Monnier. It consisted of a blue broadcloth coat, with gilt buttons, a white cravat, and a waistcoat of the same hue, buff nankeen trousers, a broad-brimmed hat, and a wide collar that was so tall that it rasped his ears. The resemblance, too, was as striking in feature, as in attire, for he had the same projecting chin and prominent nose adorned by gold-bowed spectacles.

At any other time George Roland would have been secretly amused by this rather grotesque specimen, but he was too deeply preoccupied now to pay much attention to the peculiar-looking person chance had given him for a *vis-à-vis*.

When the train paused, just beyond the bridge at Asnières, at the intersection of the Saint-Germain line, the worthy man uttered a profound sigh, and muttered between his teeth, though sufficiently loud to be distinctly heard:

"I regret that business calls me to the country-seat of the department of Seine-et-Oise to-day, instead of to the charming little town where Louis XV was born."

The major pretended that he did not think it possible that this remark was addressed to him, and surveyed the speaker very much as he would have surveyed a savage from the Island of Borneo.

"Yes," continued the stout man, imperturbably, "I should like to have another look at the scene of a crime that was perpetrated under my very eyes—and yet, without my knowledge."

This apparent contradiction excited the major's curiosity, and the idea that it might have reference to Mme. de Muire's death occurring to him, he decided to reply.

"Pardon me, sir," he began; "but I think you must be speaking to me, though I haven't the slightest idea what you mean."

"I admit that my language was rather ambiguous," replied the man, with a complacent smile; "but I thought you might guess my meaning. I was referring to an affair which all Paris was talking about three weeks ago, and of which monsieur must certainly have seen an account in the papers. A lady, a countess, was killed between Chatou and Vésinet by a bullet fired from a Saint-Germain train."

"What, were you on the train at the time?" exclaimed the major.

"Yes, sir; and the strangest thing about it all was that I knew nothing at all about it at the time. I did notice the lady who was surrounded by quite a party, but the train was going so rapidly that I only caught a glimpse of her. I did not have time to see her fall, nor did I hear the report of the pistol. It was not until the next day that I heard of the catastrophe. Take notice, too, sir, that the compartment in which I was seated was full, and that my traveling-companions saw and heard no more than I did."

"That was certainly very extraordinary, and very unfortunate, too, as you were, of course, unable to give the authorities the slightest information on the subject."

"Of course not. Had I been able to throw any light upon the mystery you may rest assured that I should have lost no time in giving my testimony before a magistrate, and, between ourselves, I am almost sorry that I did not do it, after all. I haven't much to tell, it is true; but in such cases the merest trifles sometimes serve as valuable clews."

"What did you notice?"

"Notice is not exactly the word. It was a reflection that occurred to me too late to be of any service, I fear. I recollected the next day that my neighbor in the railway-carriage acted very strangely. In the first place, he rushed into the car at Chatou, while the train was in motion, and nearly tumbled over me. Afterward, he was continually moving about, and stretching his neck to the uttermost, in order to look out of the window. In short, he acted like a lunatic. At Vésinet, he jumped out upon the platform, without waiting for the train to stop, and rushed off like a man who had just committed some terrible crime. This person, however, could not have been the assassin, as the murder was committed between the station of Chatou and Vésinet."

"Then what is your idea about him?"

"I think he was probably an accomplice."

"An accomplice, sir!" exclaimed the major. "You certainly can not think that. In what possible way could this man, who was sitting beside you, have aided the assassin, who must have been in some other compartment, if not in another car?"

"That is something I am utterly unable to explain," replied M. Prudhomme gravely, "but I pride myself on being a pretty clever physiognomist; and I am very rarely mistaken in the opinion I form of a person. It struck me at once that my neighbor had a very bad face; and you must admit that his both entering and leaving the car while the train was in motion was very singular, to say the least."

"You are nothing more nor less than a fool, my good man," thought George Roland, "and I did very wrong to take any notice of you."

"Besides," continued this brilliant logician, "it is not unreasonable to suppose that this man was the instigator of the crime, and that some other scoundrel committed it. The two miscreants probably separated at Chatou to meet in the woods near Vésinet a couple of hours afterward."

The major was no longer paying the slightest attention to the old fogy's absurd reasoning. A new idea had suddenly occurred to him. He recollected the explanation given by Médéric, a few minutes after Mme. de Muire's death, and that account harmonized so perfectly with the one given by this sexagenarian that George now thought only of clearing up the one remaining doubt that troubled him.

"What kind of a looking person was the man you took for an accomplice?" he asked, brusquely.

"Very good-looking, and dressed in the height of fashion," replied the old gentleman, "and this last fact only strengthens me in my opinion. The crime must have been committed for money by a vile subordinate; and judging from appearances, this young gentleman was quite rich enough to hire some one to do his dirty work for him."

"He was young, then?"

"Twenty-five or thirty, I should say. He was tall, dark-complexioned, and quite slim, with a long brown mustache curled at the ends. He was rather a handsome fellow, but intolerable as a neighbor. He seemed unable to keep still a second. One would have supposed that he had quicksilver in his veins, and he was continually stepping on my toes."

"Would you recognize him if you should see him again?" interrupted George.

"Yes, certainly. His was one of those faces a person is not likely to forget. But I have not met him since, unfortunately. He is probably hiding somewhere; but if I should ever happen to meet him again I shall certainly give him into custody."

"And if you were brought into his presence, would you be willing to repeat before witnesses all you have just told me?"

"Yes," replied the good man, though not without some hesitation. "But of course I should not be likely to compromise myself."

"One could hardly compromise one's self by telling the truth."

"That is true; but there are responsibilities from which one naturally shrinks; and if it be a matter of condemning a man to death, I should certainly stop to think twice. In the first place, I am a strong advocate of the abolition of capital punishment. I have been sworn as a juror several times, and I have always refused to cast a vote that might send a fellow-creature to the scaffold."

"That is your way of thinking; it isn't mine, though. Still, this is an entirely different matter. It is a question of saving an innocent man."

"Oh! in that case I should not hesitate an instant. It would be a duty I owed to humanity; and I pride myself on being a philanthropist. But excuse me, sir, I don't exactly understand what you are driving at; and before binding myself in any way I should like to know to whom I have the honor of speaking."

"I am Major Roland, a former army officer; and now you know me, I hope you will be good enough to tell me your name."

"William Postel, a retired merchant, and formerly President of the Bureau of Commerce."

"Then I have to deal with an honorable man, and I can speak without any reserve whatever. First of all, sir, you must understand that I depend upon your assistance in correcting a judicial error which may be terrible in its consequences."

"In that case you can certainly count upon me. I never can think of that terrible Lesurque case without a shudder; and I should be glad, indeed, to prevent anything like a repetition of it, though I don't exactly see how I am to do it."

"I only ask you to accompany me into the presence of a judge of instruction when we reach Versailles."

"And for what purpose, pray?"

"To request him to bring you immediately into the presence of a prisoner who is no other than the young man of whom you have just spoken—the person who traveled in the same compartment with you on the day of the tragedy at Chatou."

"There! I knew that you wanted me to assist in securing his conviction. I tell you, once for all, that you need expect no aid from me."

"On the contrary, I wish to prove his innocence; and your testimony will suffice to prove it if I can prevail upon you to accompany me. He is now in solitary confinement, but no conscientious magistrate could refuse to let you see a prisoner whose release would be assured by a word from you."

"What! by a word from me?"

"Unquestionably. You have only to say: 'I recognize this gentleman, and I solemnly swear that on the 19th of June last he entered, at Chatou, a train upon which I was traveling, and afterward left it at Vésinet.' If you were an irresponsible person the judge would perhaps pay no attention to your assertions; but when you give your name he will know that a man of undoubted respectability and well-known probity stands before him, and if, before deciding to permit the confrontation, he should desire further information about you, we shall have no difficulty in obtaining it."

"I flatter myself that it will be of a perfectly satisfactory character," said M. Postel, straightening himself up, "and if I can save an innocent man in the way you have indicated, I shall only be doing my duty. But I do not yet understand how I can be of any service to the accused, even if he should prove to be the same person that traveled with me. I shall be obliged to tell the whole truth if I say anything, and he acted so strangely that—"

"I can explain why he seemed so anxious and restless. He is accused of having fired the fatal shot himself, and your testimony will prove that this was impossible. As for the charge of complicity, I had not thought of that, I confess; but that will fall to the ground."

The worthy merchant shook his head dubiously. He still clung to his first idea, probably because he had very few of them, and it was difficult to dislodge those that had once taken possession of his brain. He felt firmly convinced that the young man who had trodden upon his toes, in his haste to leave the car, must have been steeped in crime; and all the arguments in the world would not convince him to the contrary. Obstinate people, in the end, almost always gain more or less influence over those who oppose them; and M. Postel was so positive himself that the major finally began to wonder if the worthy man might not have good grounds for the fear that his testimony would effect no material change in the condition of affairs, though it was absurd to suppose that Médéric had bribed any one to murder Mme. de Muire for him.

So the major resolved to insist that his traveling-companion should accompany him to the office of the judge of instruction. He even resolved, in case of a refusal, to compel this timid old man to tell what he knew; and to do this he would only have to ascertain his address and mention him to the investigating magistrate as a witness it would be well to summon.

"Are you really so much interested in this young man?" inquired M. Postel, sighing.

"Yes; he is the son of the brave Colonel de Mestras, who was my superior in command, and who fell on the battle-field of Gravelotte, charging at the head of his regiment," replied Major George, proudly.

"In that case, I can very easily understand the chagrin you must feel at the unfortunate position in which he is placed."

"I shall get him safely out of the scrape if you will only consent to accompany me to the Palace of Justice. I shall be infinitely obliged to you if you will; and you will be performing a most worthy action, as you will be the means of restoring to liberty and honor a worthy young man who is unjustly accused."

"I would not hesitate if I were not afraid of injuring him; but I can not help thinking that I shall do him more harm than good if I tell all I saw."

"I will take the responsibility."

The merchant was about to make some fresh objections, but before he had time to frame them into words, the train paused at Saint-Cloud, and four passengers, amongst them an officer and a lady, entered the compartment.

The conversation being of such a nature that it could not be continued in the presence of strangers, George Roland abandoned it, all the while promising himself not to lose sight of his man on the arrival of the train; and M. Postel embraced the opportunity to relapse into a majestic but prudent silence.

This highly respectable individual was not a man of impulse by any means, and he had an intense fear of finding himself involved in any disreputable affair.

The trip from Saint-Cloud to Versailles is a short one, and in about a quarter of an hour the train reached the station. The passengers alighted, and M. Postel was preparing to leave the car after touching his hat politely to the prisoner's champion; but the major took him unceremoniously by the arm and said in firm but courteous tones:

"I rely upon your promise, sir."

"I promised nothing," stammered M. Postel.

"Pardon me, but you said you would accompany me to the office of the judge of instruction if you could be of any service to the accused. I assure you that you can save him, so you can not refuse to accompany me."

"Nothing would give me greater pleasure; but I came to Versailles to conclude a business transaction with a brother merchant. He is waiting for me now—"

"Where does he live?"

"On the Avenue de Sceaux—"

"Very well, the Palace of Justice is not a step out of your way; and I know that the judge is in his office. We will request an audience, he will grant it, and you will be detained only a few moments."

The worthy man being unable to find any other excuse, did not venture to offer any further resistance, but allowed himself to be dragged off in the direction of the Palace of Justice by the energetic major.

"Ah! my dear sir," that gentleman exclaimed as he led his victim toward the Avenue Saint-Cloud, "what a noble part you are about to play! I quite envy you. To save an innocent man is an even grander thing than to win a battle."

This comparison being eminently pleasing to M. Postel's self-love, he replied with a complacent smile:

"It is a much more difficult matter sometimes."

"You are right!" exclaimed the major. "Here I have been moving heaven and earth for the past three weeks in my efforts to prove that this young man is innocent, and have not made the slightest progress thus far, for the poor fellow is still in solitary confinement. If I had not met you I do not think there would have been the slightest chance of getting him out of the scrape. Fortunately there is a Providence that watches over us continually; and this morning it inspired me with the idea of entering the same compartment with you. I feel unspeakably grateful to it, and shall continue to feel so, even if I should derive no further advantaage from it than the honor of having made your acquaintance.''

" The honor is mine, sir," replied the good man in his deepest bass voice. " I revere the army, and admire and love our soldiers. "

" Then you must be glad to come to the aid of the bravest and truest soldier I ever knew.''

" I should be proud indeed to do so; but you just told me that he was in solitary confinement, and in that case we shall not be able to see him.''

" That will not prevent us from seeing him in the presence of witnesses; and even if I, being a personal friend of his, should not be allowed to communicate with the prisoner, you, who are in a position to establish an *alibi* in his favor will certainly be allowed to. A magistrate who would refuse to bring you face to face with him would be guilty of a breach of the law.''

" But what if I should be mistaken? What if I should not be able to identify the young man? In that case, don't you think this step would prove an injury to him?''

The major had not foreseen this possibility; but he was not easily daunted. Besides, he recollected the description Médéric had given him of a stout man into whose lap he had fallen when he rushed wildly into the car at Chatou, and this description corresponded so perfectly with the former president of the Bureau of Commerce that there was little room for doubt.

" Oh! there is not the slightest danger," replied George, " at least, not so far as he is concerned; and when the magistrate learns who you are he certainly will not suspect you of being in league with the prisoner; nor will he be likely to consider a very excusable error a crime. Consequently there is nothing to prevent us from making the attempt. If we succeed, so much the better; if we fail, no harm will be done."

"So be it!" sighed M. Postel; "but if the affair turns out badly I shall wash my hands of it."

"That is understood, of course. In half an hour we shall know where we stand."

The major was too sanguine, for the old gentleman, whose movements were greatly retarded by his *embonpoint*, did not walk much more rapidly than a tortoise. They were still on the Avenue Saint-Cloud, and if they proceeded at this slow rate, they ran a great risk of not finding the judge of instruction in his office.

But there seemed to be no way of getting M. Postel along any faster, for he had to stop every minute or two to breathe, so the major was obliged to bear the delay as best he could.

When they were about half-way up the avenue, the good man asked permission to sit down and rest a moment on a bench, and there being no help for it, Major Roland consented.

During this enforced halt, the major suddenly perceived two men engaged in animated conversation under the trees about twenty yards from him. One was standing with his back toward the major, but the other was facing him, and this one wore the frock coat and cap trimmed with gold lace that forms the uniform of the employé of the Western Railway.

This fact very naturally excited the major's curiosity, and he at once proceeded to scrutinize the features of this individual who strikingly resembled the portrait that Mlle. Lanoue had drawn of the Princess Orbitello's husband. He had not time for a very prolonged survey, however, for the colloquy suddenly terminated, and the two men walked off, each in a different direction.

The railroad employé proceeded up the avenue, in the direction of the Place d'Armes, in front of the château; the other came straight toward the bench where the major was standing guard over M. Postel, and George Roland was not a little surprised to see that the man who had been standing with his back toward them was Count Golymine; surprised, but not by any means displeased, for he had just discovered him in close conversation with a man who was undoubtely the conductor mentioned by Marcelle's governess. And after a little reflection, George ceased to feel any astonishment at finding Golymine at Versailles. M. de Liscoat had warned him that Golymine was there, and George had forgotten only for an instant that he himself had made the journey chiefly in the hope of meeting the count in or about the palace.

His wish was gratified, for Golymine, who had seen him, did not seem to think of beating a retreat. On the contrary, he directed his course straight toward the spot where the major was still standing, for the latter was resolved not to leave M. Postel. whatever happened, as that gentleman might take it into his head to decamp at the first opportunity; besides, the major was not sorry to have a witness present at the impending interview.

Golymine, however, did not seem to pay the slightest attention to the good man who sat enthroned upon the bench, but bowed to the major, and said politely:

"You know who I am, sir, as the Count de Muire did me the honor to introduce me to you yesterday, so I surely can beg you to give me your attention for a few moments."

"Certainly, sir. What do you wish to say to me?"

"A most extraordinary thing has happened. I have just been summoned before the judge of instruction in this town, at the request of the unfortunate young man who is accused of the murder of Madame de Muire."

"What! at his request?"

"Yes; and he has made a very great mistake. Would

you believe it? he told the magistrate who is investigating the affair that on the evening following the crime, I was lying in wait for him at the door of his house, and that I proposed a bargain to him.''

'' I do not understand.''

'' Nor did I. It took the magistrate some time to make me understand of what this young man accused me. According to his account, I told him that I had found a revolver upon which his name was engraved, in one of the railway carriages, and that I promised not to surrender it to the authorities on condition that he would speak a good word for me, and treat me courteously when I met him at the house of the Count de Muire, and that I threatened to denounce him if he refused to consent to this arrangement. In a word, I attempted to levy a sort of blackmail upon him, and he haughtily rejected my proposals. Take notice, if you please, that I had no former acquaintance with Monsieur de Mestras, and that I did not stand in the slightest need of his assistance in conducting my negotiations with Monsieur de Muire. You had abundant proof of this fact yesterday, as you were at the Oaks while we were deciding upon the price of the piece of real estate which the count has sold to me. Take notice, too, that I had not the slightest idea where Monsieur de Mestras lived, which fact alone would have prevented me from going to call on him. The whole story is so absurd that I can not even guess his object in inventing it. To tell the truth, I am even beginning to believe that he is not in his right mind.''

'' The judge does not seem to share your opinion, as he sent for you to ask an explanation.''

'' The one I gave him was very simple. I assured him that there was not a single word of truth in Monsieur de Mestras's story, and defied the young man to produce the slightest evidence in support of his assertions; whereupon he flew into a furious passion and heaped so many insults upon me that the judge sent him back to prison. This interview with me, for which I hear the unfortunate young man has been clamoring ever since the day of his arrest, has had no other effect than to strengthen the convictions of the magistrates, who all believe him guilty. I pity him with all my heart, and knowing that you take a deep interest in' him, I felt it my duty to inform you of what had just passed in the magistrate's office.''

" I am greatly obliged to you, sir, but—"

" You probably know that some one found, a few days after the crime, a revolver that I have never seen any more than I had seen Monsieur de Mestras before he was brought into my presence in the magistrate's office.''

" Your memory has played you false. You saw him at Madame de Muire's funeral. I was present, and so were you.''

" True! and it is quite possible that I did see the young man there, but I did not know him personally, and so failed to notice him.''

" Then how did it happen that you offered him your hand?''

" I?''

" Most assuredly, and he withheld his.''

" Your eyes must have deceived you, sir; and as you are pleased to regard the matter in this light it is useless for us to discuss it further,'' replied M. de Golymine, with a piqued air. " I do not know whether or not we shall meet again at Monsieur de Muire's house, but I should prefer that my acquaintance with you would end from this instant.''

And without waiting for any response, Golymine passed on.

George Roland offered no objection, but turning to M. Postel, who had not moved during this short dialogue, he asked:

" You heard the conversation, did you not?''

" Yes, but I did not understand it.''

" But you have seen the man. Ah, well, remember his face and his words. It was he who murdered Madame de Muire. And now come and help me to save an innocent man who will suffer for that scoundrel's crime if you do not interfere."

" What!" exclaimed M. Postel, " that well-dressed, stylish-looking gentleman—"

" Has either committed murder himself, or hired some one to do it for him," replied the major. " I did doubt his guilt, but I doubt it no longer, and I shall show the miscreant no further mercy. I am going to denounce him to the judge of instruction, and you will be on hand to testify that we just saw him in close conversation with an employé of the Western Railway."

" That is true, and the gentleman seems to belong to the upper classes. But from the mere fact of seeing him in conversation with an inferior, it would be rash to conclude—"

" That he has committed an atrocious crime. You are right. But I have other proofs, and I entreat you to accompany me to the Palace without a moment's delay. If we wait any longer, we shall arrive too late, and I am anxious to end this matter to-day."

The ex-president of the Bureau of Commerce rose with a sigh. He had made up his mind to accompany the major, but he did not accompany him very cheerfully. These complications alarmed him the more from the fact that he did not understand them, and he was very much afraid that he should find himself involved in a criminal suit in which he took very little interest. He regretted having given so much license to his tongue, and he was quite right, since it was a simple imprudent admission that had caused him all this annoyance. If he had not boasted of traveling with the assassin on the 19th of June, the major would never have thought of asking for his testimony. All regrets were useless, however, for in the present condition of things there was nothing for him to do but make the best of it. So he hastened on, leaning upon the arm of George Roland, who redoubled his attentions to this valuable auxiliary.

On reaching the Palace, they learned that the judge of instruction was still in his office.

"Have you one of your visiting-cards about you?" inquired the major, turning to his companion.

The good man drew one from his note-case. Beneath his name was engraved his former title. This was precisely what George Roland had hoped for, and he at once proceeded to add these words: "Requests an interview, in order to make communication in regard to the Chatou murder." He then handed this card, with one of his own, to an usher, who returned in about five minutes to announce that the magistrate was ready to see them.

M. Postel's title had produced its effect. They entered the office together, and found themselves in the presence of a middle-aged man whose open and intelligent face had nothing alarming about it.

George knew him already from having been questioned by him on the day following Mme. de Muire's death, and had no fault to find with him with the exception of the fact that he had placed Médéric in solitary confinement.

M. Postel, who had never seen him before, began to feel a little more comfortable on finding himself face to face with an unassuming gentleman, who received him with a courtesy that was slightly tinged with deference.

The major was less graciously received, but he understood why, and hastened to say:

"Rest assured, sir, that I should not have ventured to present myself here unsummoned if my only errand had been to again request permission to visit Monsieur de Mestras in his cell. You have refused to grant me this favor twice already—"

"And I am still unable to grant it," interrupted the judge, shaking his head. "The situation has become even more complicated within the past few days, and the case is one in which the painful measure of solitary confinement must be enforced and maintained until the conclusion of the investigation. But I am strenuously endeavoring to obtain all possible light upon the subject, and it was this desire that made me consent to listen to the communication this gentleman wishes to make to me."

This evidently meant: "My consent to admit you is due simply to the fact that you are in company with a former dignitary, and it is from him alone that I wish an explanation."

The major had guessed correctly, but as he had grave doubts of the clearness of M. Postel's powers of narration, he pretended not to understand the remark, and hastily proceeded to describe the circumstances of his meeting with this highly respectable merchant who had traveled on the day of the murder in the same compartment with a young man whose personal appearance corresponded perfectly with that of Médéric de Mestras.

M. Postel confined himself to approving nods of the head, and when George had concluded the judge, who had listened very attentively, but not without an occasional grimace, seemed by no means convinced.

"I do not suspect you of the slightest desire to mislead me, nor do I entertain the slightest doubt of the truth of the statements this gentleman has made to you," he remarked. "I do not even refuse to verify them; but unfortunately this affair is so complicated that I can not take too many precautions to prevent myself from making any mistake. That is something I very narrowly escaped doing just now, for the prisoner undertook to defend himself by imputing the crime of which he is accused to another person."

"To Count Golymine, was it not?" interrupted George.

"How do you know?"

"Golymine told me so himself. I just met him on the

Avenue Saint-Cloud. He knows me from having seen me at Monsieur de Muire's house, so he had the assurance to accost me and tell me that he had just been confronted by Monsieur de Mestras in your presence—"

"He must also have told you that Monsieur de Mestras lied in pretending to have received certain overtures from him in regard to the missing revolver."

"He did tell me so, and I replied that it was he, Golymine, who told a falsehood in denying that he had ever seen Monsieur de Mestras before he met him in your office. He knew Mestras so well that at Madame de Muire's funeral, he offered him a hand, which the young man refused to take. I can produce others who will testify to this fact, if you desire it."

"That proves nothing, but you, sir, must have seen the prisoner frequently between the day of the crime and that of his arrest, and in that case he would certainly have said something to you about this nocturnal interview with Monsieur Golymine in a public square, and about this most improbable attempt at blackmail by a person whose integrity has never before been questioned."

The major was not prepared for this straightforward thrust, and it disconcerted him a little. The same objection had occurred to him more than once, and he had never been able to find a satisfactory explanation, but he was too honest to conceal the truth.

"Yes," he said, unhesitatingly, "I did see Monsieur de Mestras in his own rooms on the morning after Madame de Muire's death, and he did not say a word to me about Golymine; but immediately after the crime he discovered that he had lost on the train a revolver upon which his name was engraved. He wished to have a search made for it, and to claim it, but I advised him not to do so."

"All the more reason that he should have told you of his pretended conversation with Monsieur de Golymine, it seems to me."

"He did not do so. I have no idea why: but there is nothing to prevent you from asking him. Besides, it is in your power to convince yourself that it was utterly impossible for Monsieur de Mestras to have fired at Madame de Muire. How could he have used his revolver if he traveled from Chatou to Vésinet in the same compartment with Monsieur Postel? You can satisfy yourself of this fact, here and now, if you wish. I do not ask to be present at the interview; but I do beseech you to send for Monsieur de Mestras. If Monsieur Postel recognizes him, then Monsieur de Mestras is innocent."

The judge made no reply. He had remained standing, and so had the other gentlemen, and as he talked with them he walked up and down his office, which was lighted by two windows, one of which stood open. After reflecting some time, he paused near that one, and beckoned M. Postel to approach, as if desiring to speak to him in private.

The worthy merchant obeyed, without comprehending, and seeing that the judge was looking out of the window which opened upon an inner court-yard, he involuntarily did the same.

Almost instantly a deep flush overspread his placid face; he adjusted his spectacles in order to see more distinctly, his lips parted, and he was about to utter a loud exclamation when the magistrate seized him by the arm and hastily pulled him back.

"That is he!" murmured Postel; "that is the young man who trod upon my feet when he left the train at Vésinet."

The magistrate closed the window, then, turning to the unsummoned witness, asked:

"Are you sure of it?"

"Perfectly sure. I recognized him the minute I laid my eyes on him. I should know him among a thousand. His is one of those faces a person is not likely to forget. I am willing to swear to it, if necessary."

"Very well, sir. Will you be so kind as to hold yourself at my disposal for a day or two? I should like to bring the prisoner into your presence in the usual way, and have my clerk take down your formal deposition. The investigation will have to be begun over again, for your testimony is of the utmost importance. The identification would have been much less conclusive if I had proceeded otherwise, if I had ushered you formally into the presence of Monsieur de Mestras, for instance; but you could have no suspicion that it was he who was crossing the court-yard, and yet you recognized him instantly. The proof is conclusive."

"Yes, unquestionably," exclaimed the major, "and you will immediately declare the prisoner's innocence established."

"You must allow me to reserve my decision upon this point, sir. The mystery has not yet been cleared up, by any means, and until I have discovered the man who used the revolver, so unfortunately lost by the prisoner—"

"That man is the conductor who gave up the weapon four days after the crime, and it was Monsieur Golymine who bribed this man to assassinate Madame de Muire. I have told you so before, and I will prove it."

"You will be called upon to give your testimony on this point when I think proper, sir," said the magistrate, dryly. "The audience I granted you to-day is ended, and I must beg you to retire."

One can not dispute the decision of a magistrate when he is engaged in the exercise of his official duties, and the major left the office in a furious passion, but full of hope, for Médéric's speedy release seemed certain. In his opinion it was merely a question of time.

"Didn't I tell you that they would suspect him of complicity?" murmured Father Postel, greatly to Major Roland's surprise, as they descended the steps of the Palace side by side.

CHAPTER X.

So the major returned to Paris only moderately well satisfied with the result of his trip to Versailles. He returned alone, M. Postel having left him at the gate-way of the Palace to go and attend to some business matters.

The major had accordingly taken the address of the worthy merchant, who resided on the Rue de la Verrerie, and resolved to soon see him again, as it would henceforth be only through him that he could hope to gain news of the investigation that the magistrate was about to begin upon and entirely different basis. But he did not place much dependence upon the efforts of the former president of the Bureau of Commerce.

He depended chiefly upon himself, and yet he did not attempt to blind himself to the fact that by a rash impulse that he deeply regretted he had just barred the door of the investigating magistrate's office against him.

Médéric's situation had unquestionably improved in aspect, for he could no longer be accused of having fired the shot that killed Mme. de Muire; but as the worthy Postel had foreseen, a suspicion of complicity had instantly arisen.

An *alibi* had been established, of course; but to prove that a man has not bribed some other person to commit a crime is a much more difficult matter. Some other person is so vague! When the perpetrator of the crime is known, the aspect of the case undergoes an entire change; and this is almost always the condition in which a case is brought before the courts. The perpetrator of the crime has been arrested, and the accomplices do not appear upon the scene until afterward, when the principal denounces them, or the authorities have succeeded in discovering them; and when they are unjustly accused, they have it in their power to defend themselves by proving, for instance, that they have never had any intercourse with the culprit.

It was in this way that Médéric would have defended himself if the assassin of the countess had been under lock and key; but under the existing circumstances, what could he do? The magistrates, undoubtedly, would now say to him:

"You did not commit the murder; but you bribed some other person to commit it; and until we find the man you hired to put Madame de Muire out of the way, we can not release you."

On the other hand, Médéric, who had been kept in the strictest seclusion for three weeks, and who was entirely ignorant of the discoveries made by the major and Mlle. Lanoue, could not reply:

"Begin by arresting Count Golymine and his protégé, Maurevers. Question them, and see if they will dare to tell you that I ordered the murder—I, who have never even laid eyes on the conductor of the train, and who saw Golymine for the first time several hours after the murder."

George Roland, on his return from Versailles, found himself face to face with the same difficulty. To prove that Médéric was innocent he must first prove that Golymine and Maurevers were the culprits.

George did not feel the slightest doubt of this, since he had surprised them in secret conference; but proofs were needed, and he had none of a conclusive character to offer; besides, when he ventured to make an open accusation against the count at the close of the audience granted M. Postel, the magistrate had evidently taken offense, or, at least, had promptly silenced him.

So there was nothing left for him but to begin over again, and on leaving the railway-train at the Saint-Lazare Station, the major asked himself what he should do to repair the failure of his first attempt—a failure counter-balanced to some extent, it is true, by M. Postel's identification of the prisoner.

It would be a great disappointment to him to be obliged to return to Chatou without any good news for Mlle. Lanoue; but he did not know which way to turn to procure any. It was useless to think of extorting any information from Golymine, for open war was now declared between him and the major. Maurevers must be on duty, that is, unless he was resting at Vésinet; besides, Mlle. Lanoue was the only person who could hope for any success in that quarter.

To be sure, there was the Marquis de Brangue, who had been present at the death of the countess, and who claimed to have heard her last words. If one could believe this gentleman, who was as old, and rather more reliable than his friend Liscoat, Mme. de Muire, as she fell into his arms, had exclaimed:

" It is he!"

And these words would prove conclusively that she had both seen and recognized the man who fired at her, and from this fact those gentlemen had rather rashly concluded that Médéric de Mestras was the culprit.

Were they still of the same opinion? The major had neglected to question Liscoat upon this point; but he did not yet despair of convincing them to the contrary. He, for his part, thought the words " It is he!" might refer with equal likelihood to Golymine, if these gentlemen told the truth in asserting that Golymine had been the lover of the countess. at no very remote day; and if M. de Brangue might be brought to the same way of thinking his evidence might be of great service to Mederic.

The major accordingly said to himself that an interview with the marquis might be productive of some good. Only a short time after the crime George had announced his intention of calling upon that gentleman at an early day, and the time had perhaps come to make this visit.

The major had no particular reason to dislike M. de Brangue. That gentleman had never ventured to speak disrespectfully of Mlle. Lanoue in his presence, nor had he ever displayed as much animosity toward young Mestras as the Viscount de Liscoat. In spite of his faults, the marquis was regarded as an honorable man; and the major had every reason to believe that he was worthy of his reputation. He was an egotist, unquestionably, but he must be the possessor of some sterling qualities to be regarded as a friend by M. de Muire; besides, egotists are not prone to meddle with other people's affairs.

A brief review of these considerations made the major decide to go and see the marquis. He was not sure that the gentleman was still in Paris; but he could ascertain without much trouble, for he intended to pay a visit to the town residence of the Muires before leaving Chatou, and the marquis resided on the Rue de Madrid, which was only a few steps out of his way.

Great was his satisfaction on rounding the corner of the street mentioned to see M. de Brangue standing in the door-way of the house in which he lived, leisurely drawing on his gloves, before starting out for a walk. This seemed to be a day of meetings, and this was especially pleasing to the major, as it spared him the necessity of making a formal visit. He greatly preferred to waylay the marquis in the street, than to ring and request an interview which M. de Brangue might refuse to grant; so he quiekened his pace, perceiving with pleasure that M. de Brangue was already advancing to meet him with a smile upon his lips.

The old exquisite was extremely polite, and though he was of nearly the same age, and moved in the same circles as Liscoat, he was in the habit of showing much more courtesy to his friends and even to comparative strangers.

"I am very happy to meet you, sir," he said, shaking hands with Major George; "and I should like to make the most of my good fortune; so if you are going in the direc-

tion of the Park Mouceau, suppose we walk along together?"

" I should be charmed," replied the major, eagerly. "I
am on the way to the house of our friend Jacques."

"Then I will begin by inquiring about him. I know
that his health has not been impaired by the blow he has
sustained. Jacques is a pretty sturdy fellow, both mentally and physically; but tell me, is it true that he has sold
his charming villa to Golymine?"

" What, you have heard of that already?"

" Liscoat told me so a few moments ago. He said you
breakfasted with him this morning, and that you seemed
to be troubled by some doubts of the purchaser's financial
standing. I'll wager that Liscoat made him out a second
Crœsus."

" Rather; and I—"

" Liscoat has a sort of mania for foreigners. He knows
very little about this Golymine, who seems to me rather a
mysterious kind of person. He bears one of the oldest and
proudest names of Poland; but he has never proved to my
satisfaction that the name belongs to him."

" That is strange. Monsieur de Liscoat pretended that
you could vouch for his noble origin."

" This is saying too much; and when I see him again I
shall beg him not to burden me with a responsibility I absolutely decline to assume. The truth is, Golymine found
some persons willing to propose him for membership at the
club; but they may have taken him for what he is not. My
opinion is that Golymine is a Frenchman, and very possibly a Parisian. He established himself here only last year,
but whatever he claims to the contrary, he must have spent
his youth here, for he often alludes to events that took
place in Paris twenty years ago—matters that would never
be talked of in a foreign land. Now, if Golymine is really
a compatriot, he must have had private reasons of a weighty
nature for residing out of France until the present time."

"Then you are inclined to think that the man is an adventurer?"

"I could not swear to it, for I have no proofs of the fact; but I think so."

"If such is your opinion, marquis, I can certainly venture to tell you that I have even a worse opinion of him. I suspect him, and I hope to soon be in a position to openly accuse him, of being Madame de Muire's assassin."

"Whew!" exclaimed the marquis, half smiling, "that would be going rather too far, I think. I admit that an adventurer is not likely to shrink from any crime; but I do not see what possible object Golymine could have had in committing this particular crime. Besides, I recollect perfectly well that the poor woman, as she died in my arms, faltered the words I repeated to you a few moments afterward."

"I have not forgotten them. She said: 'It is he!' Ah, well, what of that? She knew Golymine, and she may have recognized him as the train passed."

"How did she become acquainted with him?"

"She used to meet him every summer at Aix, in Savoy. Monsieur de Liscoat even assures me that the count was her devoted admirer, if not her lover."

"I did hear him say something of the kind; but to tell the truth I had forgotten it. Still, I do not believe that Golymine has seen the countess since he came to Paris to live."

"I can not say about that; but he may have seen her unknown to any one, and as to the interest he may have had in putting her out of the way, I think I am beginning to understand that. The stocks and bonds in which Madame de Muire's private fortune was invested have all disappeared."

"Indeed!" interrupted the marquis, suddenly pausing to look George full in the face. "So that is the reason our friend is disposing of all his real estate. And you fancy that Golymine—"

" It is an idea that just occurred to me. If his relations with the countess had undergone no change, she might have intrusted these securities to him for investment, or even for sale."

" And now he will use the wife's money to purchase the property of the husband. That would be droll indeed!" said M. de Brangue, with the half-mocking, half-skeptical smile of a man of the world.

" It would be infamous," replied George, hastily, " and a scoundrel who would thus abuse the confidence of his lady love would certainly be quite capable of killing her to prevent her from claiming the fortune she had intrusted to his keeping."

" Oh, yes; I don't know which of the two crimes I should consider most ignoble. One is about as bad as the other. You present the matter to me in an entirely new light. I instinctively distrusted Golymine; but I should never have suspected him of such abominable crimes. It will be necessary to investigate this matter thoroughly in order to rid the club of such a scoundrel."

" And above all, to save an innocent man from condemnation."

" Young Mestras! That is true; I had forgotten. He is in prison, I believe."

" He has been kept in solitary confinement for three weeks. I have just returned from Versailles, but I was not allowed to see him; though he has been confronted by Golymine, who did his best to insure his conviction. The scoundrel is trying to mislead the authorities, and has succeeded admirably thus far."

" I begin to think they accused Monsieur de Mestras a little too hastily. I believed him guilty, however; and it must be admitted that I have had some grounds for the belief when I saw him come running from the direction of Vésinet."

" I have found a witness who traveled in the same compartment with him from Chatou."

"So much the better! But Liscoat said something to me about a revolver found on the train."

"By Golymine, probably, or by a rascal in his employ named Maurevers."

"Maurevers! The man's name is Maurevers?"

"Yes. He is a conductor on the Saint-Germain Railway."

"That is strange. Still we live in an age in which names have lost much of their significance. I should not even be surprised to learn that a Montmorency was acting as a stoker or brakeman somewhere."

"Pardon me; but I fail to see the connection."

"The Maurevers family is extinct; but I am related to a Baron de Méru, whose family name was Maurevers. He was much better known, however, under the name of Méru, which was that of an estate bestowed upon the family by Louis XIII. Evidently this conductor is neither closely nor remotely connected with my relative by marriage, who died some time ago; but the coincidence is none the less singular. And you say that this Maurevers—"

"Seems to hold relations of a very suspicious nature with Monsieur Golymine. I just surprised them both together at Versailles. They are evidently trying to ruin Médéric de Mestras; but I shall succeed in saving him."

"I hope so, indeed, my dear sir; and I would gladly assist you if I could, for I deeply regret having made such a mistake in regard to your young friend. It was all Liscoat's fault, however; and I should not be sorry to have an opportunity to show him that his judgment is not infallible. After accusing your protégé on the day of the crime, did he not declare that the bullet that struck the countess was intended for me? Why not for you, or Jacques, or Marcelle, or even for himself? We all have enemies, probably."

"Still there is no earthly reason why they should want to kill us; but if Madame de Muire had intrusted her private fortune to Golymine—"

" It will be necessary to prove that; and we shall find it a difficult matter, unless she made him give her a receipt, which is not very probable, or her husband would have found it before this time."

" I shall make a very careful search for it. Jacques has asked me to examine any piece of furniture in which Madame de Muire might have concealed papers, and it is for that purpose I am now going to his house."

" He acted wisely in intrusting this commission to you," said M. de Brangue, with an ironical smile. " No prudent husband will ever rummage among his wife's private papers. He might make some very disagreeable discoveries, while a trusty friend can make a judicious selection— preserve the important papers, such as receipts, leases, and contracts—and destroy all compromising letters."

" That will certainly be the plan I shall adopt. But as you have made this allusion to Madame de Muire's past, will you permit me to ask if there is any truth in Monsieur de Liscoat's assertions? He pretends that my old colonel, Médéric's father—"

" Was Madame de Muire's lover. Liscoat has told me so twenty times; but Liscoat's assertions in regard to such matters are not always worthy of credence. He loves to gossip, and to spread scandalous reports, which are not always true. I recollect that Colonel de Mestras was a frequent visitor at the Muire mansion; and I believe there was some talk about it at the time, but I, for my own part, never saw anything that would lead me to believe Liscoat's story. Still, I would not swear to the contrary any more than I would swear that Golymine has been one of the colonel's successors in the lady's affections. In such cases, the best and safest way is to express no decided opinion, either one way or the other, and that is exactly what I am doing now."

" I thank you, marquis," said the major gravely, struck by the contrast between this eminently sensible talk and M.

de Liscoat's flippancy. "You can scarcely realize how deeply I have been pained by the thought that my colonel had basely deceived his best friend; and I confess that I have felt not a little angry with this gentleman on account of his suspicions. I will even go so far as to say that I am not much surprised to find him siding with a man of Golymine's stamp."

"It is a great pity. Still it is not well to exaggerate. I have known Liscoat intimately for forty years, and he really is not a bad fellow at heart, though he is terribly vain and selfish. Age has not corrected these faults, nor that of speaking rather disrespectfully of all ladies, even though he still tries to please them. What would you say if I should tell you that at this very time he is trying to make a conquest of Marcelle de Muire's governess?"

George Roland gave a quick start; then quickly controlling himself, said coldly:

"I do not think that he will succeed."

"Nor do I," replied M. de Brangue, laughing. "But when such a fancy takes possession of him he shrinks from no means that will enable him to gratify it."

"What! even violence? I advise him not to resort to that. He will be sorry for it if he does, I swear!"

"I do not think he will go as far as that; but he is quite capable of setting a trap for the young girl. That is his way; and he has already got into several pretty unpleasant scrapes with relatives of victims."

"This time he will get into one with me. Mademoiselle Lanouc is the friend, rather than the governess, of Marcelle de Muire; and if Monsieur de Liscoat should venture to make such an attempt I shall make it my business to drive him back into the path of rectitude again."

"And you would do perfectly right. He needs a lesson badly."

"But what are his plans?"

"He has not confided them to me because he knows

that I should make fun of him; but I can guess them, especially as I have learned that he has just furnished a pretty little house near Trouville. He did not tell me so; I learned the fact through my upholsterer, of whom he too is a patron. The cage is ready. All that is lacking now is the bird; and if he knows one to his taste he will spare no pains to capture it. But here is the Muire mansion, my dear sir; and I must not think of such a thing as taking you any further. I am delighted to have had an opportunity to chat with you, and I trust you will not regret having allowed me to accompany you to the door of the house once occupied by our unfortunate friend. I thank you heartily for having enlightened me in regard to this Golymine; and I assure you that if I should be called upon to take sides for or against him, I shall certainly espouse the cause of your young friend."

———

CHAPTER XI.

With this parting assurance M. de Brangue shook hands with his companion, and then continued his walk toward the Park Morceau.

He left the major in a very uncomfortable frame of mind, though he was not sorry to have won over to the cause an influential person whom he had, up to this time, regarded as an enemy.

The major could not expect any very valuable assistance from M. de Brangue; but it was something to have converted him to more correct ideas in regard to the Chatou tragedy.

Then, too, it was something to have gained an insight into the real character and designs of the Viscount de Liscoat, to whom, unfortunately, he had first applied for information. He felt very little real fear of his machinations, however, though he resolved to warn Mlle. Lanoue, who would certainly know how to protect herself; but Médéric was still in prison, and conclusive proofs against Golymine were still wanting.

George did not yet despair of finding some during his visit to the Muire mansion, and he lost no time in entering it.

When he moved out to the Oaks to spend the summer M. de Muire had taken all his servants with him, and the house on the Boulevard Malesherbes was guarded only by the *concierge*, an old family servant, not quite as advanced in years as François, but equally faithful.

His name was Carcenac, and he had served in a regiment which at the beginning of the campaign of 1870 belonged to the same brigade as the regiment commanded by Col. Mestras. George had not been acquainted with him while he was in the army, but he knew that the worthy man had taken part in the battle of Gravelotte, and that M. de Muire had taken him into his service in memory of his friend Mestras, who fell upon this battle-field.

In physique, Carcenac was tall, slender, and dark-complexioned, with an angular face of about the thickness of a knife-blade; in character he was certainly the most taciturn *concierge* in Paris, and the most untiring in the discharge of his duties. He had never married for fear of being led to neglect his duties by domestic cares and responsibilities, and he prevented any one from gaining access to the house intrusted to his charge as effectually as three of the most formidable watch-dogs could have done.

He worshiped his employer, and was extremely fond of George Roland, whom he always addressed as major, and whom he invariably greeted with a military salute.

He liked Médéric, too, though the latter was not nearly as great a favorite as the major, from the fact that this son of the gallant colonel had not adopted his father's profession. Carcenac could not understand why such an agile, well-built fellow was not an officer of cavalry.

He was smoking in the vestibule when George presented himself, but hastily dropped his pipe to assume the prescribed attitude of a trooper in the presence of a superior in rank—both heels together, and right hand lifted to a level with his forehead, palm outward.

" How are you, my friend?" said George. " How are things going on here?"

" All right, major," replied the old soldier. " I have nothing new to report. But yes, I have. There was a gentleman here yesterday to see the house."

" Did you admit him?"

" I was obliged to. He showed me a letter from the count, giving him permission to go through the whole house from top to bottom.''

" Did he tell his name?"

" Yes; he calls himself Galoubine, or Golachine, or something of the kind. He is a Russian."

" I suspected it," muttered George. " He has lost no time, certainly. But you accompanied him, I suppose, during his tour of inspection?"

" You may rest assured that I did, major. I did not leave him for an instant. I began by closing the *porte cochère* as soon as he entered."

" Did you take him for a thief?''

" Not exactly; but I didn't like his face, I must admit. Besides, one can not be too careful with these foreigners. This one pretends that he wants to purchase the house. I don't know as the count has any idea of selling it to him; but I know that I sha'n't remain in the service of that conceited fool."

" Had you ever seen him before you showed him the house?''

" Never, major. I don't know whether the count is acquainted with him or not; but I am sure he never came here. But excuse me for asking the question, is it true that the count intends to dispose of all his real estate?"

"His wife's death has been such a blow to him that he thinks of retiring into the country, I believe."

"I will go with him wherever he goes, if he wants me."

"I think he knows that, and I shall advise him to take you with him. But I, too, have called to go through the house, though not with any intention of purchasing it. The count wishes me to bring him some papers that were left here, and as he doesn't exactly know where they are I shall be obliged to search for them. Madame de Muire's rooms are locked, I suppose?"

"Yes, major, and the count has not set foot in them since the day of the funeral. But I have the keys, and I will open the apartments for you."

"Very well, let us go up. But tell me, did the Russian see these rooms yesterday?"

"You may rest assured that he did, though I was sorry enough to be obliged to show them to him. But there was no help for it. I was obliged to carry out the count's orders. I took the Cossack there, and I thought I should never get him out of the rooms. He examined every piece of furniture so long and carefully that one might have supposed him an appraiser. If he had dared, I am sure he would have opened the desks and the bureau drawers to see what there was inside; and I could see very plainly that he was strongly inclined to offer me some money to leave him alone. If I were in the count's place I should distrust this man."

"Did he say anything about coming again when he left?"

"No, major; but if he does I shall not let him in, unless he brings me a new order signed by the count."

"That is right, and you had better see that everything is securely fastened up at night. The window of Madame de Muire's apartments overlook the garden, you recollect."

"But so do those of my lodge, and I sleep with one eye open. There is no danger that any one will get into the house in that way. Besides, you know that I have two big watch-dogs. We used to keep them tied in the stable, but since I have been here alone, I let them loose every evening, and if the Russian should take it into his head to get over the wall into the garden he would only make one good mouthful for them."

George and his guide had now reached the second floor, and Carcenac, who had a large bunch of keys in his hand, proceeded to open the door that led into the suite of apartments formerly occupied by Marcelle and her mother.

To reach Mme. de Muire's bed chamber, it was necessary to pass through Marcelle's bedroom, and also through the boudoir where Marcelle had seen Médéric for the last time. The major did not pause there, though the scene recurred to his mind very forcibly. This was no time to brood over the past, however, for he was anxious to begin his search, especially as Golymine's visit had aroused his suspicions. Golymine certainly had not examined the furniture for the purpose of estimating its value. The contents interested him much more than the furniture itself, and George, who was in the same condition, determined to finish his search that very day, for he suspected Golymine of a plot to secure papers which might ruin him.

The bed curtains in the chamber formerly occupied by the countess were closely drawn, and the tightly closed shutters admitted only a dim light that scarcely enabled a person to distinguish the articles of furniture in the room. The major began operations by having all the windows thrown open, and in a moment the entire apartment was flooded by the dazzling light of a glorious midsummer day.

George Roland had never entered this room before, not even on the day of the funeral, for the body of the deceased countess having been brought from Vésinet only an hour before the ceremony, was carried only into the hall of the mansion.

He was a little surprised to see that the furniture and ornaments of the apartment were of no artistic merit whatever, being merely handsome and expensive, without bearing the slightest stamp of individuality. The commonplace luxury and display that content the wealthy *bourgeoisie* pervaded the chamber.

And in fact the Countess de Muire, *née* Plantier, was nothing more nor less. Since her marriage with a nobleman she had learned the ways and customs of the fashionable circles into which this alliance had secured her an entrance; but taste is not so easily acquired as *savoir faire,* and she manifested a total want of it, even in her toilets, to the very great chagrin of her husband, and possibly of others.

But she had been very beautiful, and with some women beauty seems to be a compensation for all deficiencies.

Marcelle, very fortunately, resembled her only in appearance, being much more refined in her tastes and distinguished in appearance.

The major, who had not come here to make comparisons between the mother and daughter, dismissed Carcenac, adjuring him to let no one enter the house, and then set to work to fulfill the delicate mission his friend Jacques had intrusted to him.

The count had not done things by halves, for he had given the major the keys of every piece of furniture, even those the countess always kept about her, the tiny gilded keys that could be worn as jewels.

There was one that her husband had detached from a bracelet which she always wore, and which was upon her arm on the day of her death; and this, most probably, was the key to the receptacle in which Mme. de Muire kept her private papers.

Had M. de Muire made use of it to open the secret drawer to which it probably belonged? He had vouchsafed no information upon this point, but George judged, with every appearance of reason, that the search he was about to continue had not been pushed very far. Overcome with grief, and more engrossed by regrets for his daughter's disappointment than by money matters, M. de Muire had yielded to despondency, and become to a great extent resigned to financial ruin, without making any very energetic attempts to recover the missing wealth; hence, the major was not without hope that this fortune was not lost, and that a thorough search would at least enable him to ascertain what Mme. de Muire had done with it.

It was not improbable, too, that he might find some letters from Golymine, and these might, perhaps, reveal a breach of confidence on the part of this scoundrel and to the detriment of the unfortunate woman whom he had murdered in order to effectually prevent any complaint.

In the apartment there were three or four articles of furniture which might contain secret drawers. These were a large *chiffonnier*, with elaborately wrought brass handles on the drawers, a cylinder desk, a rosewood cabinet, and one of much older date, in ebony, inlaid with ivory in the Italian style of the Renaissance.

The major decided to first explore the *chiffonnier*, whose capacious drawers might contain mountains of papers. All the archives of the ancient Muire family might easily have been stored there, but the countess, who had no ancestors, used it only as a receptacle for articles of dress, and the drawers were filled to overflowing with dozens of pairs of gloves, ribbons of every color, parasols and fans; but not the slightest scrap of writing was to be found among all these gewgaws.

The rosewood cabinet contained only invitations to dinners, balls and receptions, an inventory of which was soon concluded.

The cylinder desk had evidently been used by Mme. de Muire exclusively for her business correspondence. The major found in it a large book, in which she kept an account of her receipts and expenditures, but the figures only were given. There was no clew to the source from which the receipts were derived, nor the reason of the outlays. In this ledger, which was in all other respects very neatly and systematically kept, there were only such entries as " On such a day paid out so much; received so much.''

This record, though it gave the major a pretty correct idea of the amount of the lady's income, did not throw any light upon the manner in which Marcelle's mother had invested her income, nor upon her present financial condition. He could see that up to the fifteenth of June, four days before the death of the countess, the lady's receipts had exceeded her expenditures by several thousand francs; but M. de Muire had found this money in a small safe near the bed—a safe with a combination lock with which he was familiar, his wife having often requested him to open it while she was at the sea-shore.

Certainly if she had any secrets it was not in this elegant safe in imitation of buhl that she had concealed them, so George very sensibly concluded that he might spare himself the trouble of examining it.

After exploring the secretary from top to bottom, and satisfying himself that it was of solid wood, without a lining of any sort, he proceeded to examine the ebony cabinet, which was in the form of a shrine, supported by a massive pedestal, and which stood close to the wall, which was hung with crimson silk.

This cabinet was divided into three compartments, secured by three doors that the major opened without difficulty with the same key. He then saw on the right and on the left side two rows of drawers separated by quite a deep recess which contained nothing save a miniature portrait of Marcelle as a child.

The drawers were empty.

The major, though considerably disconcerted, would not yet acknowledge himself defeated. If a secret hiding-place existed anywhere, he felt that it must be in this quaint piece of furniture. The difficulty was to find it.

He sounded the sides of the recess carefully, and pressed hard upon its floor, but without any result whatever.

At last, by dint of careful examination, he fancied he detected a slight unevenness in one of the ivory incrustations that adorned the lower part of this sort of tabernacle, and he very opportunely recollected that he had not yet found a use for the infinitesimal key which never left Mme. de Muire's person.

This key would perhaps fit into this tiny seam which might be an almost invisible lock.

The major tried it, and found that it would enter the hole, and he had scarcely given it a turn from right to left before the bottom of the cabinet suddenly dropped down, disclosing to view a row of pigeon-holes, each of which contained a bundle of letters tied with a piece of pink or blue ribbon.

These carefully preserved letters contained no valuable securities, but they would have been no more precious in George Roland's eyes if they had contained thousand franc notes, for everything seemed to indicate that they contained a complete history of the deceased lady's love affairs.

He paused a moment before touching them, however, and his hand trembled when he at last took up the first package.

There were three, but this was the largest, and must have contained nearly or quite a hundred letters, written upon thick paper, to which time had imparted a deep yellow tint.

The major had neither the time nor the wish to peruse them all, but he drew one out from beneath the ribbon that bound them, and read the missive straight through to the end. It bore no signature, not even a Christian name; but it was certainly a love letter, or at least the letter of a person who had loved and been loved too late. It was ardent, but at the same time respectful—perfectly so. There were frequent allusions to insurmountable obstacles. Had these obstacles been surmounted? To ascertain it would be necessary to peruse the entire correspondence, but George, supposing that the letters were arranged in their chronological order, drew out the last one in the bundle, and found only these words:

"Once more farewell. I love you more than ever, and I feel a presentiment that I shall never see you again. Be happy, but think of me sometimes. If I fall, my last thought will be of you."

This, too, bore no signature. Who was the writer of these letters? George Roland had seen his colonel's handwriting several times, but that was many years before, and he did not feel at all sure of his ability to recognize it after so long an interval. He said to himself, however, that a careful search among his own papers might enable him to find some order written by M. de Mestras, which he could compare with these letters addressed to the countess. At all events, Médéric must certainly possess some of his father's letters, and by and by, when he was restored to liberty, he certainly would not refuse to show them to his best friend. It was quite possible that they had been seized after his arrest, but the authorities would be obliged to restore them to him when his innocence was established.

But however this might be, the thing of paramount importance was to prove that Golymine had had an interest in removing Mme. de Muire, and in thus preventing her from reclaiming the greater part of her fortune; so deferring a further examination of this anonymous correspondence until some future day, he put the letters in his pocket, and picked up the next package.

This consisted of about twenty letters, all very short, but highly significant, and signed in full, Charles Dubrac. The billets-doux of this dashing hussar, however, had no interest for George Roland, who slipped them in his pocket with the firm intention of destroying them that very night.

The third package was nearly as voluminous as the first, but was of a much more recent date, judging from the freshness of the paper.

The signature was a single initial, a G, but nearly all of them bore at the top of the first page a count's coronet, and the major soon became satisfied that Golymine was the writer.

These letters must be read immediately and carefully, as it was almost certain that they would throw some light upon the antecedents of this pretended count and his relations with Mme. de Muire; so George, after satisfying himself that there was nothing more in the little ebony cabinet, closed it, and then seated himself by the window and proceeded to read each letter through from beginning to end.

None of them bore any date, except the day of the week, nor any address; but the oldest had certainly been written at Aix in Savoy, for there were allusions to sails upon Lake Bourget, and to excursions to the Abbey of Haute-Combe; nor did they leave the reader in any doubt as to the nature of the relations that then existed between Golymine and the countess. There had been several breaks in the correspondence, however. Once, more than two years elapsed without a meeting of the lovers, but it was easy to see that during the years in which they met only at Aix the idea of settling in France had never once entered Golymine's head.

The last letters indicated a still longer break in the correspondence; in fact, almost a rupture. The style had also undergone an entire change. To ardent expressions of tenderness had succeeded the affectionate language of a former lover, who is now only a friend. But this friend resided in Paris, and received occasional visits from Mme. de Muire. He expressed regret at his inability to visit her, and his intention of making a formal call upon M. de Muire, whom he had met again at the club, after a slight acquaintance at the springs, several years before. In those written at a still later day he made frequent allusions to business matters, and advised the countess to invest her money in the same corporation that yielded him such satisfactory returns.

The more the major read of these letters the more hopeful he became that he should find the proof he was seeking, and find it he did. The last letter ended as follows:

"It is done, my fair friend. Your money is invested as you desired, and the investment will yield you a return of at least ten per cent. this year. At our next interview I will give you the Austrian banks' receipt for the same, and in the meantime, this letter, to which I dare not sign my name, for reasons you perfectly understand, is equivalent to a receipt."

"At last!" exclaimed George, "I have you at last, you wretch! Now I can return to the Oaks. Hélène will be deeply grateful to me, and Marcelle will overwhelm me with thanks when I restore Médéric to her, as I shall certainly be able to do in a few days."

George would have done well to add: "If it be the will of God," as the Mussulman never fails to do.

The future belongs to no one, and the future had cruel disappointments in store for them all.

CHAPTER XII.

While Major George was collecting proofs against Golymine, both in Paris and Versailles, the inmates of the château were spending a very sad and gloomy day.

The Count de Muire, who seemed to be even more depressed in spirits than usual, did not make his appearance at the breakfast-table, and the two young girls after the repast was concluded, sought a shelter from the heat of the July sun in the garden, and there held a long conference together.

Marcelle seemed to take a melancholy pleasure in talking over her lost happiness, and she could talk of this only to Mlle. Lanoue, as her father had forbidden her to utter Médéric's name in his presence; and Mlle. Lanoue consoled her, comforted her, and encouraged her to hope, though with only partial success, however.

She could do no more, unless she told her friend about her visits to Mme. Maurevers, and explained the major's plans, and she had promised to say nothing about all that until she and her ally had accomplished their object.

What would be the use of awakening in the breast of Médéric's betrothed hopes that might never be realized? Much less could she tell the young girl of the unexpected declaration of love and offer of marriage that had been made to her in the forest of Vésinet. But though she guarded her secret carefully, it engrossed her mind more than she was willing to admit to herself. Resolved to remain in her present humble position rather than set foot in the flowery paths that lead young girls to wealth and dishonor, Hélène had nevertheless not entirely given up the idea of marrying some day, and she was not at all particular about marrying a man of her own age. She esteemed George Roland highly and had the most implicit confidence in him. He was very good-looking, and she admired his distinguished bearing and manly face. Mlle. Lanoue saw but one fault in him; he was too rich for her, who had nothing; but this very fault had only made her the more afraid that she might allow herself to love him.

She already began to reproach herself for having told him her life-history, not that she believed him capable of abusing her confidence, but because she feared he would mistake the feeling that had led her to reveal to him what she had never disclosed to any other person, not even to the dear pupil who concealed nothing from her.

But in spite of all her efforts during the last twenty-four hours her mind had been constantly occupied with thoughts

of this generous gentleman who had so entirely devoted
himself to the defense of a just cause. She had longed to
accompany him to Paris, whither he was going in pursuit
of further information about Golymine, and she was now
awaiting his return with impatience, the delay appearing
all the more intolerable from the fact that Marcelle, unconsciously, of course, seemed to take a strange satisfaction
in asking her the most embarrassing questions.

The poor child had begun by lamenting her mother's
death, and this very naturally led her to speak of her betrothed, who had no friend left now but Major George.

"Why does my father curse him?" she asked, trying to
read her friend's thoughts in her face. "Why, instead of
standing by him in this terrible ordeal, does he tell me that
he will never see Médéric again? He knows that Médéric
is not guilty, and that his innocence will be established
sooner or later. And, think of it, he condemns him without a hearing. He even forbids me to love him. He has
driven him from his heart."

"He yielded to the impulse of the moment," said Mlle.
Lanoue. "Think, Marcelle, what his feelings must have
been when he was told that Monsieur de Mestras was accused of this atrocious crime. He certainly hoped, and
still hopes, that Monsieur de Mestras will vindicate himself; but he is obliged to pay some regard to the opinion of
the world, and he very probably says to himself that the
world would disapprove of this marriage, even if your betrothed should be restored to liberty. This would be the
case, unquestionably, if there should remain the shadow of
a doubt in regard to your lover's innocence; but his vindication will be so startling and so conclusive that your father will feel that he owes him reparation."

"No, I know him. It is not a fear of malicious tongues
that has led him to abandon Médéric. He despises gossip
and calumny. There must be some other objection."

"What?" exclaimed Hélène, greatly astonished.

"I don't know, but I am sure there is. And my father is not the only person who is opposed to my marriage. Monsieur Roland has made no open objection, but I can see that he does not approve of it."

"He? Médéric's best friend? He who has defended him constantly for the past three weeks?"

"Yes; I am aware that he is doing everything in his power to insure Médéric's release; but I have not forgotten that my father cosulted Major Roland on the day of the arrest. The question was the date of my marriage. I proposed the fifteenth of October, but Monsieur George advised my father to wait, and when I suggested that Médéric should come and stay with us at the Oaks, the major said that it would be better for him to remain in the city as before."

"You have an admirable memory, my dear Marcelle," replied Mlle. Lanoue, forcing a smile; "and I really do not know what to say in reply. You see Monsieur Roland every day. Have you ever questioned him on the subject?"

"I have not dared," murmured the girl.

"Perhaps it is better that you should not; but wait until he has succeeded in discovering the real culprit. I think he is on the scoundrel's track; and I am sure that he went to Paris this morning in the hope of hunting him down very soon—possibly to-day."

Marcelle shook her head sadly, but silently, and Hélène saw that she was by no means satisfied.

They had been sitting together under the trees a long time, and as the sun sunk in the horizon, the coolness of the evening air began to make itself sensibly felt; so Mlle. Lanoue proposed a return to the house, and Marcelle assented. In her present state of mind it mattered very little to her whether she was out-of-doors, or in her own room, so the two girls wended their way toward the house. But Hélène had no intention of accompanying her pupil in-doors; she was anxious to see the major as soon as possible in order to learn what news he had brought from Paris, and she felt sure that his arrival would not be much longer deferred, as he intended to take the train that left the city at 5:30. She accordingly resolved to go and meet him, so telling Marcelle that she wanted to take a short walk before dinner, she advised her to go and join her father, who had just appeared upon the balcony, and then started down a road that forked about a hundred yards from the villa. It was necessary to turn to the right to reach Chatou, and to the left to reach Vésinet. Hélène intended to take the road leading to the right; but before she reached the point of intersection she saw a woman whom she did not at first recognize, making signs to her in the distance.

She paused to await her approach, and, observing this fact, the woman began to run toward Hélène, waving her arms wildly in the air, like a messenger who is the bearer of important news.

As soon as she was near enough to be heard, she cried, frantically:

"It is all over! I shall never see him again!"

Mlle. Lanoue did not understand the full import of this despairing exclamation at first, but she soon recognized Mme. Maurevers, and concluded that she must be referring to her husband.

This fallen princess rushed up with hair streaming in the wind, a torn dress, and slippers down at the heel, shrieking and gesticulating like the Neapolitan that she was.

"Calm yourself, madame," said Hélène, "and tell me what has happened, and what I can do for you?"

"Julien has been dismissed," replied the conductor's wife, in the same excited manner, "and my children will perish of hunger if you do not come to their relief."

This news of Maurevers's dismissal was not calculated to grieve Mlle. Lanoue, who would not have been sorry to hear of his arrest; but she was too kind-hearted not to sympathize with the grief of this poverty-stricken mother, whose children were crying for bread.

"I will not desert them. I promise you that, even if their father does," she said, kindly.

"He has gone, never to return."

"What has happened?"

"He was on duty all day yesterday, and spent the night in Paris. I thought everything had been satisfactorily arranged, and that nothing more would be said about that unfortunate affair of the pistol. But to-day, only about an hour ago, he came home, and he had no sooner entered the house than I saw that we were lost. He showed me a letter from the superintendent, notifying him of his dismissal, and—"

"That is very unfortunate; still, he may succeed in finding employment elsewhere."

"Oh, if that were all, I would not mind!"

"What is it, then?"

"They now accuse him of being the accomplice of the scoundrel that murdered the countess. He is afraid that he will be arrested, and as he doesn't want to go to prison, he came to tell me that he intended to—to—"

"To kill himself?"

"Yes; if he does not succeed in making his escape to a foreign land. And he will not succeed in doing that, for he has no money. He could not even give me enough to buy the children food for two days. I tried to dissuade him; I entreated him to vindicate himself; but he would not listen. He seemed to have lost his senses. After telling me this he rushed off across the fields, and I shall never see him again. I tell you, madame, there is nothing left for me to do but throw myself into the Seine with my poor children."

"Do not talk in this way, madame; God will protect them; and I am willing to do all in my power to assist them and you. But you told me that your husband had an influential friend—"

"That Russian count? Yes; he interested himself in

Julien's behalf, but when one is unfortunate one loses all one's friends; besides, I should not be surprised if this was all Golymine's work."

"How so?" inquired Hélène, hastily.

"Julien gave me to understand that it was Golymine who advised him first to keep the revolver, and afterward to surrender it to the station-keeper at Saint-Germain."

This confession was well worth remembering, and Mlle. Lanoue resolved to repeat it to the major; but she refrained from making any comment, for fear of letting Mme. Maurevers see that she intended to use it against Mme. de Muire's assassin at some future day; so she only remarked:

"In that case, you certainly have reason to hope that the foreign gentleman who gave your husband such bad advice will feel obliged to befriend him now."

"Julien counts upon that, but he is deluding himself perhaps."

"He must have gone straight to the count's house on leaving you."

"I don't know about that. He rushed off like a madman."

"But you must certainly know where the gentleman lives?"

"No; Julien never told me."

"But you know him?"

"I saw him several years ago, immediately after our marriage, when we had money; but he didn't fancy me, and I couldn't bear him. I knew that he was angry with Julien for having married me, and since we have been in France he hasn't troubled himself any more about me than if I were not in existence. If he has done anything for Julien it was only because he thought Julien might be of service to him. He will do nothing for me nor for my children."

"I think you must be mistaken. If it be really true that he has got your husband into a scrape he must be afraid that you will disclose the fact, and if you should go to see him he would not dare to refuse you assistance. Why do you not apply to him? I will procure his address for you. Monsieur de Muire knows it."

" Monsieur de Muire? the husband of the kind countess?"

" The same. Monsieur Golymine came yesterday to look at the Oaks. He thinks of purchasing it. In fact, I believe the bargain is already made."

" Then he will pay you another visit?"

" Very probably."

" If he does, mademoiselle, I beseech you not to let him go away without my seeing him. I dare not ask you to bring him to Vésinet, where I could show him how poor I am, but I ask you, in pity, to send for me while he is at the Oaks. Oh! don't be afraid; I shall not intrude at the château—dressed as I am, the servants would drive me from the door—but I will watch for him at the gate and stop the count when he comes out. I am going to make him tell me what he has done with Julien."

This unexpected proposal took Mlle. Lanoue by surprise, and she hardly knew what to reply; but she took good care not to reject it. She saw in it a means of tearing asunder the veil of mystery which enshrouded this Golymine; besides, before refusing she wished to consult Major Roland, whose return could not be much longer delayed."

" Madame," she said, after a moment's silence, " I can now promise you only one thing, which is that you shall see Count Golymine either at his own house or here. I am now expecting some one who will tell you how you can manage to meet this gentleman. Promise me, in return, not to leave Vésinet without informing me, and not to speak of me to any one."

" To whom should I be likely to speak of you!" exclaimed the descendant of the princely Orbitellos. " Who would ever think of coming to see me in the dilapidated hut in which I live? The village people think me beneath their notice, and snub me upon every occasion. Julien's friends—no, he has no friends—I mean the other railway employés, are not aware of my existence. But for you, who have so often assisted me, I should have perished of starvation, and my only hope is in you. Your words are commands for me, and I shall not leave this neighborhood so long as you remain in it. Where should I go? My own family has cast me off since I married Julien.''

'' And yet you say that your husband was well born?''

'' He is of the noblest lineage; but his relatives have done exactly what mine did. They have disowned him.''

Mlle. Lanoue felt satisfied that this man must have been guilty of grave misdemeanors to be thus ostracized, and became more and more confident that he had been implicated in Mme. de Muire's assassination, but she very wisely kept these reflections to herself.

'' What good would it do to make this unfortunate victim of an unscrupulous man still more miserable?'' she thought. '' It would be much more sensible to give her the pecuniary assistance of which she is in such sore need;'' so drawing a fifty-franc note from her pocket-book she handed it to her companion, who gratefully accepted it.

'' We now understand each other,'' remarked Hélène, '' and I hope that we shall see each other every day. Will you promise to meet me to-morrow at the same hour on this road?''

'' I will be here, mademoiselle,'' replied the *ci-devant* princess promptly. '' And even if Julien should come in search of me I will not leave without seeing you. But he will not come,'' she added, hanging her head.

It was very evident that she had ceased to believe in her husband's innocence, and even in the love of this degraded wretch who thought only of escaping well-deserved punishment without troubling himself about the fate of his wife and children.

There was more than one question that Mlle. Lanoue would have been glad to put to her companion; but just then she perceived the major hastily rounding a curve in the road; so, having many things to ask him and as many more to tell him, she did not wish their meeting to take place in Mme. Maurevers's presence.

That unfortunate woman, however grateful she might be, could not take sides against her husband; and Hélène foresaw that Major Roland would declare war upon him and pursue him to the death as soon as he learned what had taken place.

So Hélène allowed her to retrace her steps toward Vésinet, though not without giving her a cordial pressure of the hand; for although she censured this wife's infatuation for an unworthy husband, she could not help pitying the mother of three children who were worse than fatherless; and after watching her until she disappeared from sight behind a clump of trees she advanced to meet the major, who had recognized her, and who was already bowing to her in the distance. Both by his manner and expression she guessed that he was the bearer of good news; and when they met the first word she said to him was:

"Well?"

"Well, mademoiselle," replied George, joyfully, "I have not wasted my time to-day. I must tell you all about my trip to the city. It will be quite a long story, for it has been a very eventful day. But before I begin will you allow me to ask you with whom you were just talking?"

"With the wife of the conductor who found the revolver—"

"And who is Golymine's tool. I know him by sight, now; I surprised them together at Versailles."

"At Versailles! You have been to Versailles? Did you see Monsieur de Mestras?"

"Alas, no; but I found a man who can prove that Médéric is innocent. Indeed, the work is half completed already."

"Ah! how happy Marcelle will be!" exclaimed Hélène. "And it will be to you that she will owe her happiness."

"It is not yet time to announce it to her," replied the major. "It would not do to arouse any false hopes: and you will be of the same opinion, mademoiselle, when you learn what just occurred at Versailles."

And he immediately proceeded to give her a full account of his adventures after his departure from the Saint-Lazare railway station. He said nothing, however, about his breakfast with M. de Liscoat, his conversation with M. de Brangue, and, above all, his examination of the private papers of the countess, these being subjects upon which he could not speak freely to Mlle. Lanoue.

But there was nothing to prevent him from relating in detail all the incidents of his providential meeting with M. Postel, and of his interview with the investigating magistrate.

Hélène listened with an emotion she made no effort to conceal, nor could she restrain her tears when her companion began to relate how good M. Postel had recognized Médéric at the very first glance. But when the major came to the conclusion, and told her that the magistrate had refused to admit that the proof was conclusive, and had dryly requested the major to retire without promising him anything, she exclaimed scornfully:

"Is it possible that the magistrate can close his eyes to this evidence, and that Monsieur de Mestras must remain in prison until the authorities discover the assassin? Is it not enough to prove that it was not Monsieur de Mestras who fired the revolver? How dare they make this absurd charge of complicity against him?"

"It seems incredible, but such is the case, nevertheless."

"But perhaps they will never find the assassin. I suspected Maurevers, and I still suspect him, especially as his wife just told me that he had fled; but we have no proofs."

"How long since?" inquired the major, hastily.

"About an hour ago, probably. He only came home to

tell his unfortunate wife that he was afraid of being arrested, so he had made all his arrangements for flight, and that
she would never see him again.''

" Did she say anything to you about Golymine?''

" She cursed him as the cause of this, her crowning misfortune, and thinks that Golymine intends to desert her
husband after ruining him.''

" I am of an entirely different opinion. Golymine can
not desert his accomplice; and as Golymine has not left
Paris, Maurevers must still be in the city or vicinity. "

" His accomplice! Then you, too, believe that this Russian—''

" I thought at first that it was Golymine who killed
Madame de Muire; but I now think that he bribed Mau-
revers to kill her; and I know why he did it. Madame de
Muire had intrusted her fortune to Golymine.''

" Have you any proof of that?''

" I have in my pocket a letter in which he acknowledges the receipt of all Madame de Muire's bonds and
securities.''

" And does he know that this letter is in your possession?''

" No; he hasn't the slightest suspicion of the fact very
fortunately; for if he had he would be out of France before this time. "

" And you will only have to show this letter to the judge
to insure Médéric's instant release, I suppose?''

" That is exactly what I intend to do. "

" What are you waiting for?''

" Nothing; and my first impulse was to hasten back to
Versailles, and confide my discovery to this doubting judge;
but I have been thinking the matter over, and now I am a
little in doubt as to what course to pursue. "

" Why?''

" For a reason that I should not hesitate to confide to
my wife if I were married—in fact, I should certainly consult my wife—for I am sure that her decision would be the

right one; but I can hardly consult—a young, unmarried lady,'' said George, smiling.

"Say rather an old maid," stammered Hélène, blushing. "Haven't I told you that I am twenty-five?"

"One certainly would not think so," replied the major, gallantly; "but even if you were thirty I should not feel at liberty to broach such a subject to you, while—"

"Go on, if you please, sir."

"While if you were but eighteen, I could speak to you with perfect frankness if—if I were sure we were to be married this year."

This statement of the case was very plain; but it was also so delicate that Mlle. Lanoue could not take offense.

"You take an unfair advantage of the situation," she murmured.

"Possibly; but—may I speak? I await your answer."

CHAPTER XIII.

THE moment was really a solemn one, for Hélène understood perfectly well that if she answered in the affirmative it would be equivalent to a promise of marriage.

She hesitated. She dared not look at George Roland for fear that he might read her feelings in her eyes, so she stood gazing straight before her at the lofty trees, whose tops, gilded by the last rays of the setting sun, stood out clearly against the horizon.

The air was warm and balmy; the breeze sighed gently through the leafy branches, and the birds sung sweetly as they flitted from tree to tree.

Everything around Hélène seemed to conspire to touch a heart full of repressed tenderness. Reared to sacrifice herself for others, and to suppress her deepest feelings, the orphan girl seemed to suddenly enter upon a new life on hearing this brave and honorable man ask her to plight him her troth under this azure heaven—the abode of the beneficent Maker, to whom he seemed to appeal as a witness to the sincerity of his love.

There are impulses which a woman can not resist, and to which she never repents of having yielded.

"Tell me all," she murmured, shyly, at last.

George took her hand, pressed an ardent but respectful kiss upon it, then continued gayly:

"It is settled, now. I belong to you; you belong to me; we belong to each other—and for our whole life. All the rest is a mere ceremony which shall take place on any day that you will appoint. Only I beg that you will not defer it too long."

"It shall be on the day that Marcelle marries Médéric de Mestras," replied the young girl, with a covert meaning that the major understood perfectly.

"Yesterday I should have asked you to fix upon a less uncertain date," he replied. "To-day I accept your decision, for I am now sure that there is nothing to prevent their speedy marriage."

"Do you really mean it?" exclaimed Mlle. Lanoue.

"At least, nothing except the opposition of my old friend, Jacques de Muire; and I hope to soon convert him to my way of thinking. Now that you are to be my wife, I have nothing to conceal from you, so I may as well tell you here and now that I have just made some painful discoveries, which I should not feel at liberty to reveal to you if you had not promised to become Madame Roland. The fact is, I have just found a number of letters addressed to Madame de Muire by the father of Médéric de Mestras, and by two or three other persons. But I must first explain how I happened to discover them. Monsieur de Muire requested me to carefully examine every piece of furniture in his wife's apartments, in the hope that I might find papers which would give some clew to the whereabouts of the missing property; and it is very fortunate that this idea occurred to him. Heaven must have inspired it, to spare him the chagrin of learning that his wife had basely deceived him. Still, an examination of the colonel's correspondence relieved me of a terrible anxiety. His letters are not signed; but I have compared the writing with some orders I have at my rooms, penned by his hand, and I am certain that the letters are from him. I have read them, and I now know the whole history of the unfortunate passion he unwittingly aroused in Madame de Muire's heart, and he deserves the more credit for not betraying and deceiving his friend, from the fact that he returned this love. He struggled against it constantly for fifteen years and never once yielded. This was ten times more heroic than the famous charge at Gravelotte, in which he died a glorious death. His letters are *chefs d'œuvres*—the honest man speaks in every line. He could not help loving his friend's wife. We are not masters of our own hearts, and love can not be controlled. When it comes one can not tear it from one's breast as one extracts an aching tooth. But the colonel's will held this love which he could not extinguish in strict subserviency. He was too brave to be guilty of a dishonorable act, and he never became Madame de Muire's lover. He even tried to cure her of her fondness for him, and implored her to lavish all her love upon Marcelle, whom he loved ' *as well as if she had been his own daughter,*' as he remarks in one of these letters."

"Have you destroyed the letters?" interrupted Mlle. Lanoue.

"No; I shall keep them, and if any of the men who have slandered Marcelle's father dare to repeat their calumnies, I will prove to them that they are liars by showing them these letters. And if any of these shameful rumors should ever reach Jacques de Muire's ears, I shall show him, too, this correspondence, which so completely vindicates our brave friend Mestras, who died for his native land."

"I think it would be much better not to show them to Monsieur de Muire," said Mlle. Lanoue, sagely. "These letters, though they vindicate Colonel de Mestras, do not exculpate Madame de Muire, you must recollect.''

'' Oh! I shall not show them to the count unless I am compelled to do so to obtain his consent to his daughter's marriage with Médéric,'' replied the major, quickly, '' and I feel almost sure that I shall not be obliged to resort to any such measure. But under no circumstances whatever will Jacques ever see the others.''

'' The others!'' repeated the girl. '' So these were not the only letters you found?''

'' Alas, no, mademoiselle. I now come to a revelation which I could make only to the lady who is to become my wife, and to which I must entreat you to listen. It will be very painful to you, I know, but Médéric's life and Marcelle's happiness are at stake. Madame de Muire had other correspondents who were less honorable than the colonel. Monsieur Dubrac, for example.''

'' A captain in the Guards before the war!''

'' The same. Did you ever meet him?''

'' I met him two or three times immediately after I entered upon my duties as a governess in the Muire household. ''

'' Yes, and at a date that corresponds with the termination of this brief affair; I read these letters, too, and afterward burned them, for they did honor neither to the person who wrote them, nor to the person who received—and answered them. But I did not burn Count Golymine's letters.''

'' Letters! Why, I understood there was but one. ''

'' There was a package of them. The correspondence continued seven years, with frequent intermissions, however. Madame de Muire and Golymine met regularly at Aix, in Savoy.''

'' Where I have never been. ''

'' Nor has Marcelle. Jacques used to go there occasionally, but he never remained long, and so he met Count Golymine only casually. Last year he met him again, in

Paris, at a club; but he did not invite him to the house. Unfortunately, Madame de Muire had renewed her relations with this rascal whom she should have sedulously shunned. She met him secretly, I am almost certain, since I have seen the notes Golymine wrote to her, and though the old love seems to have died out, I am sure she still placed implicit confidence in him. This was undoubtedly the case, as she intrusted to him all the bonds and securities which constituted her private fortune, and for which she received no receipt except the brief allusion to the fact contained in a letter."

"Does the letter bear his signature?"

"No, unfortunately; and I am not acquainted with his handwriting, but the judge of instruction must know it, for he examined him yesterday as a witness, and he must certainly have signed his deposition. Besides, it will be an easy matter for me to procure other specimens of his handwriting, and when I am in a position to prove conclusively that these letters were from him, the magistrate will be compelled to issue an order for his arrest, for I can then explain to him how the crime was committed."

"I wish you would explain that to me."

"Willingly. I must explain to you first that the crime, even though it was premeditated, as was unquestionably the case, must have been committed on the impulse of the moment. Golymine could have had no means of knowing that Madame de Muire would go to see the train pass on the nineteenth of June; but he knew that she often indulged in that innocent pastime, and all the details of the atrocious crime had been carefully planned days, and possibly weeks, before. This Maurevers, whom he had frequently met in former years in the gambling dens of other lands, was willing to do anything for money, and is probably an excellent pistol shot. Golymine, who was aware of this fact, must have bribed him to kill the countess whenever a good opportunity offered as the train passed. Who knows how many

times the two villains made the trip together from Paris to
Saint-Germain without finding the opportunity they sought!
It presented itself at last, and under circumstances which
were particularly favorable to their designs. Médéric was
on the train; at Chatou he changed his compartment;
Maurevers, who knew him by sight—his wife told you so—
Maurevers informed Golymine of the fact, and the idea of
taking advantage of the circumstance occurred to them.
They both leaped into the railway carriage that Médéric had just hastily left, and there, by the very worst luck
I ever heard of, they found the revolver that Médéric had
lost. The name of Mestras was engraved upon it; Golymine had heard through Monsieur de Liscoat that Médéric
was betrothed to Marcelle, and that Madame de Muire was
opposed to the marriage. He saw at once the advantages
to be derived from the use of this weapon, and instead of
using the one he had brought for the purpose, Maurevers,
by Golymine's order, fired the shot with Médéric's revolver,
and his aim was only too accurate."

"Yes; it must have occurred in that way," remarked
Hélène, filled with admiration for the major's sagacity.

"Afterward they had only to cast suspicion upon Médéric, and have him accused of the very crime they themselves had committed," continued George. "They succeeded in this, as you know. But Golymine, who was the
prime mover in the affair, made one very great mistake.
He probably thought it would be advisable to avert a criminal suit, which would necessitate an investigation he had
reason to dread, and the unfortunate idea of attempting to
compromise with Médéric occurred to him."

"To compromise with Médéric," repeated Mlle. Lanoue,
greatly astonished.

"Yes; on the evening of the crime he laid in wait for
Médéric on the Place Pigalle, and when our friend was
about to enter the house, he accosted him and offered to
restore his revolver to him on condition that Médéric would

not try to injure him in the estimation of the Count de
Muire, upon whom he intended to call very speedily. ''

"I do not understand his object in making such a proposal.''

"Nor do I as yet; but you may rest assured that he
had one. He denied it, however, to the judge of instruction, whom Médéric apprised of the fact when it was too
late, and as Médéric positively rejected these overtures,
which savored strongly of blackmail, Golymine decided
three days afterward to surrender the revolver to the
station keeper at Saint-Germain, who sent it to the judge
of instruction. Golymine took good care not to appear in
this affair, however. He intrusted this dangerous mission
to Maurevers, and Maurevers probably performed it with
reluctance, for he must have feared that it would cost him
dear eventually. But its first effect was exactly what Golymine had hoped for. Médéric was immediately arrested.''

"I hope now that will soon be Maurevers's fate.''

"He is anticipating arrest, if we can believe his wife.
But Heaven only knows when Monsieur de Mestras will be
released! The judge has just refused to give orders to that
effect, and yet he must know as well as you do that Monsieur de Mestras could not have shot Madame de Muire.
Still, he can hardly refuse to give these orders when I show
him Golymine's letters.''

Then seeing that Hélène did not seem convinced, he added:

"I shall show them to him to-morrow; and they will
satisfy him that the pretended count is certainly the custodian of Madame de Muire's fortune.''

"He will also learn the bitter truth in regard to Marcelle's mother,'' said Mlle. Lanoue, sadly.

The major gave a violent start. In his anxiety to save
the son of his former colonel he had forgotten that to save
him he would be obliged to lift the veil that concealed
Mme. de Muire's disgrace.

The delinquencies of the countess were no secret to the

Viscount de Liscoat and many others, but her husband and daughter were ignorant of them.

And even if one might hope that the magistrate who held Médéric's fate in his hands would refrain from disclosing the facts, out of respect for the as yet untarnished name of the Muires, it was impossible to hope that they would not be made public on the day of the trial.

Golymine, if arrested, would certainly reveal all. He was even capable of making his former relations with the countess a means of defense, and of saying: "Why should I have killed her? I was her lover, and I owe my fortune to her. The securities I received from her were a gift to me; she would have given me much more if she had lived."

To save his head a man like Golymine would not even shrink from such an avowal as this. The authorities probably would not credit it, but there were doubtless many people who would believe it; and, whatever might be the result so far as Golymine himself was concerned, all Paris would learn the disgraceful facts.

"Then must I leave Médéric to his fate when I have it in my power to designate the assassin?" asked George Roland, after a painful silence.

"I think so," replied Hélène, much more deeply moved than she had been since the beginning of the interview. "I think that if you could consult Monsieur de Mestras he would say: 'God will establish my innocence in His own good time. I will not have the mother of my betrothed disgraced in order to prove it.'"

"Ah, well!" exclaimed the major, "I will try to save him without causing him this deep mortification and chagrin. Golymine's last letters are not of a compromising nature. They relate almost entirely to business matters; I will place these in the hands of the investigating magistrate, and destroy the others. And if Golymine dares to boast of his infamy, persons will regard the tale as an ignoble falsehood, invented by a scoundrel in dire extrem-

7

ity. It would be quite sufficient, I am sure, if I should show the last note he wrote to Madame de Muire, the note in which he stated that he had invested the property she had intrusted to him in the Austrian bank, and that he would soon send her a receipt for it. This note was not written in a very lover-like style. Read it, and see for yourself.''

Mlle. Lanouc took it, though not without some reluctance, but as she glanced at it, she murmured thoughtfully:

"It is very strange, I admit; but it really does seem to me that I have seen this handwriting before."

"Impossible!" exclaimed the major. "Madame de Muire is certainly the only person of your acquaintance to whom Golymine can ever have written; and I am quite sure that she would not have left any of his letters lying around."

"Even if she had I should not have read them,'' replied Mlle. Lanouc, "and yet the more I look at this handwriting, the more familiar it seems to me."

Nevertheless the penmanship was of a peculiar and highly distinctive character, and an expert would have drawn some strange inferences from it. It was a small, round and perfectly regular hand. Each word occupied exactly the proper amount of space; each letter was in its place; not a single stroke encroached upon the margin, or wandered too far from the line. The pen had evidently been wielded by a firm and practiced hand; still the chirography was not that of a person who concentrates all his energies upon his task. It was a very easy running hand, evidently written without the slightest effort; and yet the note was as legible as a printed page.

"You must be mistaken, mademoiselle," repeated George Roland. "Two handwritings may resemble each other as closely as two men. A person may even be unable to distinguish one from the other when he can not compare them, especially when it is a question of letters or of persons one saw years ago. I suppose this is the case with you."

"Yes, it is a very remote recollection."

"And consequently very confused; so do not attach any importance to it. You have a very recent example of these mistakes of memory. On the day of Madame de Muire's funeral, Golymine's face reminded you of the face of some one you had known in former years. Yesterday, when he called at the villa, and you had an opportunity to observe his features more closely, you discovered that you had been deceived by a chance resemblance."

The young girl made no reply, and the major, thinking that he had convinced her, continued:

"Besides, it would make little or no difference if, by some strange chance, the handwriting of this wretch has come under your eyes before. You, thank Heaven! will not be obliged to appear in this deplorable affair; but there is nothing now to prevent me from showing the investigating magistrate the letter in which Golymine acknowledges the receipt of the fortune Madame de Muire had intrusted to him for investment."

"When will you see this judge?" inquired Mlle. Lanoue, without expressing any opinion upon the expediency of this important step.

"To-morrow, mademoiselle, I shall make another trip to Versailles, and the magistrate certainly will not refuse to see me and grant me a hearing. However deeply prejudiced he may be against Médéric, he can not decline to listen to my story; besides, the deposition of the worthy man I so providentially encountered yesterday, has, I am sure, given him abundant food for reflection, and I may find him more favorably disposed toward the prisoner. But I have not an hour to lose. Golymine must even now be making his preparations to cross the frontier, and I do not intend to give him time to make his escape."

"I am not sure but that would be the very best thing we could do; for in that case the name of Muire will not be dragged through the mire."

"I will manage to prevent that, never fear; but I am determined to secure the arrest of the assassin, Maurevers, and his accomplice, Golymine. That is the only way in which we can insure Médéric's release."

"You will not leave for Versailles until after you have seen me again, promise me that?" said Hélène, hastily.

"No, mademoiselle," replied George, a little surprised at this request. "Besides, I trust that we have not seen the last of each other for this evening, as I expect to dine at the villa, and we shall consequently have an opportunity to resume our conversation. But here we are at the house. How has my friend Jacques spent the day?"

"Very dolefully, I fear. I have scarcely seen him. He did not breakfast with us this morning."

"And Marcelle?"

"Marcelle is as despondent as ever. She seems to have found fresh food for anxiety in the hesitation you displayed when the date of her intended marriage was under discussion. She fancies that you disapprove of the match, and asked me why, and I was obliged to get out of the dilemma as best I could."

"Fortunately, I can now tell her that I intend to do everything in my power to enable her to marry the man of her choice, and to convince her, I am going to tell Jacques this very evening that he will do very wrong if he persists in refusing his consent after Médéric's innocence is established. Jacques has no right to condemn his daughter to a life of celibacy; and if he continues obstinate I shall advise Marcelle to wait and marry without his consent as soon as she becomes of age."

"Where is the dear girl now?"

"We spent the afternoon in the garden, but she saw Monsieur de Muire on the balcony, and went to join him, just as I started out to meet you."

"Ah, well! let me go in. We will find them and have a little chat."

"You must dispense with my company. It is only about a quarter of an hour before dinner, and I must go up to my room and make myself presentable. Monsieur de Muire lays great stress upon dressing for dinner, you know."

"And this would be a bad time to displease him," replied George, smiling. "Now give me Golymine's letter. I want to put it carefully away in my note-book."

"Will you trust it to me until I come back?"

"Yes, certainly, on condition that you do not return it to me before the count and his daughter."

"I will promise not to do that—and if I ask you to leave it in my keeping a few moments, it is only because I have in my possession another letter with which I should like to compare it."

"Do so at your leisure, mademoiselle; but before we part for a few moments, allow me to remind you that we are betrothed. I have your promise, and you have mine."

"And I shall not break it," murmured the girl, softly.

"Then I have your permission to announce our engagement?"

"What! you would do that already?"

"Certainly. It will give me an excellent opportunity to broach the subject of Marcelle's marriage."

Hélène was about to reply but François suddenly appeared before them, and she could not continue the conversation in his presence; especially as the major stopped him to inquire if M. de Muire was still upon the balcony. So she went straight up to her room, and George Roland soon afterward wended his way to the drawing-room and found M. de Muire in the place where Mlle. Lanoue had left him. Marcelle was sitting beside him, silently weeping. She dried her eyes when she saw the major enter, smile kindly upon her, and offer his hand to M. de Muire. Something in his manner told her that he was the bearer of good news.

"How do you do, Jacques? How do you do, Marcelle?" he said, cheerfully, seating himself astride a chair. "I have been making the most of my time since I left you, and I have some good news for you."

The father and the daughter gazed at him in equal astonishment.

"I am going to be married," continued the major, tranquilly.

"You?" exclaimed the count, hardly believing his own ears.

"Yes; I am rather old, but better late than never, you know."

"Whom are you going to marry?"

"A young lady you both know and love--yes, my friend, a *young* lady. She is twenty-five, and I am forty; and she might do much better than marry a rough old trooper like me; but I assure you that she marries me of her own free will. Can't you guess who it is? Try."

Then, as Marcelle shook her head, the major continued:

"Oh, well, I had better tell you, and have done with it, particularly as there are a number of matters I want to speak to you about this evening. I am going to marry Mademoiselle Lanone."

"Hélène?" exclaimed M. de Muire and his daughter in the same breath.

"Yes. You approve my choice, do you not?"

"With all my heart!" cried Marcelle. "The news makes me very happy."

"And the two weddings will take place on the same day --the fifteenth of October—that is, unless Jacques prefers an earlier date."

"I do not understand you," replied M. de Muire, brusquely.

"I was speaking of Médéric's marriage as well as mine."

"What! do you still dare—"

"Médéric will be released in a few days, and the magistrates will humbly apologize to him for the injustice they have done him. You certainly will not be so cruel as to harden your heart against the worthy lad whom you have always loved as a son, and who has just passed through such a trying ordeal. Marcelle would never forgive you."

"Is it really you who address this language to me—you, who only a quarter of an hour before this unfortunate young man's arrest advised me to be in no haste about giving him my daughter—you, who have certainly had grave doubts of his innocence ever since he was sent to prison?"

"But I have irrefutable proofs of his innocence now. And I have yet another piece of good news for you. I no longer despair of recovering the missing stocks and bonds. I can say no more just now, however."

The count made a gesture which said as plainly as any words: "That matters very little to me," and which might refer alike to the verdict of "Not guilty" anticipated by the major, or to the hope he expressed of recovering Mme. de Muire's fortune.

Marcelle said never a word; and George Roland, rather disconcerted by the count's icy manner, was beginning to wonder if it would not be advisable for him to change the subject, when Mlle. Lanoue entered the drawing-room, closely followed by François.

She was very pale and deeply agitated, though she, of course, could not have known that the major had just announced their intended marriage.

"Dinner is served," announced the valet.

The conversation could not be resumed in the presence of a servant, so M. de Muire and his daughter rose to lead the way to the dining-room. The major offered his arm to Mlle. Lanoue. As he did so she whispered:

"I must see you to-morrow morning without fail before you leave for Versailles. I have something of the greatest importance to say to you."

THE CRY OF BLOOD.

CHAPTER XIV

On the morning following the eventful day which made Hélène Lanoue George Roland's affianced wife, Médéric's ardent defender woke very early, and in rather bad humor.

Not that he regretted engaging himself to Mlle. Lanoue, any feeling of that nature was the furthest from his thoughts, but he was greatly annoyed that he had been unable to regain possession of Golymine's letter.

The previous evening had dragged by without affording him a single moment's private conversation with his betrothed. M. de Muire had kept them both close prisoners in the drawing-room after dinner, and to the major's great astonishment the count had taken evident pains to change the subject whenever his old friend ventured an allusion to his intended marriage with the governess.

Even more persistently did the count avoid any allusion to Médéric's probable vindication; so Marcelle did not venture to broach the subject, and Hélène was equally reticent in regard to the major's plans.

Indeed, the latter seemed more sad and preoccupied than her pupil; and M. de Muire, who appeared even more depressed in spirits than usual, scarcely replied when he was spoken to, so the conversation flagged in spite of all George's efforts. At last, he proposed that the entire party should adjourn to the garden to enjoy the fresh air, in the hope of finding a chance to talk with Mlle. Lanoue, if only for a minute or two; but M. de Muire declared that the night air would be injurious to his daughter's health, so Hélène pleading a violent headache as an excuse, asked permission to retire some time before the usual hour.

Her betrothed was consequently deprived of the pleasure

of her society, and as Marcelle announced her intention of following her friend's example, there was nothing left for the major but to sit and yawn away the evening in the presence of his unreasonable friend. Finally, for want of a better way to spend his time, he wisely concluded to go to bed and secure an interview with Mlle. Lanoue early the next morning.

Her failure to return the letter excited no surprise on his part, however, for on giving it to her, he had requested her not to return it to him in the presence of witnesses; and that she fully intended to return it, he did not doubt in the least, for he attached very little importance to the comparison of handwritings upon which Hélène seemed bent.

Besides, he did not really need the letter until it was time for him to leave for Versailles, and he knew that the judge of instruction would not reach the Palace of Justice before noon.

About eight o'clock, after a restless and rather uncomfortable night, he dressed himself, and went down into the garden to smoke a cigar, while waiting for Mlle. Lanoue to make her appearance. She usually rose about nine o'clock, and rarely remained in her room after her morning toilet was completed, so he might reasonably hope to see her very soon, especially as she had requested him not to leave for Paris without seeing her, the evening before.

He waited in vain until half past nine, however, and had about decided to return to the house in the hope of meeting her in the drawing-room or on the stairs, when he saw François approaching with a blue envelope in his hand.

The receipt of a telegram is no very momentous event nowadays, but this dispatch was so unexpected that the major opened it with considerable eagerness.

It read as follows:

"The major is requested to call at the house on the Boulevard Malesherbes immediately. There have been some new developments, and I can not leave my post."

It was signed Carcenac, and George Roland asked himself in no little astonishment what all this could mean.

The old soldier did nothing rashly, and some event of great importance must have occurred to induce him to send this urgent summons to his superior officer. But what event? George shrewdly suspected that an attempt to break into the house had been discovered and frustrated by Carcenac, who was naturally anxious to report as soon as possible; but it might be something else, and being in doubt, the major decided to respond to the summons immediately and in person, and to do this he must start for Paris at once.

This little trip, however, would not prevent him, of course, from going to Versailles afterward, but the major did not want to leave without the letter, so he asked François to send one of the maid servants to Mlle. Lanoue's room, with the request that she would step down into the garden for a moment. Whereupon, François replied that Mlle. Lanoue had just gone out, arrayed in street dress, and had requested him to inform Mlle. de Muire that she would not be back much before the dinner hour.

This intelligence annoyed George very much; in fact, it even alarmed him. Where had Mlle. Lanoue gone? and above all, why had she gone without informing him of her intentions after virtually promising him an interview? She knew, too, that she ought to have returned Golymine's letter; for without it, his intended visit to the investigating magistrate would be worse than useless.

This unexpected departure was truly incomprehensible, and his trip to Versailles would have to be postponed.

"Another day of delay! Will I ever get Médéric out of prison?" growled George, stamping his foot impatiently. "And Golymine is already packing his trunks, perhaps. Ah, well! as I don't propose to waste the day, I will spend it in listening to my friend Carcenac's report, and see the judge to-morrow."

There was certainly nothing to prevent his immediate departure. His hat was upon his head, and his cane in his hand, so the major ran after the valet to bid him inform M. de Muire that he should be absent all day, and then hastened down the road leading to Chatou in order not to miss the 10:40 train for the city.

He was a brisk walker, and he soon reached the station, where an agreeable surprise awaited him. The first person he saw was Hélène, who had just purchased her ticket. She blushed a little on perceiving him, but she came straight toward him, and said:

"You must excuse me for leaving for the city without seeing you."

"I was greatly disappointed, I must confess. Last evening, you remember, you asked—"

"For an interview this morning. That is true. But just as I was about to join you in the garden, Marcelle's maid handed me a letter, calling me to Paris; and when I received it I had barely time to make the train. I am expected there at eleven o'clock to meet an old school-friend, whom I have not seen for three years, and who arrived only yesterday from Russia on her way to London, for which place she leaves to-morrow."

"It has all turned out for the best, as I meet you here," responded the major. "We can go up to town together, and you will have an opportunity to tell me all you would otherwise have told me at the Oaks. You wished to speak to me, I presume, about the handwriting you thought you recognized."

"And I think so still, though I could not find the scrap of writing with which I wished to compare it. Are you going to Versailles?"

"Not to-day. I haven't Golymine's letter with me, you recollect, and it would be useless for me to go without that."

"True; I ought to have returned it to you before leaving home, but I was in such a hurry, and unfortunately, I haven't it with me now! It is safe, however. I locked it up in a chest to which I alone have the key. I will return it to you this evening, and to-morrow, if you are still disposed to make use of it, you can take it to the judge of instruction."

"That is certainly my intention, and in the meantime I have plenty to occupy my attention in Paris. Carcenac has just sent me a telegram informing me that my presence at the Muire town house is absolutely necessary this morning. I don't know why, but I am going there, and shall remain as long as I find it necessary."

The arrival of the train interrupted the conversation.

The major selected a compartment which was partially occupied by a worthy *bourgeois* family, and Mlle. Lanoue felt grateful to him for not choosing a neighboring compartment which was vacant, and in which they might have talked more freely.

She had her own private reasons for not desiring to resume the conversation, and she thought it scarcely probable that George would say anything more to her in the presence of strangers about the letter he had intrusted to her care, or about her school-friend who had just returned to Paris.

George, on his part, deemed it quite unnecessary to explain why Carcenac's telegram had so excited his anxiety, so both had their reasons for maintaining a prudent silence.

The journey from Chatou to Paris occupied only about thirty minutes, and they made it almost in silence, but not without reflecting upon the grounds of anxiety which engrossed their minds, but which they preferred to keep to themselves.

The major was secretly wondering why Mlle. Lanoue, whose memory rarely or never failed her, should have forgotten to return Golymine's letter; and on the other hand

Mlle. Lanoue was going to Paris to carry out a plan she was unwilling to confide to her betrothed.

On reaching the Saint-Lazare Station, George had the discretion not to offer to accompany the young lady any further, and she probably was not anxious for his company, for she remarked:

"My friend is governess in a wealthy Russian family that is stopping at the Hotel Meurice, on the Rue de Rivoli. You are on your way to the Boulevard Malesherbes, consequently we are not going in the same direction, nor do I know what train I will take to return. But we shall meet again this evening at the Oaks, and there will probably be many things that I shall want to say to you."

"And that I shall want to say to you," replied George, as they shook hands.

Hélène walked away, and the major sprung into a carriage. Ten minutes afterward he was ringing at the door of the Muire mansion. Carcenac did not answer the summons very promptly, and when he did he opened the door only a little way, and peered out cautiously.

"It is you, major?" he exclaimed. "Thank you for responding to my telegram so promptly. You will find that I have not troubled you unnecessarily."

"I hope not, indeed," replied George. "But why do you take so many precautions?"

"Because since last night I have been not only a *concierge*, but a jailer."

"What! a jailer?" exclaimed George.

"Come in, come in, major, and I will tell you all about it," said Carcenac, throwing open the door.

But no sooner had the major crossed the threshold than the faithful custodian double-locked the door behind him.

"Now my mind is easy," he remarked. "No one can enter or leave the house without my permission."

"Why, what has happened since yesterday? Did any one attempt to break into the house last night?"

"If they had only attempted it I should not have ventured to telegraph to you."

"What! do you mean that some one succeeded in getting
in?"

"Over the garden wall. I prophesied as much yesterday, you recollect."

"But how about those dogs that were to devour the in-
truders?"

"It was no fault of theirs that they did not devour the
man. I untied them before I went to bed, but the man
threw some poisoned meat down into the garden from the
top of the wall, which he had reached with the aid of a
ladder, and he waited until the poison did its work before
he ventured down. The whole thing was very cleverly
planned; but fortunately, I was on hand. I am a light
sleeper, too, you know, and though I had thrown myself
down upon the bed, I had taken good care not to
undress.

"This is the whole story. About half-past eleven o'clock
I heard the dogs bark. My room is on the first floor, overlooking the garden, but though I opened the window I could
see nothing. The scoundrel had just thrown the poisoned
meat over the wall, and clambered down again out of sight.
My two dogs only growled occasionally after that. I kept
quiet in my room, but I did not close an eye, and I listened
with all my might. I said to myself: 'There is going to
be some fun to-night.' I felt perfectly well satisfied of the
fact, but I wasn't at all troubled or uneasy. My gun was
loaded, and so was my pistol, and I had sharpened up my
saber the evening before—the faithful saber that hewed
down two Prussians at Gravelotte. I had taken the precaution to extinguish my lamp, and even my pipe, on account of the odor which might have betrayed me. A
soldier is not allowed to smoke under arms in the presence
of the enemy, and I felt that an enemy was indeed prowling around my bivouac."

"Come, come, make your story as short as possible!" exclaimed George.

" I will, I will, major. Well, the clock had just struck twelve when I thought I heard a noise in the garden. I jumped up, but this time I did not open my window, but I glued my face to the pane and looked out. There was no moon, but the night being very clear, I could distinguish objects quite plainly, and the first one I perceived was one of my dogs lying on his side in the walk. He had dragged himself there to die. Then I understood why the barking had ceased, and I said to myself: 'The scoundrel who poisoned you is not far off.' I needn't assure you that I looked with all my eyes, and I soon saw a man making his way down into the garden by means of a ladder."

" You fired at him, I hope."

" I had a great desire to do so, but upon reflection I concluded that I might miss him—it is no easy matter to aim correctly at night—and if I had missed him he would have made his escape the way he came, and I should not have succeeded in capturing him, for on the other side of the wall there is only a vacant lot that extends to the Rue de Vezelay and that is inclosed at that end only by a broad fence. There are plenty of houses on both sides of us, but I did not care to arouse the neighbors; besides, I was anxious to find out what the rascal was after, and I felt sure I should have plenty of time to collar him afterward."

" Yes, it was really of the utmost importance that he should not be allowed to escape, and if you succeeded in capturing him—"

" I certainly did, major, and in a much easier way than you would have supposed possible! Would you believe it? when he reached the ground he tranquilly picked up his ladder—which was a strong, light ladder with hooks on the end, exactly like the ladders used by firemen—and crossing the garden, placed it against the wall of the house, directly under the window of the room formerly occupied by the countess."

"I understand now," muttered George Roland. "And you made no attempt to prevent it? You certainly did just right."

"I was not such a fool as to prevent him from entering the trap, so I just stood at my window, and watched his maneuvers.

"Yesterday, after you left, I took the precaution to close the shutters and draw down the curtains, but these obstacles did not deter him long. He had a little satchel containing some tools strapped across his back, and in less than five minutes he had opened the shutters with the aid of a cold chisel. Then he attacked the window. With a glazier's diamond he deftly cut out a pane of glass, so deftly, indeed, that he made no noise about it, then passing his hand through the opening, he unfastened the catch, opened the window, and climbed over the sill into the room."

"What then?"

"I waited a few seconds, then taking my revolver, I stole cautiously out into the garden. By this time he had struck a light, and was evidently hard at work, so I had only to hasten upstairs to catch him in the act. But the first thing to be done was to cut off his retreat, so I removed the ladder, which was only leaning against the wall, as he had not been able to find any support for the hooks. I hadn't the slightest difficulty in getting the ladder into the house, and then I said to myself: 'I have you now, my fine fellow!' and I did have him sure enough, major. The door leading into Madame de Muire's apartments was locked on the outside, and the window is fully twenty feet from the ground. But even if he had mustered up courage to jump out I should have had no trouble in capturing him."

"Did you go up the front stairs?"

"Yes, major. I had my loaded revolver in one hand, and a dark lantern I use in making my nightly round, in the other, and I had placed in my coat pocket a bundle of small rope. The room the scoundrel had entered was some distance from the landing, and I was sure he would not hear me, for my keys are always kept oiled, and I had on my slippers. So I crept softly through Mademoiselle Marcelle's room, and through the boudoir, and found the door of madame's room standing half open. Of course I looked in, and I saw my man hard at work. I could see him as plainly as I see you now, for he had lighted all the candles in the candelabra upon the mantel. The room was as light as day, and the scoundrel was just preparing to break open the secretary. I set my lantern down on the floor, and sprung upon him from behind, seizing him, not by the collar, but around the throat, so he could not cry out, while with my other hand I held my revolver close to his temple. He struggled to free himself, and in the struggle, he stumbled and fell; but I did not let go my hold. I pressed my knee hard down upon his stomach, and as I had half strangled him, this gave me an opportunity to bind his arms securely, before he could regain his breath."

The major glanced at the hands that had accomplished this feat, gigantic hands as brawny and muscular as those of a butcher, and secretly thought that M. de Muire had done well to intrust his house to the care of this old soldier.

"Afterward, I bound him securely to one of the posts of madame's bed," resumed Carcenac, "so securely, indeed, that I defy him to move hand or foot."

"Do you mean that he is there now?"

"Yes, of course. He can't be very comfortable. In fact, I am sure he must be terribly cramped by this time, though I did allow him to sit down. He is seated on the bed, with his legs stretched out, and his arms tied behind his back, while to make assurance doubly sure, I placed around his neck a noose of my own invention that will certainly strangle him if he attempts to get up."

"What did he say when he recovered his breath?"

"Oh, he swore like a pirate, and called me every insulting name he could think of; but I didn't take the trouble to answer him. I just lighted my pipe, and sat myself down to watch him."

"Didn't you even ask him why he broke into the house?"

"Oh! his object was apparent. He came to steal, of course. If I had not appeared upon the scene of action so unexpectedly, he would have rummaged through every piece of furniture, and made off with his booty the same way he came. What a furious passion he flew into, when he found that he was caught! But he has had a chance to calm down, during the eleven hours he has been a prisoner. He begins to realize that he has no chance of making his escape, and is anxious to know what I intend to do with him. He probably fancied that when morning came I would summon a couple of policemen, and place him in their custody; but I thought it better to hand him over to you, major, so I wrote a telegram, and sent it to the office by a lad in the neighborhood, the son of the fruit merchant across the way."

"Then I shall find the prisoner upstairs?"

"Yes, major, and you can question him at your leisure, though I can not promise that he will reply. He is a pretty hard sort of a fellow, it strikes me, and perhaps it would be better to drag him off to the station-house instead of trying to extort a confession from him here."

"What sort of a fellow is he?"

"A regular scarecrow. He has on a dirty blouse, and an old battered hat that a rag-picker would not condescend to fish out of the gutter, but his trousers are well cut and his shoes new, and this has made me wonder if the scoundrel might not be a gentleman in disguise."

"What kind of a face has he?"

"Oh! he isn't bad-looking. His hair is cut short, and he wears a goatee—a black goatee that is thickly streaked with gray. He is slender, and his hands don't look as if he had ever done any hard work. He certainly is not a laboring-man. But you are a much better judge than I am, major, and after you have seen him—"

"Let us go up and take a look at him, then," interrupted George Roland, who was now certain that the thief was one of Golymine's emissaries.

CHAPTER XV.

CARCENAC led the way up the broad staircase, but on reaching the door leading into the apartments of the deceased countess, he paused a moment to say:

"I reclosed the shutters he forced open, and it would be quite dark in the room if I hadn't taken the precaution to light a lamp which I placed on a small table near the bed, so that the light falls full on the prisoner's face."

"I am glad of it, for I want to take a good look at him. You are not to tell him who I am. I want him to take me for a commissioner of police or a magistrate."

"You don't look a bit like one, major. Still, that doesn't matter. If you wish, I will tell him that you came from the prefecture or the Palace of Justice."

"No, no; say nothing at all about it."

"As you please, major. I won't open my lips."

As he spoke, Carcenac opened the door and ushered George Roland into the sleeping-room formerly occupied by Mme. de Muire.

The man was still in the same position, and he must have become heartily tired of it, for as soon as he saw the *concierge*, he cried angrily:

"So here you are again, you dirty rascal! Have you come to kill me, or are you going to leave me here to starve, you infernal blackguard?"

"Neither, my friend," replied Carcenac, unmoved by the insults to which he seemed to have become accustomed.

The major took advantage of the opportunity thus afforded to draw a little closer to the prisoner, who was, as yet, unconscious of his presence.

Carcenac's description of the man had been correct in the main; but his features, though distorted by suffering and anger, seemed not unfamiliar to George Roland. He felt sure that he had seen this haggard face somewhere before, though it now wore an entirely different expression.

At last, by dint of racking his brain, he succeeded in recognizing in this man the person he had surprised in animated conversation with Golymine at Versailles the afternoon before; the husband of the Princess Orbitello and Golymine's tool, for though disguised to a certain extent by his new costume, the man still wore the insolent air that had struck the major at their first meeting.

Of course it was not difficult to divine his object in forcing his way into the Muire mansion. Golymine, who was naturally anxious to regain possession of his letters to the countess, had come first to reconnoiter, and concluding that his letters must be in one of the desks in the bedroom, he had made his plans accordingly, and intrusted the execution of them to Maurevers.

George Roland had both men in his power now, for a little skillful maneuvering would be sure to extort a confession from Maurevers. He accordingly set to work without delay.

"Leave us," he said, turning to the *concierge*, and then stepping forward out of the gloom.

The prisoner gazed with a frightened air at the newcomer, whose stern face certainly boded the delinquent no good, or rather he began to glare at him with the eyes of a caged wolf.

"Oh! there is no escape for you," remarked George, ironically. "You were at Versailles yesterday, and so was I."

Then, again turning to Carcenac, he added:

"Leave us, but don't go out of hearing. Remain in the next room, and if I need you I will call."

Carconac instantly obeyed, and as soon as he had disappeared, the major took a chair and seated himself in it, only a few feet from Maurevers, who was grinding his teeth in silent rage.

"You know me, of course," he began.

"I know you!" yelled the prisoner. "Why, I never even saw you before."

"You not only saw me under circumstances you are not likely to forget, but you know who I am—and I know who you are."

"Indeed!" sneered the man. "Ah, well, tell me who I am."

"Your name is Maurevers; you were formerly in the employ of the Western Railway Company, but you are now out of employment," replied George, coldly, "though you will soon be sentenced to several years of hard labor for breaking into an occupied house at night."

"Did you take the trouble to come here merely to tell me this?"

"Not entirely. You must see very plainly that there is nothing to prevent me from handing you over to the authorities. You were caught in the act, and it will only be necessary for me to notify a magistrate of the fact to insure your immediate arrest."

"Do it if you like. What are you waiting for?"

"I shall not do it unless I am obliged to. Vindicate yourself if you can. I will not deliver up an innocent man."

"But how the deuce am I to vindicate myself? I entered the house by the window, and this old bear that has charge of the place found me engaged in breaking open a secretary. I am sure to be punished, that is, unless you will have the kindness to release me and not denounce me afterward."

"Then you broke into the house to steal?"

"If I should deny it you would not believe me."

"Still, you are not a professional thief."

"No, but I have just lost my situation. I haven't a penny in the world, and when one is starving one takes whatever one can find."

"So it was money you were hunting for?"

"One would hardly suppose that it was for paper and ink."

"Tell me the truth. You were hunting for letters, were you not?"

"Letters!" exclaimed Maurevers, evidently alarmed. "Letters of exchange, you mean?"

"You are evidently anxious to pass yourself off for a common thief. Ah, well, you will find it very difficult to convince me that you, a well-born man, have sunk so low."

"How do you know that I am a well-born man?"

"The Princess Orbitello, your wife, is my informant."

"So she has betrayed me, the hussy!" exclaimed Maurevers.

Then hastily recovering himself, he added:

"You are not very shrewd if you swallowed that yarn. I am married, it is true; but I am only a poor devil. You must know that women like to boast. My wife, who isn't blessed with much sense, is all the time dreaming of princes and millions."

"Shall I relate the circumstances that attended your marriage? You met the lady at Ischia, at a time when you were a frequenter of watering-places—for you were once wealthy, and it was gambling that ruined you—and you married her against the wishes of her father, who was a Neapolitan prince of a lineage as ancient as your own."

While the major was speaking the countenance of Maurevers underwent an entire change, and it was not difficult to divine that an entire change of feeling was going on in his mind.

"Even admitting that all this be true," he said, suddenly dropping his affected coarseness of manner, " what are you driving at?"

" I am trying to make you understand that I shall be much more lenient if you will confess the truth. You may rest assured that I know all, and that if you refuse to confess to me, you will be compelled to make a confession in the presence of a magistrate. Would you like me to tell you the truth?"

" Go on."

" Well, you are the victim of a man who has already done you an irreparable injury. This man wrote Madame de Muire, the former owner of this house, some letters that compromised him very deeply. He was extremely anxious to regain possession of them, and when he learned that your dismissal had reduced you and yours to the depths of poverty, he offered you a handsome sum of money to steal the letters for him; and you were weak enough to accept an offer which he would never have made had he known that they were already in my possession."

Maurevers gave a nervous start that did not escape George Roland's vigilant eye.

" He cared nothing whatever for the danger you would incur—this man who boasts of being your benefactor, but who has been the chief cause of all your misfortunes. You have been merely his tool, but you will have to suffer in his stead, if I refuse to come to your aid."

" What do you mean by your last words?" inquired the prisoner, eagerly. " Do you propose to set me at liberty upon certain conditions?"

" I will answer that question when you have given me some pledge of your sincerity. Is it, or is it not true that it was Count Golymine who sent you here last night?"

" Count Golymine? I am acquainted with no person of that name."

" You know him so well that I caught you yesterday, at Versailles, in close conversation with him; and you have known him for years. You made his acquaintance in a foreign land.''

"At Monaco," replied Maurever, brusquely, seeing that further denial was useless.

"Very well; you have taken one step in the right direction. It is the very best thing you can do under the circumstances, for you are certainly much less culpable than this man. Now go on until the end. How much did he promise to give you for procuring these letters?"

"Twenty thousand francs in cash, and an annuity of six thousand francs, payable in Italy."

"I can hardly wonder that you allowed yourself to be tempted. If the attempt had proved successful, you would have crossed the frontier without loss of time, of course. When did you intend to leave Paris?"

"This evening; as soon as I had received my pay from Golymine."

"He is waiting for you now, then?"

"Yes, and if he does not see me to-day, he will know that I was caught."

"That would be very unfortunate, for he would hurry off, and leave you to get out of the scrape as best you could."

"Oh, he will not leave the country until he finds out what has become of me. What has he to fear? He is too rich to be suspected of being the accomplice of a thief; besides, he feels sure that I would not betray him, even if I was captured. I have been his abject slave for five long years. Ever since his influence secured me the means of earning a livelihood I have been his willing tool."

"And why? Are you in his power from any cause?"

"No; it is rather he who is in my power, for I know some pretty hard things about him. But he holds a good position in society just now, and has plenty of money, while I am only a poor scrub. I was in no situation to resist him, so I thought it best to submit."

"So you think he will be alarmed if you fail to put in an appearance this morning?"

"Certainly. I shouldn't be surprised if he even came here. He would have a very good excuse, as he talks of purchasing the house, and the count has given his permission to examine it. He came here yesterday for that purpose."

"I am aware of that, and if he should repeat his visit to-day I shall take it upon myself to receive him—and to bring him here. In your presence he will not dare to deny that he sent you here to secure possession of his letters. And if he does deny it, I trust that you will contradict him in spite of the awe with which you seem to regard him."

"Why should he deny it? Any honorable man who has been a woman's lover would endeavor to obtain possession of letters which were likely to fall into her husband's hands. And it is no crime to assist a friend under such circumstances. The end justifies the means. If you deliver me up to justice I shall tell the truth, and if I do I shall certainly get off very easily."

"You had better begin by telling me the truth."

"That is precisely what I should have done if you had acted in a different manner. Your subordinate had treated me with such brutality that I thought myself in no way bound to answer you; but now you speak to me in a gentlemanly manner, I have no desire to conceal anything from you. In fact, you already know all. I did very wrong to scale a wall, and break open a window, but it was with no evil intentions, I assure you; and Golymine is no more to blame than I am, for he was actuated solely by a desire to save a lady's reputation."

"He must be wonderfully liberal then. A cash payment of twenty thousand francs, and the six thousand francs annuity he promised you, merely to spare Monsieur de Muire the chagrin of discovering that his wife had deceived him, is a remarkable display of liberality, you must admit."

Maurevers detected the irony concealed under this praise of Golymine's generosity, and regretted his mention of the figures.

"In spite of my exalted opinion of your protector," continued the major, "I can hardly believe he would reward a service of this nature so generously."

"He knew that I would have to run a great risk, and he intended to compensate me accordingly."

"Say rather he had a personal interest in regaining possession of letters which would injure him far more than they would Madame de Muire if they should fall into a magistrate's hands."

And as Maurevers opened his lips to protest:

"Spare yourself the trouble of telling another falsehood," interrupted the major. "I found the letters and read them, and they are now in a safe place. There is one letter for which Golymine would willingly give all his earthly possessions, provided I would consent to sell it to him."

"I don't see that he would gain anything by such an exchange."

"He would escape being tried for breach of trust, for one thing. In this delightful missive, he acknowledges the receipt of a large lot of securities which the countess had intrusted to him for investment. This autograph letter is now in my possession, but if you could restore it to Golymine, I am sure that he would give you a much larger sum of money than he promised. I even believe that if I should ask him to give half of his fortune for it he would jump at my offer. But I intend to put his letter to a very different use, and after I have shown it to the government attorney, Monsieur Golymine need not hope to escape several years imprisonment."

"Why don't you say that he will be sent straight to the guillotine, and done with it?" sneered Maurevers, though his countenance certainly wore a rueful expression.

"Because juries are inclined to believe in the existence of extenuating circumstances, and because the chief executive often exercises his right to pardon; but there is a strong probability that your friend's conviction will follow, and that the penalty imposed by law will be visited upon him, and in that case you know that the law makes no difference between the accomplice and the man who commits the crime."

"I—I do not understand you," stammered the Princess Orbitello's scapegrace of a husband.

There was a moment's silence. The major had no intention of striking the decisive blow without due reflection, and Maurevers, who was expecting it, prepared to make a desperate defense.

"When I met you yesterday at Versailles," George at last said brusquely, "you were in company with Monsieur Golymine, and both of you had just left the office of the investigating magistrate."

"*He* had," replied Maurevers, unhesitatingly, "but I had not."

"That is very strange. Your wife told some one that you expected to be arrested, and that you had decided to flee."

The eyes of the prisoner flashed with anger, and if the poor princess had been within reach he would probably have made her pay dearly for this imprudent revelation.

"It seems that people censure you for retaining possession of the revolver you pretend to have found on the 5:30 train on the 19th of June. It seems, too, that you are even suspected of the murder of Madame de Muire."

"That is false!" exclaimed Maurevers, hoarsely.

"I am not your judge, but you will, I trust, excuse me if I briefly state the case as it appears to me. You bid your wife farewell on returning from Versailles, and afterward hasten to Paris, where you hide until night. You are caught in the act of breaking open a secretary that formerly contained Golymine's letters to the countess; hence it is natural to conclude that the act was only the necessary sequence to a previous and much graver crime. The authorities will certainly incline to this belief, and I need not tell you what will be your fate and that of the scoundrel who urged you not only to steal, but to commit a murder."

Maurevers hung his head, and the major read the wretch's utter discomfiture in his agitated face; but the major was resolved to extort a confession from him at any cost.

"Listen to me," he said coldly. "You are very culpable unquestionably, but not as culpable as Golymine. If any one is to lose his head it should certainly be he. It depends entirely upon me whether or not you are delivered up to justice, as you are completely in my power. But I have no hold on him yet, and if he should succeed in making his escape, it will be upon you alone that the punishment will fall. I think this would be unjust. I think the rôles should be reversed, that is to say, that he ought to be condemned, and you allowed to go and get hung elsewhere. I speak very plainly; I never think it advisable to mince words."

"Oh, not at all. Go on."

"I think your only chance of escaping the punishment you richly deserve is to assist me in insuring the conviction of the man who seems to have been your evil genius, and who has carried his rascality so far as to secure the arrest of an innocent man."

"And you will release me if I consent to do this?"

"I can not say exactly what I will do; but I know this much: if you refuse to enlighten me in regard to Golymine's past, and his recent acts, you will sleep in prison to-night."

"Enlighten you! That is easily said, and nothing would please me better, but I know nothing at all about him, or rather, I know only one thing—that Golymine was once Madame de Muire's lover, and that he is very anxious to regain possession of some letters he wrote to her. What is the cause of this anxiety on his part, he has not thought proper to tell me, and I have not asked him. You say there is a very compromising missive among these letters. I was not aware of the fact, but it does not surprise me. I admit that Golymine may have become the custodian of Madame de Muire's fortune, and that a desire to retain possession of it may have caused him to kill the lady, but I myself had no interest in putting her out of the way."

"So you would merely be accused of complicity. Golymine planned the crime, and hired you to execute it."

"If he had hired me to do it I should have money, and plenty of it, but as it is I haven't twenty francs in my pocket, and my wife and children are starving."

"But you were about to receive a very snug little sum, and a comfortable annuity. It was not enough for Golymine to get rid of the countess; he must regain possession of the letter acknowledging the receipt of her fortune, for that might ruin him; but he did not intend to pay for it in advance. So if you plead poverty as a mode of defense you will only excite ridicule. You had much better take my advice, which is to abandon all evasion and subterfuge, and answer me frankly and honestly. You are at my mercy, and I repeat that this is the only way in which you can hope to gain any mercy from me. Come, now, tell me Golymine's history, and yours."

"That would take a long time, and it is no easy matter to talk when one is lying bound like a calf on the way to the slaughter, and when one has eaten nothing for twenty-four hours. My back is broken, and I am dying of hunger. Even if I should begin the story you wish to hear I should not have strength to finish it, so I would rather not attempt it."

"I can give you some bread and wine."

"No, just a glass or two of brandy to cheer me up."

The major called Carcenac, who promptly obeyed the summons, and requested him to fetch some brandy. Carcenac obeyed without a word, though the errand was not much to his taste. As soon as Carcenac had left the room, Maurevers added:

"I am very much obliged to you, sir; and as you seem inclined to treat me like a man, and not like a dog, do me the favor to allow me the use of my hands. If you keep me bound, your valet will be obliged to place the glass at my lips, and I entreat you to spare me the slightest contact with the scoundrel who has so ill-treated me. I do not ask you to unbind me entirely. It will suffice if you will merely unfasten the rope that binds my arms to my body. The rascal has drawn it so tightly that I can not get my breath."

"Certainly, certainly," said George, little suspecting that his prisoner had any intention of abusing his kindness.

George, feeling no distrust whatever, did not even wait for Carcenac to return with the bottle of brandy that was to give fresh courage to the prisoner and induce him to speak, but rose, approached Maurevers, and began to unloose his bonds.

This task did not prove as easy as he had anticipated for Carcenac had tied the knots as securely as an old sailor. The rope that bound the prisoner's arms had been passed three times around his body and once around his neck, so that any violent effort to escape would be almost certain to produce strangulation; but the major worked on assiduously, encouraged by such expressions as the following on the part of his victim: "Softly, softly, don't be in a hurry! Don't pull the rope so tight! There, that is better. My right arm begins to feel more comfortable now. One more effort, and I shall be able to move it. But Heaven only knows when I shall be able to use it again. There isn't a particle of feeling in it now; it has become so numb."

The major did not progress very rapidly, but Carcenac would soon be on hand to assist him, Carcenac, who would have no difficulty in untying what he himself had tied.

"Will you allow me to give you some advice in regard to the best means of accomplishing your charitable undertaking, sir?" remarked Maurevers. "If you would have the goodness to lean a little further forward you would have much less trouble, and if you would stoop and pass your arm between my back and the bed-post to which your subordinate has bound me, that would be still better."

The major instantly complied with the suggestion, and while he was thus engaged in his work of deliverance, Maurevers, who was now freed from the jailer's scrutiny, cautiously slipped his right hand into his trousers pocket. He was unable to rise, as he was still fastened to the bed by a rope that had been passed around his neck and around the middle of his body, but it was not necessary for him to be upon his feet to carry out the fiendish scheme he was meditating.

His hand finally reappeared in sight, armed with a revolver.

"That is better," he remarked at last. "I feel much more comfortable now, and am ready to answer you, if you will be kind enough to rise. Excuse me, sir, for having given you so much trouble."

The wretch was only waiting for the major to turn to fire at him, and he was reserving his second bullet for Carcenac, who would soon re-enter the room, and be sure to rush to his master's aid.

Fortunately, Maurevers had not made sufficient allowance for the extraordinary presence of mind and agility of the old soldier, who entered the room just as the major was rising from his stooping posture. Seeing the barrel of the murderous weapon gleaming in the lamp-light, Carcenac traversed the distance that separated him from the prisoner in a single bound, and with a vigorous blow from the bottle in his hand, he dashed the revolver from Maurever's grasp.

"You vile eur!" he exclaimed, "so you are trying to kill the major now, are you?"

George was on his feet in the twinkling of an eye, and understood what had passed almost as quickly.

"Thank you, my brave fellow," he said warmly, turning to Carcenac.

"I wish you would let me batter the scoundrel's brains out," cried Carcenac, brandishing the brandy bottle threateningly over Maurever's head.

"No, no! I want him to live so he ean tell me what he knows. Retie the knots I was fool enough to unloose. You ean leave free the arm he has sueceeded in disengaging."

"But, major—"

"What are you afraid of? We have disarmed him."

"It is my fault that he eame so near killing you. To think that I was such a fool as not to search his pockets before binding him last night. I richly deserve to be shot myself."

"On the eontrary, you ought to be deeorated, for if you had not eome to the rescue just as you did I should have been a dead man."

As he expressed his disgust, Carcenac set to work seeuring the prisoner, who now offered no resistance either by word or look.

"Now give him a glass of brandy," said George, when the operation was successfully eoncluded.

This time Carcenae really thought that the major must have lost his senses.

"Do what I tell you," added George, "and when he has finished drinking, place the glass and the bottle there on that chair within his reach. I hope the brandy will unloose his tongue."

Maurevers did not lose a word of this conversation, but he seemed neither alarmed nor subdued. His face wore an indefinable expression, and his gleaming eyes seemed to defy George.

"To your health, sir," he said, draining the glass Carcenac had filled for him. "You are a man of rare good sense, that is evident. It was only natural for one in my position to make a desperate effort to kill you and your vassal. I failed; we will say no more about it, but I will now show you that one can gain anything from me by kindness. Question me, I will answer you frankly, and tell you all you wish to know."

George Roland resumed possession of the arm-chair in which he had previously seated himself, motioned Carcenac to a seat a little further off, and began his examination by saying:

"Let us confine ourselves strictly to facts. Was it you who shot Madame de Muire by Golymine's order?"

"No; he shot her himself."

"But you were with him when he did it, were you not?"

"No; I was in my place, which is in the imperial at the end of the train. I got off at Chatou, as I do at every station. Upon the platform I saw the young man who is now in prison at Versailles, and I noticed that he changed compartments. I saw Golymine enter the one this young man had just left as I remounted my perch. I did not witness the tragedy that occurred a little further on. I did not even hear the report of the pistol."

"But when the train reached Saint-Germain you saw Golymine again, I presume?"

"That is true, and to convince you that I have no desire to conceal anything from you, I will add that he told me all. He told me that he found a revolver in the compartment he entered at Chatou, and that the idea of dispatching the Countess de Muire having occurred to him, he had proceeded to carry it into execution."

8

"What! he made a voluntary confession to you, who would be in no way benefited by his crime, and who knew the victim only by name or possibly by sight. This is very strange, you must admit."

"I do admit it, but what I have told you is true, nevertheless. You don't know Golymine; nobody knows him except me. He is a man who is not easily daunted when he resolves to accomplish anything, and he needed my assistance in accomplishing his ends, which were: first, to cast suspicion upon another person, and secondly, to regain possession of his letters to the countess. So after he had told me all, he intrusted to my keeping the revolver, which, by the way, bore the young man's name, and bade me meet him that same evening at ten o'clock, on the Place Pigalle, in front of the house in which Monsieur de Mestras lived."

"And you went there? You witnessed the interview between him and Monsieur de Mestras?"

"From a distance. Monsieur de Mestras did not see me, and I never found out exactly what Golymine wanted of him. I have thought since that he must have made a blunder, for after the interview he did not act with his accustomed shrewdness. He ordered me first to keep the revolver, and then, four days afterward, he bade me surrender it to the station-keeper at Saint-Germain, which I did, though the act has cost me dear, as you know. I was instantly suspected of an attempt at blackmail, and yesterday, Golymine, who had been summoned to Versailles, warned me that I had better flee. At the same time he offered to save me from poverty for the rest of my natural life provided I would secure his letters for him. I was not in a position to haggle as to terms, for I had just been notified of my dismissal, so I consented to do what he asked. We met in Paris last evening, and he assisted me in my preparations for the venture. He even accompanied me to the house, and explained in full exactly what I was to do. How I was to procure a ladder, and how I was to get rid of the dogs; he even told me where Madame de Muire's bedroom was, and described minutely the articles of furniture in which she might have kept her letters."

"In short, it was he who did it all, and you have little or no cause to reproach yourself."

"Yes. I reproach myself for my weakness in acceding to his request. I was not in the man's power, and I did wrong to obey him. It would have cost me dear if you had not taken pity on me. But you can save me, for I am in no way implicated in the Chatou tragedy, and as for the attempt at theft which proved so unsuccessful, it is for you to say whether or not the authorities are ever to know anything about that."

"You forget your attempt to murder me."

"It would hardly be considered an attempt, as I did not fire. Besides, the law does not punish criminal intentions. I consider it very fortunate that I did not fire, for my only hope is in you now."

"That doubtless means that you expect me to set you at liberty in return for your confidence. Such a belief is rather premature on your part, and you can hardly wonder that I reserve my decision."

Then, turning to Carcenac, the major inquired:

"Is there any good place here to lock a person up?"

"There is a dark closet next to my room," growled the old trooper.

"Very well, take a mattress there, and some eatables, not forgetting the bottle of brandy. Unfasten the rope that binds this man to the foot of the bed, set him on his feet, and then conduct him to his place of confinement."

These orders were scrupulously obeyed. Five minutes afterward Golymine's accomplice was safely incarcerated in the dark closet, and the major, who had superintended the operation, was about to take Carcenac out into the garden to give him further instructions, when the door-bell rang violently.

CHAPTER XVI.

"ALL roads lead to Rome," says the proverb.

George Roland had taken the shortest route from the Saint-Lazare station to the Boulevard Malesherbes; Hélène Lanoue, who had no business at the Muire town house, had started off in the opposite direction; but this fact did not prevent her from finally reaching the same point after a long détour.

Hélène had not uttered an untruth in telling the major that she had received a letter summoning her to the Hôtel Meurice that morning. Falsehood was a crime of which Hélène had never been guilty in her life; but it was not merely for the pleasure of seeing an old school friend that she had taken the train; and George would have been greatly surprised had he been able to follow her movements after she crossed the pavement of the Rue d'Amsterdam.

It is true that she at first directed her steps toward the Rue de Rivoli, by way of the Rue du Havre, the Boulevard Madeleine and the Rue de la Paix.

The hotel where her friend was staying, however, was not far from the Rue Castiglione, and on reaching it Mlle. Lanoue asked to see Mlle. Védrine, the governess of the children of the Countess Borisof, who had arrived from Moscow the evening before.

In response the attendant handed her a letter from that young lady, who begged to be excused from breaking her engagement, and entreated her friend to drop in some time during the day, on the corner of the Rue Jouffroy and the Avenue de Villiers. Mlle. Védrine wrote that the countess had just leased a house there, of which she intended to take possession on her return from England, and she had now gone there in company with her daughters and their governess to decide upon some changes she desired to make in their future home.

Hélène felt very little astonishment at her friend's enforced absence, for she knew, by experience, that a governess is seldom or never mistress of her own time. She recollected, moreover, that Juliette Védrine was noted for her exquisite taste in all matters of personal and household adornment, that she had transformed the princely residence of the Borisofs in Russia, and that the countess never took up her abode anywhere without asking the advice of this young girl, who was a Frenchwoman and Parisienne to the very tips of her fingers.

Hélène was anxious to see her friend, and she resolved not to return to Chatou without visiting the Avenue de Villiers; but instead of taking a carriage or proceeding on foot toward the rather remote locality in which she might hope to find her schoolmate, Hélène turned her steps in the direction of the Champs Elysées.

The major would certainly have been sorely puzzled could he have seen her now, and been able to study the expression of her face and observe her manner. The frequenters of Parisian thoroughfares often boast of their ability to divine by a woman's attire and manner whence she comes, whither she is going, what she is thinking of, and what she is, as surely and accurately as Cuvier could reconstruct an antediluvian animal from a fragment of bone; but the most experienced of these close observers would have been at a loss to determine the social category to which Hélène Lanoue belonged, and the object of her morning promenade.

Dressed as usual in perfect taste, daintily shod, and as handsome as a queen, she might, perhaps, have been mistaken for a leader of the *demi-monde*, had it not been for the dignified almost stern air that would have daunted the boldest gallant.

She might also have been mistaken for a young married

lady who had ventured out alone to pay a visit to her dress-maker or hair-dresser; but when such ladies go out on business they walk with a rapid and resolute tread; while Mlle. Lanoue walked as slowly as if an inspection of the shop windows was her sole object; yet on the Rue de Rivoli, between the Rue Castiglione and the Rue Saint-Florentin, there is nothing except the Continental Hôtel and a few insignificant shops.

She walked straight on, however, without turning her head, or even glancing at the few pedestrians she met. Evidently her thoughts were elsewhere.

The nearer she approached the Place de la Concorde the more slow her movements became, and once she paused, as if strongly inclined to retrace her steps, but finally walked on again after a pause of a few seconds.

From this evident hesitation on the lady's part, a sagacious observer might have inferred that she was about to take some hazardous step, but that her courage had failed her at the last moment.

Impecunious persons who start out to borrow money have these moments of doubt, and often make these sudden halts before they can summon up courage to cross the threshold of the friend or banker who will perhaps open his purse or his safe for them.

But certainly it was not the fear of a refusal of this nature that engrossed Mlle. Lanoue's thoughts.

Since her entrance into Mme. de Muire's family she had known no pecuniary embarrassment. Her salary was liberal, and as she had saved a part of it each year, she now had quite a snug little sum in the keeping of the family notary.

But before leaving the Oaks Mlle. Lanoue had come to a grave decision, so grave, indeed, that she had carefully refrained from revealing it to George Roland, and she now began to perceive difficulties that almost discouraged her.

The step she was about to take was one in which she had

nothing to gain, and in which a failure would inevitably bring down a host of misfortunes upon her own head and upon the heads of her friends.

She had been trying to gather courage to make the venture ever since the evening before. All night long she had not closed her eyes, and very possibly she would not have risked it had not her friend's letter arrived just in time to turn the scale in favor of a trip to Paris, which she had hesitated to undertake until the very last moment.

On reading Mlle. Védrine's invitation, she said to herself: "It is God's will," and started off without a moment's delay, for fear she might change her mind.

This might be truly called burning one's ships behind one; still, Hélène had not yet gone so far that she could not change her mind if she chose.

She was already beginning to reproach herself for not having consulted the major, and to wonder if she had not better pay a visit to the Boulevard Malesherbes before rapping at the other door, for she knew that she would be obliged to take her intended husband into her confidence sooner or later, and to consult with him as to what it would be best to do if the suspicions which were now torturing her should prove well founded. But she said to herself that if there should prove to be no grounds for these suspicions, and if she should find that she was indeed mistaken, it would be a hundred times better for the major to remain ignorant of the terrible agony and suspense she had endured. As she was thus revolving the matter in her own mind she walked on slowly, but she walked on nevertheless, and at last reached the Place de la Concorde.

At that very moment George Roland was beginning to question Maurevers. He was not even thinking of Hélène Lanoue, and not being a clairvoyant he could not see her swiftly traversing the scorching pavement that stretches from the end of the Rue de Rivoli to the Avenue Gabriel.

Hélène had suddenly made up her mind, and was now

rushing straight on to the goal; but on reaching the corner of the Rue Boissy d'Anglas she paused for one instant in front of a sort of hanging garden which surmounts the corner of the avenue.

This garden, which is well known to frequenters of the Champs Elysées and the Bois de Boulogne, belongs to the club-house to which in happier days the Count de Muire had regularly repaired to enjoy a game of whist with his friends.

In the evening the members of the club often step out into this garden to finish their cigars, and watch the carriages as they pass on their way to the Bois, but it is not often that any one is visible there in the morning, and Hélène passed it without lifting her eyes.

The door of the club-house is a little further on, and it was there that the young girl seemed to have business. A footman in livery was yawning on the steps, and staring at the passers-by with the supercilious air of a lackey who is well satisfied with his lot.

Hélène had seen many servants of this stamp before, and the pampered menial did not intimidate her in the least; but the question she wished to put to him was one of those that a well-bred young girl does not care to address to a servant. Nevertheless, she stepped up to him and asked him for Count Golymine's address. This time if George Roland could have heard her he would have thought she had certainly lost her senses.

The footman, instead of answering her, began to laugh, with the insolent laugh that menials of this stamp indulge in when a strange lady speaks to them.

But Hélène knew how to call him to order.

"I wish to obtain the address of Count Golymine, a member of this club," she said, in a tone that made him lower his eyes. "If you are ignorant of it go and inquire. I am waiting."

The rascal's manner instantly became more respectful,

and he hastened to the *concierge's* room in quest of the desired information.

A moment afterward that functionary appeared, scrutinized Mlle. Lanouc searchingly, and becoming convinced that she was a lady, told her very politely that the count had expressly forbidden them to give his address to any one, but if madame would step into the parlor and write what she wished to say to him the letter should be taken to the count without delay.

Hélène had not anticipated this refusal, and for a moment she felt strongly inclined to abandon the dangerous project she had undertaken. That morning she had said to herself: " It is God's will!" She now said to herself: " It is not God's will!" and there seemed to be nothing left for her but to beat a retreat.

She did so, without really knowing where she was going, or suspecting that the man of whom she was in search was not far off, though for the sake of appearances she told the *concierge* that she would prefer to write to M. Golymine at home, but that she would send the letter to the club.

She then directed her steps mechanically toward the Place de la Concorde, crossing to the Avenue Gabriel to reach the welcome shade afforded by the trees on that corner of the Champs Elysées. After the rebuff that had so effectually destroyed her carefully made plans she realized the necessity of further reflection, so she seated herself on a bench, where she ran no risk of being disturbed, for at this early hour the street was almost deserted.

It was time for her to come to a final decision. She had been in positive torture ever since the afternoon before, when George Roland first showed her Golymine's letter to the countess—a letter which was in itself conclusive proof against the mysterious personage whose features and handwriting had alike aroused most unpleasant memories.

As regards the resemblance, she was still in doubt. She

had not seen the person of whom Golymine reminded her for years; she did not know where he was and she hoped she would never see him again.

But as she had remarked to her betrothed, she could compare the writing with a scrap that was in her possession. She had done so, and this comparison made while the major was chatting on the balcony with the count and his daughter, had convinced Mlle. Lanoue almost to a certainty that both had been written by the same hand. There was a slight difference, but one's handwriting changes with time, as well as one's face, though the general character remains the same. Still, the young girl, hoping almost against hope, was not yet absolutely certain.

This certainty she was anxious to acquire at any cost for reasons she could reveal to no one; and her only means of ascertaining was to secure an interview with Golymine, who filled her with both horror and loathing, since it had been proved to her beyond a doubt that this scoundrel was the murderer of Marcelle's mother.

She hated him as deeply as she liked Médéric; she knew that the latter would be set at liberty as soon as the real assassin had been discovered, and yet, by a strange fatality, she found herself obliged to seek an interview with this assassin, to question him and satisfy herself that he was not the man who had played such a prominent part in her early life.

This irresistible desire had impelled her to leave the Oaks and hasten to Paris without even knowing how she should manage to see Golymine there.

She could hardly hope to meet him in the street—such opportune meetings are rare—so she finally decided to call upon him at his rooms, though she ran a great risk of compromising herself by so doing, and as she did not know his address, she concluded to go to the club and ask for it.

Why had the people there refused to give it? Hélène was strongly inclined to think that Golymine was beginning to hide already, and that he had forbidden them to give any questioner the slightest clew to his whereabouts.

Nor was this supposition at all improbable after what had passed at Versailles the day before. Golymine, after being confronted by Médéric, must have realized his danger; and his stormy interview with the major was not calculated to reassure him. Everything seemed to indicate that he was preparing for speedy flight, and he certainly had no time to lose, for George Roland would certainly lose no time in denouncing him. In fact, he would have done so already if the fatal letter had been in his possession.

Hélène had kept this letter, but she could not keep it indefinitely; and she knew perfectly well that on the very day she returned it to her future husband the inflexible major would take it straight to the judge of instruction.

She now began to repent of not having told him the cause of her perplexity, and she resolved to do so that very evening if she returned to the Oaks without securing an interview with Golymine.

In the meantime she hardly knew what to do. The hour her friend had appointed for her call on the Avenue de Villiers had not yet arrived, and Mlle. Lanoue, who had left home very early, began to discover that she was hungry.

Nature always asserts its claims even in the deepest mental crises.

Hélène only submitted to the universal law in saying to herself that the best thing she could do for the time being was to find a restaurant.

She had only to choose, for establishments of this kind abound on the Champs Elysées, and she recollected having patronized The Royen with Mme. de Muire and her daughter on what is known as Varnishing-day at the salon, which Marcelle never missed, because she was sure to meet Médéric there, that young gentleman being an enthusiast on the subject of painting, and a tolerably fair painter himself.

Hélène, who was accustomed to going about alone, did not shrink from entering a public place and giving her order; besides, she felt very little fear of finding a crowd there, for the annual exhibition was ended, and in the heated season it is generally in the evening that Parisians take their repasts in the open air. Accordingly she rose from the bench, but before directing her steps toward the only restaurant she knew, she glanced almost unconsciously at the club-house opposite.

There she beheld a gentleman seated in a rustic chair just at the corner of the terrace that overlooks the intersection of the Avenue Gabriel and the Rue Boissy-d'Anglas. His side face was toward her, and he was smoking a big cigar, ever and anon leaning forward to look down the Faubourg Saint-Honoré.

He was evidently expecting some one, and soon, tired, doubtless, of waiting in vain for his friend to approach from that quarter, he turned his head in order to satisfy himself that no one was coming up the Avenue Gabriel.

Then, and not until then, did Hélène recognize Golymine. The *concierge* to whom she had just spoken must have known he was there, and refrained from telling her so, probably because he had received orders to be silent. However that might be the meeting was a most fortunate one for the young girl, since it spared her the necessity of calling at the house of this spurious count.

Now it would only be necessary for her to wait for him near the door of the club-house, and this she instantly resolved to do. In fact, forgetting all about her breakfast, she was about to station herself on the sidewalk near the door when M. Golymine rose and perceived her.

He evidently had good eyes and an excellent memory, for he recognized her instantly.

He bowed instantly, and with a polite gesture gave her to understand that he was delighted to see her, and that he should at once hasten to speak to her. All this, too, was perfectly proper, as he had been introduced to Mlle. Lanouc by M. de Muire, and he could hardly enter into conversation with her from the top of the terrace.

It also proved that he stood in no fear of the young governess, since he seemed to court her society rather than shun it, though it was certainly not for her he had been waiting so impatiently.

Consequently there was nothing for Hélène to do but remain where she was; and she was the more willing to do this from the fact that the place suited her perfectly, for in this quiet, but accessible spot she had nothing to fear. She felt certain that no one would interrupt the conversation, still less would Golymine attempt to take from her, by force, the letter which she had upon her person and which placed him at her mercy.

From where she stood she commanded a view of the main door-way of the club-house, so she would not fail to see Golymine in case he attempted to make his escape in the opposite direction, and she felt quite capable of running after him if he attempted to avoid the interview in that way. But he had no such intentions, for she soon perceived him coming toward her, with his hat in his hand and a smile upon his lips.

"Excuse, mademoiselle," he said, courteously, "but I could not overcome my desire to inquire about Monsieur de Muire and his charming daughter. I am told that you were just inquiring my address of the *concierge*—for it was you, was it not?"

"Yes, sir, it was," replied Hélène, looking at Golymine as a young girl rarely looks at a man.

"Then I consider myself very fortunate to have seen you, and I am ready to hear anything you may have to say to me—and to serve you in any possible way."

Instead of replying Hélène continued to scrutinize his face closely. Until now she had seen him only in the dimly lighted church and in the shadow of the great trees in the garden at the Oaks. Now she saw him in the bright sunlight, and the more closely she examined his regular features, sparkling eyes and long silky mustache, the more firmly convinced she became that her fears were well grounded.

" I can but be infinitely flattered at the amount of attention you are pleased to bestow upon me," said Golymine, smiling, considerably surprised at the persistency with which she stared at him. " Does my face remind you of any one you have seen before?"

" Yes," replied Hélène, resolutely. " Of some one I knew in my childhood."

" Indeed?" exclaimed Golymine, evidently more and more amused. " I am delighted to resemble some one you knew in your infancy—knew and loved, I presume, for children soon forget people to whom they were indifferent or whom they had cause to dislike."

" Not always."

" I trust, however, that my features do not remind you of a person against whom you have any just grievance; but should that be the case, I assure you that I have nothing in common with the person I am so unfortunate as to resemble. And if by chance you have mistaken me for that individual I can truly assure you that at the time you speak of I was in Poland, my native country—for you are not over twenty, I am sure."

" Twenty-five, sir. I was born on the 24th of March, 1859," replied Mlle. Lanoue.

" I was then at the University of Wilna, where I remained until 1866. Then I traveled through Russia, the Orient, Germany and Italy. I visited France for the first time last year."

" You are mistaken, sir, for Savoy is a part of France."

" That is true. I had forgotten that I frequented Aix for a long time before I came to Paris. I see you are aware that I often met Monsieur and Madame de Muire there."

"Yes, I know it, though I never heard either of them speak of you."

"Probably because my relations with them have never been of an intimate nature. I met Madame de Muire occasionally at the Casino, on the promenade, or on excursions to the lake, but that was all."

"But you met her after you came to Paris," said Hélène, looking searchingly at Golymine.

"No, mademoiselle. I saw her pass occasionally in her carriage, but my slight acquaintance with her did not justify a visit on my part, so I did not pay it."

"You attended her funeral, however."

"That is true. I am a member of the same club to which Monsieur de Muire belongs, and I wished to show my sympathy with him in his terrible misfortune. And now, mademoiselle, will you allow me to call your attention to the fact that you have not yet told me why you took the trouble to inquire my address at the club?"

It was impossible to evade this straightforward question, and yet Hélène was not quite prepared to answer it.

Would it be best for her to question Golymine without disclosing her motive, and try to make him confess that he was neither a count nor a Pole? or would it be advisable to begin the attack openly by showing him, not his letter to the countess, but the scrap of writing with which she had compared it, and by saying to him point-blank: "Was it not you who wrote this and appended to it a name other than that you now bear?"

The first plan presented very little chance of success, for Golymine's evasive replies indicated that he was already upon his guard. The second plan was dangerous. If Hélène showed him the scrap of writing, he would probably deny that he was the writer, and seeing that Mlle. Lanoue was hostile to him, he might immediately take measures to insure his escape from his enemies. He could do this by immediately crossing the frontier, and Médéric would not be restored to liberty for a long time, if ever.

Hélène saw the danger, but the question of Golymine's identity affected her so deeply that she could not refrain from making her venture.

It was better to know the worst than remain in this terrible state of uncertainty which prevented her from assisting George Roland in bringing Mme. de Muire's murderer to justice.

"It must certainly be a matter of interest to you," continued Golymine, "for it seems you asked the *concierge* for my address. Monsieur de Muire might have given it to you; he learned it from his notary. But you probably had your reasons for not asking him. As you were anxious to know my place of residence it must have been because you had an idea of calling at my house. I should be charmed to see you there, though I can not help feeling some surprise that such an idea should ever have occurred to you."

Before her departure from the Oaks Mlle. Lanoue had placed Golymine's letter in her bosom, but the piece of writing with which she had compared it she had slipped into a small Russia leather satchel she held in her hand.

She now opened this satchel, and taking from it a medallion portrait, she handed it to the pretended Pole, saying as she did so:

"Do you recognize this?"

"No," he replied, after glancing at it. "It is the portrait of a child about five or six years of age, and very pretty, but I am sure that I never saw the face before."

Hélène's countenance brightened; a gleam of joy and relief flashed from her eyes, but she wished to complete the test, so she suddenly showed Golymine the other side of the medallion. On this side, under a glass, was a lock of hair fastened to a bit of parchment, upon which was written these words:

"To my dear little sister, Andrée, on the fifth anniversary of her birth."

This time Golymine turned pale, and extended his hand to seize the portrait, but Hélène would not let go her hold, and he dared not take it from her by force.

"You recognize it now, do you not?" she asked.

"No," replied Golymine, though in a less steady voice.

"Then look at me."

"You! what! is it you? Impossible! There is a slight resemblance, but you are a brunette, and this little girl is a decided blonde."

"One changes a good deal in twenty years."

"But your name is Hélène."

"Andrée-Hélène-Marie. I was formerly called by the first of these three names. I took the second after my father's death."

"Andrée-Hélène Lanouc?"

"No, sir. My father's name was not Lanouc."

"What was his name?"

"I will tell you after you have told me if you do not now recognize this scrap of writing to which the name of Gaston is appended."

"Gaston, yes. That is a very pretty name. My name of Serge is much less euphonious, I must admit. Now I have answered you, keep your promise and tell me your family name."

"My father's name was Jean d'Argouges. You knew him, did you not?"

"How should I know him?" stammered Golymine, visibly troubled. "That is a noble name. Why did you abandon it?"

"Because my brother dishonored it," replied the young girl, hoarsely.

"Dishonored it? And how?"

"My brother was guilty of forgery. He fled to escape imprisonment, but he was finally captured and sentenced to ten years of hard labor. This occurred while you were completing your studies at the University of Wilna."

Golymine started violently, but he regained his ordinary composure almost instantly, and remarked with well feigned indifference:

"You do very wrong to tell me this sad story, mademoiselle. I shall not betray your confidence, but permit me to remind you of a very sage proverb, which is specially applicable in your case: 'Family troubles should never be revealed to strangers.'"

"But I may surely reveal them to those who have been the cause of them."

"I do not understand you."

"You understand me perfectly, and I defy you to pretend any longer that you are not Gaston d'Argouges."

"But in that case I should be your brother. You really do me too much honor. I should certainly be proud to have such a charming sister, but unfortunately I am the last of my race."

"Your audacity is certainly astonishing! You deny your father's name, and you have probably stolen the one you now bear, but you have not been able to change your features. I know you now, and I recognize your writing on the back of this portrait. Others, too, will recognize it, when I show it to them. You will reply that it matters very little, as twenty years have elapsed since your trial and conviction. Your offense is outlawed now, I know. You waited until it was before you returned to France."

"And consequently I should have nothing to fear if I was really the person for whom you mistake me; but you, mademoiselle, have everything to lose by making such a revelation. I shall have no difficulty whatever in proving that I am Count Golymine, while everybody will learn that you have a brother who was sent to the galleys. That in itself will be quite enough to prevent you from ever finding a husband."

"You are very much mistaken. I am about to marry, and the man to whom I am betrothed knows all. I have told him that my brother was guilty of forgery and sent to prison."

"But you did not tell him that the black sheep had suddenly reappeared upon the stage of action, I suppose?"

"Not yet, but I shall tell him."

"I fail to see what you will gain by it. Besides, even if your lover has made up his mind to marry a person of tarnished reputation, he probably will not be anxious to have the disgrace made public. However, that is his business, not mine, so I will ask your permission to leave you if there is nothing more that you desire to say to me."

While Golymine was speaking Hélène had been watching the movements of his ungloved hands, which he was never loath to show, as they were remarkably handsome.

One was toying carelessly with his scarf pin, the other was swinging a slender cane. Slender, white and remarkably well cared for, with almond-shaped nails, these aristocratic hands would certainly have done honor to a prince of the blood, and the countess had often admired them.

Suddenly, Hélène seized his right hand, so suddenly, in fact, that Golymine, in his astonishment, dropped his stick.

"Will you still attempt to deny that you are Gaston d'Argouges?" she asked, vehemently, twisting back his fingers in such a way as to disclose the thumb to view.

"Have you lost your mind?" exclaimed Golymine, trying to free himself.

He was tall and vigorous. The frail young girl who had seized his hand was no match for him in physical strength, but after all muscular power is no match for will power, and Hélène would not relax her hold.

"The scar is still there," she remarked, pointing to a marked depression and deep discoloration of the skin at the base of the thumb. "It is the result of a sword thrust given you by a man you had insulted. I can see you yet, returning home with your arm in a sling. How I cried that day when you showed me your maimed and bleeding hand.''

"All this is very touching," sneered Golymine. "Several years ago, in a duel, I was wounded in the place at which you are pointing, but I fought at Wilna with a fellow student, and I was not even aware of your existence at the time."

"Still another falsehood!" exclaimed the young girl, throwing from her in disgust the hand she had struggled so hard to secure—the hand of Mme. de Muire's murderer. "Cease to deny the evidence against you! Why do you not confess that you are my brother? What are you afraid of? We are, alone, and you know that I will not betray you."

The so-called Golymine was beginning to recover from his alarm. Indeed, he had already regained sufficient composure to be able to face the danger calmly.

He saw that Hélène was perfectly sure of the truth of her assertion, and that he would not be able to persude her that she was mistaken. This being the case, he said to himself that further denial was useless, and that it would be advisable for him to conciliate if possible the sister he had just met so inopportunely.

He recognized her now; he was even surprised that he had not recognized her before; and he now regretted that he had not bestowed more attention upon this young girl whose features could hardly have failed to remind him of Andrée d'Argouges.

Had he known that Marcelle de Muire's governess was Andrée he would have manœuvered very differently.

But though she had revealed her identity to him, he fancied that he had nothing to apprehend from her. Why should she denounce him? She would gain nothing by such a step; besides, she was naturally very kind-hearted, and she had loved him devotedly in former years—this grown-up brother who had blighted her after-life, so there was nothing to prevent her from forgiving him now.

He would have been less confident had he suspected that she knew a secret that was much more terrible than the secret of his first crime, which had been effaced by time, if not expiated.

But as yet Hélène had not said a single word about Mme. de Muire's murder; and he had not the slightest suspicion that she was about to marry the Major Roland who had taken such a prominent part against him since their meeting at Versailles.

In fact, the more he reflected the more convinced he became that his sister would not be hard upon him if he confessed his real name and his past errors. Had she not involuntarily adopted the familiar speech of their childhood, and was not this unconscious familiarity equivalent to a promise of clemency?

To obtain this hoped-for indulgence he felt sure that it would only be necessary to represent his former misdemeanors as mere youthful errors, and play the part of a repentant sinner well.

So he prepared himself for the rôle.

His countenance assumed an humble, woe-begone expression. His eyes filled with tears, for he was one of those persons who can weep at will. His lips faltered a few humble, almost beseeching words.

But unfortunately Hélène, whose patience was long since exhausted, did not give him time to conclude his appeal.

" Is it possible that you do not understand that I wish to save you?" she exclaimed, seizing him by the arm.

This was quite enough to put the pretended count instantly upon his guard.

" Save me from what?" he asked, hastily.

" From the death that awaits you upon the scaffold," was the stern reply.

This unexpected announcement aroused Golymine's defiance, and he cried, in a mocking tone:

"The deuce! I had no idea that there was any probability of my mounting the guillotine!"

"Is not that the punishment reserved for assassins?"

Golymine's face became grave again.

"And whom have I assassinated, pray?" he asked, coldly.

"Madame de Muire. It was you who shot her. I was there when you killed her."

"This is really too much! I can guess who put this absurd idea into your head, however. It was a man of whom I am not particularly fond, a Major Roland. There is no love lost between us. He has constituted himself the defender of the young man who was arrested a few days after the death of the poor countess, and he is searching everywhere for culprits. That is all very well, but I don't propose to have him implicate me in the matter, and the first time I meet him—"

"You had better avoid him, for if you fall into his hands you are lost. He will certainly deliver you up to justice. He has proofs against you."

"Proofs! what proofs?"

Hélène, carried away by excitement, was almost on the point of drawing Golymine's letter from her bosom, but she recollected herself in time, and it was well that she did, for if she had been so imprudent as to produce this fatal letter Golymine would not have failed to secure possession of it."

"You will learn only too soon if I desert you," she replied. "I alone can save you, and I, perhaps, will save you if you will accept the conditions I am going to impose."

"It is to be a treaty of peace, then?" sneered Golymine.

"You are my brother. I am certain of it now, and I do

not want to see you branded as a murderer, though I will not allow an innocent man to suffer in your stead. You will certainly be denounced to-morrow. You would have been before now had I permitted it; but to-morrow the proofs against you will be placed in the hands of the investigating magistrate, who will forthwith issue a warrant for your arrest. You are warned now; do not allow yourself to be captured. You know by experience how difficult it is to escape from the hands of the law, so flee, and at once. I give you twenty-four hours to make your escape."

"You are really too good!"

"Do not suppose for an instant that I am jesting. By the memory of the father whose name you have dishonored, I swear to you that by to-morrow afternoon the magistrate who examined you will know that you killed Madame de Muire. If you have not disappeared by that time you will be immediately arrested. But you have plenty of time to cross the frontier, and after you have once more changed your name, I hope you will never set foot on the soil of France again. Count Golymine will be adjudged guilty, as Gaston d'Argouges was adjudged guilty in former years; but the disgrace of this new conviction will not reflect upon me, for no one will know his real name. But if, on the contrary, you continue to defy the authorities by remaining in Paris, you will be cast into prison, and leave it only to be dragged before the Court of Assizes, where they will be sure to discover that you are my brother. I shall be forced to undergo further humiliation, but I shall submit to it unmurmuringly, and the honest man I am about to marry will forgive me for being your sister. Whether you depart or whether you remain you may rest assured of one thing. Marcelle de Muire's betrothed will be saved, for Monsieur Roland has abundant means of proving that you committed the crime, and he will not spare you, though I have been able to prevent him from taking any decided action in the matter up to the present time. Ever since the day I thought I recognized you in the church at Madame de Muire's funeral I have been determined to settle the doubts that tortured me. And when I learned that it was Count Golymine who killed the countess, and that he was about to be arrested, I resolved to see him and question him, and give him a chance to save his life if I found that this pretended count was really my father's son. I can not doubt it now. I am positive that the so-called Golymine is Gaston d'Argouges. I have done my duty in warning him of his danger and in imploring him to flee—to disappear forever. Now, I have nothing more to say to him."

The pretended count had listened attentively and without evincing the slightest desire to interrupt Hélène. In fact, it was quite evident that he took what she said so seriously that he was anxious to put an end to the conversation and beat a hasty retreat.

Still, he was desirous of keeping up appearances, even before this sister for whom he felt neither affection nor gratitude.

"Mademoiselle," he said with chilling irony, "I do full justice to your kind intentions. If I were your brother I should certainly fling myself into your arms; and if I really had the crime you impute to me upon my conscience I should throw myself at your feet and thank you for your affectionate counsel; but as I am not Gaston d'Argouges, and as I have murdered no one you can hardly wonder that I am anxious to take leave of you."

With these concluding words he bowed haughtily to the young girl, turned upon his heel and walked away.

Hélène made no attempt to detain him, still less did she think of following him. She stood watching him, positively confounded by such a display of audacity, but convinced that this hardened scoundrel would not fail to profit by the advice she had just given him, though he refused to confess his guilt.

Nor was she mistaken. Golymine's only thought now was to gain a place of safety.

He had made his plans, of course, in case that fate should turn against him. The meeting with the major at Versailles had put him on his guard, and his preparations for departure were already made. The securities Mme. de Muire had intrusted to him had been sold; the proceeds, in the shape of bank-notes and drafts upon New York, were in his pocket. All he had to do was to embark for America, where he expected to enjoy his ill-acquired wealth in peace.

But he was unwilling to leave the letters he had written to the countess behind him. The people of the United States are never averse to complying with the provisions of the extradition treaty, and Golymine was anxious to live on the other side of the Atlantic in peace; so he had bribed Maurevers to secure these letters for him and bring them to him at the club. But Maurevers had not made his appearance.

Had he failed in his undertaking, or was he keeping the letters in order to make his accomplice pay him still more liberally? Golymine was anxious to know. It never once occurred to him that Maurevers had been captured, and that the proofs to which Hélène had alluded was one of the letters which he himself had written to Mme. de Muire, and which had fallen into the major's hands.

In the character of a probable purchaser, Golymine, of course, had the *entrée* to the house on the Boulevard Malesherbes at any and all times, and if a robbery or an attempt at robbery had occurred during the preceding night, the *concierge* would hardly fail to mention the fact, so Golymine immediately wended his way there.

CHAPTER XVII.

GOLYMINE did not take this bold step without carefully weighing its probable consequences, however.

If the *concierge* should tell him that some one had broken into the house during the night by climbing over the garden wall, and prying open the shutters, and that the malefactor had made his escape, after breaking open the cabinets and desks in the sleeping-room of the deceased countess, Golymine would know that Maurevers had played him false. But if the *concierge* said nothing about any such attempt Golymine would know for a certainty that Maurevers had not obeyed his orders, and that his cowardly accomplice could no longer be depended upon.

Still, even if the scheme had succeeded, Golymine might hope that Maurevers, fearing that he might be tracked by the police, and being consequently anxious to reach a place of safety, had taken the morning train for Calais, in order to reach England as soon as possible.

Maurevers had money enough to take him across the frontier, in spite of what he had told his wife; and once in a place of safety, he could apprise Golymine of the fact.

There was another theory, too, that Golymine considered well worthy of credence. Maurevers loved drink, and it was quite possible that after the robbery he had gone to finish up the night in some wine-shop, where he had drank himself into a state of beastly intoxication. Golymine knew a wine-shop on the Boulevard de Courcelles where Maurevers had laid insensible under the table more than once, and Golymine resolved to go there in search of him if his visit to the Muire mansion proved futile.

Five minutes after his parting with the unfortunate young girl who had warned him of his danger, Golymine jumped into a passing cab, taking care, however, to alight from it at the corner of the Rue de Lisbonne instead of having the vehicle stop in front of the Muire mansion. He rang, too, rather cautiously, though he little suspected that the major would hear the modest summons.

It was Carcenac that opened the door; and Golymine said to him in a rather curt tone:

" I neglected to visit the garden and out-buildings yesterday. Will you show them to me to-day? You recognize me, I suppose?"

" Certainly," replied the old trooper, who, being now aware of his visitor's real character, was rejoiced to see him stepping into the same trap in which his accomplice had already been caught. "Come in, sir, and you shall see what you did not see yesterday."

Reassured by this cordial reception, Golymine required no urging to make him enter the house, and Carcenac at once proceeded to close and lock the door behind him.

From the tranquil manner of the *concierge*, Golymine had already come to the conclusion that nothing unusual had occurred in the house since the day before, and that Maurevers had shrunk from the danger of the undertaking. This being the case, he would have preferred not to enter the house, but he could not decline to do so now without exciting suspicion.

"Not that way, count," remarked Carcenac. "The carriage house and stables are on the left."

Carcenac had left the major in the garden, near the lodge window, and he was now furtively preparing a telling *coup de théâtre*.

It proved a perfect success.

As Golymine stepped out of the hall and turned to the left, he found himself face to face with Médéric de Mestras's champion.

On seeing him he involuntarily recoiled, and would gladly have beaten a retreat, but it was too late. The house door was closed; besides, Carcenac's brawny form barred the way.

George Roland, delighted that chance had at last delivered Mme. de Muire's assassin into his hands, immediately prepared to profit by his good fortune.

"This man must not be allowed to escape," he remarked to Carcenac.

"You need have no fear of that, major," replied the old trooper, complacently. "I have the other scoundrel's revolver in my pocket, and if this one tries to get away I'll put a bullet through him to prevent him from running."

"What does this mean?" began Golymine, haughtily. "Have I been lured into a trap? How dare you prevent me from going where I please? Monsieur de Muire gave me permission to visit this house, and I intend to tell him how I have been treated here. But I shall not confine myself to that; this gentleman here shall answer to me for his insolence."

"I fight with you!" replied George. "Nonsense! a gentleman does not fight with a thief and an assassin."

The pretended count turned pale, and made a hasty movement as if with the intention of springing upon the major, who faced him unflinchingly, however.

"If you move I'll blow your brains out!" cried Carcenac, leveling his pistol at Golymine.

"You see that threats are useless," remarked George Roland.

"I see very plainly that I am at your mercy. Your insults do not move me, but I want to know what you are going to do with me, for I don't suppose that you intend to keep me here indefinitely."

"You will remain here until the chief of police sends officers to arrest you, which will be this evening."

"So much the better. I can at least tell a magistrate who I am."

" The one who will examine you knows you already, and when you again appear before him, he will have proofs of both your crimes in his possession."

" So I have committed two crimes," sneered Golymine, resolved to play his part boldly to the end.

" On the 19th of June last you killed the Countess de Muire by a pistol-shot; last night you bribed one of your hirelings to steal the letters you had written to your victim. Do not attempt to deny it. Your accomplice has been captured. He has confessed all, and he will accompany you to Versailles."

Golymine saw that all was lost, and that further denial would be useless.

The hunted wolf flees as long as he has any hope of escape; but when his wiles and his strength are alike exhausted he takes his stand by a tree or rock, faces the hounds, and kills as many as he can before they strangle him.

Golymine, caught in the trap, resolved to have his revenge before submitting to the fate that now seemed inevitable.

" So be it!" he said, in sullen rage. " I will go to Versailles; I will go to prison; I will go to New Caledonia, or end my days on the gallows, if need be; but all Paris shall know that I was Madame de Muire's lover. The daughter shall know her mother's frailty, and your protégé, Mestras, will perhaps think twice before he marries her, for the news can not be much more agreeable to him than to his fool of a father-in-law."

George turned white with anger, but he, nevertheless, managed to control himself.

" And the governess will have good cause to congratulate herself as well," continued Golymine. " If she ever finds a man who is willing to marry her now, I—"

" Silence, you wretch!" roared the major.

" Ah, ha!" thought Golymine, " I have hit it this time. Yes," he resumed, " I shall be very much surprised if she ever finds a man willing to marry her when it is proved beyond a doubt that the charming Hélène Lanoue's real name is Andrée d'Argouges, and that Count Golymine is really Gaston d'Argouges, her brother.''

George Roland thought at first that this was only a heartless jest; but he soon recollected that Hélène had seemed struck by this man's resemblance to some one she said she had known in her childhood, and Golymine, perceiving the major's agitation, said to himself:

'' Good! the intended husband of whom my sister spoke is this old soldier who is so determined to see me executed. I understand the situation now.''

Then he continued aloud:

'' If you doubt my word you have only to question her. She will not conceal the truth from you any longer. I just saw her, and we recognized each other. She came to Paris expressly to warn me that you were going to denounce me, and to make me promise to leave France. She is a good-hearted little thing, and she would have saved me had not the foolish notion of coming here taken possession of me. What a shock it will be to her when she learns that you have had me arrested, you—her promised husband! Now, if you should marry her, you will have the pleasure of seeing your brother-in-law on the prisoner's bench in the Court of Assizes.''

The major was beginning to believe that the scoundrel was really telling the truth, but he wanted to question Hélène before taking any further action in the matter.

'' Come here, Carcenac,'' he cried. '' Place your revolver at this man's head, and blow his brains out if he refuses to move.''

'' Very well, major. Where am I to take him?''

'' To the same place that you took the other man.''

'' A very good idea. They can be company for each other.''

'' So you are going to shut me up with Maurevers,''

sneered Golymine. "I am not sorry, for I have a few questions to put to him; besides, it gratifies me to see that you have abandoned the idea of sending me to Versailles immediately. Believe me, sir, it would not be advisable to resort to such extreme measures; and if you will be kind enough to bring Mademoiselle Andrée d'Argouges, now known by the name of Hélène Lanoue, here, I am sure that we should eventually arrive at a satisfactory understanding."

"Hold your tongue, sir," cried Carcenac, at a sign from the major. "Forward! and no nonsense if you value your life."

Golymine offered no resistance, and in a few moments he was safely ensconced in the dark closet where Maurevers, already dead drunk, was sleeping heavily upon the floor.

"Keep an eye upon them until I come back," said the major. "I am going to the Oaks to await Mademoiselle Lanoue's return, and if you don't see me again this evening—"

"You will find me on guard just the same to-morrow morning. You would even find me here a week hence, for I shall not leave until I receive further orders. I have provisions enough on hand to last me a month."

"Very well. If they attempt to escape, kill them."

"Like dogs, major."

George hastened off without a moment's delay, for he was anxious to have an interview with Hélène as soon as possible, and he did not despair of finding her at the railway station.

CHAPTER XVIII.

HELENE had seen Golymine depart without the slightest regret. This interview with her depraved brother had disheartened and exhausted her so much that she felt utterly unable to continue the struggle against the insolent assurance of this wretch who persisted in denying his guilt instead of thanking her.

She had not succeeded in extorting from him the confession of guilt which would, perhaps, have touched her heart. She felt no further doubt of his identity, but she wanted him to confess his guilt, show some sign of penitence, and promise to henceforth lead the life of an honest man.

Had he done this how gladly she would have aided him in his flight. George Roland could not denounce him without showing the judge the compromising letter; and before returning this letter to the major, she would have waited until her unworthy brother was safe on the other side of the ocean, or at least on the other side of the Channel.

Médéric would only have to spend a few more days in prison.

But now that Gaston d'Argouges's unfortunate sister had abandoned all hope of converting the pretended count to a better state of feeling, she felt that she had no right to retard the release of an innocent man.

If George had been there, she would not have kept the letter a minute longer. She even wondered if she had not better go to the Muire mansion in search of him; but she was by no means sure of finding him there, as more than two hours had elapsed since they parted at the station on the Rue d'Amsterdam.

Moreover, a brief interview in the presence of witnesses would not answer the purpose. It was not in the presence of Carcenac, or in the street, or in a crowded railway-car that she could broach a subject that affected her so deeply. How would her betrothed like the deplorable revelation she must make to him? Did he love her well enough to marry her after he learned the truth? She was firmly resolved to tell him all, but she was anxious to prepare him for it. Before confessing her relationship to the assassin she wanted to tell him how much she had suffered, and how terrible had been her anxiety and suspense; and after the revelation she intended to release him from his engagement, implore his forgiveness— though she certainly had no reason to reproach herself—and leave the fate of Mme. de Muire's murderer in the major's hands.

Time and solitude were alike necessary for all this; the garden at the Oaks, for instance, or better yet, the path skirting the forest of Vésinet, the path where George had first told her that he loved her.

There no one would interrupt them, not even Marcelle, who never went outside the château grounds now; and they would have plenty of time for a full explanation.

They ran some risk of meeting the Princess Orbitello, it is true, for Hélène had promised to meet her there toward evening; but if she presented herself, Mlle. Lanoue could ask her to postpone their interview until the following day.

On thinking of this fallen princess, the young girl suddenly remembered that during the painful interview that had just taken place nothing whatever had been said about Maurevers, so she had no news for the poor, deserted wife, who would hear of the arrest or flight of the pretended count only too soon.

This being the case, Hélène resolved to wait for the major's return to the villa; and not to return there herself until after she had seen the old school-mate who had invited her to call at a house on the Avenue de Villiers.

She abandoned the idea of eating a regular breakfast, though she was still hungry; and entered a confectioner's on the Rue Royale, where she eat a few cakes.

She had plenty of time at her disposal, as the Countess Borisof's governess had announced her intention of spending the day at the place mentioned, and Hélène would have preferred to go there on foot, for she was a good walker; but she would have been obliged to traverse the Boulevard Malesherbes, and she feared she might meet George Roland. She had decided not to make her confession until she had had time to think over what she wished to say to him; and she felt sure that she would tell him all, in spite of this determination, if she entered into conversation with him, so she took a carriage.

On passing the Muire mansion she noticed that every window was closed, and from this fact she rather rashly concluded that the major had already attended to the matter about which Carcenac wished to consult him and left the house.

The poor girl little suspected that at that very moment her unworthy brother was an inmate of this apparently deserted house.

The carriage crossed the Boulevard de Courcelles, turned into the Avenue de Villiers, and finally paused on the corner of the Rue Jouffroy. Here Hélène alighted, paid the coachman, and sent him away, for she expected to remain with Mlle. Védrine at least an hour or two, and thought it useless to keep the carriage waiting.

" On the corner of the avenue," her friend had said in her letter, without giving the number of the house. Was it on the left-hand side of the avenue, or the right? There was a private house on each corner, and a little further on, on both sides of the street, many others.

This locality is full of them, for within the last fifteen years the desire for a house to one's self has become a positive mania with Parisians. Wealthy citizens of the middle class who were formerly content with a handsome suite of apartments on the first or second floor in the heart of the city now reside in their own houses, a long way from the Palais Royal, and even from the principal boulevards.

It was the artists that began this. They have their reasons for seeking a dwelling-place on the heights. They need the clear light that comes from the north, and that is not obtainable in the heart of Paris.

The leading members of the *demi-monde* followed them.

The ownership of a private establishment is the height

of their ambition, and Paris is indebted to them for a host
of new streets. They have even covered with ornate dwell-
ings the unimproved and barren waste upon which the ferret was still hunted in the reign of Louis Philippe.

But as it frequently happens, especially since the late
crash, that their owners are obliged to abandon them, these
houses sold at auction often pass into better hands; so all's
well that ends well.

Many artists, too, have met with reverses after amassing
snug little fortunes. America is so full of pictures for
which she has paid fabulous sums, that even the wealthiest
of her inhabitants now buy less largely and pay less liberally, so more than one painter who had become a real estate
owner has been obliged to part with his property of late.

Hélène, who knew all this, thought that the Countess
Borisof had probably taken advantage of some such crisis
to secure a bargain in this locality, but which house was it?

She had alighted from the carriage on the right hand
side of the avenue in front of a small two-story house,
modern in its style of architecture and very respectable in
appearance; and thinking this might be the house she decided to ring the bell.

She was kept waiting a few moments, but finally a middle-aged woman opened the door—a very obliging person,
apparently, for as soon as Hélène inquired for Mlle. Védrine
she lost no time in admitting her.

"Mademoiselle is at the piano," she remarked. "She
will be greatly pleased to see you, for she has been waiting
very impatiently."

"Is she alone?" inquired Hélène.

"Yes, mademoiselle; and you will have plenty of time
to talk, for the countess will not return before five o'clock.
She has gone to the Park Monceau with her daughters. I
was their governess when they were young—for I am a
Frenchwoman like yourself—and like Mademoiselle Védrine, to whom I am devoted. She is trying a new piece of

music in the little drawing-room on the floor above, and if you will follow me I will conduct you there."

Hélène knew that her friend was a fine pianiste, so she was not surprised to find her thus engaged, but she was surprised at the air of luxury that pervaded the entire establishment, even to the vestibule. The hall floor was of white marble, and upon it lay a broad strip of Turkey carpet. Near the door leading into the vestibule, in the midst of a clump of flowering shrubs and tropical plants, stood a stuffed bear holding a silver waiter, intended for visiting-cards, in one paw.

If Hélène had doubted that the house had been furnished expressly for Mme. Borisof this essentially Russian ornament would have convinced her of the fact; but it is not always well to judge by appearances. The staircase was lined with mirrors which must have reflected, at night, the light of the countess's candles upheld by onyx torches, and which led to a sort of ante-chamber hung with Cordova leather and surrounded with velvet divans.

Then came the dining-room. It had but one window, but that was embowered in verdure, and it seemed to have been intended only for *tête-à-tête* suppers, so small was it and so scantily provided with chairs.

Certainly it was no artist that had so arranged his home; and Hélène asked herself how a lady of rank and the mother of three children could have chosen such an abode. But her guide allowed her no time for reflection, for after conducting her through a silken-hung drawing-room, very unlike the imposing drawing-room of the Muire mansion, she ushered her into an even more cozy and luxurious nook which was very nearly filled by a superb grand piano.

A young lady, who was sitting at the instrument, rose as soon as Hélène entered, and running to her kissed her fondly, exclaiming as she did so:

" So here you are at last, my dear!"

" Is this really you, Juliette?" murmured Mlle. Lanoue,

who recognized her friend's features, but fancied that they wore an entirely different expression from that which had characterized them in former times.

It had been only about two years since the two young ladies met. The countess visited France quite often, and during her last sojourn in Paris the young girls had spent an hour or two together almost every day, either at the Muire mansion or the Hôtel Meurice. But since Mlle. Védrine's return to Russia she had not written a single line to Hélène Lanoue, who had written to her frequently, and marveled greatly at receiving no reply.

Hélène now was equally astonished at the great change in her old school-mate. Juliette Védrine had always been pretty: she was pretty still, but her beauty was now of an entirely different type.

Her cheeks were less rosy but fuller; her eyes were much more brilliant; her mouth had more expression, but it was a sensual expression that Hélène had never seen upon it before. The once calm and gentle face had become more mobile; the voice more shrill. Her hair, too, was arranged in an entirely different fashion. In a word, Juliette no longer looked like a modest young girl.

"How you stare at me!" she exclaimed, pressing both Hélène's hands affectionately. "I have changed very much. Confess that you think me ugly."

"By no means," replied Mlle. Lanoue. "On the contrary, I think you much more beautiful and much more lively too."

"That is true. In former years I was rather inclined to melancholy. Everything than was not tinged with rose color. The life of a governess is not always a pleasant one."

"I know it; but have you adopted some other?"

"No; for as I wrote you, I am still with the countess; but one becomes accustomed to the yoke. I have learned wisdom. Besides, my situation has improved."

"Has the countess increased your salary?"

"Yes," replied Juliette, smiling. "I am comparatively rich now, and there is nothing to prevent me from becoming really so. I have just been offered a splendid situation, which I shall probably accept, and which will allow me to reside in France, so we can see each other often."

"I shall be very glad of that. So you are not married?"

"No, indeed. Why do you ask me that?"

"Why, because—don't be angry—because you wear so many diamonds. You have them in your ears and on your fingers. What a magnificent ring!"

"Do you like it? Pray accept it. I should be delighted to give it to you."

"Many thanks, my dear friend, but such jewels are not for a poor girl like me," replied Hélène.

"They would become you; and with a face like yours you certainly ought to possess much finer ones some day. But tell me about yourself. So many things happen in the course of two years. I have a host of things to tell you, but I want to hear what you have been doing first."

"So you failed to receive my letters?"

"No, I received them; and I know you must be angry with me for not answering them. By and by I will explain why I have been so remiss. But first let me hear how you are. I know you must have had a great deal of trouble, for the first news I heard on my arrival in Paris was the death of Madame de Muire. What a terrible thing it was! And it seems that they have not yet succeeded in discovering the wretch who killed that most excellent woman. You recollect how kindly she received me when I called at her house to see you. And your pupil, that charming Marcelle, how does she bear her cruel bereavement? I admit that one of my reasons for begging you to come and see me immediately was because I was anxious to learn exactly how you were situated, and I dared not present myself at the Oaks. Sit down, my dear Hélène, and let us talk about your prospects," added Mlle. Védrine, compelling her old school-mate to take a seat beside her on a black satin sofa garnished with cushions of every hue.

Hélène offered no resistance; but she was already meditating a speedy departure from this strange house, for she felt none too much confidence in this bejeweled governess, who reminded her so little of her old school-mate. She watched her with a vague uneasiness—something as little Red Riding-hood must have watched the wolf attired in her mother's night-cap. She almost expected to see the gleam of the sharp-pointed teeth and behold the long claws; that is to say, to hear some startling words fall from Juliette's lips, or at least a painful confession.

"Now tell me all your troubles, my dearest friend," continued Mlle. Védrine, without seeming in the least aware of Hélène's uneasiness. "I say your troubles, for you must have some. In the first place, you were deeply attached to Madame de Muire; and I am sure you mourn her death very much. Still this would be a mere trifle if you could retain your situation as governess to her daughter; but you can not with propriety remain in the count's house now he is a widower, especially after Mademoiselle de Muire marries, which will be very soon if I am to believe what I hear."

"Who told you anything about her intended marriage?" asked Hélène, greatly surprised.

"Everybody in Paris is talking about it."

"But you only arrived yesterday. How could you have heard—"

"In the first place I arrived yesterday morning, and Madame Borisof has already received a number of visitors. But to return to our subject. Sooner or later, my dear Hélène, you will find yourself in the street. What do you intend to do? Will you remain a governess all your life?"

"Yes, undoubtedly; unless—"

"Unless you marry, I suppose you mean. And you are

so pretty that you certainly will not want for suitors. I have had plenty myself. If I would I might have become the wife of a very worthy man—one of our compatriots and a tutor to the Governor of Moscow's children. You see, it would have been a very suitable match."

"And you refused him! Why? Didn't you like him?"

"Yes; he was a young man and very good-looking, besides being a remarkably agreeable and intelligent fellow."

"What were your objections then?"

"He had no money."

"Like yourself."

"Yes, like myself. And it was precisely because I was no better off than he was that I refused to marry him. Poverty is all very pleasant and romantic in poetry, but in real life is frightful—hideous. It is bad enough to be poor when one is single; but to be the wife of a poor man, surrounded by a crowd of dirty, squalling, ragged brats—Ugh!"

"Can it really be Juliette Védrine who is talking in this way?" exclaimed Mlle. Lanoue. "You who used to paint such charming pictures of domestic happiness. Do you recollect our conversations under the trees in the garden during recreation hours? How we used to talk of the Prince Charming who would certainly cross our path after we left the convent. You wanted him dark-complexioned, while I preferred one with fair hair. Still both were to be young and handsome. It mattered little to us whether he was rich or not, provided he corresponded with our ideal. And the children! Don't you remember how you wanted boys, while I liked girls best?"

"All this is true, unquestionably," said Mlle. Védrine, laughing. "You have a terrible memory. I must say that I had forgotten all about those silly conversations. One may be pardoned for fostering such absurd notions at a time when one knows nothing about life; but since I have learned something about it my ideas have changed, and so will yours, if they have not already."

"I think so," replied Hélène, gravely, "and if they are mere chimeras I will remain as I am."

"I hope not, for there is not much fun in living and dying a governess. One can endure it, at your age, for every man you meet flatters and makes much of you. But by and by, when youth and beauty are gone, it will be very different. You will either have to make up your mind to starve upon the meager savings of twenty-five years of toil, or plod about the streets selling books or feather-dusters with wooden shoes on your feet—your little feet that were made to walk upon velvet—not to plod through the dust and mire!"

And as Hélène, much troubled by the conversation of this friend whose motive she was beginning to vaguely understand, answered never a word, Mlle. Védrine remarked:

"But you have found a husband, perhaps?"

"Perhaps is the very word."

"You mean probably that you have not quite decided to marry him. Well, I'll give you a word of advice. Don't marry him unless he is rich—very rich. If he is not you had better not give up your liberty. I have guarded mine, and I congratulate myself every day. If I had linked my destiny with that of the professor who asked me to marry him I should have had to scrimp and save all the rest of my days."

"So you remained with the Countess Borisof instead. I understand, and I see that you were not the loser by it, since she lavishes so many gifts upon you—for it was she, of course, who gave you these beautiful jewels."

"What! do you really believe it was that old simpleton who gave them to me?" exclaimed Juliette, bursting into a hearty laugh. "My dear, you don't know her. She has a yearly income of sixty thousand rubles, and don't spend half of it. She is the greatest miser imaginable; in fact,

such a miser that I had no end of trouble in making her
pay me my salary.”

“ But if it wasn’t Madame Borisof, who was it?” faltered
Hélène, greatly disconcerted.

“ I have made a great deal of money.”

“ How, pray?”

“ As an actress.”

“ You have gone on the stage?”

“ Yes, my dear, and I certainly have had no cause to regret leaving Madame Borisof.”

“ What! are you no longer governess to her children?”

“ No, and I haven’t been for at least eighteen months.
She treated me so badly during our last visit to France that
I left her immediately after our return to Russia.”

“ That can not be possible. Why, we are in her house
now. The woman who just opened the door for me told
me—”

“ That the countess had gone to the Park Monceau with
her three daughters, and that she would not return until
five o’clock. My excellent Gertrude was only repeating the
lesson I had taught her.”

This imprudent admission very naturally startled Hélène.
She had been caught in a trap, but she resolved not to remain in it.

“ What was the necessity of this falsehood?” she exclaimed, rising hastily.

“ I was afraid you would not come in if Gertrude told
you the truth. I had asked you to meet me at the house
of the countess, and I could not let her contradict me.”

“ Then you were also guilty of a falsehood in writing as
you did?”

“ It was unavoidable. I was so anxious to see you, and
if you had known that I had regained my independence,
you would not have come.”

“ No, certainly not, and now I know it, I shall not remain here a minute longer.”

"Come, come, don't be angry. I haven't the slightest intention of detaining you against your will. But listen to me, and after you have heard what I have to say, if you insist upon going you can do so."

"I will not listen to another word. I am going now."

"Don't make the attempt. Gertrude will not open the street door for you without my permission."

"You are in your own house, then?"

"No, this house doesn't belong to me. I own one though, and I am only staying here temporarily."

"So you own a house! Ah! I understand now why you have abandoned the humble vocation that yielded you an honest living," said Hélène bitterly.

"I don't mind your innuendoes in the least, nor do I hesitate to admit that I have strayed from the right path. I followed it as long as I could, but I finally became tired of it. It is full of thorns, and I deserve not a little credit for having torn my feet in it for five long years. I finally chose another one, in which I have as yet found nothing but roses."

"Is it possible that you can talk in this way?"

"I am frank, that is all. Yes, I have cast prudence to the winds, as the saying is, and I can not say I regret it. You can not understand it. I am now only a reprobate in your eyes. A day will come when you will pardon me, and you will do right, for I am excusable. I had nothing, and I was the hireling of an arrogant and imperious Russian who often made me feel my dependence keenly. Let those who have never known the misery and humiliation of our sad lot cast the first stone; but you, Hélène, who have passed through the same trials, should certainly be more indulgent."

"I can forgive you—but excuse you—never!"

"Ah, well. I will be content with your forgiveness, but I entreat you not to curse me nor forbid me to see you again."

"You ask an impossibility. I do not curse you; I only pity you; but as for seeing you again—"

"I know that your position demands great prudence on your part, and I should be the very first to advise you not to compromise yourself. You, I am sure, will admit that when you recollect that I denied myself the pleasure of going to the Count de Muire's to call on you; I preferred to resort to stratagem to secure an interview with you, and you ought to be grateful to me for it instead of reproaching me."

"Who is the owner of this house into which you have decoyed me?"

"It belongs to a friend of my lover."

"Your lover," repeated Hélène, sadly. "You have a lover, you, the dearest friend of my early years—you, whom I once loved as a sister."

"I love you as much as ever. If it were not so I should not have made this confession to you. Yes, I have accepted the protection of a wealthy Russian, who is worth his millions, and who gratifies my every whim. He has been recently called to St. Petersburg, where his duties as aide-de-camp to the emperor will detain him at least six months. He decided that it would be best for me to remain in Paris during his long absence, so he purchased a house for me not far from here, on the Rue Fortuny, and if you ever do me the honor to enter it you will see nothing there to shock you, I assure you."

"But you are not married, and you never will be."

"I am not so sure of that. The Russian aristocrat is not so narrow-minded as our gentlemen of rank, and I should not be the first Frenchwoman who has married a Muscovite."

"I hope so, indeed," replied Hélène sadly, "and now you have told me all, let me go."

"Not until you have told me your own plans for the future. I insist, because I am afraid that you find yourself in a very unenviable position just now. It is evident that you can not remain with Mademoiselle de Muire much longer. Have you any other place in view?"

Mlle. Lanoue shook her head.

" And if one should not offer itself what will become of you, my dear Hélène? You gave me to understand just now that you could marry if you chose. Were you in earnest?"

" I shall not answer you."

" Why?"

" Because you have lost all right to question me. In former years I concealed nothing from you, and I shall never forget the happy days when we had no secrets from each other; but that time has passed, never to return again. I did not solicit the sad revelations you have just made to me, and I assure you that I shall never betray your confidence; but I have nothing to tell you in return, and I shall try to forget that we ever met."

" At least tell me if it is true that Marcelle's betrothed is guilty? I hear that he has been arrested on the charge of having killed the poor countess."

" How did you hear that the young man was in prison?" inquired Hélène, hastily.

And seeing Juliette hesitate, Mlle. Lanoue added:

" Don't tell me again that you heard it through the friends of the Countess Borisof, who is not in Paris, as you yourself just admitted."

" Nor is Prince Werki, but I receive visits from several of his friends, and among the number there are several acquaintances of the Count de Muire, who are familiar with the tragical affair."

" Name them."

" Well, there is the Marquis de Brangue, who witnessed the shooting of the countess."

" Are you acquainted with Monsieur de Brangue?"

" Certainly. Pray do me the honor to believe that I

associate only with members of the best society. So you, too, are acquainted with the marquis."

"I hope you have never spoken to him of me," said Hélène, hastily.

"You need have no fears on that score. I am no novice, and I have taken good care not to tell him that you were once an intimate friend of mine. But a person who is equally ignorant of our former intimacy has often spoken of you to me, and always in the most complimentary terms."

"To whom do you allude?"

"To the Viscount de Liscoat. He thinks you perfectly charming, and never tires of praising your beauty, grace and intelligence."

"I am greatly obliged to him for his good opinion, but I dislike him very much."

"That is strange. It is true that he is not a young man, but he has very distinguished manners and many other good qualities."

"I have never discovered them."

"Indeed! Well, I am sorry."

"And why, pray?"

"Why, because he is immensely rich. You will probably say: 'What difference can that possibly make to me?' Remember what I said to you a few moments ago. I do not despair of being a princess some day, a real princess, after having been a sort of left-handed or morganatic one. Ah, well, it is not in Russia alone that kings marry shepherdesses, and I feel certain that you could make Monsieur de Liscoat marry you if you chose."

"I am sure that you are very much mistaken, and I am equally sure that I would not marry him if I could."

"But I assure you that he is desperately in love with you, and at his age such passions are as profound as they are rare. If I should become a princess my success will cost me dear; but you will escape the ordeal I have been obliged to undergo."

"I hate and despise the man."

"I think you misjudge him, and that you do very wrong to condemn him without knowing him better."

"I know him only too well, and I hope I shall never see him again. If he authorized any such avowal of his sentiments as you have just made to me, I am surprised that you accepted such a mission."

"If I did, it was only for your own sake. Liscoat is generosity itself. What would you say if I should tell you that you have only to say the word to become the owner of this house, which is valued at two hundred thousand francs, and of the furniture, which is worth at least sixty thousand more. Liscoat stands ready to offer you this gift, and if you like the necessary papers will be drawn up and signed to-morrow."

"Ah! this is too infamous!" exclaimed Hélène, with tears in her eyes. "How dare you propose such a shameful bargain to me! I did not suppose you had fallen so low."

"And I did not think you such a simpleton. Still, each one to his taste. If you prefer to plod along in poverty, so be it. You will regret your decision some day, when it is too late."

"Enough. Stand aside, and let me leave this house. Forget that I exist, though believe me, I shall never cease to pray for you."

"Thanks, you are really too kind. As you seem to be in such haste to depart, I will go and countermand the orders I gave Gertrude. You can surely wait here two or three minutes."

And without waiting for Mlle. Lanoue's response, Juliette Védrine lifted the *portière* and disappeared before poor Hélène could think to detain her.

It was all done so quickly that Mlle. Lanoue did not have time to follow her treacherous friend. When she recovered from the state of astonishment into which this hasty flight had thrown her she might have run after Mlle. Védrine, and perhaps overtaken her on the staircase, but it seemed to her that she was surrounded by traps of every kind, and she hardly dared to traverse the rooms that adjoined the boudoir into which she had been ushered; besides, she did not want Juliette to know that she felt afraid. She soon began to accuse herself of having been too easily frightened. She said to herself that Juliette, however depraved she might be, certainly would not venture to carry things too far. It was quite enough to have lured her innocent friend to this accursed house to listen to such infamous proposals. She certainly would not dare to make her a prisoner there against her will. "She will be back in a moment," thought Mlle. Lanoue, "and if she speaks to me I will not answer her. I shall leave the house without honoring her with another word."

CHAPTER XIX.

This thought was passing through the mind of George Roland's affianced wife when she heard a sound that made her start violently.

It came from below, and strongly resembled the noise made by the hasty closing of a heavy door.

Had this door been opened to admit some one or allow some one to pass out? There was a way for Hélène to satisfy herself on this point, and she had the presence of mind to avail herself of it.

The day was very warm, and the windows overlooking the street were open. Hélène ran to one, and, lifting the Japanese screen that protected the boudoir from the heat of the sun, she put her head out of the window.

Juliette Védrine was already rounding the corner of the street. Mlle. Lanoue reached the window just in time to see her turn into the Avenue de Villiers, and, on glancing in the opposite direction, she saw the duenna Gertrude walking slowly up the Rue Jouffroy.

Had these unscrupulous creatures imprisoned her in the house by turning the key in the lock of the door through which they had just darted like thieves who have been foiled in their attempt to plunder? Hélène's first impulse was to run down-stairs and ascertain for a certainty, and then make her escape if it were not too late; so she stepped back from the window, but on turning she hastily recoiled in astonishment and terror.

The Viscount de Liscoat stood before her in a respectful, almost imploring, attitude, with his hat in his hand, and a smile upon his lips—a half-mocking, half-insinuating smile, that aroused Mlle. Lanoue's exasperation to the highest pitch. She was less frightened now that she had been brought face to face with the danger that threatened her, and she thought only of giving the old rake the lesson he deserved.

"Your conduct is infamous, sir," she said, coldly and contemptuously. "Your accomplice enticed me here by your orders, and after attempting to drag me down into the mire into which she has fallen, she now leaves me alone with you. I knew that you were a *débauche*, but I supposed you still had some little sense of honor left. I see that I was mistaken, and I need hardly say that the feeling I now entertain for you is one of the most profound contempt, but I do not fear you in the least."

"I should certainly hope not," replied the insolent viscount, laughing. "What can you possibly have to fear? We are not living in the days when young girls are abducted by force, and this house is not a grim castle any more than I am one of the ferocious barons of mediæval times. You are in the heart of Paris, on the Rue Jouffroy, a respectable street, where one is perfectly safe from insult or violence."

"Prove this by allowing me to depart."

"You are free, mademoiselle. If you consent to grant me a hearing, it will be of your own free will, but I beseech you to allow me to tell you why I begged Mademoiselle Védrine to write to you. She was once a friend of yours, and I am anxious to convince you that she is not as guilty as you suppose."

The astute old viscount had instantly hit upon the sole pretext he could have devised to induce Hélène to listen to him.

"You will not succeed in doing that," she said, coldly; "but no matter. Speak, justify her, if you can. But first tell me is it, or is it not true that she has left the Countess Borisof to—"

"To accept the protection of Prince Werki, one of my most intimate friends? Yes; this is perfectly true. I see that you blame her, but she can certainly plead extenuating circumstances."

"That is exactly what she has done, but she has not succeeded in gaining absolution from me."

"Or in persuading you to follow her example, I am sure. Allow me, however, to say that she is the more excusable from the fact that I am satisfied her lover will marry her eventually."

"Then why did he not marry her in the first place?"

"It would have been very much better, I admit. But a man of Werki's rank and position is obliged to pay some heed to the prejudices of the circle in which he moves. Mademoiselle Védrine, you are perhaps aware, gave up teaching to accept an engagement at the French Theater in Moscow."

"She told me so, but I did not believe it."

"It is the truth, nevertheless. She achieved a brilliant success, both by her beauty and talent, for she is a born actress, and Werki fell desperately in love with her. But he could not give her his name in Russia while she was an actress, so he proposed to her that she should leave the stage and come to Paris, where he would establish her in comfortable quarters, and where she could remain until he had fulfilled his duties at the court of the Czar. He will then rejoin Mademoiselle Védrine, and if the marriage does not take place immediately it will at a very early day, I haven't the slightest doubt.''

'' I hope so, indeed, for Juliette's sake; but I do not think it at all likely. In any case, I can never forgive her for setting this trap for me, and for thinking me capable of doing as she has done. We grew up together, and she ought to have known me better.''

'' And so,'' began Liscoat, assuming a grief-stricken air, '' you would scorn an honorable man who, loving you sincerely, and having no opportunity to tell his love, has resorted to stratagem to secure an interview with you? Does not the end justify the means in such a case?''

'' Not in my eyes, sir.''

'' But I swear to you, mademoiselle, that you have inspired me with a profound passion, and I implore your pardon for having yielded to an impulse stronger than my own will. I had long been seeking an opportunity to see you without calling at the house of my poor friend, the count, who will receive no one, and learning by chance that Mademoiselle Védrine was an old school-mate, I hastened to her; I confided my secret to her, and she kindly promised to assist me. She dared not go to the Oaks for fear of not being very cordially received by your pupil and her father, and the idea of writing to you occurred to her.''

'' Then she is even more culpable than you are. But I am surprised that you should have had the hardihood to insult me by your shameful offers. You certainly ought to have realized that a man of your years would have no chance whatever of marrying me, much less of leading me astray, and you must have seen that the only feeling I had for you was one of the heartiest dislike.''

To remind this antiquated fop that he was an old man

was to wound him at his most vulnerable point; and Liscoat, who had hoped to gain a victory by gentleness and flattery, instantly changed his tactics, and threw aside his mask.

"That I fail to please you is a misfortune for which I am not entirely inconsolable," he retorted, sarcastically; "and now, will you be kind enough to listen to the rest I have to say to you? You entered this house of your own free will. I defy you to prove the contrary. There is nothing whatever to prevent you from remaining here permanently, as I offer you the entire property; but if you wish to leave the house you can do so, though you will be none the less deeply compromised, for the fact of your coming here is no secret."

"People shall also know how you enticed me here, and how I answered your insulting proposals."

"Oh! I don't doubt that you will defend yourself, and you will perhaps succeed in convincing Major Roland that, having missed the last train, you spent the night at an hotel."

"What do you mean?"

"I am anxious that you should have plenty of time to examine the house. When you have seen what a charming home you would have here, you will perhaps change your mind."

"I shall not remain here a minute longer."

"Pardon me; you will remain until to-morrow morning. A night's rest will do you good; besides, it is said, you know, that the night brings counsel. You will be entirely alone, and you will want for nothing. The bedroom is ready for your occupancy, and you will find a cold lunch awaiting you there. If you should become lonely, there are books in the library. Your imprisonment will not be rigorous, nor will it last long. To-morrow morning, about eight o'clock, Gertrude will come to release you, and there will be nothing to prevent you from leaving for the Oaks, where your friends will doubtless be charmed to see you. Nor will there be anything to prevent you from telling your friends what happened to you; and if either of them should feel inclined to make any trouble, I shall find a way to silence them."

Having said this, M. de Liscoat replaced his hat upon his head; then, seeing that Mlle. Lanoue seemed inclined to follow him, he added, coldly:

" Do not attempt to leave the house in spite of me. You would not succeed, and you had better avoid a ridiculous scene. I repeat that you have nothing to apprehend to-night, and that you will be at liberty to leave the house early to-morrow morning. I need only say that if you persist in your refusal to accept my devotion, you will never be troubled by me in the future; but I do not despair of seeing you here again to-morrow at this time."

With this parting insult the viscount disappeared, leaving Hélène to her reflections.

She realized that it would be worse than useless to engage in a struggle in which she was sure to be worsted, and that instead of following Liscoat, it would be well to make sure that his departure was not merely feigned.

So she returned to the window, where, through the slats of the lowered venetian shutter, she could see without being seen; and in a minute or two, she had the satisfaction of seeing the odious wretch leave the house, lock the door behind him, put the key in his pocket, and then amble up the Avenue de Villiers, without once turning to look back.

Hélène was now really and truly a prisoner; but she was at least relieved of one grave apprehension, for she was now certain that the detestable viscount had really left the house; but he might return; so she at once set to work to devise some means of avoiding further insult.

This would be an easy matter if the door leading from the vestibule into the hall was provided with a bolt, so Mlle. Lanoue ran down the marble stairs, and through the hall.

guarded by the stuffed bear, to satisfy herself on this point. To her very great relief she found two strong bolts, one above, the other below the lock, and she at once proceeded to draw them.

She was now safe—that is, unless the house had two outside doors—and to ascertain this she had only to explore the house from top to bottom, which she immediately proceeded to do.

She soon discovered that there was only a solid wall skillfully concealed by a dense growth of tropical plants behind the staircase, and that the hall had no other outlet.

Being already familiar with the arrangement of the lower story, which consisted of only three rooms—*en suite*—a dining-room, drawing-room, and boudoir, she went straight up to the floor above, which was divided into three rooms, like the floor above, a library, bedroom, and dressing-room.

The walls of the library, the room she came to first, was lined with ebony book-cases, filled with small but expensively bound volumes—the entire literary fruits of the gilded corruption of more than a century—which had been placed here, doubtless, to deprave those whose curiosity might impell them to open the diabolical volumes.

Hélène, without even pausing to glance at them, passed on into the bed-chamber, which was no more reassuring in its aspect.

There were mirrors everywhere, and upon a large lacquer-table was a lunch, served upon the most costly china, with crystal decanters filled with wines that rivaled the amethyst and topaz in their hues.

The dressing-room which opened out of this chamber was a marvel of luxury. The bath-tub, table, vases, and even the wainscoting were of onyx; the toilet articles, ivory and silver, and the other accessories of exquisite Sèvres.

Juliette Védrine must have had one like it in her house

on the Rue Fortuny; and Mlle. Lanoue would not even cross the threshold of this laboratory of beauty.

She was obliged to retrace her steps to ascend to the garret, where she also found three rooms—two evidently intended for holding dresses, the other as a bed-chamber for the maid.

The kitchen and servants' rooms were in the basement. She went through that, and when she had completed this hasty tour of inspection, she felt satisfied that the house had an outlet only on the Rue Jouffroy.

The architect who constructed it had certainly made the most of a very small piece of land, but the house was only a *bonbonnière,* after all, and the viscount would not ruin himself by giving it away.

Hélène troubled herself very little about its value, however. She was only thinking how she could manage to get out of this luxurious prison, and as an immediate escape seemed impossible, she returned to the boudoir, and sat herself down to solve the problem.

The first plan that presented itself to her mind seemed scarcely feasible. The Rue Jouffroy is not much frequented nor very densely populated; nevertheless there are plenty of houses and plenty of pedestrians.

Consequently there was nothing to prevent Hélène from going to the window and asking the assistance of some neighbor or passer-by. But what should she say to this stranger? How was she to explain the embarrassing situation in which she found herself? It is no easy matter to carry on a conversation from one side to the other of a broad street; besides, her account of her strange adventure might not be believed.

In these days noble maidens are no longer incarcerated in grim towers by wicked enchanters and obliged to invoke the aid of passing knights. Hélène would have been obliged to accost the first person who happened to come along, and prosaically request him to go in search of a locksmith and a policeman, who would perhaps take her for a madwoman or something worse. All things considered, she decided that this plan was impracticable, and that it would be necessary to devise some other.

Lifting the screen, she began to examine the surroundings of her prison. On the left was a vacant lot surrounded by a wooden fence; on the right there was an unfinished house, upon which no one seemed to be working. Opposite stood a private house much larger than M. Liscoat's, but apparently unoccupied, for every shutter was closed, and the family and servants had probably left Paris to spend the summer in the country or at the sea-shore.

No assistance could be expected from that quarter, consequently; and as for passers-by, Hélène soon learned to her sorrow that she could not depend upon them. She soon perceived a tall, good-looking young man walking briskly down the street, apparently a young artist on his way back to his studio. When he was about ten yards from the house he discerned Mlle. Lanoue's lovely face at the window, and instantly began to smile.

He had a pleasant face, and Hélène almost made up her mind to open a conversation with him; but artists are rather too audacious, and this one being guilty of the blunder of throwing a kiss to the pretty brunette who was gazing down at him from the window, Hélène blushed and hastily drew back.

Mortified and discouraged she threw herself on the sofa, scarcely able to restrain her tears. Was she indeed condemned to wait until Gertrude came to release her as the viscount had promised? This would not be an irremediable evil of course, as, thanks to the bolts that protected her, her persecutor could not take her by surprise. But if Gertrude obeyed her master's orders she would not make her appearance until the next morning; and the idea of spending the night in her present quarters made Mlle. Lanoue shudder.

What would M. de Muire say? What would Marcelle
say? Above all, what would Major Roland say if she did
not return to the Oaks? This inexplicable absence might
ruin her prospects forever; and it was probably upon this
possibility that the odious viscount had counted. He had
probably said to himself that poor Hélène, dismissed in disgrace by the Count de Muire and deserted by her affianced
husband, would become an easy victim to his wiles.

"No, no," she muttered, savagely, "this scoundrel
shall not get the best of me. I will leave this house, even
if I am obliged to jump out of the window. I will wait
until dark. The hour at which I return to the villa doesn't
matter, provided I return there to-night, and I shall return
unless I kill myself in my efforts to reach the ground!"

CHAPTER XX.

HAVING come to this conclusion, she immediately began
to make preparations for her flight.

The window was at least fifteen feet from the ground.
To jump from that height would involve too great a risk;
but she could make the descent in safety if she had some
kind of a support. She lost no time in searching for a
rope, that she would probably have been unable to find,
but hastily pulling down the *portière* that concealed the
door of the boudoir she tore it into strips and tied these
strips firmly together; then desiring to test the strength of
her hastily improvised fire escape, she suspended herself in
mid air by it, after fastening it securely to the railing of
the stairs, and found that it would sustain her weight.

This accomplished, there was nothing for her to do but
wait until dark—and night comes late in the month of July:
but she could not descend from the window until the street
was deserted, for any passer-by who saw her performing
this feat would be sure to cry "Stop thief!"

Hélène felt sure that this quiet street would become well-nigh deserted by nine or ten o'clock; still she had plenty of time to rest a little, and feeling the need of a repose after the trying ordeal through which she had just passed, she threw herself on the sofa and soon fell into a deep slumber.

There was no sound to disturb her for awhile, but when she did wake a strong breeze was rattling the Venetian blinds, and dashing big drops of rain in her face through the open window. Outside it was as dark as pitch.

The weather had suddenly changed; thunder was muttering in the distance, and dense black clouds were hanging over the city.

Hélène sprung up frightened, not so much by the storm as by the darkness; but she soon perceived that so far as she was concerned nothing could have been more opportune than this unforeseen tempest, for the rain had dispersed all promenaders, and kept the worthy citizens who like to stroll about the streets on summer evenings quietly at home.

Mlle. Lanoue looked out of the window and perceived, to her great delight, that the street was positively deserted. Not a person was in sight, and the only sound audible was the dull and continuous rumble of vehicles in the far distance.

"Now or never!" Hélène said to herself, and she began operations without a moment's loss of time. The attempt seemed likely to prove successful. Hélène was not heavy, and the distance was short and the rope she had manufactured reached very nearly to the ground.

Before making the venture she looked up and down the street. There was a street-lamp nearly opposite the house, and it diffused light enough for the girl to be able to see that the coast was perfectly clear.

There was nothing left for her to do but make the descent, when she suddenly asked herself what time it could be.

She had, of course, lost all idea of time during her nap,

and she could not consult her watch, for she had forgotten to put it on that morning before leaving the Oaks. She recollected having seen two or three clocks in the house, but none of them seemed to be going; besides, Hélène did not like to go upstairs without a light. It is only smokers who always carry matches in their pockets, and though there were probably some in the bedroom she did not feel inclined to go up and hunt for them.

It was of the utmost importance for her to know the time, however, for if it was past midnight she would be unable to return to Chatou that night.

She recollected that daylight was beginning to wane when she fell asleep, and she supposed she must have slept two or perhaps three hours. It becomes dark about eight o'clock in midsummer, so Hélène calculated that it must now be nearly ten o'clock, and that she could reach the Saint Lazare station in time for the 10.35 train if she made haste.

The most difficult part of her undertaking was the beginning. The window sill was no very great distance from the floor, but it was necessary to climb upon it and then swing herself from it without letting go her hold of the rope—no easy talk for a woman hampered with skirts.

Fortunately Hélène had learned calisthenics at school, and had practiced them occasionally since with Marcelle in the garden at the villa, so she was unusually agile in her movements.

When she let herself drop into space the sensation was a little startling, but she kept a tight hold on the rope, and it was not until she was within five or six feet of the ground that she noticed her support yielding a little. To escape the fall that seemed inevitable she jumped the rest of the distance, and did it so cleverly that she landed upon her feet. Still the concussion made her lose her equilibrium, and she staggered and fell to the pavement.

This fall would have been a mere trifle, however, if the

pouring rain had not changed the dust of the Rue Jouffroy into mire, so she found herself smeared with mud from head to foot. The evil was irreparable, at least for the time being; and for a moment the poor girl felt that she could not possibly return to the Oaks in such a plight. But there was no help for it, so she hastened up the Avenue de Villiers where she hoped to find a carriage to convey her to the railway station.

Aside from this slight mishap, the attempt had proved a complete success. The street was deserted, the coast was clear. There was nothing for her to do now but proceed on her way and avoid any dangerous encounters.

Mlle. Lanoue was not in the habit of going about Paris alone at night, and at first she was a little frightened to find the long avenue so completely deserted. Not a single pedestrian nor a vehicle of any kind was visible in the flickering light of the street-lamps that lined both sides of the street.

It was still raining hard, and she said to herself that in this odd part of the town all signs of life probably ceased very early, especially in such weather as this.

So she plodded bravely on through the wind and rain, and soon reached the square upon which the statue of Alexander Dumas senior was recently erected.

The quickest way to reach the Rue d'Amsterdam from this point is to turn to the left into the Boulevard Malesherbes; but Hélène turned to the right because she perceived in the distance a moving light that she took for that of a fiacre.

She began to run now, and soon found herself at the corner of the Boulevard Courcelles, which intersects the Boulevard Malesherbes at right angles.

The light had disappeared, but she found herself in front of a large omnibus that was just leaving the transfer station. Where was it going? Mlle. Lanoue did not know, but she resolved to ask the conductor, who was already perched upon the step.

As she approached, however, she heard a voice cry out:

"One more seat vacant! Step in, madame."

A woman entered the vehicle, which now had its full complement of passengers. Two men, after some grumbling, decided to climb upon the roof—a bad place in a shower—but one of them said to the other:

"We shall be drenched, but there seems to be no help for it, as this is the last omnibus."

The remark reached Hélène's ears and gave her abundant food for reflection. She knew that the omnibuses ran all the evening: if this omnibus was the last one, it must be very late.

She stepped to the door of the office, and addressing the boy who was putting up the shutters, she asked him the hour. "Quarter past twelve. The transfers are no good now," replied the lad, mistaking her for a belated passenger.

Hélène was overwhelmed with consternation. The last train for Chatou left at 12.35. She had not more than fifteen minutes at her disposal, and no amount of hurrying would get her there in time. Besides, what good would it do for her to take a train that passed through Chatou about one o'clock in the morning?

Ever since Mme. de Muire's death all the inmates of the Oaks had kept very early hours. The gates were closed, and all the servants were in bed long before midnight, so Mlle. Lanoue would have been obliged to disturb the entire household to gain an entrance. And how could she present herself before them soaked with rain and covered with mud? How could she explain her strange adventure?

She realized the necessity of postponing her return; but she could not spend the night in wandering about the streets. But where could she go? She certainly would not dare to present herself at a hotel alone at this late hour; nor would she be received in any respectable house under such circumstances and in such a plight.

Her short season of rest had cost her dear.   She thought she was saved when she succeeded in making her escape from the viscount's house, but now she felt that she was lost.   She said to herself that George would condemn her without a hearing, and that he would never marry her.

The poor girl stood there alone in the middle of the night and in the pouring rain, wondering what was to become of her, and longing to die.

Suddenly a most fortunate idea occurred to her.   The Muire town house was only about two hundred yards from the spot where she was standing.

"Why can I not seek a shelter there?" she thought. "The worthy *concierge* who was left in charge of the house will not refuse me admittance.   To-morrow morning I will send a telegram to Monsieur Roland, and as Carcenac can testify to the truth of my assertion, I will tell George all, and he will perhaps forgive me.   This is my only chance now."

Mlle. Lanoue was too much engrossed in thought to pay much attention to what was going on around her.   The omnibus had disappeared up the Boulevard de Courcelles; the office had been closed, the rain was still falling, and the poor girl supposed she was quite alone on the broad sidewalk where she had paused to reflect upon her unfortunate situation.

She had entirely failed to notice a gentleman who was coming up the street, protected by an umbrella; but he had noticed her, as was only natural, for one does not often see a handsomely dressed lady standing motionless in the street when the rain is falling in torrents.

After coming a little closer, the stranger paused, and seeing that the lady was young and pretty, he accosted her, and it was not until then that Mlle. Lanoue became conscious of his presence.

"You will be drowned, madame, if you remain here," he remarked, in a rather free and easy tone.   "Don't you see that it is raining in torrents? Fortunately, I have an umbrella that is large enough for both of us, however.''

As he spoke, he offered his arm to Hélène, supposing that she would accept it without much urging, and he was not a little surprised to see her draw back, and prepare to cross the street.

As she did so, she unconsciously stepped near enough to the street lamp for the light to fall full upon her face, which the stranger had not seen distinctly before.

" Why, I know you!'' he exclaimed; " you know me; we know each other! You are the lady I saw to-day at the window on the Rue Jouffroy. Don't you recollect that I bowed to you, and that you stepped back from the window instead of responding to the salute? Not very kind in you, was it? but our meeting this evening consoles me.''

Mlle. Lanoue had not forgotten the tall artist who had had the audacity to throw a kiss to her; she recognized him perfectly, and instantly resolved to put an immediate end to the conversation.

" It is quite possible that you have seen me before, sir,'' she said, coldly, " but that is no reason that I should listen to you here, and I must beg you to proceed on your way.''

" But our paths lead in the same direction, I suppose, as you are probably on your way back to the Rue Jouffroy, and I also reside on that highly respectable street, about half a block further down.''

" You are mistaken. I am not going to the Rue Jouffroy.''

" But you came from there.''

" Whether I did or not, I am now going only a short distance from here, and I need no escort. Will you be kind enough to leave me?''

" In such weather as this? Never! It would be positively inhuman. You are drenched from head to foot already, and you will be positively drowned before you reach your destination. If you will not accept my arm, at least accept half of my umbrella."

He was already holding it over Hélène's head, sheltering her in spite of her objections.

"I see!" he continued, gayly, "you are afraid of compromising yourself, because you don't know who I am. I will introduce myself: Pierre Dax, artist, twenty-seven years of age; born at Pamiers, in the department of Ariège, but now residing at No. 59 Rue Jouffroy, and the recipient of a medal at the exhibition this year. You know all about me now, and are satisfied, I hope, that you are not dealing with a vagabond. Take notice, too, that in exchange for all this valuable information, I do not even ask your name, nor what you were doing in that pretty little house, which doesn't bear the best of reputations, by the way."

"I was decoyed there, and afterward made a prisoner, and I have only just succeeded in making my escape from it," replied Hélène, yielding to a hasty impulse. "When you passed the house, I had more than half a mind to ask you to assist me."

"Why didn't you do it? To deliver you, I would have set fire to the house, if necessary. What you just told me, does not surprise me in the least, knowing the character of the owner of the house as I do. But I wonder at his audacity in troubling a person like yourself, and if you would like me to give him a lesson I am at your service."

"Thank you, but the wretch will never trouble me again, so I think it would be better to let the matter drop. But I shall not forget your name nor your address, and it is quite possible that I may have recourse to your testimony."

"I will testify to whatever you please; I shall certainly testify, too, that I met you in the street during a pouring rain and escorted you home, so now you can not refuse to accept my arm."

"I accept it because I see I can trust you, and because we shall not have far to go. If it were daylight, you could see the house from here."

"I am sorry to hear that. I should be only too proud to serve as your escort for a much longer time," answered the artist, gallantly.

Hélène laid the tips of her fingers upon the arm of this comparative stranger, and they traversed the Boulevard Malersherbes side by side. All her fears had vanished, and she was now endeavoring to see if any advantage could be derived from this meeting in case she should be called upon to explain the occurrence of the eventful night that might not only cost her her reputation, but ruin her whole future.

"I have a favor to ask of you," she said, at last. "After you have accompanied me to my destination, you will return to your own home, I suppose?"

"Yes."

"Well, when you pass the house in which I was held a prisoner, I want you to satisfy yourself that I made my escape by the window. To make the descent I used two curtains that I tore into strips and afterward fastened to the window sill. It must be there still."

"Very well. I will try to find a policeman, and if I do, I will certainly call his attention to the fact, and insist upon his making an investigation. He will think that some thief made his escape in that way, after plundering the house, and he will not hesitate to report the case to the commissioner of police. I understand, of course, that your name is not to be mentioned in connection with the matter, mademoiselle. I say mademoiselle, without really knowing, of course."

"You are right, however, sir, for I am not married. I hope, of course, that my name will never appear in connection with the affair, but if I should be obliged to prove that I fled from that terrible house, it is to you alone that I can look for assistance."

The artist was about to assure her of his devotion to her interests, when Mlle. Lanoue checked him by suddenly pausing and pointing to an imposing *porte cochère.*

"We have reached our journey's end," she remarked. "This is the house."

Pierre Dax, greatly surprised at the sight of this palatial abode, exclaimed:

"I congratulate you, mademoiselle. You are superbly lodged."

Then almost immediately, he added:

"Why! I know the house. It belongs to the Count de Muire."

"How do you know?" inquired Hélène, greatly surprised.

"I am acquainted with a young man, an amateur artist, who often visits here, and I have accompanied him as far as the door several times."

"What is his name?"

"His name is Mestras—Médéric de Mestras. He is a great friend of mine, but he has just got himself into a terrible scrape."

"He is innocent, nevertheless," said Mlle. Lanoue, hastily.

"I haven't the slightest doubt of it, and I am delighted to hear that you know him. It seems to be a sort of bond between us, and I begin to hope that we shall meet again some day."

"I very willingly promise you that. You shall know all, but you must ask me no questions just at this time. I am going to ring, and I don't want the *concierge* to see that I have company. Leave me now, and rest assured—"

"Are you sure that he will open the door for you?"

"Yes," replied Hélène, though in her secret heart she felt some misgivings, for she knew that Carcenac was expecting no one.

"I hope so, indeed, mademoiselle," replied Pierre Dax,

"but it is well to be prepared for any emergency. Porters are usually very sound sleepers, and if these doors should remain closed against you, you would find yourself in a very unpleasant predicament, so I will not leave you, but retire to a little distance while you ring. As soon as you are safe in the house, I shall turn my steps sadly in the direction of my humble domicile."

Mlle. Lanouc made no objection to this arrangement, especially as she felt that she owed her companion not a little gratitude. She accordingly pulled the bell with her left hand, and proffered him her right, which he shook cordially, though without pressing a kiss upon it as he was dying to do; then, faithful to his promise, he walked a short distance up the boulevard and then stopped and waited.

Hélène was left anxious and alone in front of the massive *porte cochère*. There was no sign of life in the spacious mansion, so she finally rang again, but with no better success. What would become of her if Carcenac did not wake?

She scarcely dared to ask herself this question, but rang again several times in quick succession.

At last a heavy tread resounded through the hall, and a deep voice asked:

"Who is there?"

"It is I, Mademoiselle Lanoue," cried Hélène, loud enough for her words to reach the ears of Pierre Dax. "Open the door for me, Carcenac, and at once, I beg of you."

An exclamation of surprise greeted this announcement; a big key grated in the lock, the door opened, and the old soldier appeared upon the threshold, lantern in hand.

"You! mademoiselle, at this house, and in such a condition!" he exclaimed in astonishment. "Has any misfortune befallen the family?"

"No, thank Heaven. I was to return to the Oaks this

evening, but missed the last train, so I decided to spend the night here."

"Your room is ready, mademoiselle," said Carcenac, stepping aside to let her pass.

She entered, without daring to turn and give Pierre Dax a gesture of thanks. The door closed behind her; Carcenac locked and bolted it, and then motioned Hélène to follow him.

He was always taciturn, so this silence neither surprised nor annoyed Hélène, especially as it spared her the necessity of a disagreeable explanation. He conducted her without a word to the room she had occupied ever since she assumed charge of Mlle. de Muire's education, lighted a couple of candles, bade her good-night and silently withdrew.

Hélène did not understand this strange reception, but she paid very little heed to it. She was thinking of the morrow, of her approaching interview with George Roland, who would hardly fail to ask an explanation of her absence, and of Gaston d'Argouges, the unworthy brother who had been the cause of all her misfortunes.

The poor girl little suspected that he was under the same roof with her.

CHAPTER XXI.

WHILE Mlle. Lanoue was passing through these strange experiences, Major George was not reposing upon a bed of roses, by any means.

He had hastened from the Muire town house with the intention of seeing Hélène as soon as possible and ascertaining if Golymiue was really her brother, for George still doubted it, and before delivering the wretch up to justice, he wished to become satisfied on this point, and this certainty could be obtained only by questioning Mlle. Lanoue on the subject.

He had very little chance of meeting her at the Saint-

Lazare Station, and he chafed at the idea of being obliged to return to the Oaks and wait for her, without knowing the hour at which she would be likely to arrive, so suddenly recollecting that Hélène had gone to call upon an old school-mate who was stopping at the Hotel Meurice, and thinking it probable that the interview would prove a long one, the major concluded to call at the hotel before taking the train, and see if his betrothed was still there.

Mlle. Lanoue had not mentioned the Countess Borisof's name, but the information she had given him was sufficient to enable him to make the necessary inquiries of the hotel employés.

So he took a carriage, and was driven straight to the Rue de Rivoli, where he inquired for a Russian lady who had arrived there the day before, in company with her children and a French governess. The servants assured him that no such lady was staying there, and when he insisted the clerk remarked that a Russian countess, accompanied by three daughters, had spent several months at the hotel two years before, but that she had not been there since, nor had she written to engage rooms.

Then, noting the major's astonishment, the clerk added that the countess had probably been delayed on the way, for a young lady had called that very morning to see the French governess, who must be in the city, however, as a letter from her had been left at the hotel, addressed to Mlle. Lanoue, and as this letter had been intended for the very person who had called to see the governess, it was handed to her, and nothing had been seen of her since.

George Roland was greatly disconcerted, and even a little alarmed. It was evident that Hélène had not invented this story of a summons to Paris, but George hardly knew what to think of the proceedings of this friend who had written to Mlle. Lanoue that she wished to see her at the Hotel Meurice, when she had not even set foot there, and when the foreign lady whose daughters she was educating was still in Russia.

Nevertheless, the major finally came to the conclusion that all this was merely the result of a misunderstanding, and that Hélène having failed to find her friend, had probably hastened back to Vésinet where he had better rejoin her as soon as possible.

The same carriage conveyed him to the station on the Rue d'Amsterdam, which he reached at the very moment when Mlle. Lanoue reached the door of the little house on the Rue Jouffroy.

A fresh disappointment awaited him at the villa, for Hélène had not returned, and he found there only M. de Muire and his daughter, who seemed even more depressed in spirits than usual. His former misgivings returned with increased force, and he felt strongly inclined to hasten back to Paris in quest of the absent one; but where should he go to look for her? Besides, she might return at any moment, so it would be wiser to wait, which he finally made up his mind to do, though sorely against his will.

It is needless to say that the hours seemed well-nigh interminable to him. He had not even the resource of conversing with his friend Jacques, still less with Mareclle, who seemed to become more and more deeply absorbed in her own grief.

Both the father and daughter appeared to be unconscious of Mlle. Lanoue's absence, and the major took good care not to say anything about his anxiety for fear of being obliged to enter into an explanation which he wished to avoid, if possible, so he needs must bear alone the burden of suspense caused by Hélène's prolonged absence.

This state of enforced inaction, too, was all the harder to bear when he remembered that the assassin and his accomplice were at last in his power—that the two scoundrels would be utterly unable to deny their guilt now, and that although Médéric was still in prison, it would only be necessary to show Golymine's letter to the magistrate to insure the young man's immediate release.

Hélène had kept this damaging letter, and George Roland was beginning to understand why. If Golymine had told the truth in asserting that Mlle. Lanouc was his sister, her reasons for keeping the letter were apparent, and it was hard to doubt that Golymine had told the truth, under the circumstances.

George recalled the first disclosures of his betrothed. She had spoken of this disreputable brother of whom she had heard nothing whatever for twenty years. She had also confessed that the name she bore was not her own, and George now recollected vividly the agitation depicted upon her face when she first beheld Golymine.

Evidently she had resolved to ascertain the truth, and to see him again before the major caused his arrest; and she must have seen him, for Golymine had just declared that she had sought an interview with him for the express purpose of urging him to leave the country.

George had told himself all this at the Muire town-house, when he gave Carcenac orders to imprison the scoundrel with Maurevers, but he did not then realize the inevitable consequences of this unfortunate discovery. They had become apparent now, and he did not know how to extricate himself from the embarrassing position in which Mlle. Lanouc's imprudent step had placed him.

He was resolved not to desert Médéric under any circumstances; but he could not save him without delivering up to justice the brother of the girl he loved—the brother, who had avowed his intention of proclaiming that poor Hélène's real name was Andrée d'Argouges, and that she was the sister of an assassin.

The threat uttered by Golymine as Carcenac pushed him into the dark closet where Maurevers was sleeping off the effects of the brandy he had drunk, still rang in the major's ears.

"You will have the pleasure of seeing your brother-in-law tried as a felon," the venomous scoundrel had cried; and he was quite capable of boasting of his relationship to Major Roland if the major married Hélène.

Not that the major had any idea of breaking his engagement. His promise became all the more sacred in his eyes in proportion as his betrothed became more unfortunate. Nor was he angry with her for having tried to save her brother. He even resolved not to decide the scoundrel's fate until after he had consulted her.

But he became more and more astonished that she was so long in returning to the Oaks. It seemed to him that she would naturally feel a desire to confide in her best friend, to tell him about her interview with Golymine, and ask his advice. He little suspected that she had been lured into a trap; but the idea of doubting her never occurred to him for an instant, for he had implicit confidence in her, and would sooner have believed her dead than unfaithful.

But each hour, as it dragged wearily by, increased his anxiety, and toward the close of the afternoon, unable to endure the suspense any longer, he left the villa with the intention of walking down to Chatou to await the arrival of the trains. He did this not only to quiet his impatience, but because he was anxious to secure an interview with Mlle. Lanoue, before her return to the château.

About a hundred yards from the gate of the château, he was accosted by a shabbily dressed woman who was standing by the road-side, apparently waiting for some one.

He had never seen her before, but he recognized her by the description Hélène had given him of the princess, who was leading such a deplorable existence at Vésinet.

"You have just left the Oaks, sir?" she said, brusquely, "so you must know whether or not Mademoiselle Lanoue is there."

"No; she is in Paris."

"But she will return to-night, will she not?"

"Undoubtedly. What do you want with her?"

"She granted me an interview here yesterday."

"I know; I was on my way home from the depot, and saw you in the distance. She told me who you were."

"Did she also tell you that she had promised to obtain for me, in Paris, the address of a man who has got my husband into trouble, but who might get him out of it, if he would?"

"No; but I feel sure that you are referring to Count Golymine."

"What, do you know him?"

"Yes; and I know your husband also. He was formerly in the employ of the Western Railway Company."

"But lost his situation. Ah, sir, if you could only tell me what has become of him?"

"Are you so very anxious to see him again?"

"No; he left my children and me without so much as a crust of bread. I do not want him to be captured by the police, but, so far as I am concerned, I do not care if I never hear his name again. It is the other man I want to see."

"Golmyine?"

"Yes, in order that I may compel him to render us some assistance. It is his fault that my husband has reduced us to beggary."

"Golymine will do nothing for you."

"Then I shall denounce him. I know all about him."

"He could do nothing for you, even if he would, and Mademoiselle Lanoue will not bring you his address, for the very good reason that no one knows exactly where he is just at this time."

"Then he has fled, coward that he is! I might have known that he would desert Julien as soon as he got him into trouble."

"Julien!" repeated the major, inquiringly, for he had never heard her husband's Christian name before.

"Yes, Julien de Maurevers, Baron de Méru, whom I married because he was a nobleman. Ah, well, if that fiend, Golymine, has taken himself off, I shall apply to the Marquis de Brangue."

Of all names that the poor woman could have uttered, that of the Marquis de Brangue was the one the major least expected to hear; and yet the title of Baron de Méru she had just mentioned, awakened a vague recollection in George Roland's mind.

"The marquis has disinherited his nephew," she continued, passionately, "and he did perfectly right; but if he has a spark of humanity, he will not allow his nephew's wife and children to starve."

"What, your husband is—"

"The legitimate son of Baron Maurevers de Méru, whose patent of nobility dates back to the Crusades, and of Mademoiselle Herminie de Brangue, the only sister of the marquis."

The major suddenly recollected that during his conversation with M. de Brangue, on the Boulevard Malesherbes, the evening before, he had learned that one of that gentleman's relatives by marriage had borne the name this woman had just mentioned. The marquis had not said that this relative was his brother-in-law, and it was not difficult to understand why he had refrained from specifying the degree of relationship that united him to the father of a scoundrel of the deepest dye; but he was undoubtedly the uncle of this Julien de Maurevers, for this unfortunate princess could not have invented this genealogy which corresponded so perfectly with the statements of M. de Brangue.

This discovery opened an entirely different horizon to the major's astonished gaze. He recollected now the entire conversation with the marquis, and now drew from it deductions that differed widely from those which had first presented themselves to his mind.

"Yes, sir," continued the poor woman, becoming more and more excited; "my poor children are the grand-nephews of a man worth his millions. He has never done anything for them; but—"

"Is he aware of their existence?" interrupted George.

"No. I was married in Naples, ten years ago, but Julien had quarreled with his uncle before that, and I married him against the wishes of my family; so we sent out no invitations to the wedding. Afterward, when we returned to France, where my husband, through the influence of Golymine, secured the situation he so lately held, the marquis knew nothing about it, and Julien was too proud to ask any assistance of him."

With the exception of her husband's relationship to the marquis, Mme. Maurevers had told the major no news, for she had previously related her story to Mlle. Lanoue, who had repeated it to George Roland.

"So Monsieur de Brangue could not have rendered us any assistance, even if he had been so inclined," she continued. "Besides, I feel that my husband deserves his fate—as I deserve mine, since I was foolish enough to marry him. If I were alone in the world, I would not complain. I should try to make my way back to my own country, where I have some cousins, who would not allow me to starve. But I have three children. They are guilty of no wrong-doing. They did not ask to be brought into the world, and yet they have suffered ever since they were born. They have been punished for their father's crimes too long already, and their great-uncle owes them some reparation. I can prove to him that they have an undoubted right to the name of Maurevers de Méru, like their grandmother, who was his only sister, and he will not dare to repulse them. Julien once made me promise never to ask his uncle's assistance, but Julien has deserted us. His desertion absolves me from my promise, and it is not his accomplice, Golymine, I shall appeal to now, but the Marquis de

Brangue. You must know him, as he is a frequent visitor at Monsieur de Muire's house, and you probably know where he lives. My husband knew, but he would not tell me; but you, sir, will surely give me the address."

"I will do more," replied George Roland, touched by the sorrow of this mother pleading for her children; "I will go and see Monsieur de Brangue, tell him that you are left entirely without resources, and ask him to come to your assistance. He has never heard of you, and probably he would refuse to see you, especially as your husband's name would not be an open sesame to Monsieur de Brangue's heart, while he would listen to me if you would place me in a position to prove the relationship you claim."

"I have my marriage certificate, the certificate of Julien's birth, and the certificate of the deaths of my father and mother."

"That is all that is needed, and if you will intrust these papers to me—"

"I will bring them to the villa this evening."

"To-morrow morning will do. You reside in Vésinet, Mademoiselle Lanoue tells me."

"Yes; near the railroad, in a wretched hovel you would perhaps have some difficulty in finding."

"Mademoiselle Lanoue could show me the way."

"Mademoiselle Lanoue? Ah! how glad I should be to see her. And you think she will return this evening?"

"I hope so."

"But if she should not, you might be at a loss; and I don't want you to be obliged to waste your time in searching for me in the village, so you had better let me bring the papers to you to-morrow morning. I will be here before the departure of the first train."

"Very well, for that is probably the train I shall take. I have some other important matters to attend to in Paris, so I can not go straight to the house of Monsieur de

Brangue, but I promise you that I will see him some time in the course of the day."

"I only ask for money enough to take me to Naples with my children. If you can persuade him to give me that, I shall bless you forever, sir."

" Whatever his answer may be, I promise you that you shall return to your native land, madame," said the major. "If Monsieur de Brangue refuses, I will give you the money myself. Mademoiselle Lanoue takes a deep interest in you, and that in itself is more than enough to insure you my sympathy and assistance. And now let me advise you not to wait for her here any longer. It is getting late, and she will dine in the city, probably."

"Your word is my law," replied the Italian princess, promptly. "I will return to my children. Believe me, we shall all remember your name in our prayers."

"Pray for her as well," murmured the major, who was much less easy in mind than he pretended to be.

He knew very well that Mlle. Lanoue had had no intention of dining in Paris, and that if she had remained there it had been sorely against her will. He was really beginning to believe that some misfortune had befallen her; and Mme. Maurevers's sorrows troubled him much less than Hélène's mysterious absence.

When the princess turned her steps in the direction of Vésinet, he directed his toward Chatou, not with any hope of meeting Mlle. Lanoue on the way, but because he had become too anxious and impatient to remain inactive.

So he walked on, and before he reached the station he had ample time for reflection.

The case of Maurevers very naturally occurred to his mind, and he asked himself what he should do with the scoundrel after he had informed the marquis that one of Mme. de Muire's assassins was his own nephew. He had left Maurevers imprisoned with Golymine under the surveillance of Carcenac, but he could not leave him there long; and on the other hand he could come to no decision until after he had seen Mlle. Lanoue. Still, if her return should be delayed even a single day he would find himself compelled to decide without consulting her. Still this was the least of his troubles, for the thought of the risk she was running in Paris worried him most of all.

At the station, where he arrived about sunset, everybody knew him, and they made no objection to his stationing himself on the platform, though he had purchased no ticket. The station-master approached him to inquire about the health of the inmates of the château, and soon alluded to the affair of the 19th of June, which had not been forgotten by any one in the neighborhood, especially not by the employés of the line, as they had been indirectly connected with it.

George took advantage of this opportunity to inquire about Maurevers, and he was surprised to learn that the dismissal and subsequent disappearance of this man were already known to all the railroad employés. No one doubted that he had fired the bullet that killed Mme. de Muire, and all expressed a wish for his speedy capture.

Nothing was said about his wife, and the major felt satisfied that all these worthy men were ignorant of the fact that she was living in the village of Vésinet.

They all evinced a great interest in Médéric de Mestras, and the station-master strongly censured the arrest of that young man who, he said, was no more guilty of the crime than the keeper of the draw on the Asnières bridge, who had not left his post on the day of the murder.

"It is really too bad!" said the worthy man, in conclusion, "but this state of things won't last long, very fortunately. He will be released as soon as that scoundrel Maurevers is caught."

George certainly hoped so, and he had it in his power to hand over the real culprits to justice; but just at that moment Hélène was engrossing his every thought, especially as train after train passed without bringing her. After the arrival of the eight o'clock train the major became discouraged, and decided to return to the Oaks.

It was dark when he reached the villa. He had forgotten all about dinner—his anxiety had deprived him of all appetite—and not caring to disturb the gloomy meditations of the Count de Muire, he began to wander aimlessly about the garden.

He certainly had no expectation of meeting Marcelle there, and he could scarcely believe his eyes when he saw her emerge from a clump of shrubbery in which she and Hélène were fond of sitting on summer evenings; but he recognized her even in the dim starlight, and hastened toward her.

"I am so glad you have come!" she exclaimed vehemently. "I was just returning to the house. I have had a terrible fright; and if you had not come I should not have remained here a minute longer. I am no coward, as you know, but—"

"Why, what has happened?" inquired George hastily. "Have you seen any one in the grove?"

"No, not in the grove."

"But where, then? Pray explain."

"It happened in this way. I was anxious to see you; and after dining alone in my own room the idea that I might perhaps find you in the garden occurred to me, so I came down. You were not here, so I went and seated myself over there on that bench only a few steps from the little gate that leads into the forest. The gate, you recollect, is an iron one, and has not been used for a long time. No one has been able to open it; and my father intended to have the place walled up, but he has neglected to give the order."

"Did any one attempt to climb over it?"

"No; that would be a very difficult matter. It is narrow, but it is also very high, and a man would find it no easy task to climb over it."

"What did happen, then?"

"I heard some one shaking it violently as if trying to get it open, and it seemed to me that I could see a dark form on the other side of the bars. Then I became frightened and ran away."

"Without satisfying yourself that some one was really there?"

"I did not dare. A few months ago I should have gone straight to the gate, for it is very strong, and I should have run no risk in approaching it; but now there are times when I am utterly unable to reason calmly. It is nervousness, I suppose. At all events, I lost my wits completely, and could think only of escaping from a danger which was perhaps purely imaginary. Still I am none the less glad to have met you if only to ask your advice."

"My advice?"

"Yes. Ought I to tell my father or the servants?"

"That is hardly necessary it seems to me, now I am here. Will you wait here a moment while I go and reconnoiter?"

"Take care. What if it should be a thief?"

"In that case he would take himself off on my approach, you may rest assured of that. Besides, even if he should show fight, you needn't be alarmed, for I have a pistol in my pocket. But no thief would think of coming at this hour while everybody is up and moving about. Still it would be well to know who the rascal is; so remain here. Don't stir; I will be back in a moment."

Marcelle was anxious to have the mystery solved, so she made no further attempt to detain the major.

The moon had not yet risen; but it was a cloudless night, and in the bright star-light objects could be distinguished at some little distance; so as George approached the gate he could see that there was no one there. He concluded therefore that Marcelle must have been mistaken; but to satisfy himself he went close up to the gate and peered through the bars into the road beyond.

On the other side of this road was a dense forest, and as the major could see no one in the road the person who was prowling about might have taken refuge there. He fancied that he could hear cautious footsteps not far off, but the sound ceased almost instantly, and he thought his ears must have deceived him.

After a long and careful survey he became convinced that there was no one there, and returned to Mlle. de Muire, who was waiting for him in the same place.

"The man you saw must have been some passer-by who paused a moment to look in at the lighted windows and then quietly continued on his way," the major remarked on joining her. "He must be some distance off already."

"A passer-by would hardly have shaken the gate," remarked Marcelle.

"He might have done so unintentionally. Still, however that may be, there is certainly no cause for alarm; though if it would make you feel any easier, when we return to the house we will tell the gardener and the footman to keep a sharp lookout for tramps, so if any one should take it into his head to climb over the gate he will meet with a warm reception."

"You are right of course. What cowards solitude makes of us," said the young girl sadly. "I shall have to accustom myself to it though, as it seems likely to be my fate. My father has not addressed a word to me to-day. I could not see you, as you did not return in time for dinner; and to crown my misfortunes, Hélène went to Paris this morning. She has not returned, and her absence is beginning to alarm me."

It alarmed the major even more, but he took good care to conceal his anxiety from Mlle. de Muire. In fact he did his best to reassure her, and to excuse Mlle. Lanouc, whom Marcelle evidently blamed in her secret heart.

"She went up to town in the same train that I did," he remarked.

"Yes, by one of the early trains, and without saying a word to me," replied Marcelle; "and I must admit that I feel a little incensed at her for her abrupt departure."

"You should excuse it. She was summoned to Paris by an old school-mate whom she had not seen for a long time, and who wrote notifying Hélène of her arrival and speedy departure—"

"It must be Juliette Védrine!" exclaimed the young girl.

"I don't know about that. Mademoiselle Lanoue did not mention her name."

"She is governess to the Countess Borisof's children."

"I think so. The lady is a Russian, is she not?"

"Yes; and Juliette Védrine went to school with Hélène. I know her. She called at the house quite often two years ago. I never liked her; and I am surprised that my dear Hélène, who is so different from her in every way, should be so anxious to see her."

"Possibly it was because you don't fancy this governess that Mademoiselle Lanoue left this morning without informing you. But may I ask you why you dislike Mademoiselle Védrine so much?"

"I can hardly explain my aversion. Probably it was instinctive rather than reasonable, but it always seemed to me that she would be a bad adviser for Hélène."

This explanation was not calculated to reassure George Roland, but he did not dare to pursue the investigation any further, and he was about to change the subject, when Marcelle added:

"But Hélène does not return! Where can she be? She is acquainted with no one in Paris; I am afraid that she must have met with an accident."

The major did not know what to say in reply.

"Misfortunes certainly could not come as thick and fast as all that," he finally managed to stammer with a forced laugh. "Everything will be satisfactorily explained to-morrow, I am sure."

Then after a slight pause he added:

"I feel convinced, on the contrary, that God has at last taken pity on us, for I can now assure you that Médéric will soon be restored to us."

"You gave me that assurance last night," replied Marcelle sadly, "but you did not state your grounds for this belief."

"Mademoiselle Lanone came in just as I was about to explain, and all the rest of the evening your father changed the subject whenever I tried to speak of your marriage or of mine."

"I don't think that he disapproves of yours," replied Marcelle; "but you will marry Hélène whether or no, as you can dispense with his approval; but I shall never marry Médéric, for my father will never give his consent."

"He will when I prove to him that Médéric has been the innocent victim of a judicial error. Médéric will soon be set at liberty. Yesterday I could only hope it, now I am sure of what I say, and I can tell you why. The real culprits are in my power, and I can deliver them up to justice at any moment."

"What are you waiting for?"

"It will be done to-morrow; that is, unless—"

The major did not finish the sentence, for Marcelle suddenly clutched his arm. He understood the full significance of this sudden pressure, and hastily turned his head.

They were still standing in the path, and Marcelle was facing the gate, which was only about twenty yards from them.

"The man has come back," she whispered.

"I see him," replied George, "and I must find out what he is after. If I go toward him he will disappear again. But I know a way to catch him. Let us walk toward the house. When we reach the terrace, you must sit down on the bench which commands a view of the gate; I will run across the court-yard, and around on the outside of the garden and catch the rascal in the act of playing the spy—for he is certainly playing the spy—for he sees us, and yet remains there. No thief would act in this way, and I am anxious to know the meaning of these maneuvers.''

'' Let me go with you.''

'' No, you would only be in my way. By remaining here you will not only be out of danger, but able to keep an eye on this suspicious individual while I make the circuit of the garden wall. He will have no idea that I am stealing a march on him, until I collar him, pistol in hand. He will offer no resistance, I assure you. Besides, I begin to think that it is not an enemy, and who knows? he may, perhaps, have come to bring us news of the absent one.''

'' If I could believe that—''

'' You will soon know what to think. Here is the bench. Take a seat on it, and wait for me.''

One is always strongly inclined to believe what one wishes to believe, and the theory advanced by George Roland quite reconciled Mademoiselle de Muire to his departure, and he left her after a parting glance in the direction of the gate where the man was still standing.

The major traversed the archway leading from the garden to the front court-yard, where he met the coachman and footman, smoking their pipes in the cool evening air, and he was not sorry to see them there, for in his secret heart he was by no means convinced of the truth of his assurance to Marcelle, and he might have need of the servants' assistance.

He did not wish to ask their aid unless he was positively obliged to do so, however; for he said to himself that Mlle. Lanoue might have sent a messenger to the Oaks, with orders to communicate with the major without the knowledge of any of the other inmates of the villa, for since the strange events that had marked the day just spent in Paris, George Roland was prepared for anything except what was about to happen.

Then, too, he had taken all needful precautions in case he should find himself in the presence of a reckless tramp, for he had satisfied himself that his pistol was loaded and in perfect order.

It was his intention to dart upon the man, collar him before he had time to offer any resistance and compel him to state his business.

The garden was much longer than it was broad, and the gate at which the mysterious visitor was standing was only a short distance from the side wall along whose base the major was stealthily creeping; for instead of taking the macadamized road, he had stolen along the strip of grass that bordered it on one side.

He reached the corner without making any sound that would betray his approach, then he paused to listen, and it seemed to him that he could hear some one shaking the gate.

It was time to interfere, and George darted forward, but unfortunately, just as he turned the corner he stepped upon a pebble, and stumbled. Hearing the sound the man turned and cast a hurried glance in the direction from which it proceeded; then, letting go his hold upon the bars, he fled as swiftly as his legs would carry him.

This did not suit the major, who was anxious to question the intruder, and who felt strongly tempted to send a bullet after him to stay his flight; but he had the presence of mind to recollect that the report of a pistol would bring all the inmates of the villa to the spot, so instead of firing, he gave chase to the fugitive, who was only a short distance ahead of him.

Though the man was unusually agile in his movements, the major was endowed with an extraordinary amount of endurance, and felt confident that the fugitive would tire before he did; and this would probably have been the case if the chase had been through an open country; but the road soon began to wind in and out through the forest, and it had scarcely begun to do so when the man disappeared from sight.

He had evidently taken refuge in the woods, but he could not be far off, for George, who had been close upon his heels a moment before, could no longer hear the sound of the fugitive's footsteps. It was probable, therefore, that he had concealed himself behind the trunk of a tree, or in a clump of tall shrubs, and that he intended to emerge, and retrace his steps as soon as the enemy had passed.

But the major was prepared for this *ruse*, and instead of hastening on, he stopped short on the edge of the woods, snapped the trigger of his pistol, and called out loudly:

"I know where you are. If you attempt to run I'll fire; but if you'll come out I won't harm you."

There was no response to this appeal, however, except a slight rustling in the bushes that surrounded the base of a tall oak, and the major leveled his pistol at the spot.

It required some courage to stand there as a target, for the fugitive might be armed, and it would be all the more easy for him to fire with deadly effect from the fact that the moon had just risen above a few light clouds that fringed the eastern horizon, and its pale light now fell obliquely on George Roland's face.

But the major was determined to solve the mystery, and he never even thought of the danger to which he was exposing himself. After a long silence a voice that made him start violently, replied:

"Don't fire! I am coming."

Almost at the same instant a human form rose from out of the bushes, a few steps further on, and rushed toward the major, waving its arms wildly in the air, while a glad voice cried:

"Ah, major, if I had only known it was you!"

This time George Roland recognized the voice, and starting back in astonishment, he exclaimed:

"What! you have made your escape, and on the very

day before you were to be released? Unfortunate youth that you are!''

'' But I have been released. ''

'' What?''

'' I am telling you the plain truth. The judge of instruction sent for me about two o'clock, and announced that I was identified yesterday while in the prison courtyard by a worthy man who traveled in the same compartment with me, from Chatou to Vésinet, on the afternoon of the 19th of June. The magistrate went on to say that I was about to be confronted by this man, for he had been summoned to Versailles, and when I was ushered into his presence I positively threw my arms around his neck and hugged him. The identification was complete. I had to sign a final deposition, and at six o'clock the prison doors were thrown open for me, and I departed without asking any more questions. I had but one desire—to see you and Marcelle again. I left Versailles at seven o'clock. At eight I was in Paris. There was nothing to keep me there, for I knew that you were all at the Oaks, so I didn't even leave the railway station, but took the 8:35 train for Vésinet. I did not want to get off at Chatou, because the people at the station would have been sure to recognize me, and ply me with questions, while at Vésinet my arrival would excite no remark.''

'' I can scarcely wonder at your desire to preserve your incognito, but why didn't you present yourself openly at the villa?''

'' Because I didn't know how I would be received. You must recollect that I have been kept in solitary confinement for three weeks, so I am ignorant of all that has occurred since my arrest. I have not forgotten how Monsieur de Muire treated me in the presence of the officer who came to arrest me on the day of Madame de Muire's funeral. He believed me guilty then, and I have no reason to suppose that he has changed his opinion.''

"He will change it if he has not done so already," replied the major, evasively. "You acted wisely, perhaps, in not dropping in upon him unexpectedly, this evening, but what was there to prevent your asking for me? You must know that I have never ceased to be your friend."

"Oh, yes, I know that. The good man who identified me told me what a valiant defender I had in you. It is to you that I owe my release, and it was you, above all others, that I came to the Oaks to see. But I did not dare to speak to any of the servants; I was afraid that they would inform the Count de Muire."

"So you tried poking your nose through the bars of the gate at which I caught you. A great idea that! What the deuce did you hope to accomplish by that maneuver?"

"I hoped that you would come down into the garden to take a smoke, as you are in the habit of doing, and if I had recognized you I should have called you."

"And at first you saw no one but Marcelle. A nice scare you gave her! But you must have seen me a few moments afterward."

"I took you for somebody else. It was so dark."

"For whom, pray? You certainly could not have mistaken me for Marcelle's father."

"No, but Monsieur de Liscoat is about your size, and Golymine, too, and being in doubt—"

"Liscoat hasn't set foot here since Madame de Muire's death. As for Golymine— But this is no time to discuss those people. Why did you remain when you perceived that Marcelle was not alone?"

"I flattered myself that she would suspect who it was that was watching her through the bars, that she would return to the house with her companion, leave him there, and then come back to the garden. Then, of course, I should have called her."

"You were playing a dangerous game; for I thought

strongly of sending a bullet through you; but fortunately I did not fire."

"And I recognized your voice after I hid in the trees, and so came out."

"It was time. Well, here you are at last! You certainly can boast of having caused me plenty of sleepless nights during the past month. But I bear you no ill will on that account. Come to my arms, you young rascal!"

Médéric instantly accepted the major's invitation, for it would be hard to say which of the two men was the most deeply moved. But even the transports of friendship can not calm the anxiety of a lover, and Médéric took advantage of the embrace to ask:

"Tell me, I beg of you, does Marcelle still love me?"

"Marcelle is a brave girl," replied the major, "and her feelings have not changed. She loves you even more devotedly than in days gone by."

"Now I can breathe again," cried Médéric. "I could not exist any longer without news of her. I was tortured by a thousand doubts and fears. You can not imagine how much I have suffered."

"She has suffered as much as you have—more, perhaps—for you suffered only from loneliness, being sustained by a knowledge of your innocence, which would surely be established, sooner or later. Marcelle has never once doubted it, but she saw that her father did, and she has shown a strength of character rare, indeed, in a girl of her age."

"Can I see her?"

"Of course you can see her, but you had better not enter the villa this evening."

"I understand. Her father is there—"

"And he must be prepared to receive you before you are ushered into his presence. He is strongly prejudiced against you, but I am sure that he will get over it in a few days."

"But you left Marcelle in the garden, did you not?"

"Yes, and she must be anxiously awaiting my return. She little suspects that you are here, and if you should appear before her suddenly, the shock might be too great."

"What! would you have me go away without seeing her?"

"No, come with me."

They were talking near a turn in the road, about two hundred yards from the garden, and as the major spoke, he took Médéric's arm and led him back the same way they came.

"I am going to tell her that you are here," said George, "and I think I shall have no trouble in persuading her to come to the gate, where you can talk to her through the bars, but that must be all this time."

"That will be enough to make me the happiest of men, and it is to you that I shall be indebted for this happiness."

"Don't thank me; but promise to obey me in everything until I succeed in getting you married. There is a good deal to be done before that day comes, I assure you. In the meantime, after the interview I am going to secure for you, you must accompany me to Paris. I will explain my reasons presently."

"I will do whatever you wish; I am sure I have no desire to leave you. I have a host of things to say to you."

"And so have I to you. Now you must station yourself close to the wall, near the gate, and remain there until I bring Marcelle down to the gate. When I call you, you must come, not before."

"I understand."

"And I warn you that I intend to be present at the interview."

"I am sure I have no objections, major. You know very well that Marcelle and I have no secrets from you."

They walked briskly on, and they were only about twenty yards from the gate when Médéric exclaimed:

"There she is now! I see her."

A slight form was indeed distinctly visible behind the bars, upon which the moonlight was now falling.

"Her anxiety would not allow her to remain where I left her," remarked the major. "It is all for the best, however, as I shall not be obliged to return to the house."

Then, seeing his companion make a sudden movement as if with the intention of rushing to the gate, he added:

"No; you are to remain here, and give me time to warn her. Don't presume to move without my permission. When the right time comes, I will call you."

The lover submitted, and the major walked rapidly toward the young girl, who recognized him and greeted him with the words:

"Here you are at last, thank Heaven! I have been in a perfect agony of fear ever since I saw you give chase to the man."

"I caught him!" replied George, gayly.

"And he is standing there in the road. So he is not an enemy, after all?"

"Quite the contrary."

"Then why doesn't he approach if his intentions are friendly?"

"Because he dares not. It is so long since he saw you."

"Of whom are you speaking?" asked Marcelle, in a voice that trembled with emotion.

"Can't you guess?"

"Médéric? But no, that is impossible!"

"I was as much surprised as you are, when I recognized him. It was quite time for him to reveal his identity, for I was on the point of firing at him."

"So he has escaped?"

"No; the judge released him, and the poor fellow was

no sooner out of prison than he hastened here. Will you see him?''

"Will I see him? Call him—but no; I had better go around through the court-yard and join him.''

"No, no, don't do that. The servants are there, and your father might come down. Médéric only asks to speak to you through the bars, and—see, here he comes.''

The major had hastened matters. Diplomacy was not his forte, and instead of gradually preparing the young girl for the news, he had blurted it out, after all.

Marcelle pressed her face close against the bars, and Médéric imprinted an ardent kiss upon her brow. George Roland did not interrupt the transports of the lovers, nor hinder the interchange of the incoherent words that seemed to be so fraught with eloquence to them; but when they began to discuss the situation, he said, gently:

"My dear Marcelle, our friend is restored to us, and he shall not leave us again, I promise you; so you will have plenty of time to talk over the past and the future by and by, and if you will take my advice, you will make this first interview a short one. I must take Médéric back to Paris. I shall spend the night there; and to-morrow I shall see your father and do my best to convince him that he owes the man he has so misjudged some reparation. This reparation must be his consent to your marriage. But you must allow me to be guided entirely by my own judgment in the matter; that is to say, you must allow me to act as I see fit, and choose the time that I consider most favorable.''

"We leave everything to you," exclaimed Mlle. de Muire; "and now, do not let me detain you another minute. I only ask permission to tell Hélène the good news. She will soon return, and she will be very sorry to find that she has missed seeing you.''

"Yes; you will probably see her before I do,'' replied George; "and, if you do, ask her not to leave the villa until she has seen me, for I must have a talk with her. She will understand why.''

"Marcelle!" cried a voice from the other end of the garden. "Marcelle, where are you?"

"It is your father," whispered the major. "He is on the piazza. He will come down into the garden. He must not see us. Hurry back to the house, and not a word to him about what has happened. If he inquires for me, tell him that I have returned to Paris. We will see you again to-morrow. Come, Médéric."

The lovers realized the necessity of obeying the friend who was interesting himself in their behalf, so Marcelle hastened to the house, and Médéric followed his old friend, who remarked:

"Let us avoid passing the court-yard by going up to Vésinet to take the train. That will be the safest way."

His companion agreed with him, and turning, they walked swiftly and silently in the direction of the village mentioned.

Médéric, rejoicing once more in the knowledge that he was loved, could think of nothing but the short, though blissful, interview which had just been interrupted by the voice of the Count de Muire; but the major was engrossed with thoughts of the morrow which seemed likely to prove such an eventful one.

Whatever might have become of Mlle. Lanoue, it would be absolutely necessary to come to some decision in regard to the prisoners Carcenac was guarding, and George was utterly at a loss as to what it would be best to do with Golymine and Maurevers.

When he imprisoned them both in a dark closet in the Muire town-house, it had been with the firm intention of delivering them up to justice; but now Médéric was free, he was hardly willing to resort to such extreme measures. He said to himself that, instead of deeply grieving Mlle. Lanoue, and braving the scandal of a trial before the Court of Assizes, it would be better to get the two scoundrels out of the country, after preventing all danger of a return by extorting a written confession of their guilt from them. It was not necessary to have them convicted of the crime in order to prove Médéric's innocence now, for the investigating magistrate, convinced of the truth of M. Postel's testimony, had just admitted the existence of an incontestable *alibi*.

Consequently, the situation had undergone a complete change, and George Roland was becoming more and more convinced that the conviction of the real culprits would be attended by more disadvantages than advantages.

The progress of the two friends was rapid, and the lights of the little station of Vésinet had become visible when Médéric said in a low tone, and without pausing:

"I think some one is following us."

The major glanced behind him, and seeing no one, replied:

"You must be mistaken."

"No; I am sure that some one is walking along the edge of the forest. I have heard the dead branches crack repeatedly. I heard the sound first near the place where I concealed myself."

"But who the deuce would follow us?"

"I haven't the slightest idea, but I know that my ears have not deceived me. At first, the sound came from a long way behind us; then it gradually came nearer, and for some time it has been keeping pace with us. You do not hear it now, because the person who makes it is in advance of us."

"But, in that case, he can not be following us," laughed the major, who attached no importance to this discovery.

Médéric said no more, and about ten minutes afterward they reached the station. During their walk, the wind had risen, and the sky had become overcast.

The weather had suddenly grown threatening, and in the

waiting-room there was only a single man, seated upon a bench, a man whom Médéric began to scrutinize with great attention.

There was nothing remarkable about the man, however. He was of middle age, neither handsomely nor shabbily dressed, neither tall nor short, and the possessor of a rather insignificant face. In fact, he looked very like a department clerk, or a denizen of suburban Paris, and seemed to have just seated himself to await the arrival of the train. Between his knees he held a stout cane, and he had just lighted a penny cigar.

"What are you staring at that man for?" inquired the major. "Do you know him?"

"No," replied Médéric; "but I think it was he who just followed us through the woods."

"You are dreaming. No one followed us. The sound you heard was the wind sighing in the branches. You must have noticed that a storm is coming up."

"I may be mistaken in asserting that this man followed us; but I am, at least, certain of one thing; this man left the train at this same station when I did, three-quarters of an hour ago. He left Paris in the same train that brought me here."

"What of it? I see nothing very extraordinary about that."

"But I am surprised to find him here at the very moment of our arrival. When one comes to Vésinet at night, it is not usually to spend an hour. Persons generally remain here until the next day, or, at least, until the departure of the last train."

"Your reasoning is certainly very remarkable. If you bestow so much attention upon every stranger you meet, you certainly will have plenty to occupy you. This man doesn't seem to be troubling himself in the least about us, and what possible object could he have had in following us?"

"You are right, undoubtedly. I scent danger everywhere now. Still, you can hardly wonder at it; I have just spent three weeks in prison, and my brain has become a little muddled."

"The ticket-office has opened," interrupted the major. "I will go and purchase the tickets, for I suppose you have no money about you."

"Yes, I have. The fact that I paid my fare from Versailles here is sufficient proof of that. Before he opened the prison-doors for me, the chief jailer returned me twelve louis that happened to be in my pocket at the time of my arrest."

George Roland had already started for the ticket-office to purchase two first-class tickets. The stranger, who followed him closely, purchased a second-class ticket.

In a few minutes, the whistle of a locomotive was heard, the doors of the waiting-room were opened, and the occupants stepped out upon the platform. When the train arrived, Médéric saw the mysterious individual climb into the imperial.

"I certainly misjudged him," he thought. "The poor devil is not troubling himself about us."

Four persons were already installed in the compartment which our friends entered, and Médéric could not resume the discussion of his affairs in the presence of strangers.

The two friends exchanged glances when the train passed the spot where the countess was killed, but that was all.

On their arrival in Paris, Médéric wished to go straight to his rooms on the Place Pigalle, but the major was anxious to first pay a visit to the Muire mansion, in order to ascertain how his prisoners were behaving; so the two walked up the Rue d'Amsterdam together, without noticing that the rain was beginning to fall.

When they reached the corner of the Rue de Londres, George paused and said:

"I must leave you now for an hour or two, but I will

come and spend the rest of the night with you. You have a bed at my disposal, have you not?"

"Yes, certainly; that is, unless the authorities sold my furniture at auction while I was enjoying the hospitality they so generously accorded me at Versailles."

"It is a comfort to me to see that you have the heart to jest after your late experience."

"I was in no jesting mood when I got off the train at Vésinet, I assure you; but since I have seen Marcelle, I am so happy that I have forgotten all my troubles. They are ended now. I trust—"

"Look down there, under the arcade at the entrance to the Passage Tivoli," interrupted the major.

Médéric glanced in the direction indicated.

"Why, there is my man!" he exclaimed. "He is pretending to light a cigar; but he is furtively watching us. I am certain now that he is shadowing us."

"I begin to think so myself, though I am sure I can't imagine his object."

"Nor can I. The police shadow people before they arrest them; but they don't shadow a prisoner who has just been released."

"I think I understand the situation now. You were released so that the police could watch you."

"It would have been much easier to keep me in prison, it seems to me."

"Yes, but the judge of instruction would have known no more than he knows now. He saw that he would not succeed in extorting any more information from you, but he had not learned all he wished to know. On the other hand he could not detain you indefinitely, especially after Monsieur Postel's deposition. That worthy man's testimony proved that the fatal shot was not fired by you. But a suspicion that you might have been an accomplice still rankled in the mind of the magistrate, and he said to himself, 'I have but one means of satisfying my doubts. I will set this young man at liberty. He will think himself safe, and he will not hesitate to frequent the society of his friends and acquaintances. The superintendent of police will detail one of his cleverest detectives to watch him. This detective will render a daily report, and I shall know what my prisoner does every hour of the day. I shall know whom he sees; and if he bribed any one to kill Madame de Muire I shall soon lay my hand upon his accomplice, for they will be sure to meet.'"

"In that case the spy must know that I have seen you and Mademoiselle de Muire already."

"Unquestionably. You can not expect to take a single step now without having a detective at your heels."

"He will have his labor for his pains, that is all."

"That is true. Still I would advise you to go out as little as possible until you have received further instructions from me. I am about to deliver up the real culprits."

"You know them?"

"Yes; but just at the present moment my hands are tied. This state of things will not last much longer, however. I can say no more just now except to beg you to remain a prisoner in your own rooms for awhile."

"That will be no easy matter, after being deprived of exercise in the open air so long! Still as you insist I must be content to inhale the fresh air from my window, though I hope you will often drop in to tell me how affairs are progressing."

"You need feel no anxiety on that score; besides, I have decided not to leave you after all. I have changed my mind, and now think that I will accompany you home and remain with you until to-morrow morning. I am anxious to watch this man's maneuvers. Let us walk on."

They did so; but they had scarcely crossed the Rue de Londres when they perceived that the mysterious stranger had left the shelter of the arcade and was still following them.

This fact was the more significant as it was now raining hard and as the man had neither an overcoat nor umbrella to protect him from the inclemency of the weather.

The major and his companion were no better off, but they cared very little about getting wet provided they speedily reached the Place Pigalle, but their pursuer must be acting in obedience to orders to thus brave the storm.

As they walked on at the same brisk pace and chose the shortest route they soon reached their destination. Médéric experienced a very natural pleasure upon again beholding the house in which he had lived for several years.

The *concierge* uttered a loud exclamation of surprise on perceiving him, and was rather inclined to take him either for a ghost or a fugitive from justice; but Médéric soon corrected the mistake, and taking his candle and key tranquilly wended his way up to his rooms on the fourth floor, followed by George Roland, who found the stairs rather steep for his less active limbs.

Médéric had the satisfaction of finding his apartments exactly as he had left them. Everything was in perfect order and not an ornament was missing.

The very first thing the major did was to open a window and look out upon the square. He had considerable difficulty in discerning the spy, but he finally discovered him seated at the window of the nearest *café*, and pointing him out to Médéric, he asked:

"At what hour do the restaurants close in this part of the town?"

"At half past one o'clock. They will turn the rascal out then, and a fine time he will have of it if this rain continues," replied Médéric, rubbing his hands complacently.

"Let us hope that he will go home and go to bed. I am going myself, and I would advise you to do the same. You must be tired, and I must prepare for the morrow. That will be the decisive day."

Médéric would have preferred to talk, but it was evident

that nothing more could be gotten out of the major, so he gave up his own sleeping-room to his friend and took possession of a small camp-bed in the studio where he tossed restlessly to and fro, while George Roland in the adjoining room snored as heavily as the great Condé on the eve of the battle of Rocroy.

CHAPTER XXII.

As soon as Carcenac had left her, Hélène Lanoue knelt and thanked God for saving her from the greatest peril to which she had ever been exposed. She prayed, too, long and earnestly for those she loved, and even for her brother, the scoundrel who had so blighted her life and endangered her future.

She believed him out of harm's reach now, and did not regret having warned him, for she felt sure that the escape of the real culprit would not prevent the major from proving Médéric's innocence.

She also congratulated herself upon having conceived the idea of taking refuge in the Muire mansion. Carcenac could testify that she had arrived there about midnight, and in case she should be called upon to explain why she had presented herself there at that late hour and in such a deplorable plight she could appeal to Pierre Dax, who had avowed his willingness to testify to her escape by the window from the house in which Liscoat had imprisoned her.

She was now safe in her own room, in the room which she had occupied for six years, and in which she had left both linen and clothing when she removed to the Oaks in the early part of the summer.

She could consequently proceed to make the change of clothing which was indispensable, for she was covered with mud and drenched to the skin; but after doing so she dressed again instead of going to bed, for she wished to leave as early in the morning as possible. When her toilet was completed she threw herself down upon the bed, where she soon fell into a doze, though she had slept several hours in the house into which Juliette Védrine had enticed her.

The sun rises early in July; and when she opened her eyes it was broad daylight. There was a clock in the room, and it was going, thanks to Carcenac, to whom the winding of all the time-pieces in the house had been intrusted in the master's absence.

Hélène saw that it was five o'clock. She knew that the first train for Chatou did not leave Paris until 7.20 A.M., consequently she had plenty of time at her disposal; but she did not care to remain in bed any longer, and finally decided to go down-stairs and have a chat with Carcenac.

In fact it was very necessary that she should have a conversation with him before her departure, if only to ascertain what had called the major to the house the day before, and if he would be likely to return there that morning.

Feeling a longing for the fresh morning air she went to the window to open it. This window overlooked the garden, and as she glanced out Hélène perceived Carcenac slowly pacing up and down a path that skirted the house wall.

The measured steps with which he advanced to the end of the house and then returned made him appear very much like a soldier on guard, and to complete the resemblance he carried upon one shoulder an army musket, a *chassepot* that he must have picked up on some battlefield during the war of 1870.

Hélène knew that the old trooper was a vigilant guardian of the property intrusted to his charge, but she was surprised to see him armed in this way.

Had he been ordered to prevent the possible escape of some prisoner? It certainly seemed so—but what prisoner?

Mlle. Lanoue could not imagine. She resolved to satisfy

herself on this point, however, and hastening down the little staircase leading directly to the garden, she had hardly set foot on the gravel walk before she found herself face to face with Careenac.

He appeared slightly annoyed at the meeting, but instantly raised his cap and politely inquired how she had passed the night.

"Very comfortably," she replied. "But what are you doing here with that gun?"

"My duty, mademoiselle. I am *concierge*, and as there is no one but me in the house, my turn to stand guard comes every day."

"And every night, it seems to me. I woke you at midnight, and I find you up at sunrise."

"I didn't go to bed at all last night. The major told me not to."

"Major Roland? You have seen him, then?"

"Yes, mademoiselle. He was here yesterday morning. I sent for him."

"I know it. We came up to Paris by the same train. Did he remain here long?"

"About two hours. He then returned to Chatou. When he left he told me that if he did not return last night he would certainly be here to-day."

"This morning, perhaps."

"Probably. I promised him that he should find me at my post, and I am, as you see, mademoiselle."

This announcement of George Roland's speedy return changed Mlle. Lanoue's plans. If she returned to Chatou by the morning train she was more than likely to pass the person she wished to see on the road, so it would be better for her to wait for him in the Muire mansion.

"In that case, I will remain here until he arrives," she remarked.

"As you please, mademoiselle," replied Careenac, laconically.

He turned to resume his promenade, but she checked him by saying:

"What is going on here?"

"Why—nothing, mademoiselle."

"Why did you telegraph for Monsieur Roland?"

"Didn't he tell you?"

"I am sure he would have told me if I had asked him."

"Ah! well, then ask him when he comes, mademoiselle, and he will tell you."

Hélène saw that she would not be able to extort any information from the obstinate old trooper, so she did not insist, but she had not abandoned all hope of ascertaining what he refused to tell her.

"You are right," she said, smiling. "I had better apply to Monsieur Roland. I will now walk about the garden a little and then go back to my own room. Don't forget to inform me of the major's arrival."

"I will not fail to do so, mademoiselle. I will tell him that you are upstairs, and that you wish to see him."

"That is all I ask."

As she uttered these words, Hélène turned away and began to walk slowly up and down the paths, which were still wet with dew.

The garden was much smaller, and not nearly as well shaded as that at the villa, for in the heart of Paris trees grow much more slowly than in the country, and the house had been built only about twenty years; still one could occasionally find a shelter from the sun behind the clumps of shrubbery that had been planted near the walks.

The young girl finally seated herself on a bench in the shade of a large euonymous bush where she could watch the movements of the *concierge*, who never wandered far from a certain window in the *rez-de-chaussée*, the blinds of which stood open.

"That is the window of his own room," Hélène said to

herself. "He must have shut some one up there and is now standing guard over them. A strange place he has chosen! though unless he had taken the cellar for a prison he could hardly have selected a better place, for there is a large dark closet opening out of his room. There is but one other door in the room—the door opening into the hall at the foot of the main stairway. This door is probably locked; if it were not I could slip into his room without his seeing me and find out what is going on. At all events it will do no harm to try."

Impelled by a curiosity which was certainly not unpardonable under the circumstances, Mlle. Lanoue rose and resumed her promenade, but finally returned to the starting-point, where she again encountered the untiring sentry.

"I am going up to my own room now," she remarked. "I took cold last night, and I find the air a little damp."

"That is true, mademoiselle," replied Carcenac, without making any allusion to her evening promenade in a pouring rain. He had evidently decided not to question her in regard to her adventures of the evening before.

Hélène, instead of taking the back stairway by which she had descended to the garden entered the arched passage that led from the garden to the *porte cochère;* but thinking that the old trooper might be watching her she made no attempt to enter the lodge, but contented herself with glancing at the door as she passed, and to her great surprise, she saw that it was open. She did not pause, however, very fortunately, for as she turned to the right, apparently for the purpose of ascending the main stairway, she saw that Carcenac was standing at the other end of the passage watching her.

Instead of mounting the stairs, however, she stood for several minutes on the lower step, listening to the measured tread of the sentinel, who had now transferred his beat to the back hall; then, choosing a moment when Carcenac had just reached the further end of his beat, she slipped into the lodge and concealed herself in the corner next the window, where she could not be seen from without.

The room was vacant, and at first Hélène thought she must be mistaken in supposing that any prisoner was confined in Carcenac's *sanctum*, but soon she heard a sound that was half groan and half yawn on the other side of the partition that separated the dark closet from Carcenac's room.

Then a voice that made her start exclaimed:

"Here, you brute, wake up! It is time. How many days must you have to recover from the brandy you have drunk?"

"Let me alone," growled another voice, the husky voice of an intoxicated man awaking from a long and heavy sleep.

"Shall I have to kick you to make you get up?"

"Go to the devil! I am very comfortable as I am."

"That is quite possible, but I want to speak to you."

"Speak to me! What for?"

"So we can come to an understanding about what we are to say before we answer the man who is going to question us."

"He has questioned me already. If he tries it again I shall say nothing. It's of no use. We are caught, and there's nothing for us to do but make the best of it."

"It is all your doings, our getting caught. Now, we must devise some way of getting out of the scrape."

"I defy you to do it. The door is too heavy and strong for us to have any chance of bursting it open; besides, our jailer guards us too closely."

"I have no idea of bursting open the door, nor is it upon our jailer that I depend for my release."

"Upon whom are you depending, then?"

"Get up if you want to know. I have to yell at you to make you hear me, there on the floor, and some one may overhear our conversation."

Some one in fact was hearing it, but not Carcenac, for he had again extended his beat to the garden, and little suspected what was passing on the other side of the house wall, for his prisoners had given no sign of life during the night and he supposed them still asleep.

But Mlle. Lanoue, who had stolen into the adjoining room, was not losing a single word of the dialogue, and she had recognized the voice of her brother—the brother to whom she had granted ample time to escape the penalty of his crime.

How he happened to be a prisoner in the Muire mansion Hélène could not imagine; but though the other voice was unknown to her, she was beginning to believe it was the voice of Maurevers; and it was only necessary for her to listen to what followed to become convinced of the fact.

"All right! all right!" growled the husky voice. "Just lend me a hand, will you?"

A loud scrambling followed, and it was evident that the drunken man found it no easy matter to resume an upright position.

"You make a hog of yourself, pretty thoroughly, while you're about it," said Golymine, angrily. "You have been snoring away here for dear knows how many hours. It is time to wake up now, and tell me what I want to know."

"I have nothing to tell you," muttered Maurevers, who had not yet entirely recovered from his intoxication. "You sent me here; I came. It is no fault of mine that I fell into the wolf's jaws; it is yours. You ought to have warned me when you gave me your orders."

"I did warn you that the house was guarded."

"And I took my precautions accordingly. In fact I flatter myself that I went to work very adroitly. I began by throwing poisoned meat to the dogs. After they were disposed of I got over the garden wall with the aid of a ladder, by which I afterward climbed to the bedroom window. I entered the room, and was just going to break open the secretary when the old trooper sprung upon me from behind and throttled me. If you had been in my place you would have come off no better than I did."

"And afterward the major arrived—that arrogant prig we met at Versailles."

"Yes, and I tried my best to blow his brains out with the revolver you loaned me."

"And failed?"

"The other man sprung upon me and disarmed me."

"I suspected as much. Well, after that, what happened?"

"After that he tried to extort a confession from me. He began by assuring me that he knew perfectly well that I had broken into the house to obtain possession of some letters you had written to the countess."

"The devil he did! Well, did you admit it?"

"No, on the contrary, I denied it; but he silenced me by telling me that he had read the letters himself, and that I came too late. It seems that he had been here and taken possession of your correspondence the day before, and when he told me that, I knew that all was lost."

"And then you betrayed me?"

"Betrayed is not the word. I admitted that I had acted at your orders; I couldn't do otherwise, under the circumstances; but I assured him that though you had bribed me to steal the letters addressed to Madame de Muire, it was only to shield the reputation of the unfortunate countess, and to prevent her husband from finding them."

"And of course he didn't believe a word of it. But the examination did not end there, I suppose. He must have said something to you about the murder. What did you say to him when he questioned you about the Chatou affair?"

"I told him the truth."

"What do you call the truth?"

"I told him that it was you who fired the fatal shot."

"Is that all?"

"Yes, for the very good reason that I knew nothing more."

"You might have added that I was acting in your interest."

"That is not true. I had nothing to gain by the death of the countess, while you hoped to secure undisputed possession of the money she had intrusted to you."

"But you know perfectly well that I did not aim at Madame de Muire. I hit her by accident."

Hélène, who was still listening, hoped for a moment that her brother had been guilty of an unintentional crime; but the illusion was of short duration.

"You forget that the idea of firing from the train originated with you," continued Gaston d'Argouges, "and nothing would have pleased you better than a chance to fire the shot yourself. That would have prevented any necessity of sharing the profits, on your part. But you doubted your skill, and really it was no easy task, as I missed my aim, I, who am noted for my skill as a pistol-shot."

"You did not miss your aim, for it was at the countess that you aimed."

"That is false. I aimed at your uncle, and if my bullet had not swerved from its course you would have come into possession of a very handsome fortune. To be sure you had agreed to divide with me, but even one half of the Marquis de Brangue's property is well worth having."

"The Marquis de Brangue!" murmured Golymine's unhappy sister.

She had not heard Mme. de Maurever's last revelation, and she was amazed to learn that this scoundrel was the Marquis de Brangue's nephew.

But she learned, at the same time, that her brother's crime was even more dastardly than she had supposed, since he had committed murder at the instigation of another villain, like the Italian *bravi* of the sixteenth century, hired cut-throats, who killed persons to order at stated prices.

"Yes," exclaimed Maurevers, "you made the bargain, but you did not stick to it. Nothing will ever make me believe that you did not kill the countess on purpose. You said to yourself that my uncle had probably disinherited me, and that I had no chance of securing any of his property. The bonds and securities you had stolen from the countess were a much surer thing; and she must be killed to prevent her from claiming them, so your choice was quickly made. But I killed no one. I am only charged with an attempt at robbery, and when I say that it was you who urged me to commit the offense—"

"You think you will get off very easily," sneered Gaston d'Argouges. "You forget that I have in my pocket a contract signed by you, in which you agree to give me one-half of the property you receive after your uncle's death. If you take sides against me I shall not hesitate to show this document, which proves your complicity beyond any possibility of doubt."

"If you dare to do that—"

"Silence, idiot, and listen to the rest I have to say to you. You have allowed yourself to be caught, and I am the only person who can get you out of the scrape, but if you wish me to succeed you must obey me implicitly."

"You want to order me about—you, who have been guilty of blunders a thousand times greater than mine! If you had not insisted upon my surrendering that fellow's revolver to the station-keeper at Saint-Germain, we should not be in the predicament we are now. You blame me for getting caught, but you got caught yourself, you, who think yourself so shrewd, and you have only yourself to thank for it, for you had no business here, but just came and tumbled into the trap."

"It is very fortunate for you that I did, for if I were not

here you would leave this house only to go to prison. As it is, the man who captured us will never dare to send us there. You would not doubt my word if you had heard what I said to him while his valet was pushing me into this dark hole, but you were too drunk to hear anything."

"I heard you say something about a young lady whose name I did not catch."

"A young lady whom the major is about to marry—my sister."

"Your sister!"

"Precisely. I can produce proofs of the fact, if necessary, but it is not necessary. I saw her yesterday; we recognized each other, and if need be, she will testify that we are children of the same father and mother. Do you think now that she will allow him to deliver me up to justice?"

"You, no! but how about me? I shall have to suffer for both of us, if I don't look out. I don't intend to submit to anything of the kind, however. I have no confidence in you, and I want you to return the contract I was foolish enough to sign."

"I will return it to you when we are safely out of this house, and out of France."

"No, I want you to return it to me now."

"I shall do nothing of the kind."

"Take care! Don't go too far."

"So you dare to threaten me! I don't mind it in the least, my dear, but if you don't stop it, I'll call our jailer."

"Call him, you scoundrel," yelled Maurevers. "He will only find your carcass, for I am going to strangle you."

"Help! help!" cried Golymine.

But the words died in his throat, and only Andrée d'Argouges heard the despairing cry.

This cry destroyed the last vestige of Hélène's self-control. It did not occur to her that it would be a most fortunate *dénouement* if the two scoundrels should cut each other's throats. She had only one thought; to defend her brother, who was calling for assistance—and a most insane idea it was, for even if she could have thrown herself between the two combatants it would have cost her her life. But she was utterly incapable of reasoning now, and she rushed wildly forward to open the door of the dark closet.

She felt wildly for the key, but it was not in the lock. Carcenac had taken it away with him after securing his prisoners, so she began to hammer upon the door with her clinched hands, hoping to put an end to the combat by announcing the presence of some one. But this had a contrary effect, for they only fought all the more desperately in order to end the conflict before any one could separate them.

Gaston d'Argouges, though half-strangled, had succeeded in freeing himself from his opponent's grasp, and was now making a furious attack upon Maurevers, who defended himself with all the energy of desperation. They hurled the most opprobrious epithets at each other, and the sound of broken glass soon mingled with their curses.

They had fallen upon a pile of empty bottles that Carcenac had placed in the dark closet, and the conflict still went on—a conflict like that between two wild beasts, in which teeth and nails were used indiscriminately.

Andrée heard them pause, panting for breath, now and then, but soon the struggle would begin again, and she would hear them threatening each other.

They were on their feet again, but they had not let go their hold on each other's throats, and they soon fell heavily against the door upon which Andrée was wildly beating.

"Wretch!" shouted Golymine, trying to shake off Maurevers, who was clinging to his opponent's garments, "I have something to quiet you with now."

"And I have something to let the blood out of you, you villain!" cried Maurevers.

A dull thud closely followed this exclamation.

The blow had fallen; a powerful blow with a bottle upon the skull of the Princess Orbitello's dissipated husband.

"Die, cur!" yelled Gaston d'Argouges, as his accomplice fell to the floor.

Then, almost instantly, and in a weaker voice, he added:

"The traitor has stabbed me! I am dying!"

Andrée, in despair, rushed to the window to call Carcenac. She should have done that at first, but her wonted presence of mind had deserted her, and the conflict had lasted only two or three minutes.

Carcenac had just paused a moment to listen, for he fancied he heard a sound. When he saw the form of the governess at the open window, and heard her cry for help, he flew into a violent passion.

"What are you doing here?" he cried, angrily, as he burst into the room.

Poor Andrée could only point to the door of the closet and falter:

"The two men in there—they are killing each other!"

"What if they are? You are meddling with matters that do not concern you. Ah, well, mademoiselle, you will now oblige me by returning to your own room, and this time you will not leave it without my permission, for I am going to lock you in. We will see what the major says about your conduct."

The poor girl made no attempt to defend herself; the idea of seeing her brother's dead body filled her with such horror that she was only too glad to escape from the place. So she allowed herself to be conducted upstairs by Carcenac, who locked her in as he had threatened, and then hastened down-stairs.

He was just entering the lodge when some one rang violently at the front-door. He expected no one at this early hour, but the visitor might persist in ringing, so he ran to open the door, and was surprised to see George Roland standing on the step.

"Oh, major, how glad I am to see you!" cried Carcenac. "I had no idea you would come so soon. It is hardly six o'clock, and the first train hasn't left Chatou yet."

"I spent the night in Paris," replied George. "How about the prisoners?"

"They behaved very well during the night; but they began to fight just now, and I was about to enter their cell when you rang."

"You are armed, I see."

For Carcenac had not laid aside his *chassepot* when he conducted the governess to her room.

"I have my revolver," continued the major. "Let us see what they are about. I want to question them before I send for a magistrate."

"It is time we got rid of them, I think myself. I haven't slept a wink since night before last, and if they remain here another day, you will be obliged to take my place."

As he spoke, the old trooper drew a key from his pocket, opened the door, and cried:

"Advance, prisoners!"

There was no response.

"Have I got to drive you out with a club?" Carcenac continued, angrily.

The same unbroken silence reigned as before.

George, losing patience, was about to enter the closet, when Carcenac hastily interposed.

"Not without a light, major," he exclaimed. "They may be hiding in a corner with the intention of rushing upon us. Let me strike a light. It may be they have killed each other, after all."

As he spoke, he lighted two candles and a lantern.

"Impossible! the one you put in there first was securely bound," remarked George Roland.

"But the other man may have untied him, major. They were very friendly at first. The thief had his bottle of brandy with him, you recollect, and he must have drained it, for he snored heavily until morning. But he probably woke in bad humor, for, just now, he began to quarrel with his companion."

"Let us see," interrupted George, picking up a candle.

Carcenac insisted upon entering the closet first, in order to protect the major in case of an attack, but not a sound was heard, and George Roland soon discovered the bodies lying motionless on the floor, which was thickly strewn with fragments of broken bottles.

"I was right," exclaimed Carcenac, setting down his lantern, in order to examine the body nearest him.

Maurevers was lying stiff and cold beside Golymine, who had shattered his skull by a powerful blow from a bottle. The latter was still breathing, though his former accomplice had buried in his stomach the blade of a kitchen-knife that he had found while they were struggling on the floor.

George did not feel inclined to waste any compassion on the wretches.

"They will not have to go before the Court of Assizes, now," he remarked, without any display of false sensibility, "and this is certainly the very best thing that could have happened both for them and for us."

"I think so, too," growled Carcenac; "but we can not keep their carcasses here. Who knows but we may be accused of killing them? But, no; I have a witness who heard them fighting and finally killing each other."

"A witness! are you not alone in the house? What witness?"

"Mademoiselle Lanoue, major. It was she who called to me from the window, and told me they were fighting."

"How long has she been here?"

"She spent the night here. It was not far from twelve o'clock when she came, in the very worst of the storm. She was wet to the skin. She told me she had missed the last train, and wanted to spend the night here, so I showed her up to her own room. I don't know whether she slept

any or not, but this morning about five o'clock she came
down into the garden. Afterward she must have slipped
into the lodge, for she called me when the quarrel began.''

"Where is she now?''

"In her own room. I locked her in.''

"Very well, give me the key, and while I have a talk
with Mademoiselle Lanoue search the pockets of these
men, and if you find any papers, bring them to me.''

"You shall be obeyed, major.''

CHAPTER XXIII.

GEORGE ROLAND could think only of Hélène now. He
knew, at last, that she was safe, but he was impatient to
hear an account of her adventures from her own lips. He
was anxious, too, to speak to her about the brother whose
sinful career had just been brought to such an abrupt termination.

He found the girl in tears, and on seeing him she turned
so pale that he thought she was going to swoon. He sprung
forward to support her, but releasing herself from his in-
folding arms, and rising to her feet, she asked, in a hollow
voice:

"He is dead, is he not?''

"They are both dead,'' replied George. "Yesterday,
when I arrested Golymine, he boasted of being your brother. Did he speak the truth?''

"Yes; I recognized him by a scar on his hand, and I
hoped that he would be able to make his escape.''

"That was evidently his intention, but God did not will
that the murder of Madame de Muire should remain unpunished, nor would He permit the wretch to bring further
disgrace upon your father's name. Let us thank God, and
weep no more. Justice is done at last, and Médéric is
saved!''

"Monsieur de Mestras! What, do you think he will be released?"

"He has been. You will see him to-day. Marcelle has already seen him. And it is not to me that he owes his release, for you have not returned the letter I intrusted to you."

"The letter!" repeated Mlle. d'Argouges, laying her hand on her bosom. "True, I kept it. Here it is."

"It is fortunate that you did not burn it," remarked George. "Golymine is dead, and no one will ever know that he is your brother, so there is nothing now to prevent me from showing the judge of instruction the letter in which he acknowledged the receipt of Madame de Muire's personal property."

"But what good will it do?" inquired the young girl. "Monsieur de Mestras is free, you say, consequently his innocence must have been established."

"Not entirely, I fear. He has been released from prison, but he is liable to be arrested again, unless I can prove that the real assassin was the man who called himself Count Golymine. And how can I prove that without this letter?"

Before Hélène had a chance to reply, Carcenac burst into the room.

"I bring you here all I found in the pockets of scoundrel number two," he exclaimed. "The other fellow had in his pockets only a pipe, a bag of tobacco, and three one-hundred sous pieces, but the pockets of the pretended count were stuffed with bank-notes, as you see."

Carcenac laid upon the table three rolls of bank-notes which must have contained two or three hundred thousand francs each, and a pocket-book stuffed with drafts and letters of exchange on New York. The major had only to glance at them, to see that Golymine had recently sold an immense amount of stocks and bonds. There was even a list giving the numbers of the securities, and this list seemed to have been written by the hand of the countess.

After a brief examination of these valuable papers, George Roland glanced up at Mlle. d'Argouges, and said:

"I have here all the proofs that are needed. You can burn the letter, mademoiselle."

Then, turning to Carcenac, he added:

"Return to your post. I will join you in about ten minutes."

The old trooper left the room, and the major found himself once more alone with Andrée.

They both felt that the hour for a full explanation had come, but George hesitated to ask it. Andrée gave it, however, without the asking.

"I owe you an account of the way I spent my time yesterday, after leaving you," she began.

"You owe me nothing of the kind, mademoiselle," interrupted George, pleasantly.

"But I prefer to render it. We have plighted our troth, and though your feelings in regard to the matter may have changed, I wish you to know what happened to me. I warn you, however, that you will have to be content with my word alone, and that I shall refrain from giving the names of the persons who figured in the strange story I am about to relate to you."

"As you please, mademoiselle," said the major, rather surprised at this preamble; "but I assure you that I have no explanation to ask."

"When I have finished my story, you will understand why I am unwilling to mention any names," continued Andrée, without paying any apparent attention to the interruption. "On leaving you at the Saint-Lazare Station, I went straight to the Hôtel Meurice, where I expected to find the friend who had written to me."

"But you did not find her?"

"How do you know?" inquired Andrée, hastily.

"Because I, too, went to the Hotel Meurice yesterday. I wanted to find you to tell you that I had secured Madame de Muire's murderers. The servants at the hotel told me that a young lady had called there, and that a letter addressed to Mademoiselle Lanoue had been given her."

"The letter was from an old school-mate begging me to call upon her in a distant part of the town," said Andrée.

"And you went?"

"Not immediately. I went first to a club house on the Champs Elysées to ask Monsieur Golymine's address. He happened to be sitting on the terrace, and he came down and I had a long conversation with him under the trees on the Avenue Gabriel. He denied that he was my brother to the very last; but I knew better, and I hoped that after my warning he would lose no time in leaving France."

"He intended to do so. He told me so when he boasted of the relationship between you. But pardon me for again interrupting you."

"Afterward I took a carriage and drove to the house my old school-mate had designated."

"And there you found yourself in a trap. I understand; Marcelle told me about this Mademoiselle Védrine, whom she met two years ago, and of whom she retains a very unfavorable impression."

"Why didn't she warn me? If she had I should not have accepted the treacherous invitation. Yes, Juliette Védrine adopted this means of enticing me to a house owned by a shameless libertine. She left me there alone. The wretch came in, and when I rejected his odious proposals with the deepest indignation and dislike he did not dare to resort to violence, but went away, leaving me a prisoner, and it was not until nearly midnight that I succeeded in making my escape."

"Did any one release you?" asked George, looking searchingly at the girl.

"No," replied Andrée, meeting his gaze unflinchingly. "I escaped from the house by the window with the aid of some curtains I had knotted together."

"And no one saw you perform this feat? What time was it?"

"Nearly midnight, and the rain was falling in torrents. The Rue Jouffroy was deserted at the time."

"The Rue Jouffroy? Isn't that a small street leading into the Avenue de Villiers?"

"Yes; and the little house in which I was made a prisoner stands at the corner of the two streets. I had no other means of escape, and I could not employ that in the daytime. Fortunately I reached the ground in safety. It was too late to return to Chatou—the last train had left—so I hurried here as fast as I could. Carcenac opened the door for me and conducted me to my old room, where I spent the night. It was not until this morning that I discovered he was guarding two prisoners. I entered the lodge unseen by him, listened, and soon recognized my brother's voice. He and Maurevers were mutually blaming each other for their capture; then they began to fight. I called for help—Carcenac came—"

"I know the rest," interrupted George. "Now tell me the name of the man who insulted you."

"You promised me you would not ask it," replied Mlle. d'Argouges, "and I have sworn not to tell you."

"Why?"

"Because, if you knew who the wretch was you would challenge him; and I do not want you to stake your life against his. The odds would not be equal."

"I know him. It was the Viscount de Liscoat."

"Who told you so?"

"His friend the Marquis de Brangue warned me that the viscount had designs upon you. The marquis spoke of a little house that Liscoat was furnishing near Trouville. Brangue was mistaken, it seems, as the house is in Paris. That doesn't matter, however. The old scoundrel shall answer to me for his insolence."

"He does not deserve that you should do him the honor

to fight with him," said Andrée quickly, " and I beseech you—"

Just then the door leading into the hall was again opened by Carcenac, who put in his head and said, with a slightly embarrassed air:

" There is a gentleman down-stairs who wishes to see Mademoiselle Lanoue. That is to say—he did not mention mademoiselle's name, but he wishes to see the young lady he escorted to the door of this house last night.''

If Carcenac was actuated by any malicious motive in announcing this inopportune visit in the presence of his beloved major, he had the satisfaction of perceiving that he had succeeded in deeply annoying both the governess and George Roland.

Such a thing as love without jealousy does not exist, and the story of Andrée's strange adventure had aroused a slight feeling of distrust in George's mind. The major turned pale and looked inquiringly at Andrée d'Argouges.

She did not attempt to conceal the embarrassment caused by the unexpected arrival of the worthy fellow who had acted as her escort the evening before; but she soon recovered her composure, for she knew that she had no reason to reproach herself.

" Come, sir," she said, turning to her betrothed, " it is best for you to be present at an interview which I can not refuse to grant.''

And without waiting for the major's reply she left the room, and there was nothing for him to do but follow her.

Pierre Dax was awaiting her at the foot of the stairs, and seemed rather surprised when he saw the stern face of the major; but he was no whit disconcerted, and as he possessed plenty of shrewdness and mother wit, he wasted no time in apologies, but gave a clear and brief account of the incidents that had made him the protector of an entire stranger the evening before, and that authorized him to call this morning to inquire if the lady's health had suffered in consequence of her long walk in the rain.

He concluded by giving his name, and announcing that he was an intimate friend of Médéric de Mestras.

This was more than sufficient to dispel the last lingering doubt from the mind of the major. He cordially offered the artist his hand, and Pierre Dax, encouraged by this token of sympathy, went on to say that on returning home after escorting the young lady to the Muire mansion, he had called a policeman's attention to the fact that the curtains were still hanging from a window of the little house at the intersection of the Rue Jouffroy and the Avenue de Villiers.

This interview had taken place in the hall, and Carcenac had not understood a single word of it; but the major reproached himself severely for having doubted his betrothed for an instant.

"I thank you most sincerely, sir," he said, "for what you have done for Mademoiselle Lanoue, who will soon be my wife, and I have some good news to announce to you. Your friend and mine, Médéric de Mestras, is free, and I hope that you will soon have the pleasure of seeing him."

"This is news indeed!" muttered Carcenac, who could hardly believe his ears.

Andrée d'Argouges was too much agitated to speak; but Pierre Dax was about to congratulate the major warmly when a stentorian voice—the voice of an aristocratic coachman—thundered out:

"Open the door if you please!"

The party had been too deeply engaged in conversation to notice the sound of approaching carriage-wheels, but Carcenac could not be deceived.

"It is the count!" he cried.

"Well, open the door," said the major coolly. And as Carcenac started to obey George turned to Andrée d'Argouges and Pierre Dax, and added:

"Will you both be so kind as to step upstairs. I should like to see Monsieur de Muire alone. You, sir, of course, are at liberty to leave whenever you please; but I hope we shall soon meet again. As for you, my dear Hélène, I must beg you to wait for me upstairs."

Hélène was already on the staircase closely followed by Pierre Dax, who always bowed gracefully to circumstances even when he did not thoroughly understand the situation, as was certainly the case in the present instance.

George Roland then hastened forward to assist his old friend to alight from the carriage. As he did so he remarked:

"You did not expect to find me here, my dear Jacques, and I had even less idea of seeing you in town to-day; but our meeting is most fortunate, as I have some very important news for you. Will you step out into the garden with me?"

"If you wish it," replied the count rather coolly, "but I warn you I have very little time at my disposal. I have written to my notary, promising to be at his office at nine o'clock."

M. de Muire seemed to have grown many years older since George Roland saw him last. His eyes were sunken, and his tall form less erect; adversity had bowed him as the tempest bows the oak.

"He will be himself again when he learns that God has punished the assassin, and that Médéric is innocent," thought the major. "But the deuce take me if I know how to begin!"

They walked along side by side, and when they had taken their seats upon the same bench the governess had selected for a resting-place two hours before, M. de Muire remarked:

"Count Golymine, who talked so strongly of purchasing the Oaks, and perhaps this house as well, has neither called upon me since nor written to me about the matter. Hence I conclude that he has changed his mind, and that it is not worth while to wait for him any longer, so I am going to ask Desbois to sell both pieces of property at auction in the Chamber of Notaries immediately. I am anxious to retire to the country as soon as possible.''

'' You are acting too hastily; and if you will listen to me a moment you will see that—''

'' But the life I am leading is insupportable. ''

'' There will soon be a change for the better, believe me. In the first place, I have recovered Marcelle's fortune, and she is as rich as before her mother's death.''

'' What! you have found the money? It was concealed in some desk or secretary, I suppose?''

'' No; I have discovered the man who stole the money and who murdered your wife. This man was the Count Golymine, to whom you wished to sell your country seat residence.''

'' You are mad!'' exclaimed M. de Muire.

'' Not in the least. Golymine had an accomplice. They have just killed each other here in your house. I found two or three million francs in Golymine's pockets. He was making preparations to cross the frontier. Ask Carcenac if you do not believe me. ''

The count looked at George with a really frightened air. He evidently regarded him as a man who had just been attacked by a fit of mental aberration.

'' Golymine used to visit Aix, in Savoy, every year, '' continued the major. '' It was there, I believe, that the poor countess introduced him to you; but she never told you that he had so thoroughly won her confidence that she asked him to invest her money in the foreign banking-house in which he pretended to be a partner. Afterward her suspicions must have been aroused. Some one may have told her that the pretended Polish nobleman was only an adventurer of the worst kind. At all events, she certainly demanded a return of the immense sum she had intrusted to him, and it was then that—with the assistance of another scoundrel—he fired the shot that saved him from any further demands on her part. You think I am relating a romance, but I have proofs of the truth of all I say—and I am anxious to show these proofs without delay to the judge of instruction who arrested poor Médéric."

George Roland fully expected to be subjected to a cross examination by his old friend after these startling disclosures, but to his great astonishment M. de Muire requested no further explanation. Did he mistrust that Golymine had been the lover of the unfortunate countess? George suspected so, and he lost no time in returning to the subject of Médéric.

"He has been released," he continued. "The prison doors were thrown open for him yesterday."

"I know it," interrupted the count. "Marcelle has told me all."

"She has acted wisely, though only last evening I advised her to be silent, fearing that Médéric had been set at liberty only temporarily. There are not the slightest grounds for any anxiety on that score now. The real culprits are dead; but before their death they confessed their guilt. Médéric will be here in a few minutes, and he will ask you to give him your daughter's hand in marriage. Shall you refuse his petition?"

"I shall tell him as I have told Marcelle, that I will never give my consent to her marriage with a man who has been accused of murdering her mother."

"You said that because you thought it possible that he might have killed her; but his innocence is well now apparent to every one, even to his bitterest enemies. You certainly owe him some reparation for your injustice to him, besides you have no right to condemn your daughter to everlasting misery."

"You must certainly allow me time to reflect, and above all, to satisfy myself of the truth of your statements. I am not obliged to take your word for all this."

"Insult me, my friend, if you like; it is all the same to me, provided you will allow me to convince you. The bodies of the assassins are here. Come and look at them. Question Carcenac—question Mademoiselle Lanoue—they will tell you all that has occurred in this house during the last thirty-six hours."

"What! is Mademoiselle Lanoue here?"

"Yes; I will call her."

The major beckoned to Carcenac, who was standing in the open door-way; and Carcenac was about to advance to receive the order when the front door-bell rang, and he stopped short. George, understanding the reason, called out to him to open the door, and the old trooper promptly obeyed.

"It must be Médéric," remarked the major. "I left him at his rooms, but requested him to join me here a little later. In the name of our old friendship, I implore you to see him, however painful the meeting may be to you. This is the decisive moment; you will certainly regret it, by and by, if you condemn him without a hearing."

The new-comer was not Médéric, however, for there suddenly appeared in the hallway a gentleman whom the major had never seen before, but whom the count instantly recognized, for the recollection of this person's first visit would never be effaced from his memory.

"You are either deceiving yourself or you are deceiving me," the count said bitterly. "That man is the person who arrested Médéric three weeks ago. He is the chief of the detective service, and he would not show himself here if your protégé's innocence was established as you pretend."

"It will be very soon if it is not already," replied George Roland. "I consider it a most fortunate thing that this man should have taken it into his head to call this morning. We will wait for him here, but let me do the talking, if you please."

After exchanging a few words with Carcenac the stranger, who was very neatly dressed in black, stepped out into the garden and walked straight toward the two gentlemen who had risen on perceiving him.

"I am very glad to meet you here, Monsieur le Comte," he began, "though it is certainly an unexpected pleasure. It was Major Roland of whom I was in search, and as I find him here—"

"What! do you know me?" exclaimed George, quickly.

"I know everybody," replied the chief of the detective service, smiling. "That is my business. I know, too, all that you have been doing since Monsieur de Mestras's release."

"I did, in fact, notice that some one was playing the spy on me," replied the major, haughtily.

"Not on you, sir. I received orders from the judge of instruction to have Monsieur de Mestras followed by a detective. Of course I had no option in the matter."

"And the detective followed me at the same time."

"You are right. He followed you to the apartments of Monsieur de Mestras on the Place Pigalle; and this morning a second detective was detailed to follow you. I just learned from him that you had entered the Muire mansion, so I am here."

"Very well, sir. What do you wish to say to me?"

"I have some news of a very agreeable nature to communicate. The information we were in pursuit of has reached the police head-quarters, and we know now that this so-called Count Golymine was once tried and convicted of forgery under a different name. We also know that Conductor Maurevers is a scoundrel, though he belongs to an old and honored family. Hence it is by no means improbable that these two miscreants committed the murder at Chatou. Search is now being made for them, and as soon as they are arrested, I have every reason to believe that the innocence of Monsieur de Mestras will be established beyond any possible doubt. The detective who is now waiting for him at his door will dog his footsteps to-day, but it will probably be for the last time, for the entire force is on the alert, and the scoundrels we are seeking will soon be captured, though we have lost track of them since yesterday.''

"Would you like to see them?" asked Roland, suddenly.

"See them! What do you mean?"

"They are in this house. Come with me; I will show them to you, and when you have identified them I will explain why they murdered the Countess de Muire, and show you conclusive proofs of the truth of my assertions. You will, I am sure, permit me to act as guide to this gentleman," he added, turning to the count, "and you will surely be kind enough to wait here until I can return to proclaim Médéric's innocence."

M. de Muire made no response, so taking silence for consent, the major departed with the chief of the detective service.

The count saw them disappear in company with Carcenac, and almost at the same instant Pierre Dax, who had just taken leave of Andrée, came down-stairs. The outside door having been left open, the young artist took advantage of the opportunity to slip quietly out, and M. de Muire only caught a glimpse of his retreating form.

But Marcelle's father little suspected the fresh surprise that had been prepared for him by the kind Providence that aids the unfortunate and protects the innocent.

CHAPTER XXIV.

The Count de Muire had had a long and stormy interview with his daughter the evening before.

Summoned into his presence almost at the very moment of her parting with Médéric, Marcelle, quite forgetting

George Roland's prudent counsels, confessed all to her father, who immediately flew into a furious passion. He absolutely refused to believe that Médéric had been released, but accused him of having made his escape surreptitiously, and even went so far as to threaten to inform the authorities at Versailles that he had been prowling around the Oaks at night.

After this outburst of anger he positively forbade Marcelle to hold any further communication with her lover, whereupon Marcelle promptly replied that nothing could prevent her from keeping her promise to Médéric de Mestras.

The father and daughter parted in anger, and the count resolved to put an immediate end to this intolerable state of affairs by selling his property, and taking Marcelle to Brittany, where he still owned a small estate upon which he intended to live in the strictest seclusion at least for a time.

After informing Marcelle of this determination he immediately set to work to carry it into execution. Rising at a very early hour, he drove to Paris, without seeing his daughter, who was still abed and asleep—at least, he supposed so. He had just given his notary orders to sell at any price, and now intended to go straight back to the villa and take his daughter away the next day, without informing his friend George.

M. de Maire did not make sufficient allowance for the energy and strength of will of this nineteen-year-old girl who had sworn to keep her promise to Médéric. She allowed her father to depart unhindered, then hastily dressed herself and walked to Chatou. She reached the station some time before the departure of the first train for Paris, and at seven o'clock she reached that city, stepped into a carriage and ordered the coachman to drive her to the Place Pigalle.

When she reached Médéric's apartments the major had

been gone about ten minutes. She would have preferred to find him there, but his absence did not trouble her, for she had implicit confidence in her betrothed.

What did the two lovers say to each other during the half hour they spent together? Everything and nothing. What do the birds say when they bill and coo in the leafy branches? M. de Muire might have seen and heard them without finding aught to censure, however. ·

Just then, seated in the garden adjoining his house on the Boulevard Malesherbes, he was listening to George Roland as he pleaded the cause of his old colonel's son, but he would not allow himself to be persuaded.

And afterward, even the assurances of the chief of the detective service failed to entirely overcome his doubts of Médéric's innocence.

Still, he could not leave the house before the return of this official, and he, after satisfying himself of the death of the culprits, stopped to listen to the major's story and examine the money and papers found in Golymine's pockets. All this took some time, and the count was beginning to lose patience when the two gentlemen at last reappeared.

They were accompanied by Andrée d'Argouges, who had testified that the assassins quarreled on account of a contract signed by Maurevers which Golymine refused to surrender.

The chief of the detective service was now fully convinced of their guilt, and of Médéric's innocence. He was anxious to convince M. de Muire of the fact, and as M. de Muire would probably not be satisfied with a mere assurance on his part, it would be necessary to produce proofs that the crime could have been committed only by the two scoundrels who had just killed each other.

One may belong to the police force, and yet possess plenty of delicacy and tact; and this chief of an army that wages a relentless war against villainy, and that all honest men ought to bless instead of despise, was a man of feeling, and after listening to George's frank explanation, he understood the whole situation perfectly.

M. de Muire must be convinced of Médéric's innocence without allowing him to suspect his wife's former relations with Golymine; and the major had already paved the way by telling his friend Jacques that the pretended nobleman's relations with the countess had been of a business nature. The official took the cue, and made it appear that Maurevers's attempt to steal the letters had been merely for the purpose of securing possession of a receipt signed by Golymine—a receipt that the thief had succeeded in destroying. The quarrel was the natural result of this breach of confidence on Golymine's part, and now the two scoundrels were dead and the fortune of their victim had been recovered, it would be useless to carry the matter any further.

So far as M. de Mestras was concerned, the investigation was ended. The surveillance to which he had been subjected would cease immediately; and the chief of the secret service announced his intention of doing everything in his power to prevent the affair from becoming generally known. It would be impossible to conceal it entirely, however, as Golymine's tragical death would be sure to create considerable excitement in the circles into which he had gained an entrance, but Parisians have very short memories.

"It will create a good deal of talk for a few days, but in a month it will be forgotten," remarked the chief; "and we will see to it that the Count de Muire's name does not appear in any of the newspaper accounts of the catastrophe. We will represent the affair as an attempt at robbery, followed by a quarrel over the spoils, between the two accomplices—a quarrel which terminated in the death of both of them; and no outsider will perceive any connection between this affair and that of the shooting."

He concluded by advising M. de Muire to leave Paris for awhile. Such a step, on his part, would excite no comment at this season of the year; and he had the sea-

shore and the springs to choose from. During his absence
public curiosity would abate, and by his return the whole
affair would be nearly forgotten.

M. de Muire listened without saying a word, but it was
easy to see by his face that he was inclined to heed this
very sensible advice.

The giver of it had the major on his right hand, and
Hélène on his left. Careenae, by George Roland's order,
had gone to stand guard over the money and drafts which
had been left on the table in Hélène's room.

Pierre Dax had not closed the outside door on leaving the
house, and passers-by might have watched the conference
from a distance, for it took place in the garden, and the
doors at both ends of the hall were open, but they did not
stop to gaze at persons who only seemed to be talking
quietly.

A carriage stood in front of the door, a carriage occupied by two detectives who had accompanied their chief to
render him any assistance that might be necessary.

A third detective, the one who had followed the major
from the Place Pigalle, was walking up and down the sidewalk in front of the house, awaiting further orders. The
poor devil had had no sleep the night before, and he was
longing to be released from duty when he saw the comrade
he had left on guard before the house in which M. de
Mestras lived coming up the boulevard.

This comrade was still engaged in the discharge of his
duties, however; for though he had left his post, it was only
to follow Médéric, who, after a consultation with Maroelle,
had decided to seek George Roland's advice and protection.
Marcelle was leaning on the arm of her betrothed, and did
not seem to be troubling herself in the least about the man
who was dogging their steps.

The detective having been detailed for this duty that
same morning, Médéric had never seen him before; but on
crossing the street in front of M. de Muire's house, he saw

and recognized the man who had followed him several hours the evening before. Médéric was not at all surprised to find him here, however, though he refrained from pointing him out to Mlle. de Muire. The two lovers were seeking the major, in order to place themselves under his protection.

They knew he was at the Muire mansion. Everything else was of trifling importance.

They entered the house boldly, but had scarcely crossed the threshold when they paused in astonishment on perceiving the group that concealed M. de Muire from their sight.

George Roland, Hélène Lanoue, and the chief of the detective service, were all standing with their backs to the new-comer, but they instantly recognized the major and his betrothed.

It was too late to beat a retreat, whoever the third individual might be, so, summoning up all their courage, they walked straight toward their friends, and reached them just in time to hear the count say:

"Why does he not come, then? Why is he hiding, if he has no reason to reproach himself?"

"Here I am!" cried Médéric, pushing aside his defenders, and throwing himself at the feet of the startled count.

The *coup de théâtre*, however, was rendered much less effective by the fact that Marcelle appeared upon the scene almost at the same moment.

Hélène and the major received her with open arms, quite forgetting to ask whence she came, but her father, though he had not repulsed Médéric, hastily sprung up with a frowning brow on beholding his daughter.

"Have pity, too, on me!" entreated the girl. "I love him, and you know that he is innocent."

Médéric was already upon his feet, and clinging to him, she continued in a beseeching voice:

"If you curse us, it will kill me."

The count, conquered, opened his arms.

"Unite them now," said George, taking Marcelle's hand and placing it in that of Médéric.

Hélène burst into tears, and even the chief of the secret service felt a mist gather over his eyes.

The comical note was sounded by Carcenac, who, witnessing the reconciliation from Hélène's window in the second story, shouted wildly:

"Hurrah for Major Roland! Hurrah for the son of Colonel de Mestras!"

His shouts brought the coachman out of the stable, whither he had gone to rest and feed his horses, and George thinking the scene had lasted long enough, and that it was time for M. de Muire to return to the Oaks with his daughter and Mlle. Lanoue, bade him harness, at the same time promising to rejoin his friends at the villa as soon as the chief of the detective service would allow him to do so.

CHAPTER XXV.

BUT the major had completed only a part of his task. He had just saved an innocent man; he must now punish a guilty one.

Twenty minutes after the reconciliation that had just made every one so happy, the Count de Muire, his daughter, and her governess were bowling swiftly along toward Chatou.

The major, the chief of the detective service, and Médéric, remained in close consultation in the garden.

The official had summoned his subordinates and issued his orders. No further surveillance was to be exercised, so far as M. de Mestras was concerned, but the Muire mansion was to be closely guarded until the bodies had been removed. Two men would suffice for that task, however, so the others were to go and notify the officials at police head-quarters.

The investigating magistrate at Versailles must also be notified, not because it would be necessary for him to investigate the case any further, but because it was of the utmost importance that he should be immediately apprised of the facts that established Médéric's innocence.

"This last is a duty that devolves upon me," said the chief of the detective service; "and Monsieur de Mestras had better accompany me. When the magistrate hears my report, he will immediately render a formal verdict of not guilty; and this action on his part will be final. I have taken the responsibility of dismissing the detectives who were detailed to watch Monsieur de Mestras. They will not trouble him again, and so far as he is concerned, the case will be ended to-day."

Médéric could do no less than thank the kind-hearted man who had espoused his cause so warmly, and obey him. He announced his perfect willingness to accompany the officer, and even declared that to him the journey would seem nothing more or less than a pleasure-trip.

What a difference there was between this and the trip he had made in the same company three weeks before!

The official announced his intention of awaiting the arrival of the commissioner of police before starting for Versailles with M. de Mestras; but it was deemed advisable to deposit the large sum of money found upon Golymine's person in a place of safety, and they finally decided to place it in the cabinet from which George Roland had taken the letters, and which Maurevers had not had time to break open.

Carcenac was to guard this article of furniture for the present, and the chief of the secret service was to keep the key.

These arrangements having been concluded, there was nothing further to detain the major, so he shook hands with Médéric, after making an appointment to meet him at the Oaks, and then took leave of the chief of the detective service with the warmest expressions of gratitude.

Mlle. Lanoue had no sooner concluded the story of her adventures than the major resolved to seek an interview with the man who had so grossly insulted her, demand an explanation, and then punish the scoundrel as he deserved; and as he would not be able to see Médéric again before evening, the major thought he could not employ the rest of the day to better advantage than in arranging a hostile meeting with Liscoat.

But though one may have very serious and just grounds of offense against a man, one can not improvise a duel, as it were. One must find one's seconds, and explain the case to them; and this necessity placed George Roland in a rather embarrassing position, for he would be obliged to mix Mlle. Lanoue up in the affair, relate her adventures on the Rue Jouffroy, and even explain why he had a right, as the young lady's intended husband, to avenge the insult offered to a girl who had no near relative to protect her.

After some reflection, he decided to apply to M. de Brangue. The marquis was an honorable man; he knew the Viscount de Liscoat's character, and of what he was capable; and in a recent conversation with George, he had alluded to the viscount's admiration for Mlle. de Muire's governess, and his plans in regard to her; consequently the marquis was prepared to listen to the major's revelations, and he certainly could not refuse to act as his second, even against an old friend.

M. de Brangue lived only a short distance from the Muire mansion, and George Roland could hardly fail to find him at home at this early hour; but, to his very great surprise, he had hardly left the house with the intention of going straight to the residence of the marquis, when he was accosted by the widow of Maurevers.

"You surely have not forgotten that I was to meet you

this morning on the road near the Oaks," she remarked. "I waited for you there until I got tired, and then I ventured to question one of the servants, who told me that you went back to Paris last evening, and that Mademoiselle Lanoue had not returned to the château. I can endure this suspense no longer; my children are starving, and I am come to remind you of your promise. Take me to the house of my husband's uncle, to the house of the Marquis de Brangue."

"So be it," replied the major, promptly. "Come with me. I am on my way there now."

He felt that this unfortunate woman would serve as an excellent excuse for calling on the marquis, and that it would be well to settle the matter as soon as possible.

So he hastened toward the Rue de Madrid, accompanied by the former princess, who looked extremely shabby, though she had dressed herself in her best.

He did not inform her of her husband's tragical death, knowing that she would learn the truth only too soon through the papers, nor did he address a single word to her during their walk, which was not a long one, however.

"Here are Julien's papers," she remarked, when they finally paused before the house of the marquis. "I intrust them to you. Plead my children's cause for me. I will await his answer here in the street."

This arrangement suited the major exactly, for he did not care to present himself in company with such a shabbily dressed person; besides, he preferred to explain the situation to M. de Brangue untrammeled by the presence of witnesses.

So he left the last of the Orbitellos at the door, and ascended alone to the second floor, where the marquis occupied a handsome suite of apartments. Here he handed his card to a stylish valet, who immediately ushered him into M. de Brangue's presence.

The old beau, who had just finished his toilet, received

the major with a courtesy in which no little astonishment
was apparent. George did not give him time to complete
the polite phrase: "May I ask to what I am indebted for
the honor of this visit?" but went straight to the point.
After briefly apologizing to the marquis for the liberty he
was taking, he told that gentleman the whole history of
Julien de Maurevers, the only son of Mlle. Herminie de
Brangue, from his marriage to his tragical death. With
this account was necessarily mingled the equally strange
history of Golymine, not omitting the part these two men
had played in the Countess de Muire's murder.

The marquis listened to this long narrative with all the
coolness of a *grand seigneur* who feels that his own position
is much too secure to be affected by the acts of a disreputable relative. His first words were:

"Liscoat was right. It was for me that the bullet that
killed Madame de Muire was intended. My charming
nephew expected to inherit my fortune, and was consequently anxious to hasten my departure to another world.
He reckoned without his host, however, for my will was
made long ago."

"He leaves a widow and three children," remarked
George.

"His wife is some unscrupulous and designing woman,
undoubtedly."

"On the contrary, here are papers which prove that she
is really the daughter of Prince Orbitello, of Naples, and
that she was legally married to Julien de Maurevers in that
city. She now entreats you to give her bread for your
grand-nephews."

The marquis took the papers.

"Very well, sir; I will think the matter over," he said,
coldly. "You may, however, assure this woman that if
her children really have a right to the name my sister bore,
I shall not allow them to want."

"I think I have only done my duty in constituting myself the bearer of this unfortunate woman's petition," replied the major, no whit disconcerted; "and I hope, Monsieur le Marquis, that you will now allow me to mention the chief object of my visit. It is in relation to the Viscount de Liscoat that I wish to speak to you."

" Go on, sir."

" You told me, day before yesterday, that Monsieur de Liscoat had designs upon Mlle. de Muire's governess. You added that he was not quite capable of forcibly abducting her, and when I told you that I should call him to an account if he ever attempted such a thing, you replied that I would be doing perfectly right, and that he needed a lesson badly."

" All this is perfectly true. But what are you aiming at, if you please?"

" I came here to tell you that Monsieur de Liscoat set an infamous trap for Mademoiselle Lanoue, that he enticed her to a house where he afterward made her a prisoner, and from which she escaped only by a miracle."

" Such conduct was dastardly on his part, and I shall not hesitate to tell him so."

" Will you say to him, at the same time, that Mademoiselle Lanoue will soon be my wife—that in insulting her he insulted me, and that he must grant me satisfaction?"

" I will, indeed."

" And if he accepts my challenge, as I do not doubt he will, will you, Monsieur le Marquis, do me the honor to act as my second?"

M. de Brangue seemed greatly surprised at this request, and it is quite probable that he was about to respond by a refusal, when his valet entered, and informed him in a low tone that the Viscount de Liscoat wished to see him.

" Ask him to wait a moment," replied the marquis.

Then, as soon as the servant had retired, he turned to the major, and said:

" A mere chance has just brought here the person you

accuse of an act that is utterly unworthy of any honorable man. He has been my friend, but he will cease to be if it be conclusively proved to me that he has so conducted himself. Under the circumstances, you can scarcely wonder that I wish to question him myself, before taking sides against him. If you were present, he would probably refuse to defend himself; but I want you to listen to the conversation I am about to have with him. Will you be kind enough to step into the smoking-room? I will call you when I think the right time has come to bring you both face to face."

Under any other circumstances the major would have indignantly refused to act the part of a listener; but in some cases the end justifies the means, so he left the room in which M. de Brangue had received him, and as soon as the *portière* which separated it from the smoking-room had fallen behind his retreating form, the marquis hastened to admit the Viscount de Liscoat, who entered, exclaiming:

"Ah! my dear fellow, I have a long story to tell you, and some strange news for you as well. You are alone, I hope?"

"You can see for yourself," replied the marquis evasively.

"Well, I will begin by telling you my greatest piece of news. The wonderful Golymine has disappeared. He has fled, leaving victims everywhere. It has been proved beyond a doubt that this pretended descendant of the Jagallons was only a common swindler. They even say that he obtained possession of the fortune of that old simpleton of a countess, and that is the reason her husband is retrenching."

"I have heard all this before!"

"Indeed! who could have given you so much information? I just heard it by the merest chance from the steward of the club, whom I met in the street, and who told me that the chief of police had sent for him to inquire if Golymine cheated at cards. Ah, well, Golymine's end doesn't surprise me in the least. I always regarded him as a sort of sharper."

"What! you who were always praising him! Really, this is too much!"

"Oh, I may have been deceived in regard to him at first; but I have had my suspicions for a long time. Besides, it makes very little difference to me if this impostor does go to the devil—or to the penitentiary—which amounts to the same thing. It is not about him that I want to talk to you."

"About whom, then?"

"About myself, my dear fellow. I am sadly in need of advice. I have just had an unpleasant adventure that seems likely to get me into trouble."

"What new piece of folly have you been guilty of?"

"I have spoken to you a hundred times about that beautiful Hélène Lanoue, Marcelle de Muire's governess. You have seen her, and know that she is as handsome as a picture. I have often tried in a quiet way to make her understand that it was utter folly for her to waste her time in teaching stupid children when she might lead a life of luxury, and queen it royally over the *jeunesse dorée* of Paris."

"How did she receive these suggestions?"

"She pretended that she didn't understand me; and having seen plenty of these make-believe innocents before I decided to resort to stronger measures."

"That is to abduct her, I suppose?"

"I didn't dare to go quite as far as that on account of that old fogy of a Jacques, and also on account of the family friend, Major Roland, who seems to have constituted himself the girl's champion. The other day, while breakfasting with him at Durand's, I happened to speak of her rather familiarly, and he seemed to be almost on the point of demanding satisfaction for my pleasantry. I did not care to get into any trouble with this paragon of virt-

ue, so I resolved to win the young lady by gentle means,
if possible. I finally succeeded in unearthing an old school-
mate of hers—a certain Juliette Védrine, who was formerly
a governess in the family of the Countess Borisof, but who
has recently found a protector in the person of Prince
Werki, a tall Russian you must have met at the club."

"I know him; but he is not in Paris now."

"No, but Juliette is. She has taken up her abode on
the Rue Fortuny; and I am on very good terms with her,
so I implored her to assist me in softening the heart of the
obdurate fair one, and she cheerfully consented. She accordingly wrote to Mademoiselle Lanoue, asking her to call
and see her at a little house on the Rue Jouffroy that belongs to me, and the young lady fell into the trap."

The further Liscoat proceeded with his story the darker
the face of the marquis became. The honorable man
could hardly restrain his indignation; but he wished to
know all, so he said not a word.

"And then trouble began," continued Liscoat, who still
believed that he was talking to an approving auditor. "I
did my best to tame my captive. My embassadress, Juliette,
had tried to pave the way for me but without success. I
pleaded my cause in person, but was even more ungra-
ciously received. The fair Hélène was so indignant and
repulsed my advances with such disdain that I was compelled to beat a retreat."

"It was certainly the best thing you could do under the
circumstances."

"Yes; and I ought to have kept away from the house
afterward; but I said to myself, 'the night brings counsel,
and to-morrow I shall find the young lady more tractable,'
so I locked the outside door and put the key in my pocket."

"And thus violated an article of the penal code."

"I don't care anything about the penal code; but I find
myself in a very unpleasant predicament. On paying a
visit to the house on the Rue Jouffroy just now I found it

in the possession of a justice of the peace. The bird had made her escape during the night by the window, with the assistance of some curtains she had knotted securely together. A couple of policemen who were passing happened to see the rope hanging from the open window, and supposing that some thief had made use of it to gain an entrance into the house they reported the case, and a magistrate was engaged in investigating it. I had considerable difficulty in convincing him that nothing had been stolen, and I assured him that the whole affair was a perfect mystery to me. He went away finally, but I should not be surprised if he began another investigation; and if he does I shall certainly find myself in a pretty bad fix. Nor is this all. Mademoiselle Lanoue must have returned to the villa before this, and even if she does not relate her adventure to Jacques de Muirc she will certainly relate it to this Major Roland, whom I strongly suspect of being in love with her and of being a suitor for her hand."

" That is very probable," replied M. de Brangue coldly. " But I can do nothing for you. What do you expect of me?"

" A little advice. What do you think of the situation?"

" If you really wish to know I will tell you. I think that a nobleman who conducts himself as you have done deserves to be cut by all his acquaintances."

" You are severe, my dear fellow. You yourself, who now take such high moral grounds, may have been guilty of a like misdemeanor in former years."

" Never! And as you have consulted me, I advise you to repair your wrong-doing by asking pardon of those you have offended."

" What! I suppose I could, if need be, apologize to the virtuous damsel, but you certainly would not advise me to confess my fault in the presence of all the inmates of the villa with a rope around my waist and a candle in my hand, as in the Middle Ages."

"That is not necessary, of course. You have deeply wounded an honorable man who will soon become Mademoiselle Lanoue's husband, and it is only right that you should express regret for having so grossly insulted her betrothed."

"How ridiculous! He would take me for a coward, or at least for a fool. I had rather fight."

"Let us fight, then," cried George, bursting into the room.

"You here, sir!" exclaimed Liscoat.

"It was at my request that Major Roland entered the smoking-room," interposed the marquis; "and if you refuse to make the apology due him I shall act as his second, and shall certainly hope that he will kill you as you deserve."

Liscoat hesitated. He had turned as pale as death, though certainly not with fear, for this shameless libertine at least had the merit of being brave. He felt that he had been guilty of an infamous act, but his pride prevented him from confessing it. He finally consented to heed the voice of conscience, however, and said, though with a very perceptible effort:

"I confess that my conduct has been most culpable, and I deeply regret having offended a young lady of irreproachable character, and an honorable man whom I highly esteem."

"That will do, sir," responded George dryly.

"Good!" exclaimed M. de Brangue. "Thank you, major; Liscoat, I forgive you, for I hope this unfortunate affair will lead to a complete reform in your case."

"Reform!" repeated Liscoat. "I shall not be content with that: I shall turn anchorite."

"Better late than never," said the marquis, gravely.

Then pressing George Roland's hand he added:

"I entreat you to present my most sincere respects to Mademoiselle Lanoue, and to tell my old friend, Jacques de Muire, that I shall call on him very soon. It will certainly give me great pleasure to meet Monsieur Médéric de Mestras at the Oaks. Will you also have the goodness to inform the widow and orphans you have recommended to my care that they need feel no further anxiety in regard to their future. They, too, are innocent, and I shall not forget them.''

*　　*　　*　　*　　*　　*　　*

A year has elapsed since the murder of the Countess de Muire.

In the month of October Marcelle was married to Médéric in the little church at Vésinet. Major Roland and Andrée d'Argouges were united in marriage on the following day.

Both happy couples spent the winter in Italy.

M. de Muire did not accompany them, but he has regained much of his former cheerfulness, for his friends have conspired to keep him in ignorance of the fact that his wife ever deceived him; and the chief of the detective service, with the assistance of the magistrates, managed to keep the real history of Golymine and Maurevers a secret.

The affair was the general topic of conversation for a week or ten days; now it is well-nigh forgotten. Worthy M. Postel is the only person who delights in entertaining his friends and neighbors with accounts of the tragedy of Vésinet, in which he played the part of a special providence. He often boasts of it, and is not a little proud of having been invited to Mlle. de Muire's wedding.

Pierre Dax served as one of the witnesses at Médéric's marriage, and has since become the intimate friend of the major.

The Marquis de Brangue has sent the *ci-devant* Princess Orbitello and her children to Naples. He grants them, too, a liberal allowance, and will not forget them in his will.''

There is justice in heaven, people say; but sometimes

there is justice on earth as well, for Marcelle and Médéric, Andrée and George are as happy as mortals can be here below.

" The blood of our kings cries out, and is not heard,"

says Racine, in " Athalie."

The blood of Louise Plantier, Countess de Muire, was certainly less precious than that of the kings of Judah, and yet it did not cry in vain for vengeance.

Andrée's unworthy brother and the Marquis de Brangue's degraded nephew died a violent death.

In this instance, at least, God has punished the wicked and rewarded the good in this world, and Carcenac, who is very pious, like all old soldiers, never ceases to bless His name.

THE END.